"The Duplication Factor is a fine piece to read. Very broad, very rich. Expansive. Great characters, high stakes. A page turner. It has elements of Sci-Fi, thriller, and romance. It is filled with three-dimensional characters with rich back stories and justified motivations. On the page and scene level, this is an easy read. There's a nice command of description and dialogue as well as an ever forward moving story progression. The characters all have definite objectives. Structurally it is inventive, and emotionally it covers all the bases."

— Grey Line Entertainment, Pasadena, CA

The Duplication Factor

by Terry Wright

2019, TWB Press
www.twbpress.com

The Duplication Factor
Copyright © 2002 by Terry Wright

Published by TWB Press

Cover Art by Terry Wright

ISBN 978-1-944045-59-3

PART ONE

The Lost Diamonds

Chapter One

Cedar Lake, Indiana, July 1969

*T*he best-laid plans of mice and men often blew up in his face. That's what Dr. Eugene Marshall thought as he watched the pregnant cow buck and bellow, her wails of pain echoing through the basement laboratory at Blythe University. Like a wild beast, she fought the ropes lassoed around her neck, panicked, not because of the students trying to restrain her, but because of an enormous and undulating swell in her belly.

The stench of manure made Eugene's stomach sick. "Don't die on me," he muttered as hay dust swirled from the steel-railed pen and burned his throat. He wished he were back in his room, plopped in front of the TV, watching the liftoff of Apollo 11. Instead, he had this emergency to deal with, which happened to be just as important as any trip to the moon. The future of the human genome hung on the wails of this bawling cow.

"Pull harder," he shouted to his students.

Four young men struggled with the ropes, a chore to which they were ill suited. These guys were no cowboys. Instead of blue jeans and boots, they wore white lab coats and penny loafers. They were college boys, bioengineers. This was their class project, a project gone horribly wrong.

"Get her on the ground."

In the ensuing tug-of-war, they managed to pull the cow off her feet. She slammed to the floor on her left side. A cloud of hay dust leaped into the air and drifted like fog under the bright halogen ceiling lamps. Her hooves flailed like battering rams. Clumsily, the students snared her right hocks with ropes that hung from hooks on the ceiling.

Now Eugene got his first clear view of her swollen abdomen. It was twice its normal size, grotesquely deformed and churning from within. Terror welled in her white-rimmed brown eyes. Bellowing, she tried to regain her feet, panic and pain taking their toll on any remaining sanity she may have possessed.

Eugene steadied his trembling hand, the one that held the scalpel. As soon as his students had the cow safely restrained, he would rush in and make the incision. He expected a monster to spill out on the hay-strewn floor.

The head of Blythe's genetics department, Dr. John Larson, sprinted in, his face creased with concern. "Can you save it?"

"She's dying, John."

Larson climbed the gate rails, getting dust on his perfectly pressed black suit and polka dot tie. "It's the sixth one."

"Your restriction enzyme isn't working."

"There you go again. Blame it on me."

Damn right, Eugene thought.

The cow bawled.

Eugene's neck hairs prickled. He wanted to relieve her suffering. Her calf was killing her, kicking and ripping her insides apart. She wasn't making it easy for him to help her. Two weeks ago, only three months into gestation, everything was normal. Then yesterday this sudden growth spurt came on. He'd monitored her closely during the night, but by morning it became clear—the calf had to come out.

"Get a rope on her left hind leg," Larson shouted.

Two students scrambled through the hay. One held the tangled end of a rope. The other grabbed the cow's thrashing leg. They managed to get a loop around her hock without getting killed.

"Pull it tight."

The cow hacked, choking on drool.

"Careful," Eugene said.

Lying hogtied in the hay, she heaved with great breaths,

nostrils flaring. Eugene knew she was losing the fight for her life. Six out of twenty were too many to lose. Fourteen of these pregnancies had come to term normally. Five had turned to disaster, like this one now, all ending in death for the cows and their calves.

He thought about them for a moment, the losers in this genetic lottery. To him, science was a mix of success and failure, the difference being the knowledge he gained. However, he couldn't figure out what caused these sudden growth spurts, how to predict them, or how to prevent them. The animals died, and he had learned nothing.

Failure.

A chill skittered up his spine. He knew he had to solve this problem. They couldn't risk it in the next phase of the experiments. It would be too dangerous, too inhuman.

Larson shook his fist. "You're wasting too much time," he shouted at the students. "Shoot her."

"No." Eugene glared at his boss. "The surrogates have to survive."

"They're expendable."

"Think of the paperwork. The reports. The Board is going to have a fit. You can't keep killing the cows."

"So what? It's just a dumb animal."

"The next phase of the experiments, John. Are we going to kill the women, too?"

Larson's eyes narrowed. "I'm not concerned about the next phase or this dumb animal. She won't calm down, and I want that clone alive."

Frustrated, Eugene shifted his gaze to the cow lying in the hay, bellowing in misery. Larson was right, of course, but did he have to be so damned callous about it? Somewhere during the course of things he'd made a tradeoff: compassion for dedication. His research agenda had taken precedence over any show of human kindness. As supervisor of these experiments, Eugene wondered if he was just as guilty. The possibility tied a knot in his stomach. Were they nothing more than a couple of mad scientists making monsters in their secret laboratory?

The cow went into seizures, legs stiff and trembling, throat convulsing. Blood spurted from her mouth. Eugene knew a bullet would be the merciful thing to do, but he didn't like feeling responsible for her death. Worse, he feared he would be responsible for more deaths to come. Glaring at Larson, he made on last plea. "We weren't going to do it this way."

"We'll do it, Eugene, whatever way we have to." Larson pointed to the lead student, Chet Brady. "You heard me."

Slowly, Chet pulled out a gun. Eugene didn't know anything about guns. This one was black and looked heavy. The sullen-faced student stepped up to the pitiful animal.

Eugene wondered who was more pitiful now, the condemned cow or the mad scientists.

Chet raised the gun, hesitated.

Wincing in anticipation of the blast, Eugene wanted to run all the way back to Vermont, back home to a time before he knew Blythe University existed, before he'd accepted this position as Chief of Obstetrics, but he couldn't bring himself to leave. Cedar Lake, Indiana, was in the heart of the nation's agricultural belt. Their hybrid corn and wheat fed a hungry world. He had a job to do, a research agenda like none to be found anywhere else. The challenges had been rewarding, sure, but lately, he'd had his regrets. The duplication factor was chipping away at his sense of morality: what was right, what was wrong, what was an acceptable risk, an acceptable loss. There were good days and bad days. This was turning out to be one of the bad days.

"Do it," Larson shouted.

The gun went off with a bang that echoed through the basement. The cow huffed and fell silent, but her abdomen still churned from the kicking and rolling calf. The clone.

Without looking at Larson, Eugene climbed over the gate and dropped to the floor. An acrid smell of gunpowder lingered in the air.

He knew a gunshot was the only way to euthanize the cow; an injection would've killed the calf too. Chet had angled the shot away from the students in case of a ricochet. Safety first.

Two students joined him. They straddled the throbbing carcass, a procedure that wasn't new to them. This was the sixth time.

Swallowing his disdain for what he had to do in the name of science, Eugene knelt and made the cut. There was no delicacy to his work, no precision, just a butcher's gash through the abdominal wall. Blood and fluid gushed out and flowed to the floor.

As the students spread open the ragged incision, the huge calf kicked and thrashed its way out of the carcass, flinging blood and amniotic fluid across the pen. It squalled like a demonic beast, struggled to its knobby legs, and charged the students. They scrambled through the hay and climbed the pen rails to safety.

Eugene jumped on the gate, his heart beating wildly. He sat next to Larson on the top rail, shook his head, and watched the clone lumber around the pen, bawling, kicking, and charging the rails. Its black coat dripped fluid and blood, and the umbilical cord and placenta dragged behind it through the hay.

There was no doubt in Eugene's mind. The clone was just as mean as its donor, Hurricane, one of the deadliest bulls on the rodeo circuit. He'd killed three cowboys and maimed countless others. And like the clones that came before, this calf was more active than a normal calf, more mentally alert—but deformed.

Watching it storm around the pen, Eugene took inventory of its physical defects. Its eyes were set crooked on its head, the left one much lower than the right. And the left side of its head had two ears, one flopping with each stride. Its gait was lopsided because its left hind leg was shorter than the right. Eugene turned his eyes away, not wanting to see any more of the monster they had made.

He remembered watching Dr. Larson clone Hurricane's cells, peering into the microscope as he worked delicate instruments and manipulated tiny nuclei submerged in a batch of his restriction enzyme, BZ-20. Immediately, the cell divided: once, twice, four times, eight times, sixteen. The resultant zygote was a perfect duplicate of the donor's cells. After growing for fourteen days in a test tube spiked with BZ-20, the viable embryo was ready for Eugene to implant in the surrogate cow's uterus. It had all gone well—until now—until this monster emerged. Eugene feared it was his fault, though he preferred to think the outcome was out of his control. Maybe a higher force was telling him that their work here was not in the best interest of mankind.

"How about that," Larson said. "We've got another live one."

"It'll be a miserable existence, John. A thirty-three percent failure rate is not acceptable."

But Larson's wide smile relayed satisfaction with this new addition to their small herd of cloned calves, each plagued with one affliction or another. "He survived. That's all I care about."

"But your BZ-20 isn't working."

"Look at him. He's just as mean as his old man."

"He's crippled, John. We've got to stop using that enzyme. There are others..."

"And settle for an ordinary clone? Forget it. An exact duplicate, remember? Right down to the fingerprints."

"You and your damn ego."

Larson frowned. "We've got to do it better than anyone else. Arber got all the credit for discovering restriction enzymes. I was that close." He pinched his thumb and index finger together. "And what about those bastards, Shapiero and Beckwith. They took credit for isolating the first gene. Hell, I did that long before they even thought it was possible. I'll be damned if those guys are going to get all the credit."

"So what? We're way ahead of them."

"That's because my enzyme is better."

Looking at the crippled clone, Eugene had his doubts about that. "You should publish your research. Everyone will know—"

"All in good time." Larson swatted dust from his lapels. "When the duplication factor hits the science journals, the world will be dumbstruck. Our human clones won't just be identical twins of their donors. They'll be exact duplicates. Nobody will ever beat that."

"But we have a moral obligation—"

"Don't start," Larson snapped. "This is about science. Science exacts a toll on morality. A few lab rats have to die in the name of progress."

Eugene flinched. "We're not talking about rats here, John. We're talking about human clones."

"What's the difference?"

"Christ." Eugene didn't want to get into that argument again. Holding his temper, he glanced at the students sitting along the top rail, their attention on the mad clone tromping through the hay. Pride radiated from their eyes, conveying an eagerness for the project to proceed. He looked at Larson. "Fix BZ-20 or we can't go on to the next phase."

"What's the matter, Eugene?" Larson grinned. "Your clone will have two out of three chances to survive."

"And zero chances of being normal. We're not using BZ-20 on my cells."

"You're right, of course." Larson adjusted his tie. "I'll need to refine the enzyme again. The next batch, BZ-21."

"Use it on your own cells."

"That's not an option," Larson said. "Conflict of interest...you know."

"Not me, not you. Then who are we going to clone?"

Larson thought about that for a moment then licked his lower lip. "We need to find some poor sap who's going to die."

The clone bawled.

Eugene shuddered. Mad scientists and monsters.

Chapter Two

Chicago

" *Thirty seconds and counting.* "
William Tuliver, the CEO of Diamond Auto Parts, looked up from the television broadcast as Sally walked into his dimly lit office. The curtains were drawn, and a glow from the screen lit the frown on her lightly freckled face.

"Your appointment is in half an hour." She approached his desk with grace and determination, her flower-print dress hugging the curves of her five-foot-three frame. "You should be on your way."

"T minus 25 seconds."

William shifted his weight in his executive chair, hoping she didn't notice him wince from the pain in his right hip. "After this is over." He pulled the knot loose on his broad paisley tie and undid the top button of his heavily starched white shirt.

On the screen: Kennedy Space Center. A Saturn 5 rocket sat poised for flight on launch pad 39-A. Vapor spewed from a liquid oxygen valve high above the third stage. The six million pound spacecraft was loaded for the moon.

"Twenty seconds and counting."

Sally glared at the television set, jammed her hands on her hips. "Is this more important than your health?"

Brushing fingers through his thick mat of gray hair, William sighed. She was acting like one of his nagging ex-wives. "Nothing is more important than my health. It's just that this is more pressing, not something you'll see every day."

"But what about your hip?"

"*T minus 15 seconds. Guidance is internal.*"

"It actually feels better today. By the time I get to the doctor's office it won't hurt at all. You know how that goes."

She huffed. "It's been bugging you for weeks."

"Arthritis, I tell you."

"At your age, it could be anything."

"Hey. Watch it. Sixty's not old."

"*10-9-8, ignition-sequence-start.*"

Smoke and fire erupted under the massive rocket as five F-1 engines lit.

"*2-1-Zero. All engines running.*"

The umbilicals fell away, and the launch pad glowed like the face of the sun. Clouds of steam from the noise suppression system churned high above the harnessed spacecraft.

"Wow," Sally said, leaning against the desk.

The awesome power rocked Kennedy Space Center and exploded into William's office, vibrating the walls. He tried to imagine how thunderous it sounded to those who were watching in Florida.

"*We have liftoff. Thirty-two minutes past the hour. Liftoff of Apollo 11.*"

"There they go." William felt proud as a patriot on Veterans Day. Goose bumps skittered up his arms. Sixty years ago, his parents had given up their horse and buggy for a newfangled machine called the Model T. Technology had changed a lot in his lifetime, and he was glad to have been a witness to it, if not a driving force for it.

"*The tower is clear.*"

The 364-foot rocket thundered into Florida's blue sky, its flaming tail flickering like a welding torch atop a towering column of smoke. The first stage booster, pushing seven and one-half million pounds of thrust, burned 214,000 gallons of fuel each minute of its fiery leap to the heavens.

Terry Wright

The spectacular display of American technology made William smile. "Will you look at that? There's nothing we can't do, Sally. Just think of it. In eleven minutes they'll be orbiting the earth at 15,300 miles an hour."

"And you'll be late for your appointment."

"It can wait." He grabbed a painful breath. "Doctors are never on time anyway. Besides, this is history in the making."

A ribbon of smoke arced across the sky. Through the roar of rocket engines rumbling from the television, an astronaut's voice came over the radio. *"We got a roll program."*

"Altitude, two miles," the Houston controller announced.

"Andrew is waiting downstairs." Sally tapped her foot on the carpet.

William looked up from the newscast. "The limo isn't going anywhere without me." He couldn't help but notice Sally's unnerving glare and the glow of rocket fire reflecting from her hazel eyes. Dazzling. He flashed her a wink and returned his attention to the moon shot.

"Downrange one mile. Altitude, four miles high." The controller took a breath. *"Velocity, two-thousand-one-hundred-ninety-five feet per second."*

The rocket engines' roar didn't seem to be getting any farther away. William squirmed in his chair, trying to reposition his weight off his right hip. It felt like a million needles pricking him from the inside. Trying to ignore it, he contemplated the mission ahead of the astronauts. Neil Armstrong and Ed Aldrin were going to land on the moon. "You know, Sally, if they pull this off, I'll bet *anything* is possible."

She cracked a sly grin. "Including marriage?"

He swallowed dryly. "Okay, almost anything." Three times he'd been married. Three times he'd failed. Now, he'd rather face a firing squad—

"Eight miles downrange, twelve miles high. Velocity, four thousand feet per second."

Or be shot to the moon. Though his divorces were emotionally trying and expensive, he wasn't left with any animosity toward women. Just his ex-wives. And Sally, over the past ten years, had become his best friend as well as his lover. He wasn't about to marry her and ruin a good thing.

A beep echoed from NASA's radio. *"You are 'go' for staging."* The rumble rolled off in the distance as the rocket streaked higher and higher, dragging its tail of smoke. *"Downrange, thirty-five miles, thirty miles high. Standing by for the outboard engine cut down now...and ignition."*

At 5,330 miles an hour, the first stage separated with a billowing puff of smoke followed by the glow of the second stage J-2 rocket engines. Framed by a long-range camera, the rocket streaked toward Earth's outer atmosphere.

Sally moved to the windows and opened the curtains. Summer sunshine flooded the office. "Okay, that's enough. They're on their way to the moon, and you're on your way to Dr. Webber's."

William stood, and wobbling a little from his painful hip, reached for his diamond-studded black walnut cane propped against the desk. Engraved hieroglyphics on the Rhino-horn handle felt rough on the palm of his hand. He shuffled to the window with a slight limp and leaned on the cane. The drone of rocket engines reverberated from the TV behind him. "All this fuss over some lousy arthritis."

"Aspirin isn't helping you anymore." She put her arm around his waist. "I'm worried." Her shoulder-length red hair glistened in the sunlight shining in through the plate-glass window.

With Sally tucked under his arm, he scanned the Chicago skyline, a splendid view from his suite atop the Diamond Building. The Chicago River snaked through the city, sixty-six stories below, a living artery pumping nutrients to a massive body of concrete, glass, and steel. He looked at Sally again. "What are you worried about?"

Her moist eyes were fixed on his. "You've been exhausted and not eating like you should."

He patted his slightly rounded belly. "I've lost twelve pounds."

"In three weeks." She wrinkled her nose. "That's not healthy, William."

He knew she was right. Wracked by a fear of what might be wrong with him, he barely heard Houston give Apollo 11 the *go* for third staging. "Okay. So I haven't been feeling so hot lately." He minimized his concerns. Denial was his first line of defense. "It'll pass."

"I hope you're right." She smiled a little. "I've got big plans for you. Someday, you'll see that I *am* different from the others."

"I already do, Sally. It's just that...well...changes are hard to make. I feel safe leaving things just as they are."

She took hold of his arm. "We're not getting any younger, William. I'm thirty already. If we're ever going to have a baby, it'll have to be soon."

A lump stuck in his throat. He didn't want to be a father. There was no time for it. He'd convinced himself of that long ago, though he knew the real reason for his reluctance. Having children meant taking risks, big risks. Children die and parents suffer. How well he knew that pain. He'd watched his mother succumb to it after his brother was killed. Children weren't worth the risk. "I wish you'd stop bugging me about that."

"Never."

His hip responded with a sharp pain. "Why not?"

"Because it's something I want to do, William. I want to feel our child growing inside me, to feel that love, to give that love. It's a woman thing."

"Why my baby?"

She looked up at him with one eyebrow bent. "You really don't know, do you?"

He shook his head, really didn't want to know. His mind was made up, but he couldn't help but notice how her eyes glowed warm as the sunshine coming in through the windows.

"You treat me with more love and kindness than I've ever

dreamed possible. Your strength lies in your heart, William. You'd rather go for a walk with me in Paradise Park than go fishing with the guys. And you're so damn sexy. Those big brown eyes take my breath away, make me want to do things to you...well...you know." She smiled. "I didn't fall in love with you for your brains."

Mustering a phony look of surprise, he said, "And all this time I thought it was for the money."

Playfully, she poked him in the ribs. "Keep your money, honey. I'll take the body."

He blinked. What good was that? His body was falling apart. Too bad he couldn't make spare parts for it the same way he'd made spare parts for cars all these years. He chuckled at the thought: *spare parts for humans?* "Guess that means you won't have any use for me if I'm all crippled up."

She pulled him closer. "I'll take you any way you come, if you'll let me."

"Easy for you to say."

"There's nothing I wouldn't do for you, William. I love you." Tears welled in her eyes.

His heart felt warmed by her words though he had little luck with the subject of love. His mother told him it was because he was too self-centered to truly love someone. What did she know? "I love you too, Sally."

"I know."

From the television, the drone of rocket engines faded in the distance.

She gave him a pat on the fanny. "You'd better get going."

Chapter Three

Descending in the penthouse elevator, William tightened the knot on his tie. As his fingers fumbled with the buttons on his gray suit coat, his mind grappled with his reluctance to commit to Sally. She was the best woman he'd ever known. However, he remembered feeling the same way about his three former wives before those marriages crumbled. He was wrong then. He could be wrong now. How could he ever trust his feelings again?

Hanging the diamond-studded cane on his left forearm, he leaned back against the elevator wall, trying to keep his weight off his right hip. The nonstop ride ended in the lobby, and the doors slid open with a chime. Chin up, he stepped out.

"Morning, William," the guard said from his position behind the security desk. "Catch the liftoff?"

"Sure did, Ron." William tried to hide the limp in his walk as he approached the reception counter. "It was splendid."

Ron grinned. "Makes me proud to be an American."

"Expensive trip...going to the moon...but worth it. The whole world was watching." He signed the *OUT* register. "Have you seen Andrew?"

"At the fountain, I think."

William frowned. He didn't feel like walking that far but headed for the exit with determination.

"Have a nice day," Ron said.

Yeah, right...a nice day at the doctor's? Not likely.

Revolving doors creaked as he pushed his way outside. Muggy summer heat hit him like a boxing glove. The sound of splashing water filled the air, from his prized fountain.

Under the carport, he spotted his black '59 Cadillac limo parked unattended in the space marked *Executive One Only*. He'd once considered buying a new 1970 model, but they didn't come with fins. Fins made Cadillacs look special. He reached through the open driver door window and honked the horn. The blare didn't cause Andrew to appear.

Sighing, William set on his sunglasses and stepped onto a sunlit marble deck that overlooked a park that fronted the Diamond Building. He leaned on his cane and took in the view.

Thirty semicircular marble steps led down to the green grass of Paradise Park, his oasis in a desert of commerce. The sweet scent of freshly mowed grass drifted in the air. Majestic oak trees, rustling in the breeze, lined the sidewalks leading to the pool and its magnificent fountain where four turbo-electric pumps fed sixteen geysers that shot water a hundred feet into the air. Cascading back down to the pool, the resultant splashing sound reminded him of a tropical waterfall. Hearing it lightened his spirits. The meaning behind it comforted his soul.

"William."

He saw Andrew Cobb running up the sidewalk from the direction of the fountain. William waved his cane and watched his lanky aide scramble up the marble steps. A warm feeling glowed inside. He felt fortunate to have such a loyal companion. For twenty-plus years, Andrew was less like an employee to him and more like a brother, a welcome stand-in for the brother he'd lost long ago. Ten years his junior and six-foot-skinny, Andrew was an avid tennis player. They'd played many a rousing match against each other until this damn hip interfered.

Waiting for him to reach the upper deck, William turned around and looked up the side of his towering building. Its rigid face of glistening glass and polished steel stood as a monument to his auto parts empire. In glowing blue letters, *DIAMOND* radiated from the top floor for the entire city to see. His wasn't the tallest building in Chicago, but to him, it was the most beautiful. He'd made a lot of money making spare auto parts, and the way he foresaw things, a lot more was to be made in the future. He just hoped the pain in his hip wouldn't interfere with that too.

"Whew," Andrew said, gasping as he finally made it up to the marble deck. Sweat beaded his forehead, made prominent by a receding hairline of stingy blond hair. His narrow face and wedge-shaped nose were beet-red from the summer heat, the steep climb, and another hangover.

William chuckled at the sight of him. "See what happens when you slack off at the tennis club?"

"I beat your ass...last time," he managed between breaths.

"It was a good game. Too bad you don't have *me* to run you all over the court anymore."

"So...this is...your fault," Andrew managed.

"You look like you had a rough night."

"Ah...the usual...poker...cigars...a bourbon or two—"

"If I know you, two too many."

"I'm all right."

William nodded toward the fountain. "What were you doing down there anyway?"

"Collectin' money from Gilbert...in the pumpin' station. He owed me a C note from last night's game. I'd seen his truck in the drive and didn't want him to skip out. Got a chance to see the place, though. I tell yah, a guy could get lost down there." He wheezed. "I didn't realize it was so big with all them stairs, halls, tunnels, and pipes."

"Gilbert gave you the grand tour, huh?"

"Braggin' mostly." Andrew wiped sweat from his brow with the back of his hand. "But I got my money while I was waitin' for you. Killed two birds, yah know."

"Time well spent." William pointed his cane toward the fountain, its diamond-clear water jetting into the air with a roar. "The pumping station goes down four-stories under the pool, all encased in concrete. Every system has a backup. I spared no expense."

"So it runs all the time," Andrew added.

"Without interruption, like the Eternal Flame at Arlington, only wet. I expect it to work for generations to come."

"Must mean somethin' special to you, boss. I mean...go through all that expense for a fountain. I understand Kennedy's Eternal Flame and all, it's for the whole country, but this—."

"I don't want to talk about it."

"Yeah, you never do."

A sharp pain reminded him of his hip. What if...God forbid...what if he was dying? He didn't want to believe it, but still, what if? He looked at Andrew. Maybe now he should know the fountain's special meaning, even if it was personal and a bit eccentric. Leaning on his cane, he threw back his shoulders. "I call my fountain *Mothers' Tears*."

Andrew's narrow eyebrows arched. "Why do they call it Paradise Park Fountain?"

"I built it for my mother..." William blinked back a tear as he remembered the sounds of her sobbing from behind the closed bedroom door, night after night—after Pearl Harbor. He shook his head to get his mind back on track. "And every mother who has cried for her children, children lost to war, poverty, and disease, the three things American technology has failed to conquer. But I have great hopes, Andrew, great hopes for America's future. So, you see, the city can call my fountain whatever it likes."

"Jeeze, boss. For a reason like that, I'd think you'd have your name plastered all over it."

"Trust me. I have my name plastered all over enough stuff. Now, other than Sally, you're the only one who knows the true meaning of my fountain. I expect you'll keep it that way."

"I'm honored."

"Good." William tapped his cane on the marble deck. "Let's go. I'm already late."

Chapter Four

E levator doors slid open, revealing William's outer office and Sally looking up from her desk at him, her eyes wide with expectation. He thought she must've been surprised to see him this way, collar unbuttoned and sleeves rolled up to his elbows. With his suit coat slung over his left shoulder, he limped out of the elevator, the diamond-studded cane clutched in his right hand.

"How did it go?" Sally asked as the elevator doors slid closed behind him.

Not knowing what to say, he headed into his office. How was he going to tell her?

She followed him as far as the door. "William?"

Throwing his coat across the back of his chair, he grumped. "Doctors. They're never satisfied. They strip you, poke you, prod you, take your blood and your money, and still they want more."

Sally leaned on the doorframe. "What did he say?"

He ripped off a wad of cotton taped to the inside of his arm, tossed it in the trash can, and fell into his chair. He didn't care how much it hurt. Setting the cane across his lap, he decided to tell her the least of it. "Webber wants me at Westside Medical Center on the twentieth...eight o'clock, for more tests."

Sally frowned. "Oh dear."

"And I can't eat for twelve hours before the appointment."

"What did he say he was looking for?"

"It's too early to tell."

Her eyes narrowed. "It isn't arthritis, is it."

William didn't want to think about it. He clicked on the TV, hoped she'd get the hint and leave him alone. Apollo 11 was hurtling toward the moon. He likened the astronauts' journey to his own, fraught with danger with an unknown outcome. Settling back in his chair, he had to get his mind on something other than his hip.

Sally disappeared from his doorway.

Feeling suddenly alone, he wished she hadn't gone. He wanted to tell her he was afraid, but no matter what was wrong with him, he was going to fight it. He was going to beat it.

Using models, a TV announcer demonstrated how the Command Module was going to separate from the booster, turn around, dock with the Lunar Module, and extract it from the innards of the third stage. Though the maneuver was critical and dangerous, it was nowhere near as exciting as the launch.

Bored, William switched through the channels. A news station caught his eye. On screen, a young woman with brown hair sat behind a counter. Next to her, a monitor showed the picture of a stubbly-faced baldheaded man, a familiar, frightening face. William felt a jab in his hip.

"The governor's office has issued a statement," she said. "The date will be set shortly. Again, Morris Brennon, Illinois' most notorious mass murderer has lost his last appeal, paving the way for his execution. Eight years ago, he was convicted for the 1959 ax-murders of three nurses in Champaign. Though prosecutors believe he's responsible for more than a hundred similar murders, they're not going to spend the money to try him for all of them, saying, and I quote: We only need to fry him once."

"It's about time," William said, his heart suddenly heavy with the weight of those memories, the bloodbath of a decade ago, the death of his parents at the hands of Morris Brennon and his lethal ax. The police had said he'd followed them home from the store, an elderly couple picked at random, defenseless. He watched the house for a while, then that night, he broke in, killed them in their bedroom. And why? Nothing was taken, so burglary wasn't the motive. He'd done it just for the fun of killing them; that was the only reason.

Murder in the first degree.

Back then, William attended the trial every day, hoping they'd say something, just a mention of his parent's names. But they didn't. There were too many victims. So three nurses in Champaign, Morris Brennon's first victims, got all the attention. After the trial, it was only a matter of time before his appeals were exhausted. American justice was slow but sure. The death penalty was well suited for Morris Brennon.

There was a time when William wanted to throw the switch himself, if they would have let him, but he didn't feel that way any longer. The years of waiting had calloused him. His parents were gone. Nothing would ever bring them back. Morris Brennon would pay for what he did. He'd be executed, and he'd be dead. He was someone else's problem. William had to grab onto his cane to stop his hands from trembling.

"Next up," the newswoman said, "can Arab oil producers really put the squeeze on US commuters? Stay tuned.

Chapter Five

Moments later, Sally's voice came over the intercom. "William, the Dragon Man is in the lobby." Her voice sounded choppy, wrung with emotion. "Ron wants to know if it's okay to send him up."

William turned off the TV, shut out the past to make room for the present—and an unknown future. The Dragon Man? As if today hadn't been problematic enough. Carl Savage was a ruthless lawyer hired by the stockholders to present their wishes to the CEO of Diamond Auto Parts, or more like badger him. The weasel was just a puppet for some Japanese consortium trying to sway Diamond's investors to sell out their stock. But as long as William held the majority, their efforts to take over the company would be in vain. Like his hip, the problem wasn't going to go away on its own. "Do we have their last offer?"

"I'll get it."

Sally walked in with a file folder, her eyes red and tear-swollen. She avoided his gaze as she set the file on his desk, so he decided not to let on that he knew she'd been crying. Though her sadness tore at his heart, he forced himself to ignore it, like the pain in his hip that seemed destined to cause so much sorrow.

Fighting off his own apprehensions, he took a deep breath, picked up the folder and flipped it open. "None of this matters." He examined a column of figures. "Diamond is an American company. I'm not selling it to the Japanese." He turned a page and looked up at Sally. "And today I'm going to spell it out for them. *N - O*."

She smiled halfheartedly. "Go get 'em, tiger."

"Grrrr."

She walked out, acting strong. So was he.

Skimming through the pages of proposals and figures, he shook his head. A few million for this, a few million for that, a lot of million for the other. At stake was his control of a corporation with a billion-plus in assets. The *sweat equity* alone was worth twice their feeble offers. Disgusted with the cheap-shot tactics the Japanese were using to buy up American companies, he grumbled, "Only on my death bed," and closed the file. Did we really win World War II, or was corporate America just a different battleground? Reaching for the intercom button, "Sally," he said. "Tell Ron to send the bloodsucker up."

A moment passed. "He's on the elevator now."

"And he'll be on his way back down sooner than he thinks." Releasing the button, William leaned back in his chair and looked toward the vacant doorway. The pace of his heartbeat rose as he awaited the confrontation. Like the pain in his hip, the persistence of his investors had become more than just an irritation.

Before long, the short fat frame of The Dragon Man appeared at the door. Scraggly shoulder-length hair hung from under his brown fedora. He wore a long gray coat, unbuttoned, the hem skimming the floor. Either his black vest was a size too big, or he was packing a holstered pistol.

"Afternoon," Carl said in a gruff voice that didn't fit his pudgy size. "Mind if I come in?" Stiff legged and hunched forward at the waist, he walked in as if he had a bad back and a crook in his neck.

"What is it this time, Carl?"

"You look like dog shit, William."

"It's Mr. Tuliver to you." He caught a whiff of the fat man's cheap cologne. "At least I don't smell like a French whore."

Carl's bushy black eyebrows arched. "I'm here to help you."

"Help yourself to the window ledge."

"You can't get rid of me that easy." Carl pulled off his hat and tossed it on the desk. Sweat glistened on his forehead and trickled down from his temples to a thin mustache.

William had to laugh. "Does your mother always dress you this funny?"

"It's hot as hell's fire out there." Carl peeled off his coat and slung it across a chair.

"By all means, make yourself comfortable." William pressed the intercom button. "Sally, do we have any arsenic or strychnine for our guest?"

"You don't get it, do you?" Carl sat his fat ass on the corner of the desk. "With my connections, you can retire in style." He talked with his hands in constant motion. "We got a deal here that'll make you rich."

"I'm already rich, Carl. It's this country *I'm* worried about. Traitors like you would sell us off, bit by bit. Pretty soon we'll be casting ballots written in Japanese and riding Arab camels to work. My guess is you'll be swinging some deal with them, too."

"The camels?"

"What else will be left?"

Carl twitched his mustache. "So what? You'll be rolling in dough."

"Or camel crap and sushi."

With a sneer, Carl pinched the fat under his chin. "I'll find a way to make a fortune off that, too. Supply and demand, you know the rules. If something is in demand, I'll find the supplier, for a price, of course."

"And if your mother wanted a soul?"

Carl's eyebrows lifted. "Already sold it. Made the deal myself, nice and legal-like."

William frowned. "So that's why they call you The Dragon Man. You'd have your own mother burning in hell."

"Nope." His tobacco-stained teeth showed through a crafty grin. "Insurance company gave me that nickname. I'm a legend at thirty-two. But hey, it wasn't my fault I was representing a bunch of belly-up companies when the fires broke out."

"So, I see. The Dragon Man leaves a trail of burned out buildings wherever he goes. Insurance pays off in the aftermath."

"The bastards went from rags to riches." Carl jumped down from the desk, his fat belly straining the belt that barely held up his slacks. "For that, I'll take the credit, and the nickname."

"Deservedly so, I'm sure." William felt uneasy about what he had heard. Shifting the diamond-studded cane in his lap, he repositioned his hip in the chair, trying to ease his discomfort. He thought about getting up, walking out the stiffness but decided against it. He dared not reveal any weakness to Carl. "So now you're a legal goon for the consortium. Big career change."

"I go where the money is. Made some big deals along the way, too. And I can do the same for you. We're not talkin' chicken shit here, William. These guys are serious players." He paced in front of the desk, his hands constantly moving. "Big bucks in it for both of us, I tell yah."

William shook his head. The nauseating little creep was making his stomach sick. Diamond's investors and the Japanese had picked the right man to do their bidding. Shifting in his seat, William took a painful breath. "If they're so serious, then why the puny offers?"

Carl stopped, and leaning on the desk with the palms of his hands, he glared at William like a cat poised to pounce on a mouse. "Competition in the spare parts business is going to be gruesome. Everybody and his grandma will be selling. The Japanese have Diamond down as a *short-term* investment. It won't be worth squat in twenty years."

William's hip throbbed. "That's not so, fat boy. They're looking for an outlet to peddle their import parts. Flood the market with cheap Japanese cars, create the demand, and bingo, they're set with Diamond: warehousing, distribution, and retail outlets across the country. They'll laugh at us all the way to the bank."

Carl grumped. "So what's it to you?"

"American jobs," William shot back. "The responsibility of

corporate America should be to its workers, the people who make it all possible, not to its board of directors, investors, and sharks like you. Turning a fast buck is bad for business, and as long as I'm alive, Diamond will stand for those principles. Is that clear?"

Carl stepped away from the desk. His grin turned to a frown that wrinkled the fat on his forehead. "Spoken like a true American, but it don't hold water with me, buck-o. Every man has his price. Even you."

"Not likely."

The fat man's face twisted into a scowl that could have made the dead crawl. "We'll get this company, one way or the other."

A wave of hot adrenaline spilled into William's veins. "Are you threatening me?" His hip throbbed.

"We don't make threats, William. A hostile takeover will leave you on *The Loop* with the rest of the bums."

"I'll block any attempt you make. Tell the Japanese they'll have to look elsewhere for their sucker, and while you're at it, teach them some English. Start with the word *no. N-O.* As in not only *NO,* but up their asses *NO.* And yours, too." He shoved the file folder toward Carl. "Now get the hell out of here before I sic Sally on you. She takes care of all my light work."

Carl bared his teeth. "There are other ways to force you to sell." He tossed his card on the desk and grabbed his hat and coat. "You'll be crawling on your knees when you're ready to talk business. They don't call me the Dragon Man for nothin'."

As Carl stormed out of the office, William pulled himself to his feet and followed him as far as the door. Clutching the cane, he wanted to beat the fat bastard to death with it. "Don't try anything stupid, Carl."

Behind her reception desk, Sally stood. "Leave him alone, Carl. He's got enough problems to worry about."

Carl stepped inside the elevator and pointed a hairy-knuckled finger at William. "His problems are just beginning, lady."

The doors slid closed, and the elevator dinged him down.

Chapter Six

Westside Medical Center

On July 20th, William lay flat on his back on a gurney. The tart smell of antiseptic hung heavy in the air. He was there to find out what was wrong with him. Doctors had spent the morning scanning every inch of his body, prodding and poking places he never knew he had. Now, an orderly's face, clean-shaven and smiling, appeared above him. The gurney began rolling down a hallway. "Where to?" William asked, forcing a smile.

"Your room. We're finished for today."

"Then wheel me straight to the front door."

The orderly chuckled. "After all the radioisotopes we injected into you, it's best you stay here tonight. We don't want you going into fits without us."

"Fits?"

"Just in case, so relax."

The gurney banged through a set of double doors, jarring William enough to unsettle his stomach. Or perhaps all the stuff they'd been pumping into him was making him nauseous. For whatever reason, his guts were rolling like Lake Michigan in a gale. "I don't feel so good."

"Breathe deep."

Fighting nausea, he gulped air. The motion of the gurney wasn't helping matters. An empty stomach had suddenly become a blessing. A few deep breaths later, the feeling subsided as the gurney took a turn down another hallway. The ceiling lights were much dimmer.

"Be sure to drink a lot of water, even if your liver starts swimming. It'll help flush out your system."

William managed a nod.

The orderly pushed the gurney into an elevator and hit a button. "Sorry about all the private rooms being taken."

"It's only for one night."

The elevator jerked to a stop on the eighth floor, and the doors slid open.

"*Dr. Carter. Report to ER*," echoed down the hall as the gurney rolled past a nurses' station and through a gray door.

"William."

Sally's voice sounded like music. She stood at his side now, her warm hand on his arm, looking down at him through eyes clouded with worry. A hundred questions hung on her brow.

He patted her hand. "I'm okay."

"You look terrible. What did they do to you?"

"You know, the poking and prodding stuff again."

The orderly helped him slide off the gurney and onto a bed.

William winced. He tried to keep the split in the back of his hospital gown from showing his crack to the world. "I felt better before I got here. I think these doctors are making me sicker."

Nodding, the orderly said, "Sometimes you have to make a mess to clean up a mess." He cranked up the bed and pushed a pillow under William's head. "There's your water pitcher." He pointed to the bed stand. "The bathroom is over there. Use them both. The doc will see you later." He left the room without looking back, the door swinging closed behind him.

Sally fussed with a fallen lock of William's hair as he looked around the room. The bathroom was directly across from the bed. To his right, just beyond the water pitcher on the bed-stand, a white curtain hung from a track on the ceiling. He could hear the shallow breathing of a patient sleeping on the other side. A round black-rimmed clock on the wall said 3:00. Next to it, a platform supported a small TV, its screen dark. He wanted it turned on to pass the time and run interference for the questions he knew Sally was busting to ask.

"That thing work?"

"Tell me what they did to you down there. What took so long?" She poured him a glass of water from the pitcher and turned on the TV, which slowly came into focus. Two commentators, wearing headsets, sat behind a counter back-dropped by a large NASA emblem. The sound was set so low he couldn't hear what they were saying.

William rearranged his bed sheet, took the glass of water, and chugged half of it down. "Turn that up." He motioned to the TV.

"Not until you tell me."

"Fine. If you must know the gory details, they shot me up with this big needle full of blue stuff. Burned like hell when it went in my arm. I thought I was going to puke."

Sally's upper lip curled.

"Then they put my bare ass on a cold table and took a bunch of x-rays in positions I think you'd like to have seen."

That got a smile out of her.

"I'm just glad it's over."

"Now we wait." She tucked in his top sheet. "Comfortable?" She patted his pillow.

Her smile reminded him of his mother's, when he was eight and had the flu, warm but worried. He looked at the television, the voiceless faces lighting his curiosity. "Now can I listen to the TV?"

"Grump." She turned up the volume.

"At sixty miles high, Neil Armstrong and Buzz Aldrin executed the first burn of the Lunar Module," the commentator explained. "That's dropped them out of orbit, and gravity is pulling them toward the moon's surface."

"How about that," William said, excited that he wasn't going to miss the moon landing, the astronaut's adventure a welcome distraction from his health problems.

Sally leaned on the bed and took his hand, looked at him, fussed with his hair. Why couldn't she just watch the show?

The commentator said, "When they reach fifty thousand feet, they'll be over the Sea of Tranquility where they'll begin a twelve minute powered descent. Let's listen in on their open-mic transmissions."

The screen changed to an animation of the Lunar Module, Eagle, free-falling toward the gray, pockmarked lunar surface.

William chugged the rest of his water and handed the glass to Sally. "Barkeep. Hit me with another. Make it a double."

"I wish Dr. Webber would hurry up. Not knowing is driving me crazy."

"He's got enough blood and pictures to keep himself busy for a while. Relax. We'll know soon enough. Watch this."

NASA's radio beeped. "*Eagle, Houston, twenty miles,*" the controller announced.

"Drink up, dear." She handed him the filled water glass.

He took a swig, though not as aggressively with this glass as the first one. He started feeling better, watching the drama unfold on the moon. He felt lucky to witness it.

"*Ten miles,*" Houston said.

Sally asked, "Do you think they can pull this off?"

"You bet *we* can."

Suddenly, the drone of the Lunar Module's descent engine filled the small room. It sounded feeble compared to the blast of Saturn 5 engines. A glowing comic-strip flame appeared under the animated lander.

"*Eagle, Houston. Five minutes.*"

"Houston has just informed Armstrong of the fuel remaining," the commentator explained for his viewers.

And William added for him, "If they're not down in five minutes they'll run out of fuel and crash. I can see it now." He placed two fingers on his temple like a fortuneteller at a fair. "A moonlit summer night, two lovers strolling hand-in-hand. They gaze up at the moon and suddenly realize that two dead astronauts are still up there."

Sally's face drooped. "What a morbid thought."

"The romantic allure of the moon would never be the same."

She squeezed his hand. "Then they better not screw up. You know how much I love those moonlight walks with you in Paradise Park."

"Me too." He wondered if he'd ever do that with her again.

The radio beeped. "*On manual,*" Armstrong said.

"Neil Armstrong is now at the controls for the final phase of the landing," the commentator said. Steering thrusters made popping sounds like .22 caliber gunshots scattered throughout the radio static and engine drone.

William drank down the last of his water and handed Sally the glass.

"More?"

He shook his head as the animation on the television screen played out the landing.

"*Two minutes.*"

"Can they do it in two minutes?" Sally asked.

"They'd better."

"*Down at 15, 400 feet high, down at 9...*"

William's heart pounded.

"*Altitude light on. 220 feet. Coming down nicely.*"

As the descent engine droned in the background amidst the popping of the steering thrusters, William stared at the animation, worried that the fuel would run out.

"*60 seconds.*"

"One minute of fuel left." His stomach started churning again. Already, the animated landing sequence depicted the Eagle resting on the lunar surface. The engine flame was gone, and the dust had settled.

"They should've been down by now."

Sally gripped his hand tighter.

The Duplication Factor

"*Lights on. 40 feet. Kicking up some dust.*"

"*40 seconds.*" The controller's voice was laced with anxiety.

As precious seconds ticked away, William felt a knot tightening in his stomach, his hip throbbing. "Come on."

"*Faint shadow. Drifting to the right a little.*"

"*20 seconds.*"

"*Contact light on. Engine stop.*"

The airway went silent as a funeral parlor.

"What happened?" William held his breath.

The radio beeped. "*Houston, Tranquility Base here. The Eagle has landed.*"

"All right. They did it." William smiled with pride and clapped for their success. It was an incredible achievement for America.

Even Sally was smiling.

"There's nothing we can't do, Sally."

"Seems like you might be right."

"*Roger, Tranquility, we copy you on the ground,*" the Houston controller said. "*Be advised there are a lot of smiling faces in this room...and all over the world.*"

"You bet there are." William thrust his fists into the air like a victorious prizefighter. The whole world had just witnessed America's ingenuity. It was a proud day for—

The door swung open, and the orderly backed in, struggling with a wheelchair.

William wondered what was going on, why the interruption. "What is it?"

After maneuvering the wheelchair into the room, the orderly propped open the door. "Mr. Tuliver, we're going for another ride."

"I thought you said we were through."

"Dr. Webber wants to see you in his office."

William's heart banged against his ribs. The emotional thrill of the moon landing suddenly spiraled downward into a black abyss of fear. "I don't want to see him right now."

"Let's go anyway." Sally patted his shoulder.

"But they just landed on the moon."

"The astronaut's glory will have to be savored by the rest of the world." She turned off the TV.

In the sudden silence, William again heard the shallow breathing of someone in the next bed. Was that *his* future, oblivious to the world around him? He motioned toward the curtain with a jerk of his head. "That poor guy missed the whole thing. I hope I don't end up like him."

"Maybe we better start praying that you don't."

The orderly helped William sit up. His bare feet dangled above the floor.

"I don't think praying help." He took a deep breath, again fighting a sudden wave of nausea. "The last time I asked God for anything was when my parents were killed. How badly I wanted my mother to find the peace she thought was waiting for her in heaven."

Sally pulled the bed sheet off his lap. "How do you know she didn't?"

"I don't know that she did, either."

"What do you think happened to them after they died?"

"Lights out, forever engulfed in black unconsciousness with no hint of ever having existed." When his feet hit the cold floor, the fear of that empty eternity gave him a chill. Even at sixty, he was too young to die. He'd amassed a fortune over his lifetime. He wanted the time to enjoy spending it. This could be the fight of his life. "I intend to beat this...any way I can."

"We'll beat it together."

He stumbled toward the wheelchair, and dreading the future he was about to face, didn't care if the whole world saw his crack.

Creaking, the wheelchair rolled down a long hallway toward Dr. Webber's office. Sally walked beside William, her hand on his shoulder. Though her touch was comforting, it didn't quell his anxiety.

Moments later, the orderly turned the wheelchair down another corridor where Dr. Webber stood at the door to his office, his face long, his eyes dark hollows of fatigue. William thought he was looking into the face of the Grim Reaper. His stomach sunk.

At the office door, Dr. Webber put a hand on Sally's arm. "Please, wait out here."

"But I..."

"She can come in, doctor," William said.

"After we talk—"

"But, she—"

Dr. Webber put his index finger up. "You know the rules. She's not family."

"Screw the rules." He didn't want to go in there without her.

Sally stepped back. "Go ahead, William. I'll wait here."

"No."

"It's all right."

This was one argument he wasn't going to win. "I love you."

She blew him a kiss.

The orderly pushed the wheelchair through the door, past a cluttered desk, and down a hall to a room with x-rays lined up on a lighted wall. Eerie photos of bones, surrounded by misty body forms, had been put together like a giant puzzle to look like a whole skeleton. The sharp smell of photo developer lingered in the air.

"Are those mine?"

The orderly left the room and the door squeaked closed.

"Unfortunately." Dr. Webber's lab coat hung unbuttoned. Perspiration and worry dominated his face.

William got to his feet, dizzy from fright, and limped to the x-rays. "What's all this mean?"

Dr. Webber stood at his side. "Acute lymphoblastic leukemia, William. Malignant cells in your bone marrow." He pointed to the right pelvis. "See how black these bones are? The marrow is infested with cancer, destroying its ability to produce white blood cells."

William's heart fell into his stomach. "Cancer?"

"Your body's natural defenses are failing. That's why you've been feeling weak. You have no appetite, and you're losing weight."

He pointed to an x-ray of William's left arm. "This marrow hasn't been affected yet. See how clear it is?"

William forced himself to compare the films, not wanting to accept the horrifying truth. A blackness in his pelvis bones seemed to be webbing outward, staining his femur bones and the lumbar vertebrae at the base of his spine. The lower bones of his rib cage were also infected. He could clearly see the killer was spreading. Looking at Dr. Webber, a feeling of hopelessness swept over him. "I'm a goner."

The doctor touched William's shoulder. "The good news is it hasn't metastasized...spread to your organs. We can hold it off with drugs and radiation treatments for a while, but there's really no way to stop it entirely."

"Why not?"

"Your tests came back *positive* for chromosomal abnormalities."

"Chromo what?"

"It's hereditary, William, a fatal flaw in your genes."

"Then fix it."

"Do you have any idea how complicated DNA is?"

"So what?"

"It's impossible to fix."

"They just put a man on the moon, for Christ's sake. Nothing's impossible."

"We don't have the technology."

Fighting panic, slowly, William returned to the wheelchair, his heart pounding, neck sweating. He tried pushing the reality out of his mind, but like a rubber band, it kept snapping back. He was going to die. "I have no options?"

"A bone marrow transplant."

"You can do that?"

"It's an experimental procedure, mind you. The first successful bone marrow transplant was performed last year...in Minnesota. A boy received marrow from his sister. He's doing very well."

"Then let's do it." William slapped the arm of his wheelchair, a ray of hope now glimmering inside.

Dr. Webber leaned against the counter. "It's not that easy. We've only had success with family member donors, mother, father, or sibling. You're the sole survivor of your family, William. A non-family donor must be a perfect match, and even then there's no guarantee."

"Meaning?"

"Your body will reject the bone marrow."

"But there's an anti-rejection drug for that, right?"

"Imuran, yes, but it's expensive and plagued with side effects."

"Worse than dying?"

"Point taken." Webber smiled for the first time. "My assistants are searching for possible donors right now." He put a hand on William's shoulder. "It's a tedious process, may take a while. Then again, we might get lucky."

William felt faint. "If not, how long do I have?"

"A year. Maybe."

"That's all?"

"With treatment, mind you."

"And without it?"

"Six months tops."

"Christ."

"It's the best we can do, William. Do you want me to call Sally in now?"

A lump stuck in William's throat. He had no idea how he was going to explain this to her. "Just wheel me out of here. I'll tell her after you find out about the bone marrow. I don't want her to hold any false hopes."

Chapter Seven

The black '59 Cadillac limo pulled out of Westside Medical Center's parking lot and turned northbound on the Eisenhower Expressway. Sally sat in the back seat, alone. Andrew was driving. William stayed behind—for more tests, he'd said. *Go home, Sally, there's nothing you can do here.*

Traffic whizzed by the windows.

She recalled William's face when he'd come out of the meeting with Dr. Webber. Did he think he could hide the look of despair in his eyes? She leaned forward, tapped Andrew's shoulder. "What did William tell you?"

"Nothin', ma'am." Working the bone-white steering wheel, he glanced at her via the rearview mirror. "Just told me to take you home."

She flopped back into the seat and folded her arms. Her jaw muscles twitched. If William had told Andrew not to tell her anything, he would remain silent, even if he were being tortured. Such was the loyalty between the two men. But she didn't understand what William thought he would gain by keeping the doctor's prognosis from her now.

Speeding along, the limo came upon a school bus full of children, some of them pressing their faces to the windows, their eyes wide. One little girl with red flowing hair and braces smiled at Sally, sparking the memory of her youth and a time when she rode on a bus from New Orleans to Elwood, Illinois. It was a sad time in her life, just after Mother died, when Sally was eight years old.

Before that, for more than three years they'd survived on the streets of New Orleans. Her mother, Rose, blamed herself for her husband's death, Sally's father, even though no one could have talked him down from the bridge that night. The police tried for several hours before they brought Rose to the scene. She pleaded with him to come down—begged him not to jump.

With tears in her eyes, Rose had told her the story of how he clung to a cable, leaned out over the water, and confessed that his business had failed. Bawling, he told her he'd cashed in all their savings bonds, stock certificates, and life insurance policies. Even after withdrawing all the money from Sally's college fund, he said it wasn't enough to save his company. He couldn't save himself from the indignity of what was to come; he couldn't bear the responsibility of failing.

She told him those things didn't matter, that she loved him anyway. "We can make it through this together," she'd promised him. But no matter how hard she tried, Rose was unable to convince her husband to climb down from that bridge, if not for her sake, then for Sally's. "We love you," she told him.

"I'm sorry," he said and let go of the cable.

After that black night, strangers came to the house and took everything: the furniture, the paintings, the car, everything but their clothes, which they crammed into plastic bags and piled on the curb. Rose put the bags into an abandoned shopping cart, and Sally remembered walking alongside it, her fingers clutching the basket and her mother crying as she pushed all that they owned away from the only home Sally ever knew.

At first, New Orleans wasn't a bad place to be homeless. The weather was generally fair, compared to Chicago. The nights were warm and muggy. The days were hot and muggy. It rained sometimes, made life uncomfortable. But when it was cold, when ice storms sagged power lines and broke tree branches, Rose found her daughter shelter in the mission, or when it was full, in the abandoned windowless buildings of the old French quarter. It wasn't too bad— until Mother got sick.

The doctors said she died of pneumonia. They told her Mother couldn't breathe anymore. And they said the bus would take her to Aunt Clara's farm in Elwood. There were lots of farms in Illinois. She couldn't help but wonder if there were homeless people in Illinois, too.

As the limo pulled ahead of the bus, Sally waved goodbye to the children, thinking how happy they looked. She thought back to her childhood in Elwood. Aunt Clara and Uncle Clifford managed the best they could with what little they had on their farm. Dairy cows for milk, chickens for eggs, and pigs for bacon. "Breakfast's what farmin's all about," Uncle Clifford told her. She could still smell his chewing-tobacco breath and picture the brass spittoon on the floor by his rocker. She remembered how he always wore the same clothes: blue jean bib overalls, a white t-shirt, and muddy brown boots. And on a nail by the back door of the farmhouse, Uncle Clifford always hung a big brush. He said he used it to brush the cows' teeth, something he got up early every morning to do. Though she'd never actually seen him brushing the cows' teeth, the brush was always dripping wet every morning, hanging by the back door as she headed off to school.

Aunt Clara stood on the porch, waving goodbye. She possessed the hardened features of a woman who could have ridden covered wagons west a hundred fifty years ago. Life on the farm had creased her face, browned her skin, and streaked her hair with gray. But Sally would always remember Aunt Clara as the one who made the farmhouse come alive with the color and fragrance of flowers, and from the kitchen, the most wonderful aromas of fresh-baked bread, ham and split pea soup, and apple pie. The farmhouse seemed as if it were on a different planet than the smelly barnyard, thanks to Aunt Clara.

Back then, Sally wasn't a complainer. On the streets, she'd learned that complaining did nothing to change things. She was happy to be out of the soup lines, the mission showers, and the endless maze of alleys in New Orleans. Her mother taught her how to survive on her own.

The limo turned left on Lakeshore Drive and sped along the windswept bank of Lake Michigan. In the hazy distance, barges floated on white-capped water. It happened out there, on Lake Michigan one spring day, she remembered, when William Tuliver rode the Sea-Lane Ferry into her life. He and Andrew Cobb had been drinking as they shuttled to a party on the Mary D. Light, an 86-foot yacht moored off Whitefish Bay.

"I'm celebrating my third divorce," William said. "Want to help me ring in the dawn of my new freedom?"

"Why should I?" she asked playfully.

"Because I love your red hair."

The Mary D. Light was one hell of a party.

Now, sitting in the back seat of his limo, she remembered how William was, at first, just a man of means to her. Unlike her father, the man who had jumped off a bridge, William was successful. In the past, she had always rejected the farmhands and college boys that came her way. They were frivolous, concerned only with the moment and without a clear vision of their own futures, much less hers. In them she saw the possibility of ending up like her mother, abandoned and alone. William, on the other hand, was the kind of man she could count on, the kind of man who wouldn't give up on himself, the kind of man she needed in her life.

Not too long after the Mary D. Light, William offered her a job working with him in the Diamond Building. So what if he was more of a father figure to her when all this began? Over time, her feelings for him grew, blossomed into the most wonderful relationship of her life.

Her heartbeat faltered as she realized it was all about to end.

Chapter Eight

In his dimly lit hospital room, William roused from a restless sleep. He'd heard the door latch click and the creak of hinges. Bright light from the hallway silhouetted Andrew Cobb's lanky frame.

"Boss?"

"It's all right, Andrew. Please, come in."

He closed the door. "Thought you were sleepin'."

"Did you get Sally home okay?"

Andrew lowered his eyes. "You should've told her what's going on."

William pushed the sheet down to his waist and hit the button to motor the bed up to a sitting position. "There's nothing to tell her."

"You don't have to lie to me, boss." Andrew plopped into a chair next to the bed. "Bullshit her all you want."

William showed him an uneasy smile. "I couldn't just come out and tell her I'm...d..." The word lodged in his throat. "Dying."

Andrew jerked upright in his chair. "What?"

"Relax. There still may be a chance. So why give Sally half the story? When I have all the facts, I'll tell her."

"Does the same go for me?" He got up and stood at William's bedside. "I sure hope not."

William locked eyes with Andrew's. "It's some kind of genetic leukemia."

Andrew's shoulders drooped. He put a hand on William's shoulder. "Is there a cure?"

"Doc says I need a bone marrow transplant."

"Never heard of it."

"It's experimental. He's trying to find a donor."

Andrew held out his forearm, fist clenched. "You can have some of mine."

"No thanks," William said. "As much as you drink, it's probably pickled."

He looked at his arm suspiciously. "You think?"

"Besides, it won't match mine. Our blood types are different. Remember the Red Cross blood drive?"

"They wouldn't let me drink for a week."

"I just have to wait and see what the doc can find."

Andrew sat in the chair again. "Then I'll wait with you." He clicked on the TV. "But you really should have told Sally."

"Yeah, yeah..."

The television brightened the room. Locked in conversation regarding the upcoming moonwalk, commentators sounded like play-by-play announcers for a football game that was about to begin. "After Neil is on the porch, he'll have to take ten steps down the ladder to the surface of the moon."

"And once they get the TV camera operating," the other commentator added, "we should be able to watch that historical event as it happens. Let's listen in. They're about to get started."

Andrew settled back, crossed his spidery legs. "This should help pass the time."

William wondered how much time he had left to pass.

"*Houston. This is Neil. Radio Check.*"

NASA's radio beeped. "*Verify TV circuit breaker in.*"

"*Ah, check.*"

"*Roger. We're getting a picture.*" His voice sang with the excitement of a child with a new toy. "*We can make out a fair amount of detail.*"

"It's great," William said, taking it all in as if it were the last historic thing he'd ever witness. The black and white transmission showed the Lunar Module's ladder extending down to about a foot above the moon's gray surface. Shadows cast from the lander shaded some of the scene, which looked like a still picture taken from a science fiction movie. He stared at the television screen, expecting a breeze to rustle the insulation on the Lunar Module or whip dust into the air. But nothing moved on the surface of the moon.

"Okay, Houston. I'm on the porch."

Creaking, the door swung open, flooding the room with light from the hall.

William flinched, saw Dr. Webber come in. He switched on the ceiling light. "Sorry for the interruption."

The forlorn look on the doctor's face told William he was about to get some more bad news. "What's wrong?"

Dr. Webber stood at the foot of the bed. "There are no donors, William."

His stomach turned upside down. "None?"

"I put your name on a waiting list."

"How long do I have to wait?"

"It's hard to say. Remember, the procedure is relatively new. Worse, it's not yet been successful with non-family donors, and it's never been used to treat leukemia."

William hated the way doctors beat around the bush. "How long until my name comes up on the list?"

"Nine months, tops."

"And you're sure I'm going to live that long?"

"With treatment...yes. But we could be cutting it close."

How stupid, William thought. His life depended on a list? "It's not good enough." He clenched a fist. "I'm wealthy, damn it. I'll pay extra. I need the operation right away."

Dr. Webber frowned. "It's out of my hands."

"I'll go over your head."

Andrew got out of his chair. "Take it easy, boss."

"Don't tell me to take it easy. I don't want to die."

"It's the best we can do, William." The doctor marked

something on a clipboard, hung it on the bedpost. "I suggest you take your friend's advice."

"I suggest you do your job."

"Look," Andrew said, pointing to the TV. "They're going to walk on the moon."

"Screw the moon," William shouted. "It's my life we're talking about here." But Andrew and Dr. Webber weren't listening to him. They were watching the TV.

Houston radioed Eagle. *"Okay, Neil. We can see you coming down the ladder now."*

William looked up at the screen, saw dark boots appear on the upper rung. He felt emotionally torn between his dilemma and the incredible image before him. What good was walking on the moon? Didn't they know the world was coming to an end? His world. It might as well be everyone's world. If he didn't think of something, he was going to die. Everything else was just a distraction from his problem, even the space man with a large pack on his back. He became fully visible on the screen, making history when history didn't matter anymore. Not to William. He was going to lose everything—his life—his fortune—

"I'm at the foot of the ladder," Neil reported.

Forcing himself to concentrate on the problem at hand, William thought about his conversation with Sally—about having a baby. He didn't have a family, but he could make one of his own—in nine months. Wouldn't the baby's bone marrow match his? He looked at the doctor who was still watching the television. "What if Sally and I have a child? You know, we can make our own donor."

Dr. Webber answered without looking away from the screen. "You'll have a one-in-four chance of a match."

"Those are lousy odds."

Webber nodded but continued watching TV. "Especially considering your marital status, gestation period and, of course, your life expectancy. But it's not a bad idea."

"Is there any way to guarantee a match?"

"I'm not a miracle worker."

"So you're just going to give up on me?"

At that, Dr. Webber turned from the TV. "You have to be patient. Stick with Sally. Have a child. Take your chances. It's your best option."

"There's got to be another way."

"Sure...if you can clone yourself."

William's throat went dry. Clone myself?

Neil Armstrong jumped down to the surface of the moon, his footprint embedded in lunar dust and history. *"That's one small step for man. One giant leap for mankind."*

William blinked, his mind in a whirl. There it was—on television—a man walking on the moon. How incredible was that? It meant one thing. Nothing was impossible. He remembered wishing he could make spare parts for his body, the way he'd made spare parts for cars. Human cloning could be a way to do that, a hundred percent guaranteed match. But he didn't know the first thing about cloning. Did anyone? The next question seemed laughable, but necessary. "Where can I get myself cloned?"

Andrew speared him with a sharp glare. "What did you say?"

"If scientists can put a man on the moon, they can find a way to clone a human."

Dr. Webber turned toward the door. "I wasn't serious."

"Look up there." William pointed to the TV, his heart racing. "With the right technology, anything is possible."

Webber grabbed the doorknob. "Where are you going to find that kind of technology?"

"Surely there are books on the subject, articles written by researchers, universities with government grants—"

"Cloning is not a practical endeavor," Dr. Webber said. "More of an inside joke...science fiction at best."

"Don't discount the power of science to turn fiction into reality, doctor. It's happening on the moon right now."

"Be realistic." Dr. Webber opened the door. "If cloning were being done anywhere, it would be totally secret. You'll never find anyone to help you. Have a baby with Sally."

William didn't like the odds. Cloning kept banging around in his head like a sparrow in a cage. "I know someone who might be able to help me."

Andrew frowned. "What are you thinkin', boss?"

"The Dragon Man." William pushed himself upright on the bed, grasping at ideas out of thin air. "I've got something he wants, Diamond Auto Parts."

"Come on, boss, think about what you're sayin'. You're not going to give up your company. And even if cloning is possible, Carl Savage can't be trusted."

"What do you expect me to do, lie down and die? I'm not that kind of person. I'll fight for what I want."

"It'll take a deal with the devil to get what you want."

"Are you with me or against me, Andrew?"

"I gotta go against you, boss. I'm sorry. It's not going to work. Besides, I'm not so sure it's even right."

William didn't need Andrew's approval anyway. "So be it."

Dr. Webber huffed. "Most of us have better things to do than clone humans and walk on the moon." Stepping through the doorway, he glanced back at William. "Treatments. I suggest we get started tomorrow."

He clicked off the light and closed the door, leaving the room illuminated by the televised moonscape.

Chapter Nine

Paradise Park, Chicago

A cold wind off Lake Michigan rustled the oak trees overhead as William sat on the white-marble edge of *Mothers' Tears*. The breeze felt cool on his face, and cascading water slapped the pool's surface with a rhythm that warmed his heart. He gazed up at the jets of water, their pinnacles giving off a fine mist to the winds aloft. Sparkling droplets drifted down over the park and refracted the afternoon sunlight into a rainbow. Its magnificent arc of colors seemed to touch the grass in a glow of gold. It was as if *Mothers' Tears* was showing him her finest hour, the hour before the storm.

He checked his watch. *3:05*. Two weeks ago, he'd called Carl Savage and pressed him for a meeting. Now, sick from radiation treatments and nauseating drugs, William had managed to get here on time. But the Dragon Man was late.

Unnerved about waiting, he pried himself to his feet with his diamond-studded cane. Relying on it for support, he limped along the edge of his fountain and its sparkling pool, pausing when coins on the bottom caught his attention, glistening reminders of wishes once made. He wondered what those wishes might have been: a new love, a new car, a new life. How about a cure for a horrible disease? He thought a cure had to be worth a coin. From his pocket, he pulled out a quarter and flipped it into the water. After watching it settle to the bottom with the others, he tested his hip. It still hurt.

Wishful thinking wasn't going to solve his problem. It would take action. His fate was in his hands now, but in order to survive, he had to trust Carl Savage. The Dragon Man was despicable, but he was capable. He knew how to get things done, had contacts in high places, and he wasn't afraid to bend the rules, if not break them entirely. Carl was the right man to help him, all right, but still, William would have to be careful.

Limping to the bronze placard that identified Paradise Park Fountain, William stopped and rubbed the side of his neck. Maybe he should have put his name on his fountain. Now he was destined to lose *Mothers' Tears*, along with everything else he had accomplished in his lifetime. It wasn't fair.

A flock of pigeons foraging on the lawn suddenly leaped into the air, batting their wings and startling him. His quickened heartbeat slowly recovered as he watched the birds fly gracefully through the park, darting left and right. He felt insignificant to them. They'd been here for decades, before he'd built his Diamond Building, before Paradise Park, and they'd be here long after he was gone. The cycle of life, he was part of it, on the downhill side. He didn't like it. Begrudgingly, he continued his arduous walk around his prized fountain.

When he made it back to where he'd started, he spotted Carl lumbering down the marble steps from the upper deck. A wisp of smoke swirled from a cigar clenched between his teeth. William braced himself on his cane and watched the fat man descend.

At the bottom step, Carl stopped, his rounded chest heaving as he reorganized something under his vest. He lifted his hat and wiped sweat from his brow then waddled toward him. "It's your dime, Tuliver. You better not be wasting my time." He pulled the cigar from his teeth and sucked in a raspy breath. "What's on your mind?"

Limping to the marble poolside, William sat on a section shaded by a big oak. Carl plopped down next to him and flicked cigar ashes onto the deck. The breeze rolled the embers away.

William caught a whiff of the Dragon Man's cheap cologne. "When are you going to switch aftershaves?"

Carl sneered. "I didn't come all the way down here to discuss my toiletries. If you're looking for a better offer from the Japanese, forget it. They're sick of your patriot games."

"Don't get your panties in a wad, Carl." William took a deep breath. "There's something I need you to do for me."

Carl's brows arched, lifting his hat brim. "Like what?"

"A while back, you shot off your mouth about supply and demand, remember?"

"So?"

"I need you to find something...something I need."

"What's in it for me?"

"Money."

Carl snorted. "I'm not interested in your money." He stood. "Just Diamond Auto Parts."

William grabbed Carl's coat sleeve. "If you find what I'm looking for..." he swallowed. "Diamond will be in the deal." He couldn't believe he'd said the words.

Carl's eyes lit up. "Diamond?" He spoke the word softly, barely audible over the splashing fountain. "Diamond?" He repeated the word as though he were savoring it like fine wine. "You'd sell Diamond to the Japanese?" He sat down, grinning. "Is that what I heard you say?"

"That's right." William wanted to pull the words back, grab them out of the air, and stuff them back down his throat, but it was too late. Besides, he knew this was something he had to do, as painful as it was.

"I'll be damned." Carl propped his elbows on his thighs, inhaled on the saliva-soaked end of his cigar, and spit. Smoke swirled from his nostrils and rushed away on the breeze. "All that talk...American jobs, fast bucks, and principles—"

"Things are different now."

"It was all bullshit."

"No."

Disbelief washed across Carl's fat face. "A man in your

position doesn't flip-flop overnight."

William knew Carl wouldn't resist getting in a few barbs. "Let's just say my priorities have changed."

"Horsepuckey."

"Look." William held out his cane. "You think this is a fashion statement?"

The lawyer looked the cane up and down with wanting eyes. "I wondered about that...when I saw you favoring your hip. Old age must be a bitch."

"It's not old age, Carl. I'm dying. The big C."

Carl's face lit up with a smile that reached his eyes. "You don't say?"

"You find favor with that?"

He shrugged. "I may be slow, but I'm not stupid. Your bad luck is my good luck."

"This isn't about luck. It's about doing what's necessary. All my life I've lived by my principles. Now I have to make a trade-off, my principles for my life."

"Sounds like a personal problem. I'm only interested in how Diamond fits into the deal."

"I need a bone marrow transplant. It's a long shot but a chance, nonetheless."

Grabbing the cigar from his mouth, Carl frowned. "I don't get it. You gotta sell your corporation to the Japanese for a transplant? Must be one damned expensive operation."

"The operation is nothing. It's coming up with a donor that's the hard part."

Carl leaned back. "Don't look at me."

"Don't worry, fat boy. I'd sooner die than walk around with your bone marrow inside me."

"Then just what the hell do you need me for?"

"A genetic research facility is the only place I can get a suitable donor. I need you to find one for me."

"What's wrong with the Yellow Pages?"

"They don't advertise cloning in the book, Carl."

"Cloning? Are you nuts?"

"Maybe."

The fat man fell silent, his eyes locked on the gray ash of his smoldering cigar. Splashing fountain water and rustling tree leaves were the only sounds. "Why would you dump your principles to save your ass?"

"It's my selfish nature," William decided to tell him. Put all his cards on the table. Be frank. Be open. "That's what my mother told me. I've always looked out for *Number One* first. Not like James."

"Who's James?"

"My brother, now there was a patriot. He was ten years younger than me, and he died for his principles...or for America's principles. Whichever it was, he was just as dead at the bottom of Pearl Harbor. I'll never forget how my mother cried, how she wailed as if the world had ended." He glanced up at his fountain, remembered those long nights.

A gust of wind swept through the park. Carl held his hat brim. "Did she like him best?"

"She thought I was too self-centered to give a damn about what James died for."

"Did you?"

"I buried myself in my work."

"I don't get it." Carl took a drag on the dwindling cigar and blew smoke into the breeze. "If Diamond was your way of dealing with your brother's death, why give it up?"

William pulled the cane to his chest. "What good will it do me when I'm dead? I have no heirs. May as well sell it." The words hurt deep in his chest, words he thought he'd never say, but it was the only thing he could do. If he survived the cancer, he'd start spending his money, take Sally on a cruise. Go to Europe. Egypt. If not—

Smiling, Carl patted William's shoulder. "You're doing the right thing, Tuliver. And believe it or not, the Japanese aren't the enemy anymore. They'll do a lot of great things for Diamond, and for America too, someday."

"The Japanese will always be my enemy. They murdered my brother."

"Let bygones be bygones. What's it to you, anyway? You'll be worm food and the world will still be turning without you."

"Don't bet on it," William said. "Find a research lab that'll clone me, and I can be cured."

Carl stood and threw down the cigar butt. "Count me out, Tuliver."

"What?"

"I blew off the notion the first time you said it." He flailed his hands like an Italian politician. "Are you out of your mind? Clone you?" He started walking away, the wind tearing at his long coat. "I'm gonna send you a bill for wasting my time."

"That's fine." William tried to get up but couldn't. "Charge me double. Just hear me out."

Carl stopped, stood there a moment with his back to William, and then slowly turned around. "There ain't no such thing as cloning. They can't do that yet."

William pointed to the sky. "Walk on the moon? You going to tell me they can't do that either? Find the lab, Carl. I need my clone's bone marrow to survive this cancer. I've got less than a year. Whether I live or die, you make a deal with the Japanese. Either way, it's a win-win situation for you."

Carl strutted back toward him. "Either way?" His steps had a slight bounce to them. "What's the catch?"

"No catch."

"Let me get this straight. All I gotta do is find you a cloning lab of some kind, and you'll sell Diamond to the consortium."

"And you get a big commission check."

Carl squinted. "Where am I gonna find a lab that can clone humans?"

"Supply and demand. Those are your words. Time to put your money where your big mouth is, Carl. I think you'll prove yourself worthy."

"But...but what leverage will I have with a lab, you know, to convince them to do it...if they thought they could, that is."

"Offer them research money, a lot if you have to. Make your best deal. I'll back you. Then go to the Japanese and tell them I'll accept their last offer on two conditions."

Carl frowned. "Here comes the catch."

"First, payment up front, in diamonds. No cash, no checks, no stock options, no payment plans."

"Two-hundred-thirty-seven million dollars in diamonds?" He whistled. "That's a lot of rocks."

"Diamonds in exchange for Diamond Auto Parts. It's only fitting." William felt his past slipping away, his future spinning out of control. "Top quality diamonds."

Carl tipped his hat. "What else?"

"Paradise Park Fountain is to be held in trust by the consortium, funded and operated without interruption, forever."

Carl shook his head. "Forever's a long time, Tuliver."

"So's dying."

Chapter Ten

Menard State Prison, Chester, Illinois

C&K all the way!

There they were, three nurses, standing in front of him, tempting him with their smiles, arms outstretched, calling his name.

"Morr-rris...Morr-rris."

White uniforms lay neatly folded at their feet, their socks and panties, too. Naked flesh made his pulse race, the curves and crevices, nipples erect and wanting. His heart pounded.

C&K all the way!

"Morr-rris...Morr-rris."

Their sweet voices filled the air like the harmony of a choir. Calling. Swooning. Beckoning. Yes. They wanted him. He wanted them, too, all of them, their hair in his fingers, their sweat on his tongue, and their blood on his hands.

C&K all the way!

"Morr-rris...Morris!"

They wanted to give it all to him. Begging. Pleading. Moaning. Screaming. *C&K...*

"Morris."

...all the way...

Bang, bang, bang!

"Morris."

What...huh?

"Get your ass up, Morris."

A sharp pain shrieked from his ribs. Morris's eyes popped open. He saw cell bars, lime-green cement, a single bulb glowing from the ceiling. "What the hell?"

"Get up."

Fred Flanagan. The son of a bitch had stolen his dream. On top of that, the bastard was jabbing him in the ribs with a nightstick. Morris grabbed it, leaped from his cot. "I'll rip your fucking heart out."

Flanagan tried to pull the nightstick back through the bars. "Just try it, fat boy." A stiff-armed tug-of-war ensued.

As Morris wrestled with the nightstick, a wonderful sensation came over him. The smooth, lacquered finish reminded him of his old ax handle. Ah, yes, the perfect tool for murder: random destruction with each swing. The memory sent ripples of delight through his whole body. How he missed the crunching sound of breaking bones and the crimson spray of blood.

"Stop it, Morris. Damn you."

Though he didn't want to give in to the guard, Morris knew the wimp would call in his buddies. They'd beat him to a pulp. So he let go. "Stick it up your ass."

Flanagan bared his teeth. "Twenty-nine days and I'll be rid of you, you psycho. Do you have to be an asshole to the end?"

"You can count on it." Morris gripped the bars with both hands, his bloodstream burning. "Cage a wild animal and you're gonna get bitten, sooner or later. And I'd just as soon kill you as look at you." He squeezed the bars. "I want the hell out of this shit box, dead or alive, it don't matter to me. I ain't scared of your damn chair."

"Oh, you will be," Fred replied with a growl. "And I'll be there when they throw the switch. I'll be sitting in the front row, watchin' you fry."

"I hope you puke."

"Fuck you." Flanagan snarled. "Now get your ass ready. She'll be here in five minutes. Clean up that ugly mug and put on a shirt."

Morris flipped him a finger. "I'm going like this. If the bitch don't like it, tough shit."

"A shirt, Morris, and tuck it in real neat." Flanagan disappeared down the corridor.

Morris sat on the cot and patted the bandage on his right forearm. Satisfied it was still secure, he glanced around the dingy cell he'd called *Home Sweet Home* for the past eight years. Death Row, Menard State Prison, Level B, Cell 5, this was his little world: his beloved cot, his beloved sink, and his beloved crapper. Every day it was the same thing, day in and day out. Other than the occasional fly or cockroach that haplessly wandered in, there was nothing around here to kill.

Buttoning his starch-stiff prison shirt, he heard chains rattle from down the hall. Shackles. Everywhere he went they chained his legs together and his wrists to his waist. They were scared to death of him...and for damn good reason.

Flanagan keyed the lock. "You know the drill, Morris, on your feet and against the wall. We don't want to keep the lady waiting." The cell door opened with a squeal that echoed down the corridor.

Morris took a deep breath. Six months of this crap. She kept coming back, but he never told her a damn thing. This time it was going to be different. Morris assumed the position, and Fred administered the chains.

Clanking with each step, he shuffled his two hundred ninety pound frame down the hallway and into the visitor's room, which looked more like an interrogation chamber with its mirrored wall, long wooden table, and the big steel chair bolted to the floor. Flanagan pushed him into the chair. It felt cold, hard, and uncomfortable, like everything else in his little world.

Flanagan locked the heavy leg irons to the chair and leaned in to Morris's ear. "You be real nice to the young lady, you hear? I'll be right outside."

"Go to hell."

The door closed with a thud. Morris waited in silence, scanning the drab off-white room. The smell of old cigarette smoke lingered in the air. A single shaded bulb dangled over his head. Its bright glare reflected off the mirrored wall in front of him. His bald head gleamed as he smiled into the mirror—in case any of them bastards were behind it, watching.

On the other side of the table, a metal folding chair awaited the sweet ass of Karen Carlyle. She'd told him she was a journalist, an investigative reporter looking to boost her career by interviewing the notorious Morris Brennon. She was a bitch. She never let up, always asking questions, trying to get into his brain, find out what happened to the nurses. He hated her, but she'd been a steady visitor. He'd told her he'd talk, someday. If she wanted the byline, she'd have to show up. Maybe she'd get lucky, maybe not. He had a surprise for her today.

Eyeing the bandage on his forearm, he recalled his only other visitor, some smartass doctor from Blythe University who said he wanted samples of Morris's cells. Fuck you, he had told him. But the doc explained how he thought a flaw in Morris's genes might have caused him to do all those killings. Made perfect sense. Got him out of that stinking cell for an hour when they took him to the infirmary where the doctor collected some tissue samples. Epidermis, whatever that was, would prove that Morris had screwed up genes. It was something that could happen to anybody. Killers were born every day. Who cared?

The door swung open, and the sound of high heels clicking on tile got his attention. He turned and silently watched her walk in, her light brown hair bouncing on her shoulders with each step. She carried a red file folder tucked under her arm. Red was for death row. The geeks had a color for everything.

Watching her walk by, his eyes swept her body up and down. She was a fine bitch, dark skinned, like she vacationed in Florida. Her big brown eyes glistened in the light that hung above him. He made eye contact with her, batted his eyebrows seductively. She disengaged. He watched her move like fluid around the table. She seemed unshaken by his stare. He bet she'd be sweating hailstones if it weren't for these chains. Rattling the links, he hoped she'd flinch, but she didn't.

She set a tape recorder on the table and sat in the folding chair. After opening the file in front of her, she put on a pair of dainty reading glasses. "Hello, Morris. Feel like talking today?"

"Nice blouse," he said with a growl. "If it was buttoned up around your neck any tighter you'd be chokin'. What's the matter? Afraid to show Morris a little skin?"

"Well, that's a start." She eyed the recorder. "Shall I turn this on?"

Morris nodded. "You'll want to get every word of this."

Her eyebrows arched in approval. With a click, she pushed the button that started the tape reels rotating. A faint whirring sound invaded the silence.

"Hurt your arm?" She pointed at the bandage.

He eyed the doctor's workmanship. Slicker than hell, he'd cut out a chunk of that epidermis stuff. It was for some experiment where the students at the university would clone his cells to make another one of him. They were going to use some kind of enzyme that would make the clone exactly like him, a duplicate. If the brat turned out to be a killer, it would prove Morris's lust for murder was hereditary. What a crock, but if the doc was right, Morris Brennon would be back someday, all two hundred and ninety pounds of him. He smiled as he looked at the bandage. "It's nothing."

"You're running out of time, Morris."

"So they tell me." He chuckled.

"They're going to electrocute you in twenty-nine days. You're only thirty years old. How do you feel about that?"

Morris glanced at the recorder. It looked invasive, but it was necessary—this time. "Life without freedom ain't worth squat," more for the recorder than the bitch. "They did me a favor, you know, slapping me with a death sentence. Life in prison would have been the real punishment. I'd rather be dead."

She turned a page in the folder. "You surprise me, Morris. I've been here to see you six times. You've always played mute. Why talk to me now?"

"I got something to say."

She smiled. "So let's hear it."

"It wasn't my fault that I killed those people."

Her smile faded. "Of course not, Morris. It never is."

"I couldn't help myself."

"Sure, Morris. Are you apologizing?"

"Why should I apologize for something I had no control over?"

"So you're not sorry."

"I did what I had to do. That's what I want you to tell everybody."

"And what are you going to do for me?"

Cocky bitch. "I'll give you what you came for." He leaned forward, rattling the chains. "The gory details."

She licked her upper lip. "All right, Morris. This is your chance to tell the world. What made you kill those girls?"

"Nothing *made* me do it," he said, thinking of the doctor's theory. "I was born to do it."

She frowned. "That's it? You're a born killer? You want me to write that? My readers aren't going to buy it."

"You want your story or not?"

"All right, Morris...go ahead. Tell me how it is that you're a born killer."

She better listen good. He was only gonna tell her once, from the beginning. "My mother told me that I was a mean kid. I frightened her. She said, when I was born, I made hissing noises from my throat. And she wouldn't nurse me 'cause I tried to rip off her tits. She said I hurt her real bad. I scratched her. I kicked her. That's what she said I was like from the start, like it was instinct to cause pain. I turned out to be a barbarian, raping and murdering in the wrong millennium."

Karen shook her head and wrote something in the file.

Put aback by her lack of response, he wanted her to believe him, but how? *The devil is in the details, they say.* She'd have to believe him then. But no matter what, he could never tell her about the game, his game, the game he'd invented all by himself. Catch them and Kill them. *C&K all the way* he would say. His game had to be kept a secret; no one else would understand the rules.

"Why did you hurt your mother?" Karen asked.

"It makes me feel good...you know...to hurt someone, to kill someone. I love that feeling. As long as I can remember, I wanted it. I needed it."

With a heavy sigh, she made another note in the file. "When did you first start *wanting it*?"

He thought about the first time he'd played the game. *C&K all the way.* "When I was about five," he said flatly. "I cut the legs off my kitten. I can still remember how funny that stupid animal looked, flopping around, trying to run, and meowing its fool head off. I watched it bleed to death."

She shot him a disapproving glare over the frame of her glasses.

"Don't worry. I buried all the pieces."

She grimaced. "What did your mother say when your pet turned up missing?"

Morris remembered and chuckled.

"What's so funny?"

"I told her the kitty ran away. Ran away. Get it? No legs." Morris laughed hardily, the image flickering in his mind like an old picture show.

Karen's lower lip trembled. "You find humor in that?"

"Don't you?"

Her mouth fell open. "God, Morris."

He grinned. Now he had her attention. It was time to make her believe. "Try to imagine it, baby, the burning desire to kill."

"I can't." She dropped her gaze to the folder. "It's not normal."

He wanted her to know it was out of his control. It was instinct.

Natural. Primeval. Like fucking. "What's it like, Karen? You know, when you're getting laid?"

Her head jerked up, eyes like darts. "What?"

"You know. The fire. The heat. The wanting. In the throes of passion, you want nothing else. Nothing will satisfy you but the act itself. The raw, body sweating, heart pounding, orgasmic convulsions of pleasure. And when it's over, how do you feel? Are you satisfied, or do you want more?"

"So it's a sexual thing?"

"For me, killing and sex are the same thing."

Coolly, Karen turned a page. "It says here, you raped most of your victims, sodomized them."

"I like it like that," Morris replied. If she was looking for sensationalism, he had plenty of that for her, too. "Sometimes I fucked them first, but when it was over, I wasn't satisfied. Turns out sex was just foreplay." He leaned forward on his chains. "The real ecstasy came from taking their lives. The bloodier it was, the better it was. You can't imagine the adrenaline rush, the power, the thrill. I get off on killing, baby. Don't knock it 'til you tried it."

She looked down at her folder, her knuckles turning white from gripping the pen. "And the men and children you murdered, did you have to rape them, too?"

"Not all of them." He smirked.

As she wrote in the file, he noticed her pen quivering. Her breasts rose wantonly as she pulled in a deep breath. He knew she was trying to stay calm, but she couldn't fool him. He could tell when a woman was on the verge of panic.

"Do you have any recollection of abuse...sexual abuse?"

"You're kidding."

"Did your mother ever...well...touch you inappropriately?"

"My mother is dead."

"Your father, perhaps?"

"I never knew my father, some longshoreman from Germany. He knocked up my mother and left her."

"Then did anyone else abuse you, an uncle maybe, or a neighborhood boy?"

"Don't make me laugh." He rattled his chains. "You still don't get it, lady. Nobody did anything to make me this way. I sexually abused myself. Do you want to know what I liked to do with my dick?"

"I know what you did with it, Morris. You raped two of your classmates, Tina and Sharon, in junior high."

"They asked for it."

"You really believe that?"

"They were wearing miniskirts. What did they expect?"

She scanned a record in her file. "You got no jail time."

"I was a juvenile."

"My guess is there were others."

"I was careful after that."

"But you didn't kill them."

"I didn't know any better."

She pulled the glasses down her nose and glared at him. "So what was different about the nurses?"

"The nurses?" He tried to act stupid. He'd never forget his three nurses. *C&K all the way.*

"In Champaign, the women you were convicted of killing. The ones that are sending you to the chair."

"What about them?"

"Tell me what happened."

"This is what you came for, isn't it?"

"My readers want to know."

The tape recorder whirred. "You'll tell them it wasn't my fault?"

"What do you care what they think?"

"I don't. I just want you to tell them I had no choice. I want them to know it's possible. The boy next door might be another one like me, a born killer."

"Have it your way, Morris. It wasn't your fault."

"We got a deal?"

"Sure. What happened with the nurses?"

Morris studied her eyes. She didn't blink, so he decided to trust her. "They were my first, yah know."

Like a child about to open a birthday present, she leaned forward in anticipation. This was what she wanted to hear. He was going to make her wish she'd never asked. "Because of them bitches, I lost my inhibitions, my innocence, my virginity. I'll always remember the day we met."

"You mean the day you killed them."

"The day I took them...all of them. Best part was, I didn't plan it. It just happened. All my fantasies came true that day in the shed."

She flicked back a lock of hair. "How did you end up in the shed?"

"I left the feed store early that day. Felt restless, I guess. Parked the Edsel off County Line Road and went for a walk in the woods. Something was bugging me. Had been for a long time. If Mr. Jensen had picked up his order like he was supposed to, I wouldn't have gotten off early. I wouldn't have been there in the woods. I wouldn't have known what was missing in my life. Good thing, huh?"

"How do you figure? In twenty-nine days you're going to be put to death for what you did that day."

Morris shifted in his chair, the chains clanking. "Death ain't no big deal. It's living in prison that's hell. People worry about dying all their lives. I'm not afraid of it. Besides, I did them nurses a favor."

"You murdered them, Morris. Why can't you admit it? And you were brutal about it, Jesus, merciless." She poked her finger on a page in the folder. "Right here, in the report, it says you decapitated Debra Simmons with an ax."

He puffed out his chest. "She was the prettiest. She had to die first."

Karen's face turned sullen. Her eyes narrowed. Slowly, she leaned back in her chair and crossed her arms. "Go ahead."

Morris blinked. "I heard laughing and giggling in the woods

where I was. It came from a house in the clearing. I could see it through the trees, red roof, red brick, nice place. I was real quiet sneaking through the bushes. They were there, the three of them, in the backyard. I watched for a while, saw them prancing around the patio in their bikinis, chasing each other with a garden hose, splashing in the wading pool like birds in a birdbath. I was a cat."

"How long did you watch them?"

"Maybe an hour. Then they spread a blanket on the grass and laid there in the sun, napping. I got bored. I wanted more."

Closing his eyes, the memories of Champaign replayed.

"I made my way through the bushes toward a wooden shed in the corner of the back yard. It looked more like a rundown garage with and old door that hung loose on rusted hinges. Firewood was piled high against the wall, and weeds grew everywhere. Peeling paint told me no one had been taking care of the place."

Karen sat upright. The recorder whirred.

"Music from their radio covered the sound of my footsteps, but I thought for sure they'd hear my heart pounding in my chest. My blood was on fire, and my fingers tingled.

"When I got to that broken door and squeezed my way inside, I could only see by the light coming in through a small window. The old shed was chucked full of junk. Ropes and cords hung from the rafters, and a piss-stained mattress was propped up against a wall. A bunch of boxes and two wooden chairs had been stacked up next to a table that leaned on a bad leg. There was a washing machine in the corner, all dusty and dented, and a bench with tools hanging above it on the wall—probably put there by some guy who once cared about how pretty they looked. Now they were covered with dust, which told me the man of the house had split. How lucky could I get?"

"So you knew the women were defenseless."

"I was nervous anyway. I bumped into that rickety table I was telling you about. The damn thing tipped and fell into a stack of boxes full of pop bottles. A car wreck couldn't have made more noise. I tell you, I held my breath, and one of them bitches yelled out, 'Sheila, that damn raccoon is in the shed again.' My throat went dry. That's when Deb says, 'I'll get it this time.' Shit, I was gonna get busted."

"Why didn't you just run out of there, run away?"

"Crossed my mind, sure, but when I reached the window, I saw Deb getting up from the blanket. She had to tuck her titties back into her bikini top as she came toward the shed. I can still see her long brown hair trailing behind her as she bounced across the lawn in her bare feet, looking tall and leggy. No way I was going to run away from that."

Morris opened his eyes at the recollection of how he'd feared being discovered. A bead of sweat trickled down his face. He focused on the reporter across the table. "They'd call the cops. I couldn't let them do that, so I hid until Deb came in.

"She screamed when she saw me, and the others came running. They had me cornered. I grabbed an ax off the bench. They froze, their eyes open wide with fear. Suddenly, I was in control."

Karen stared at him, a nervous twitch on her lower lip. "When did you realize what you had done?"

The recorder whirred. The tape real was halfway through.

"The ax...it was dripping blood." Morris closed his eyes and returned to his memories. "Them wooden chairs creaked from Sheila and Janet fighting the ropes I had tied them up with. And they begged me. They pleaded. They screamed. I was ready. I kicked aside the boxes, threw the nasty mattress on the floor, and pushed Deb down on it, ass up." Morris opened his eyes again, just in time to see Karen's face turn pallid.

"She was bleeding," Morris said. "Mostly 'cause the ropes were cutting into her wrists. I'd tied her hands behind her back. She was trying to get up on her knees, and her big butt was sticking up in the air. That was more than I could stand. I ripped off her bikini and grabbed her ass. God she was a fine bitch. She let out a scream, so I turned her over. She was beautiful. Naked. Subdued. Writhing on the mattress.

"My heart was poundin' something fierce. Each breath I took came hard and fast. Her screams were like music, in harmony with Sheila and Janet's wailing. Oh, they all wanted me, you know. They begged me. They pleaded. It was like some kind of symphony swirling in my head, but I knew it wouldn't last. It couldn't last. Like every orgasm, it had to end. It was sheer ecstasy when I slammed that ax into Deb's throat."

Karen's breath hitched. She wanted the gory details; now she was getting them.

"A stream of blood gushed out. It startled me...at first, but it thrilled me at the same time, if you know what I mean."

Karen looked down, shook her head.

"I held life and death in my hands. The ax. The power. I swung it at her neck again, but I missed. Her jaw shattered instead, and next thing I knew, I smelled somethin' awful. The bitch shit all over herself. But that wasn't gonna stop me. I swung again. The ax went into her chest and got stuck there. I put my foot on her breast and yanked out the ax. A rush of air came out and sprayed blood all over me.

"I was shaking mad by then, and gasping. I took another swing. This time her head cut loose, rolled across the floor, and thumped against that old washing machine. I just stood there holding my breath, watching her neck drip on the floor. All of a sudden, Deb didn't look as pretty as she did before. But her big blue eyes were staring up at me with that wanton look.

"That's when I felt a throb in my loins and looked down at my bloody jeans. Man, I had a giant hard-on." Morris's heart raced. The memories became a feeding frenzy. "Sheila and Janet stopped screaming. They stunk of urine and whimpered while I did Deb in the ass. They never said another word. I think they knew they were next."

"God, Morris," Karen said, looking ill, her eyes wide and mouth agape. She set down her pen. "Why did you sodomize her headless corpse?"

Morris batted his eyebrows. "Can't a guy have any fun?"

She held her breath and stared at him, silent. Morris watched her lips slowly form a smile that didn't reach her eyes. She slammed the file folder shut, pressed the *off* button on the recorder, and slid her chair away from the table. "You're sick, Morris. My readers are going to love this."

"But you're going to tell 'em it wasn't my fault."

"Oh, it was your fault, all right. We all make choices, Morris. You made yours." She pulled the glasses off her face and cast him a cold glare. "And I for one am glad you're going to the chair."

Morris clenched his jaw. The ungrateful bitch got her goddamn story, and then she reneged on her part of the deal. She wasn't going to tell the story his way. Of all the nerve—

"You fucking bitch. How dare you?" He clenched his fists, and with his chest puffed out and biceps bulging, he tried to break the chains that shackled him to the steel chair. "I'll get you for this," he shouted with a hiss. "I'm coming back, bitch. You'll see me again, I promise, when you least expect it."

She stepped backward, hand on her heart, eyes ringed in white.

He leaned forward, glaring. Drool dangled from the corner of his mouth. "I'll know what came in your mail yesterday, what you had for dinner last night, what your hubby said to you after he fucked you in the ass."

"You're crazy, Morris."

"You just keep on thinkin' that, bitch." He eyed the bandage on his forearm.

Chapter Eleven

A month later, William was sitting in the back seat of his Cadillac Limo as it sped toward the Diamond Building when a special news broadcast came on the radio. "This morning, Morris Brennon was executed in the electric chair at Menard State Prison."

"It's over, boss," Andrew said, looking at him via the rearview mirror.

"Turn it off," William insisted. With the diamond-studded cane pressed between his knees, he felt empty inside. His mother was gone, and his father, and now their murderer was dead. William thought he'd be elated at the news, but instead he was left emotionally numb. His hip ached, and he felt nauseous from the treatments he was receiving for his cancer. Though the doctors had told him to go home and rest, he couldn't wait to get back to his office and the cushy chair behind his desk. He wasn't going to give up any semblance of normalcy in his life until it became impossible for him to get around under his own power.

In the lobby of the Diamond Building, William relied heavily on his cane as he walked to the security desk. "Hello, Ron." He signed the logbook.

"You don't look so good," the guard replied. "Shouldn't you be home in bed?"

As William set down the pen, he noticed that Carl Savage had signed in thirty minutes ago. "What's he doing here?"

"Sally said it was all right to send him up."

"Christ." William headed for the elevator at a brisk and painful pace. When the doors slid open at the foyer to his office, Sally was standing there waiting for him.

"He's in your office," she said and peered toward the door.

"What does he want?"

"He wouldn't tell me, just walked around looking at everything."

The smell of cigar smoke tainted the air. "You stay here." William headed to his office, his heart beating hard. At the door, he stopped and looked inside. Carl was sitting at William's desk, feet propped up and a cloud of smoke hovering over his fat head.

"I don't allow smoking in my office, Carl."

"Correction, William," Carl said and took a big drag on his cigar. "My office."

"Get out of my chair." William closed the door and hobbled to his desk. "Or I'll have Ron throw your fat ass out of here."

Grinning, Carl stood. "So this is the thanks I get."

Moving behind his desk, William gave the hoggish lawyer a poke with the cane. "Go on. You're stinking up my office."

"I brought you something." Carl indicated a briefcase on the desk that William hadn't noticed. "Diamonds for Diamond, you said."

"Huh?" Unable to catch his breath, William stared at the briefcase and Carl's attitude became suddenly clear. "The diamonds?"

Carl opened the briefcase. Inside, a black velvet bag bulging with precious stones sat atop a stack of legal papers. "The Japanese accepted your offer."

Looking up, William felt a rush of anxiety. "Aren't you forgetting something?"

From the pouch on the briefcase lid, Carl removed a folder and tossed it on the desktop. "Blythe University, Cedar Lake, Indiana. Your salvation, William."

"You found a cloning lab?"

"Better get out your checkbook. It wasn't cheap."

In disbelief, William sat in his chair and opened the folder. Everything was there. A synopsis on Blythe University stated that the facility was situated in the middle of the Midwest's agricultural belt. They specialized in the genetic reengineering of corn and wheat, making them more resistant to insects and disease. Their hybrid cattle grew up faster and fatter. Postgraduate programs included experimental projects in microbiology and nuclei transplantation. They were on the cutting edge of cloning technology.

Another pamphlet touted the expertise of Blythe University's staff. Dr. John Larson headed up the department. His chief obstetrics doctor was Eugene Marshall. Their credentials were impeccable.

Then there were contracts, consent forms, disclaimers, and financial agreements that totaled forty-seven million dollars. Everything appeared to be legal and proper.

Astounded, William looked up at Carl. "How did you do it?"

"Senator Bennett had a line on this place. He's from Indiana, you know. Got the Department of Defense in his back pocket."

"I hear he's a crook."

"He's just trying to get some special funding for the DoD through Congress." Carl took a drag on his cigar. "So what if he used special interest money. Besides, Blythe University is his biggest contributor."

"What's with the Department of Defense?"

Carl grinned. "He's got them on a tight leash."

"Good. I want the military to have this cloning technology, whatever these doctors come up with. No more mothers' sons are going to war if I can help it."

"Cloning you is going to be hard enough, much less a battalion of soldiers. All you gotta do is sign these papers. I'll take care of the rest."

"You'd better not let me down."

"It's all nice and legal like." Carl handed him a pen. "Start signing."

Pen in hand, William looked over the papers. The legal jargon was hard to understand. He didn't trust the fine print.

As he tried to make sense of the documents, Carl strutted around the office, first going to the plate-glass windows and looking out over Chicago, then to the wall-mounted TV, and then he glanced at the other walls and the ceiling. "What do you think?" he asked flatly. "Would oriental tapestries look better on this wall or on that one over there?" He pointed with the smoldering stub of his cigar. "Oh, and how about a few bonsai trees on your old desk? I think a row of potted Japanese ferns would look great over there."

A sting of contempt stabbed William's heart. Carl knew how William hated the Japanese, how they'd killed his brother at Pearl Harbor and sent his mother into a downward spiral of depression and grief from which she never recovered. The fat man was sticking it to him, rubbing his nose in it.

Carl took in a lungful of air, his barrel chest expanding. "I can smell the incense burning now. Ah yes, William. Nothing like a little Shamisen music to set the mood."

That was enough. William bolted to his feet. "Get out."

Carl lumbered back to the desk and slammed down his fist. "Sign the papers, Tuliver. A deal's a deal."

"You're a rotten bastard."

"If you don't sign, you'll be rottin' six feet under."

The thought of that fate quickly quelled William's rage. This wasn't about principles anymore, he knew. It was about staying alive. There was enough money in the deal with the Japanese consortium for William to retire in style. He could take Sally to some Pacific island where they could bask in the sunshine and savor the smell of salty fresh air from the deck of a yacht. They could swim in secluded lagoons and fish for tuna and marlin. On any whim, they could travel to Europe, to Egypt, to Brazil. Their future was bright. All he had to do was beat this cancer. A little ribbing from Carl was a small itch to scratch. At that, William sat down and signed all the papers without reading them thoroughly.

Satisfied, Carl tossed him the bag of diamonds. "Don't spend them all at once."

When Carl left, William called Sally in. "Close the door."

She approached his desk, a curious twist in her eyebrows. "William?"

He stood and slowly moved around the desk to take her hand. "Everything is set." He led her to the windows overlooking Chicago. "Except one detail."

Her red hair glistened in the sunshine. "What are you talking about?"

Now he gazed into her hazel eyes. "Will you carry my baby?"

Stepping back, she put her hand on her heart. "A baby? Oh yes, William, of course I'll—"

"Not just any baby."

She flinched. "What other kind is there?"

"This isn't easy to explain." He told her about the bone marrow transplant that could save his life.

"You can have some of my bone marrow."

"It won't work." He explained how Morris Brennon had killed his parents, his best chance for survival. "So I need to make my own bone marrow."

Sally gasped. "So you want us to have a baby so you can take the poor thing's bone marrow? Is that what you're saying?"

"Not really."

"I should hope not."

"There's only a one-in-four chance that our baby's marrow would match mine."

"Then what are talking about?"

He held her shoulders and looked into her eyes. "I'm talking about a clone, my clone."

"Oh, for crying out loud. Are you insane?"

"Its bone marrow would be exactly like mine."

Her eyes were wide with disbelief. "How are you going to get a clone?"

He told her about Blythe University and the deal Carl Savage had made with the doctors there and the deal he'd made with the Japanese. "It's the only way, Sally. I need you to give birth to my clone."

"That's not the kind of baby I had in mind, William."

It became obvious that she wasn't going to make this easy, but he couldn't take no for an answer. "You told me there wasn't anything you wouldn't do for me."

"But—"

"You stood right here, Sally. You told me you loved me." He had to be hard on her, straightforward. Push her buttons. Get his way. "Don't tell me you didn't mean it."

"Of course I meant it, William." She stroked his arm. "But not like this. I couldn't let you—"

"Then I'm going to die, Sally." *Pile on the guilt.* "You may as well say goodbye right now. I don't have a prayer in hell—"

"That's not fair." She turned her back to him. "You can't put that on me."

He stepped behind her and encircled her waist with his arms. Time to pull his punches. "Look to the future," he whispered in her ear. "We'll raise the child together, travel the world, you and me, Sally. And my clone."

"But I wanted a baby that is part of me and part of you. What's so hard to understand about that?" She turned around, tears welling in her eyes. "Why can't we have our own baby?"

"It's no guarantee I'll live."

"We'll take our chances."

"We can always have another baby, Sally, but I have to survive this cancer first. This is the best way."

"How's the clone going to feel about this?"

"We're talking about saving my life, Sally," he said softly. "Does it really matter what the clone thinks?"

"It's still a child. A baby. What are you going to do, break its bones for the marrow?"

"The doctors told me they use a needle," he said, knowing full well he'd had no such conversation with them. "And they don't need much. When he's old enough, we'll tell him the truth. In the meantime, we'll go on with our lives together. He'll be like a son to us. No one will know otherwise."

She folded her arms across her chest. "Does that mean we're going to get married?"

"Of course," he replied, knowing that hesitating would have been costly. "As soon as we can after I'm better."

"Promise?"

"Yes."

She threw her arms around his neck. "Then I'll do it for you, William, for us, for our future."

Thank God. He hugged her, hoping his lies would go unpunished.

Chapter Twelve

Blythe University

On the day William left Chicago, the Japanese were moving into the Diamond Building. He likened them to a swarm of ants invading another's anthill. The whole affair left a bitter feeling in the pit of his stomach.

He told Ron that they were off to have a baby. He didn't say where because he didn't want Andrew to know what they were doing. Andrew had voiced his disapproval, so William thought it best to keep their plans from him.

It only took a week to get settled in at Blythe University. Here in the Indiana heartland, William found hope for his future. All the things he'd left behind mattered less and less as the days passed into weeks and then months. There were tests and more tests and surgeries and more tests, radiation treatments and pills, and more tests. Some days he was so sick he couldn't sit up in bed.

Sally had it bad, too. Harvesting egg cells from her ovaries was a brutal operation, not just once, but several times the doctors went in for more. Through it all, she didn't complain.

Meanwhile, Dr. Marshall and Dr. Larson attended to their every need. Larson was more businesslike, impeccably dressed, but with a strange affinity for patterned ties. Marshall had a personable quality about his bedside manner. He was especially attentive to Sally.

Three months had gone by when Dr. Marshall came into his room, followed by Sally, all smiles. A student assistant, Chet Brady, brought champagne and glasses for everyone.

"We did it," Sally said and hugged William. "I'm pregnant."

It was the happiest day of William's stay at Blythe University. Energized with the news, he got out of bed and put on a robe, and with the help of his cane, he and Sally took a stroll on the university grounds, through the wooded courtyard and down to a creek that meandered across a field and disappeared under a perimeter wall made of stacked and mortared stones. By the time he got back to his room, he was exhausted. It was the last long walk William would ever take. He became wheelchair-bound after that, but in spite of this setback, he maintained confidence in the doctors and his plan for survival.

Everything was going according to that plan until five months later, when William had an extremely bad day of nausea and diarrhea. He began experiencing seizures and blackouts, and his condition seemed to worsen by the hour. Dr. Marshall came into his room, a look of doom on his face. "We thought we had a handle on your cancer." He touched William's arm. "But I don't think you'll live long enough to see your clone."

William sat up, head spinning. "That's not true. I'm going to beat this..." He fell back to the pillow, thought about Sally—their plans. He'd failed. How could he protect her from the heartbreak?

"I want you to understand something," Dr. Marshall said.

"What's so hard to understand?" William breathed. "I'm going to die."

"But there's something you don't know about your clone."

"I know it took you guys too long to clone me. It's your fault."

Dr. Marshall shook his head. "Before you condemn us, hear me out. Your cells weren't simply cloned, William, we duplicated them with the restriction enzyme BZ-21."

"So?" William didn't care how they did it. It had all been a waste anyway.

"It means your clone is an exact duplicate of you."

"Clone...duplicate, what's the difference?"

Terry Wright

Pulling up a chair, Dr. Marshall sat at William's bedside. "A clone is an identical twin of the donor. Clones occur in nature all the time. However, a duplicate is entirely different. It's a carbon copy of the donor, right down to nose hairs and fingerprints, and if I'm right about this, personality too, though Dr. Larson doesn't agree with me."

"My clone is a duplicate of me?"

"Your clone *is* you," Dr. Marshall replied. "You're going to be born again. You'll have a second chance at life."

"And I'm going to remember who I was?"

"Not exactly...actually, we don't know. However, we intend to find out. So don't give up all hope, William. Chances are good that you are coming back, exactly like you are."

Outrageous, William thought. "I don't believe you."

"Then it's your loss." Dr. Marshall stood, leaned over him. "I'm just trying to help. Believe what you want."

Gritting his teeth, William grabbed the front of Dr. Marshall's white lab coat. "All right," he rasped, still trying to comprehend the possibility of being reborn, living life over again. "But you've got to promise me—"

"Take it easy." Dr. Marshall tried to pull away.

"Don't say a word about this to Sally. Don't you dare tell her I'm going to die before my clone is born, you hear? It'll kill her."

"Calm down." The doctor wrestled himself free of William's grasp.

William fell back, exhausted. "Don't tell her."

"We shouldn't lie to her."

"Who's footing the bill for this?"

"She's my patient...I can't lie—"

"If you tell her, I'll cut off your funds. You'll be on the street looking for work. Make up your mind...your career or your patient."

Dr. Marshall's shoulders sagged. "I get your point, William. Whatever you say."

"Make sure Dr. Larson understands, too. No slipups."

When the doctor left the room, William clutched his bedcovers and mulled over what he'd heard. If Dr. Marshall was right, William was going to be reborn, but there had to be a way to guide him back to his past—to his fortune and the diamonds. He had to leave the clone a note, a story—a book. That's it...a book to lead the clone back to his past life, a book about William Tuliver, a book about the diamonds. "The Lost Diamonds," he said aloud. Filled with a new hope, he pushed the pager button by his pillow.

Moments later, Chet Brady came in. "Yes, Mr. Tuliver?"

"I need a pad...and a pen."

Terry Wright

Chapter Thirteen

Four months later, in the basement of Blythe University, Sally's screams echoed through the corridors, the shrill sound of the coming of a new life. From his bed in a small room down the hall, William was unable to get up, to go to her. He could only lie there and listen.

Andrew sat in a bedside chair, his face etched with worry. "How are you doin', boss?"

"N-no tennis today," William replied in a feeble voice. "You'd beat me anyway. Look at me, ninety pounds, and all my hair fell out." The radiation treatments had been brutal. His bones ached, and every movement was agony, each breath torture.

"Are you sure you don't want somethin'...you know...for the pain?"

"No." He'd stopped taking pain medication so he could be alert for the birth of his clone. Against all odds, he'd survived to see this day. Now he wondered how much longer he could hang on. Straining his neck, he looked out the doorway and down the brightly lit corridor beyond. It was empty. All the assistants and doctors were with Sally.

She screamed again. He heard someone shouting *push*. William wanted to be with her. He cursed his body for failing him. Slowly, he moved his head and stared up at the ceiling. Filled with dread, he spoke to Andrew softly, happy that he'd come all the way from Chicago. "I'm afraid."

"You've never been afraid of anything," Andrew replied in a voice clouded with sadness.

But he was wrong. Death terrified William. It was the unknown, that dark place called eternity that took his brother, his mother and his father—and now him. He had never known fear like this before. It washed over him like tidal waves. He was succumbing to it. Nature was taking its course, and powerless to fight it, he feared this night would end like no other night in his life. He didn't want to leave his fortune behind. He didn't want to leave Sally alone.

"Sally," he cried out and trembled.

"Take it easy," Andrew said.

His heart raced. "She loves me."

"I know."

"You don't understand." William forced himself to calm down. He'd been such a jerk, the way he'd put her love to the test. Back when he told her of his plan to clone himself, he'd made it all sound flawless, dolled up everything, and added lots of smiles and assurances. She really did love him. He knew that as surely as he knew the cancer was taking him away from her.

She screamed again.

He gasped painfully.

"She's okay, William. Try to relax."

Swallowing dryly, his memories were a blur. On that black day of the Apollo 11 moon landing, Dr. Webber had told him no bone marrow donors were available and flippantly mentioned cloning, Andrew had voiced his opposition to the idea, so William didn't tell him what they had done. Now, knocking on death's door, William felt guilty. Surely Andrew would understand. He looked into his best friend's eyes. "Remember when I told you there had to be another way to beat this cancer?"

"At the hospital, sure, you were talkin' about havin' a child...but didn't the doc say there was only a one-in-four chance of the baby's bone marrow matching yours?"

"I didn't settle for those odds."

"But Sally's pregnant with your child."

"It's not our child, Andrew."

He flinched. "I don't understand."

"It's my clone."

Andrew's mouth fell open. "You didn't."

"I had to."

"So you came here...to this...what kind of place is this?"

"They're dedicated to the science of cloning here."

"How could you?"

Sally screamed, causing Andrew to wince.

"It was the only way," William said.

"Why did you keep this from me?"

"Because you were against me. You made the choice."

"Then why are you tellin' me now?"

Painfully, William moved his head and returned his gaze to the ceiling. He had to tell him now. "I'm proud of what we've accomplished here. Before, scientists thought this technology was beyond their reach, but in reality it wasn't any different than landing on the moon. It wasn't as impossible as they thought. But just think, Andrew, a clone with fresh bone marrow. My salvation." William took a shallow breath and looked again at Andrew, hoping to find some understanding in his blank expression. There was none.

"Did Carl Savage find this place?" he asked.

"With Senator Bennett's help."

"Bennett? The guy's a crook."

"I made them a deal, Andrew..." William coughed. "I financed the cloning experiments, and they let me be their first subject. Carl made sure everything was legal. I must've signed a hundred papers. When everything was set, Senator Bennett called the Department of Defense..."

Andrew's jaw dropped. "The government is in on this?"

"It's top-secret, I assure you."

"That can't be a good thing."

"I did it for my brother."

"But he died in the war."

"So did my mother...in a way. She was never the same after

that." William struggled to get another breath. "In the future, as a result of what I've done here, no more mothers' sons will have to go to war."

"An army of clones? Is that what you're saying?"

"It'll be my legacy to America."

"You gotta be nuts."

"Let history be the judge of that. Meanwhile, Carl walked away with the Diamond Auto Parts deal."

"Now they've got me haulin' Japanese hotshots all over town." Andrew huffed. "I gave 'em notice."

"I'm sorry to hear that."

"Gives me more drinkin' time."

"Don't let it get the best of you, Andrew."

"Why did Sally go along with this? I mean...I get where Carl is comin' from. He's a maggot in the manure. There's nothin' he won't do for a fast buck. But Sally, what's in it for her?"

William coughed. "A baby."

Andrew screwed up his face. "That's it? A baby? There's gotta be more to it than that."

"No." William looked away. He knew there was more. There was a promise.

Now Andrew leaned forward in his chair. "Are you bullshittin' me again, William?"

"All right," he said, knowing he couldn't fool Andrew. "I told her we would get married."

"Nobody said anything about a wedding. I didn't bring a tux."

William sighed. "Don't worry. There'll be no wedding."

"But if Sally thinks you're going to marry her—"

"She doesn't know...I...I'm going to die."

"What?"

"The clone has come too late. My cancer has spread."

Andrew stiffened. "There's nothing they can do?"

"No." A shot of regret rifled through William's pain-wracked body. "It wasn't supposed to work out this way."

"How long have you known?"

"Four months."

"When are you going to learn, William? You should tell Sally the truth."

"I couldn't."

"But you filled her with false hope."

"I didn't want to disappoint her."

"Now what'll she do when you're gone?"

"There's a trust fund."

"Like that's gonna fix anything. What else can go wrong with this stupid plan of yours?"

"Everything has gone wrong, Andrew. N-Now the clone is my only hope."

"But you said it's too late."

"That's why I asked you to come here."

Andrew leaned back, frowning. "I don't understand."

"The doctors used a special enzyme when they cloned my cells. The clone isn't just identical to me...like a twin...it's me."

"That's ridiculous. How can...?"

Sally's scream cut him off.

"Push."

"Don't you see? I'm being born again. I get a second chance at life."

Andrew shot him a sour look.

William wheezed. "If Dr. Marshall's right about this enzyme, that's me in there." He indicated the room down the hall. "Being reborn."

"Push."

Sally screamed.

"Jesus," Andrew said. "Why is she in so much pain?"

"She's not taking any medication."

"No spinal tap?"

"Nothing."

"But she's suffering in there."

William lifted his trembling hand and touched Andrew's arm. "I told her I wanted a natural childbirth, the way I was born the first time."

"Oh, no. The poor woman."

As William caught Andrew's disapproving glare, he thought about his mother and father and wondered if they would approve of his rebirth. A year ago, their bone marrow might have saved him, but in reality, when Morris Brennon murdered them, he had also condemned William to death. The fact that Morris had been executed for his crimes was now of little solace.

Throat burning, William coughed.

Andrew rubbed William's frail arm.

Though he said nothing, his touch felt comforting. William turned his head toward the nightstand where he'd set the book he'd written. *The Lost Diamonds*. In one hundred twenty pages he'd told the story of his life, complete with clues to his hidden fortune, clues only he would understand. He had one book printed, and he sent the original manuscript to the copyright registration office at the Library of Congress. "Hand me my book," he told Andrew.

Andrew examined it before he gave it to William. "You wrote this?"

William held the book with weak fingers. "If Dr. Marshall is right about the clone, this book will help him find out about me, his real identity. There's only one copy."

"Did you tell him he's a clone?"

"Huh?"

"In the book, did you tell him?"

"No. Sally will tell him, but in case something happens to her, he'll have this book to find out he's really me, William Tuliver, reborn."

"God, boss. That sounds weird."

"I've got it all planned." William looked at the title printed boldly across the cover. *The Lost Diamonds*. He hoped to recover them when he returned, take up his life again.

The book slipped from his hands.

Andrew placed it on the nightstand. "It's never going to work."

"Of course it is."

"Too many things can go wrong."

William let out a painful breath. Andrew was right, but the book and the diamonds were the only way to be sure the clone would seek out his past. Leaving the diamonds in a bank vault or money in a trust fund would have been too easy. The clone might not look any further than the bank statements. This way, guided by the book and lured by the diamonds, he would have a chance to discover who he really was, and by the time he found the diamonds, he will have learned the truth about himself. William locked eyes with Andrew. "Swear you'll never tell anyone about this."

"It's too bizarre, William. Who'd believe me?"

"You've been like a brother to me...Andrew. Don't let me down now. Promise you won't say a word."

Andrew regarded William for a moment then patted his hand. "Your secret's safe with me, boss. I won't say anything. Besides, I don't want anybody thinkin' I'm crazy like you."

William managed a wan smile and pointed a trembling finger toward the diamond-studded cane propped in the corner. "There...my cane...take it. Please...keep it for me...until I get back."

"How will you find me?"

"If I don't...you'll know my plan failed. Take the cane with you...to your grave."

"I'll spend eternity with it, boss."

"Let's hope that won't be necessary." William stared at the ceiling and wondered if the clone would recognize his own words, his own feelings, and his own history in *The Lost Diamonds*. And other questions bombarded his brain. As a duplicated person, would he remember his former life, the Diamond Building and *Mothers' Tears*? Would he still love Sally? He knew these things depended upon Dr. Larson's enzyme working properly.

If not, William would never see his diamonds again.

Chapter Fourteen

own the hall, Sally lay on a delivery table with her knees in the air and her bare feet in the stirrups. Trembling, she heard the doctor telling her to push, and she pushed with all her strength. But it wasn't enough to end the labor. She ached, puffing short breaths, preparing for the next agonizing wave of contractions.

"You're doing fine, Sally," Eugene said, standing next to her. He wiped her forehead with a damp towel, a look of compassion in his eyes. Nine months ago, he had implanted the zygote into her uterus and monitored her pregnancy throughout. Tonight, all their work was culminating in a new life for William, a new life she desperately wanted restored. She missed him, the way he was before he fell ill.

Dr. Marshall smiled and held her hand, leaving the towel on her forehead.

"This is harder than I thought it would be." She puffed and gripped his hand tightly.

"The first one usually is."

"When will William be here?"

"He's just down the hall. When Geoff is born, we'll take him to William's room."

Sally closed her eyes. They had decided to name the clone Geoffrey Scott Michaels. It had been a tough decision. They'd thought about William Tuliver, Jr., but given the circumstances, a direct link to this cloning might do more harm than good, especially if the media were to get wind of what they had done. And should anything happen to them, *The Lost Diamonds* would be Geoffrey's only link to William.

Wincing in pain, another contraction wracked her body. She held her breath and pushed harder. Though surrounded by doctors and technicians who'd been with her from the start, she knew they couldn't help her. This was something she had to do on her own. For William, she gladly gave him this service. She was finally having a baby.

The doctors wanted to do it the easy way—the safe way, by cesarean. It would have been less stressful on the clone. But William had insisted on a natural childbirth. The debate went on for months until he threatened to cut off further funding if he didn't get his way. Larson agreed in favor of the money.

Her abdominal muscles contracted. She screamed. She pushed. It wasn't getting any easier.

Dr. Marshall glanced at the heart monitor recording Geoff's cardiac rhythm. He looked satisfied, which made her feel a little better. She followed his eyes as he glanced up to the delivery room control center where Dr. Larson was watching them through the observation window. Carl Savage was standing next to him, along with another man dressed in a military uniform. Larson pointed to his watch and frowned. Dr. Marshall shrugged and returned his attention to Sally. "You're doing great."

She forced a smile and wondered what planet he was living on.

Chapter Fifteen

11:30

The night dragged on for Dr. Larson. His mouth was dry, and his eyes burned from lack of sleep as he paced across the control center that overlooked the birthing room. He wore his usual black suit coat, slacks, and a paisley tie. His patent-leather shoes ticked on the tile floor with each step. As director of the cloning laboratory at Blythe University since its inception in 1952, he and his team were familiar with late hours, long days, and disappointments. However, their many accomplishments in cloning plants, and then animals, left them eager for the challenges of human cell duplication. His new enzyme, BZ-21, now faced its most grueling test. Had it produced the ultimate clone?

He felt grumpy, not because he was tired, but because of the crowded conditions in his control center. A Colonel from the Pentagon and a fat lawyer from Chicago were breathing up all his air. He didn't want them here, not tonight, but the Department of Defense had insisted. They were interested in the birth of this clone, which could have been a history-making event if the Board of Trustees hadn't muzzled Larson and his team. Everyone was worried about any moral scrutiny this project might bring down on the university. The press could be brutal, and religious fanatics would be up in arms. He had to assure the Board and the Department of Defense that the project would not be made public. For now, as much as he wanted to publish his findings and make a big name for himself, he would have to be content conducting his research in secret.

"What's taking them so long?" Colonel Harrison asked.

"Just relax." Larson turned another lap in front of the observation window. The Tuliver project had been the most challenging of all their cloning experiments. It had taken three hundred and seven attempts to produce the viable zygote that became Tuliver's clone. The Colonel couldn't possibly have any appreciation for the technology involved in the process: harvesting Sally's egg cells, removing their nuclei, which stripped the eggs of her identity, and then implanting the nuclei from William's cells into Sally's barren eggs. It was tedious work fraught with failures, until tonight.

Larson stopped pacing and glared into the Colonel's gray eyes, eyes that had seen a lot of sadness, or anger, or both. The Colonel was thirty-five years old, Larson surmised, and standing six-foot-two, he was an intimidating man in his sharply pressed uniform. Even so, Larson wasn't about to let him berate the Tuliver project. "The clone will come in its own time, Colonel."

"The process is too complicated. You have to find a better way." The Colonel rocked back on his heels, his attention still on the goings-on below.

Larson shoved his hands into his pockets and resumed pacing. He wasn't going to waste his breath explaining the complexities of BZ-21 to the Colonel. Besides, he had an attitude problem. He didn't realize that it took more than a decade to put a man on the moon, and NASA succeeded only because the government had pumped massive amounts of money into the project. BZ-21 had taken longer to develop and with far fewer dollars to work with. If the Colonel wanted faster results, he'd have to step up to the teller's window.

However, as much as Larson wanted to tell him to take a bubble bath in formaldehyde, he decided to forego that approach in favor of kissing up to the man with the money. Now standing at the Colonel's side, Larson said, "The duplication factor is complicated, but eventually, we'll find an easier way. You have to understand—"

"I understand one thing, doctor. It's never going to fly at the

Pentagon."

"Colonel, this research isn't any different than putting a man on the moon. It's expensive and time consuming."

"A waste of both, if you ask me."

"Then what are you doing here?"

"Observing. It's my job."

Carl Savage had been quiet until now. "Then try opening your mind and closing your mouth, Colonel."

Harrison shot the fat man a dagger-like glare, and Larson stepped between them. "Think of the problems we face, culturing zygotes, testing enzymes, working with things that can only be seen under a microscope."

"It's ridiculous."

"It's science, Colonel."

"The army can't be waiting around for some surrogate to give birth to a clone, and then stand by while it grows up to be a soldier. I don't care what Carl says."

The lawyer frowned and wagged his stubby finger at the Colonel. "Give these guys a chance to work out the kinks. You'll be a hero."

"An army of cloned soldiers? Give me a break."

"William Tuliver wanted you boneheads to have this technology," Carl spat. "He didn't want any more mothers to suffer like his mother suffered when his brother was killed at Pearl Harbor."

"Mothers' sons have been dying for their countries throughout history, Carl. How the hell did you talk Senator Bennett into wasting the Pentagon's time with this crap?"

Carl grinned. "He owed me a favor."

"And a consulting fee, I'm sure."

"That's none of your business, Colonel."

"Will you two stop it?" Larson shouted. "You're giving me a headache."

With that, Carl put a sympathetic hand on the Colonel's

shoulder. "Something like this might have saved your son."

"How'd you know about him?" Harrison barked.

"I make it a point to know everything about my clients."

Larson cleared his throat. "What are you talking about?"

"His son was killed in Vietnam," Carl said. "Last month."

"It's the goddamned politicians," the Colonel shouted. "They killed him with all their pussy-footing around, kissin' up to them Communist bastards. And the President. I could strangle him."

"Then help these guys out, Colonel," Carl said. "Maybe you can spare someone else the kind of grief you're going through."

Harrison stepped away from the window. "An army of cloned soldiers going off to war with nobody back home to care what becomes of them. It's science fiction, for Christ's sake."

"It's William Tuliver's wish," Carl reminded them.

"Doesn't he realize America is in a mess? We're sending troops into Cambodia, the National Guard is shooting students at Kent State, and the silent majority is all over our butts. Christ. We've got bigger problems."

"We have to start someplace," Larson said.

Harrison pursed his lips, glanced at Carl, and then at Larson. "The way I see it, in order for this to work, you'll have to cut the conception time, accelerate the maturity rate, and for God's sake, get rid of the surrogates. Eight years from egg to soldier or the DoD will never buy it."

Larson frowned. "Eight years? That's impossible."

"Eight years is *not* an unreasonable time frame in which to build a new weapon system."

"This isn't a bomber, Colonel."

Harrison rubbed his chin. "How long will it take you to work out the bugs?"

Larson didn't know if the problems could ever be solved. If not, the DoD would never be satisfied. However, opportunity was knocking at Blythe University's door. If nothing else, he had to think of his career. Government funding for this project would certainly make the Board of Trustees happy, and in return, the money would bolster his job security. Future success or failure would be inconsequential in the long run, but to get the money now, he'd promise them anything. "Twenty years," Larson said, hoping not to discourage the Colonel.

"That's a long time."

"Remember your son," Carl put in.

"My son, yes." Harrison held his breath a moment then nodded. "Very well. I'll recommend appropriations under the Pentagon's top-secret defense research budget. I'm sure Carl can get Senator Bennett to push it through committee."

Carl nodded, his fat chin undulating. "Of course."

At that, the Colonel walked to the door. "And this project is to remain top-secret, Larson, so just in case you get any ideas about making yourself famous, I'm stationing a security force here permanently. Their orders are *shoot to kill*. The clone goes nowhere. Got that?"

"It's not leaving the lab," Larson said. "Ever."

"Good luck." Harrison walked out with Carl waddling behind him. As the door swung closed, Larson felt a jolt of anger. Because of Tuliver and his high and mighty patriotism, their research project now had an agenda. A new weapon system, an army of cloned soldiers: that was a big order. An eight-year duplication factor seemed like an impossibility, but the influx of government money would be good, good for his project and good for his career, for the next twenty years, anyway.

But those were tomorrow's concerns. He turned his attention to the birthing room below. Tonight, Sally and William were the real-life players in this new technology. He wondered if their motivations were worthy of the price they would pay. Tuliver was near death, and the clone would never leave the university, two details Sally knew nothing about.

A sudden burst of activity erupted below. Larson felt a reviving wave of enthusiasm. The new weapon system was coming.

Chapter Sixteen

In the birthing room, "He's crowning," an assistant announced.

Groaning, Sally pushed as hard as she could and wondered why she ever agreed to do this. She'd had enough. She wanted to go home now, forget the whole thing. Her insides felt as if they were clamped in a vise, cramping and contracting around a basketball that someone had shoved up inside her.

"Another big push, Sally," Dr. Marshall said softly in her ear.

"What the hell do you think I'm doing?" She clenched her jaw and sucked air between her teeth.

Geoffrey's head popped out of the birth canal, and the contractions stopped. A wave of relief came over her. But according to Dr. Marshall, this was like the eye of the hurricane, a lull in the storm before the worst part of all: the shoulders.

Working with a suction tool, Dr. Marshall cleared the baby's mouth and nose of fluid. "Almost there, Sally."

Her muscles contracted again. She gulped air and wished she were dead. Suddenly, the basketball felt more like a football. Geoffrey's shoulders had slipped through.

"One more push, Sally."

She let the next contraction be her lead and pushed. Then it was over. Dr. Marshall lifted the baby by his tiny feet, and with one pat on his back, Geoffrey's shrill cry echoed through the birthing room.

Sally relaxed every muscle in her body and cried tears of joy and relief. Eugene laid the sopping newborn on her stomach, the umbilical cord still intact. His skin was pink and wrinkled and glistening wet. "He's beautiful." She smiled and set a gentle hand on his tiny shoulder.

He sneezed.

All her maternal instincts engaged. Compassion, love, and a mother's nurturing burst from her heart for her son. The smile on her face gave away her feelings to the delivery team. They gathered around the gurney to share the moment. She'd never felt this happy before.

Then Geoffrey's eyes popped open. Sally's breath hitched. There was something wrong. Those brown eyes, they were William's eyes—looking up at her, oddly fixed and focused, studying her. How could that be? Normal newborns didn't do that. They couldn't be so alert. Panic seized her. This child was not her son. This wasn't a normal baby. It was William Tuliver's clone. His eyes kept staring at her, examining her. Racked with a sudden tremble, her maternal feelings plummeted like a rock down a well. She wanted the doctor to take the clone away, but mesmerized by his stare, she couldn't stop staring back at him. Her heart raced, and she felt afraid.

As if sensing that fear, Dr. Marshall lifted the clone off her stomach. He tied the umbilical cord. Still in shock, she turned her head away, unable to watch, but she heard the snip of scissors that freed her from the clone. Relief swept over her.

An assistant took Geoffrey to the prep table. "Seven pounds, three and a half ounces. Twenty inches," she announced.

Dr. Marshall looked at the clock as he filled in the birth certificate.

Sally followed his eyes. *11:52 p.m.* It was August 20th.

"He's a fine baby boy, Sally." Dr. Marshall folded the birth certificate and put it in his pocket. "You did good." He tousled her hair.

While the assistants finished their post-delivery procedures, Sally watched Geoffrey lying on the prep table. He wasn't crying or fussing. His eyes followed the doctor's movements and those of the assistants and students milling around him. It was as if he had conscious thought, switching his focus back and forth between the things that interested him. It was the strangest thing. "Is he all right?"

Dr. Marshall nodded.

"But how can that tiny thing's bone marrow save William?"

The doctor didn't answer. He just went about his duties, checking over Geoffrey and writing notes in a tablet.

Meanwhile, Geoffrey kicked both feet and made a *goo goo* sound. Sally's heart skipped as she accepted the stark reality of this child. She wondered how she could have been led to believe cloning William was the right thing to do. And now she couldn't comprehend the doctors dissecting this child for spare parts—just so William could survive. How could he think his life was worth the suffering of a child, even if it was a clone? Clones felt pain. Even a needle piercing its tiny bones was too much for her to fathom. She couldn't condone it. She wouldn't allow it.

Then a sudden realization hit her. If she refused to allow the bone marrow transplant, William would die. Then all she'd have left was his clone. He'd grow up, look just like William. With that thought, a creepy feeling wormed through her stomach.

Wondering what she'd gotten herself into, she knew this wasn't the time to ponder William's fate. Though she was exhausted and in pain, she decided the child's well-being was more important than her doubts. Exhaling, she reached out for Geoffrey. "May I see him again?"

Dr. Marshall lifted the infant clone from the prep table, wrapped him in a white blanket, and handed him to her. The bundle was light in her arms. She held him close to her chest, felt his warmth. "Hurry. Let's take him to William."

Moments later, the assistants pushed the gurney out of the birthing room and rolled it down the corridor toward William's room. A worn wheel shuddered back and forth with an irritating clicking sound. Dr. Marshall walked alongside her, his hand on her arm. Though his touch was reassuring, she didn't look at him.

At William's doorway, they stopped. She heard shallow breathing.

Andrew bolted up from a bedside chair, wide-eyed, holding the diamond-studded cane.

"William?" she called out.

Andrew's gaze was locked on the child, but William stared at the ceiling as though he were afraid to look at his clone.

"William. I have brought him for you to see." The gurney rolled into the room and stopped alongside his bed. "Look. He has your eyes."

***

William turned his head and looked at the child. Geoffrey was staring at him intensely. "They *are* my eyes," he managed in a weak voice. There was little power left in his lungs to speak. "Raise me up, Andrew."

Motor whining, the bed rose to Sally's eye level. He leaned forward, and with his arms quivering from pain, he reached for the child. Sally and the doctor helped situate the baby clone in William's feeble embrace.

For several minutes silence dominated the room. He stared into the child's eyes and contemplated the miracle that his money had produced, a duplicate of himself, exact in every detail, the way he was sixty-one years ago, cradled in his mother's arms. Renewed.

Restraining tears, his pain dissolved to numbness, as if his affliction wasn't real anymore. Only the child filled his senses: pink skin, puffy cheeks, a wisp of thin hair, and he inhaled the distinct scent of a newborn. He heard the soft wheezing of each breath the baby took. His little fingers were curled into tight fists, his tiny pink thumbnails clearly visible. In those respects, his clone looked as normal as any newborn, yet strangely, it stared at him with an eerie sense of recognition.

"Isn't he beautiful?" Sally asked.

The infant flinched in response to Sally's voice, but William found the strength to hold him firmly. Minutes passed that seemed like hours. Slowly, the child's face began to blur. William felt lightheaded. Satisfied his plan was in place, he looked at Sally. "Thank you."

Her smile warmed his heart.

Then his eyes rolled back, he gasped, and as he held himself in his arms, he died.

Chapter Seventeen

S ally clenched her hands under her chin. "William? William!" The infant clone began to roll toward the edge of the bed. Dr. Marshall caught him, and without a moment's hesitation, he handed Geoffrey to Chet Brady. "Get him out of here."

Pulling a corner of the baby blanket over Geoff's head, Chet hurried out of the room.

"Wait," Sally cried out. "Come back." Her stomach cramped. She glared at Dr. Marshall. "Where's he taking Geoffrey?"

With a long face, the doctor placed two fingers on William's neck and shook his head.

"Oh, God, no." Tears streamed down her face without restraint. It wasn't possible. It didn't happen. William can't be dead. Not now. Not after all they'd been through. "Do something."

Dr. Marshall pulled the sheet over William's head and stepped back. "Let's go."

"Aren't you going to try to resuscitate him?"

"It's no use, Sally. He ran out of time."

"What are you talking about? You're a doctor. Save him."

The assistants started pushing the gurney into the corridor, wheels clicking. Mute, Eugene walked alongside her. She had to crane her neck to see him. "What do you mean he was out of time?"

"You've had a long day, Sally. Save your questions for tomorrow, when you're rested."

"Somebody better tell me what's going on around here." She tried to sit up, but the doctor forced her back down. "Where have they taken Geoffrey?" she screamed. "Why did William die? His condition wasn't that serious."

The doctor bit his lower lip, kept walking.

Rage tore through her. "You fucking lied to me?"

"Settle down," Eugene said. "You're going to hemorrhage."

"I can't believe you bastards—"

"Hush."

"Don't you dare hush me." Her insides were on fire, her thoughts running amuck. What the hell were these bastards up to?

When the gurney rolled into her room, Dr. Marshall turned to an assistant and whispered something into his ear. He nodded and left. The other assistants lifted Sally from the gurney and slid her onto the bed, then in a rush, pushed the gurney out and disappeared. As the clicking of wheels faded down the hall, Sally glared at Dr. Marshall—the lying bastard.

He patted her pillow and pulled up the bed sheet. "Get some rest." He gently stroked her hair.

She batted his hand away. "I don't want rest, I want...I want William." Uncontrollable sobbing consumed her.

Dr. Marshall handed her a tissue. "He didn't make it, Sally. I'm sorry." His voice was soft, compassionate.

Wiping her eyes, she sniffled. "But I don't understand." She blew her nose in the tissue, looked up toward heaven and called out, "William. What went wrong?" Tears flowed. Blowing her nose again, she tried to compose herself, but sadness held a firm grip on her heart.

Dr. Marshall took her hand. Their eyes met. "Sally, listen to me. I know it's a shock, but the cancer spread much faster than we anticipated."

"You knew all along, didn't you."

"Four months ago, we suspected William wouldn't make it to see the birth of his clone. He insisted that we not tell you how critical his condition had become."

"Not tell me?" She jerked her hand free of Dr. Marshall's gentle grasp. "Damn it. I was carrying his clone. Doesn't that give me the right to know everything? I'm your patient. It's your responsibility to be honest with me...no matter what."

"I couldn't go against William's wishes."

"I thought there was time..." She wiped tears from her eyes, "time for us to share Geoffrey. Now there's nothing. You should've told me the truth, damn it."

"Please, Sally. Settle down."

"Fuck you."

Dr. Marshall inhaled as if to respond, but an assistant entered the room and handed him a hypodermic needle filled with a clear liquid.

Her temples throbbed. "What's that?"

"Just something to help you sleep." He pointed the needle upward and squirted a few drops from the tip. "I was hoping you wouldn't need this."

"No," she shouted. She wasn't finished talking to him. It wasn't fair—using a drug to end the conversation. "Keep that thing away from me."

"Don't make it hard on yourself." He signaled the assistant around to the other side of her bed.

"Get out," she yelled and began flailing her arms.

They subdued her.

"Let go of me." She kicked. "You bastards."

As they held her down, the needle pierced her forearm like a bee sting. Defiantly, she glared into the eyes of the man she once trusted. She once believed Dr. Marshall truly cared about her. But he'd deceived her. They all had. Hate stabbed her heart. The sedative began to dull her senses. Hard as she tried, she couldn't keep his lying face in focus. "This isn't over."

"Just relax, Sally. Take it easy."

His voice echoed down a long tunnel.

Her will to fight slipped away. Euphoria soothed her mind like a soft melody. She gave in to the sensation. The room began to rotate, slowly at first, and then faster and faster, colors and shadows combined into hypnotizing swirls of light, clouds, fog, and silent darkness.

***

Sally went limp on the bed. Eugene retracted the empty hypodermic, pressed a cotton ball on the wound, and watched her eyes rotate in their sockets. With the palm of his hand, he brushed her eyelids closed. Dabbing the cotton, he saw the puncture wound had clotted, and then tossed the cotton into the trashcan. Picking up the tissue she'd dropped on the bed in the struggle, he wiped away a glistening tear from her cheek, sighed, and handed the syringe to the assistant. "Help the others clean up the delivery room and get some rest."

"Is she going to be okay?"

"Tomorrow."

The door closed, and Eugene returned his attention to the woman he had attended over the past year. Saddened by this sudden turn of events, he wished things were different. Though the science of this project was important to him, so was the humanity, the one-on-one connection between doctor and patient. Only now did he realize he'd failed at that.

"You bastards!"

Her words replayed in his mind and cut deep into his heart. Taking her limp hand, he said, "It's not me, Sally. I'm not the bastard. I love you too much." God, if he could have told her that when she was awake. So many times when they were together alone he'd wanted to tell her—but how could he? If Larson found out—or Tuliver—it would have jeopardized his career, his position at the university. Doctor rule number one: never fall in love with your patient. How could he have let that happen? But it did. It was wrong, he knew, so he'd kept his feelings to himself.

Looking at her now, sleeping, he admitted she wasn't the most beautiful woman he had ever seen, rather plain, a few freckles on her nose, and she'd kept her red hair shorter than he liked. He'd never seen her wear makeup. But she was always a joy to be around, optimistic, cheerful—in spite of what she was going through—for William, a man so self-centered that he didn't really appreciate her inner beauty. Eugene did, he saw it all, her spirit, her strength, and her loyalty to an old man who didn't deserve her.

And Dr. Larson didn't appreciate her much either. To him, she was a necessary inconvenience: a walking womb, a guinea pig in an experiment like the other lab rats and cows. He showed no compassion, no concern for her, just cold dedication. "I warned him," he whispered to sleeping Sally. "I warned William, too. I told them we should tell you the truth. Forgive me, darling."

As he leaned forward to kiss her cheek, the door banged open. Flinching, he turned and saw Dr. Larson.

"What's going on?" he asked, sweeping into the room like a wraith.

"She's resting now." Eugene released her warm hand.

Larson moved to the bed and looked down at her. "She's had a rough day. I hear she didn't take William's passing well."

"That and the lies."

"We never lied to her, Eugene. Tuliver may have, but not us."

"She trusted us, John. We should have told her the truth."

Larson walked back to the door. "We had good reason not to tell her everything. It was our benefactor's wish, remember?"

"She didn't know about William, and we didn't tell her. Lies by omission are lies just the same."

Larson jabbed a finger at Eugene. "What do you think she would have done if she knew what this was all about? You think she would have gone along with this project if she knew that the clone would never set foot in the outside world? Hell no. She thought this was some kind of family affair. Would she have agreed to go through all this and walk away, leaving the clone here for us to do with as we pleased? Never, I suspect."

"And Tuliver wouldn't have agreed to it either."

"Tuliver couldn't see beyond his own needs. He was naive to

think we would bust our butts on this project and let Sally walk out the door with our investment."

"Then you should have told them upfront, let them decide if the clone's freedom was worth the bone marrow."

"And risk losing the project and the money that came with it? That's not in *my* job description, doctor. Carl Savage slipped Tuliver the bogus contract like a poisoned pill."

"And he died oblivious to what the two of you had done." Eugene shook his head. "It wasn't the right thing to do."

Larson shook his fist. "We all knew Tuliver should've gotten Sally pregnant—had a child of his own, the normal way—take his chances. But no, the odds of a bone marrow match weren't good enough for him. His selfishness worked to our advantage, and I couldn't care less about his motivations." He pointed to Sally asleep on the bed. "She got herself into this for all the wrong reasons. The old man used her to save his own skin. He won't get any sympathy from me."

"And Sally, any sympathy for her?"

Larson grabbed the doorknob. "Sympathy is your department, Eugene. I have a clone to attend." He walked out and left the door open.

Eugene again turned to Sally. Tomorrow he would have to tell her the truth: when she leaves Blythe University, she'll be leaving without Geoffrey. His contribution to science was yet to be made. Larson planned hundreds of medical experiments on the clone of William Tuliver, and as long as the world was unaware of Geoffrey's existence, Larson could get away with it.

Sadness gripped Eugene. It wasn't fair. He knew that Sally would lose the child she was led to believe would be hers to keep. She had no legal claim to him, thanks to Carl Savage and his bogus contract. There was no way she could save Geoffrey from Dr. Larson—not without help, anyway. Unless..?

Fumbling with an idea, Eugene reached into his pocket and retrieved the birth certificate he'd filled out earlier. *Cook County,*

Illinois, it read, a formality for Sally's sake, more than anything. They had no intentions of filing it. He saw where he'd written: *"Mother: Sally Mayfield, Father: Unknown."* Under different circumstances, Eugene would have gladly put his name on that line. *"Father: Eugene Marshall."* But as things were, it didn't matter. The birth certificate was a meaningless piece of paper without the seal of the county commissioner.

Why not? He decided to file the birth certificate with the county clerk. Then Geoffrey Scott Michaels' existence would be on record. Someone would be accountable for him—someday. There would be no more lies by omission.

All Eugene had to do was keep Larson in the dark about it.

Chapter Eighteen

T he morning sun hung low on the horizon, its dull rays fighting to penetrate a thick blanket of fog that shrouded the pastures and meadowlands skirting Blythe University's stone-hedged perimeter. Larson couldn't sleep. He stood on the balcony outside his bedroom, coffee cup in hand, and took in the view. Nestled on the western shore of Cedar Lake, the chancellery building stood like an English monastery transplanted from the eighteenth century. To the south of its mystic spire and stone walls, cattle grazed on dew-slicked grass and bellowed to each other as they meandered along an irrigation canal that snaked its way through the countryside. Groups of dairy cows huddled together under clumps of trees along the muddy bank. From somewhere in the distance, a rooster crowed. The late August morning air felt sharp on his skin, icy, a prelude to the coming of autumn.

However, Larson knew this morning was very different from any other morning on the campus of Blythe University. During the night, the first human clone was born.

In robe and slippers, he paced the balcony as he looked out over the misty farmland below. Cold air bristled the stubble on his face. He felt older than his forty years. But he loved it here. He loved the country, the peacefulness of this place he called home.

Leaning on the railing, he watched the cows slog through the creek, bellowing. Some cows wore yellow ear-tags, those that were cloned in the lab two years ago. He spotted the latest addition to his herd, a calf lumbering along with a discernable limp. Larson wondered what color ear-tags he should use for the human clones.

The Duplication Factor

Geoffrey Scott Michaels, case number 1010C, would be the only clone with a name. Names were too personal. The next human clones would be referred to only by their case numbers, just like all the other genetic experiments at Blythe University.

As he watched the cows move along, a military jeep rattled into view, down on the dirt road that skirted the stone wall around the university. The sight sent a jolt of anger through his chest. Colonel Harrison's security presence on campus would send the wrong message to the students. The Department of Defense's agenda could interfere with the university's charter mandating education and research. However, to safeguard their cloning technology, Larson realized Colonel Harrison was a necessary inconvenience. But that didn't make it any easier to accept.

Melanie appeared at the balcony door, her long blond hair kissed by the cool breeze. She wore a paisley-print robe that hung loosely from her shoulders and open down the front. Leaning against the doorframe, she crossed her arms. "What's the matter?"

He pulled out a chair from under the patio table and sat. "I thought you were sleeping."

"I was...until a cold spot came creeping under my covers. You were gone. I got worried."

"You don't say." He put his feet on the next chair, arranged the robe over his bare legs, and sipped his coffee.

Barefooted, Melanie padded across the patio and sat on the table, facing him, crossed her legs and leaned back on her hands. The untied robe fell open, revealing her swollen breasts and protruding abdomen. She didn't seem to mind the cold air against her exposed skin.

"You're going to catch a chill," Larson said, like any good doctor would in a show of concern.

Melanie arched her back and gazed at the sun, its yellow glow filtered by the churning fog. "I love the mornings, John. Wish we could spend more of them together."

"Yeah, yeah." He sipped his coffee, hoping she wasn't going to get mushy on him this early in the morning.

She looked at him as though she could see all the way through his rock-hard demeanor.

Her piercing stare made him uncomfortable. "Go back to bed."

"It was last night, wasn't it?" she whispered.

"What?"

"Sally." She leaned forward. "She had her baby."

"The clone. Not her baby."

"I knew it." Her eyes opened wide with excitement. "You were gone so long. How did it go?"

He blew at the steam rising from his cup. "Okay...except for Tuliver. The old man checked out."

Melanie dropped her gaze. "How sad." She put her hand on her belly and caressed the bulging orb.

He suspected she was thinking about Sally's ordeal. Childbirth. Though understandably apprehensive about it, she had said she was looking forward to it, but not the way Sally had agreed.

"Is she okay?" Melanie asked without looking up.

"Eugene gave her a stiff nightcap. But don't worry, a spinal tap will make your labor a cakewalk compared to what she went through."

"I can't imagine—"

"Then shut up about it."

She sneered at him for his curt reply and continued to stroke her stomach, then gasped. "Oh, John. Look. He's awake. Look."

For a brief moment, he saw her abdomen quiver and roll as the fetus moved around in his cramped quarters. Then it went still. Melanie lifted her eyes. Larson could tell by her faraway gaze that she was awestruck by the sensation.

"Who is he, John?"

"Nobody you know." He frowned. And nobody she would want to know. Morris Brennon was a man she wouldn't have survived meeting. He'd killed over a hundred people: men, women, and children, murdered them all without mercy, without remorse.

The Duplication Factor

Larson thought back to the day he met the killer on death row at Menard State Prison in Illinois. Morris was waiting for his time in the electric chair. And no one deserved it more. Being that the ax was his favorite murder weapon, he'd left a bloody trail of misery across the Midwest. But he was just what Larson was looking for, an obscure cell donor for his next human clone. Morris wouldn't be around to cause any problems or point a finger at Blythe University. And he was happy to oblige. By the time they threw the switch, Larson had the tissue samples he needed, and Morris was sure he would be back. His last words, *See ya all later,* made no sense to any of those who'd witnessed his welcome demise.

"John? I'd like to know."

"You're not supposed to ask. Read the contract."

"I just wonder sometimes." She uncrossed her legs and sat on the edge of the table. "But I can still do another one after this, right?"

He finished the last sip of his coffee. "Maybe."

"I hope so."

"What's the hurry?"

"The pay is good, that's all."

"I thought as much." He leaned back in his chair and looked her up and down, admiring his handiwork. "But someday you'll want a real child, don't you think?"

She shrugged. "Maybe."

With a smirk, he shook his head and turned to the creek. The bellowing cows had moved somewhere upstream, now concealed in the mist. While he watched the silent fog drift by, he thought about his plans for today, the medical experiments he was going to conduct on the clone of William Tuliver.

Larson had a lot to learn before 1122B was born.

Chapter Nineteen

Across campus in a basement bedroom, Sally awoke from her medicated sleep to graveyard silence. Her eyelids fluttered as she tried to open them. Eventually, darkness began to give way to a glow from a nightlight. Everything looked blurry, as though she was peering through a glass of water. She blinked, but everything remained out of focus. Feeling dizzy, she wanted to move but couldn't make her body respond. She drew in a breath, wondered why her chest felt heavy as a load of bricks. Exhaling, she heard a moan from her throat that startled her. Her tongue felt numb and dry. Pulling her right hand up to her face, she tried to feel her lips. Her fingers tingled.

"Oh, God," she mumbled.

"Sally?" a voice said.

She flinched. Who's there? A man's voice.

"Welcome back to the land of the living."

A familiar voice but her groggy mind couldn't place it. "I'm thirsty," she managed. "Water."

A strong arm lifted her head from the pillow. Her lips touched a glass. Cool water splashed on her tongue. She swallowed, choked, and coughed.

"Try again," the gentle voice said.

She got down a couple tasteless swallows.

"Better?" he asked.

"What happened?"

"Not now." He lowered her head to the pillow.

The room wobbled. She took another deep breath. Body pains

became evident as her grogginess subsided. Was she hit by a truck? Bile burned the back of her throat. "Oh no." Her stomach cramped. She rolled her head to the side and vomited. "I'm sorry." She spit, wondered where the bedpan came from.

"It's the damn drug," his voice said, holding the bedpan. "It'll pass."

That voice. Again she tried to remember it, saw a face appear above her, silhouetted in the nightlight's glow. Was he an angel?

"Am I dead?"

"You'll have to get better to die."

"What time is it?"

"Early. Go back to sleep."

That voice. Soothing. She trained her gaze on his dark face, his blurry mysterious features. Handsome. She blinked. For an instant, her focus sharpened, then quickly faded. Another blink brought another image. This time she saw him. It was Chet Brady. "How long have you been here?"

"Most of the night." He dabbed spittle from her mouth with a tissue. "I couldn't sleep." He dropped the tissue into the bedpan and set the mess aside. "You had me worried."

"I don't mean to be a bother."

"Never."

She closed her eyes. Chet Brady. She should have known it would be him. He was a gentle man with black hair, high cheekbones, and a square jaw that made him look tough, like a mobster, but he was short in stature with a thick chest and muscular arms. He'd talked about getting a nose job someday. That was Chet Brady, always making fun of his big nose, always joking around. Always thoughtful. Sometimes he would sneak her jawbreakers from the big machine in the cafeteria. He treated her like a little sister. And here he was, taking care of her again, as usual. She licked her upper lip and wondered why he'd stayed with her all night. Maybe he wanted to take over for William—for William— Her eyes popped open. Was he dead...or had she only dreamed he'd died? "William."

Chet took her hand. "I'm sorry, Sally."

Then she remembered the baby. "Geoffrey?" They took him away. She tried to sit up. *Pain.* "Where is he?"

Chet lowered his eyes. "In Larson's lab."

"Oh, God. Geoffrey," she cried out, turning her face away from Chet's angelic glow. "William, what are we going to do now?"

"Please, Sally. That won't help." He rubbed the back of her hand. "Everything will work out."

Easy for him to say. She fought back another bout of nausea. Sick. Tired. Heartbroken. She wanted William back. She wanted Geoffrey. She needed help.

"Go back to sleep."

Tears stung her eyes as she closed them, exhaled, and let the residual effects of the drug take her away.

***

Satisfied that Sally had fallen asleep, Chet slowly released her hand. Leaning back in his chair, he watched her gentle breathing. The dim nightlight cast an eerie glow around the room. Her hospital bed, draped with white sheets and a green wool blanket, was the centerpiece of her room's meager decor: a brown cushion couch, a magazine-cluttered coffee table, and a little dinette. An old black and white TV had been her only link to the outside world for the past year.

A warm feeling came over him as he remembered how excited he was the day he met her. After enduring a grueling schedule of night classes and extracurricular exams, he'd received his assignment to the Tuliver Project. The old man was a bore, but Sally, Chet had taken to her like a sister. Being only in his first year of postgraduate studies, he felt privileged to work with her, and William, as well as Dr. Larson's genetic research team, and now Geoffrey, the first human clone. He shook his head in disbelief.

He wanted to tell the world, but he couldn't. He was sworn to secrecy. He couldn't even tell his wife. No one. Those were the rules, and he gladly accepted them. It wasn't too much to ask for such a great honor.

Sally stirred. "William," she murmured.

Leaning forward, he checked to see if she was waking up again. She moaned something else he couldn't understand. Satisfied she was still sleeping, he stood and stretched, wishing he was asleep, preferably next to Mrs. Brady.

He paced, working out the stiffness in his back and leg muscles, and thought about his wife. This time of morning she'd be awake, coffee cup in hand, standing at the window of their modest ranch house north of Gary, Indiana, looking out over Lake Michigan. He wished he were there, holding her, inhaling the perfume on her neck, feeling the softness of her skin—God. Why did he torture himself this way? His education, he remembered. That's what this was all about. There was life after Vietnam, the Marines, and Special Forces. He'd served his country. It wasn't his fault he was wounded, sent home. Now, a Master's degree in bioengineering took precedent over everything.

Sally squirmed in her sleep.

He thought she was having a nightmare.

Chapter Twenty

*S*ergeant Pepper's Lonely Hearts Club Band* echoed through Eugene's bedroom. He peered out from under his covers and looked at the clock radio on the nightstand. *7:00 AM.*

"Already?" Hating *The Beatles* for waking him, he shut off the alarm. Time to get up. He didn't want to get up.

Rolling over, he cast a sleepy gaze around the room. His slacks, shirt, and smock lay in a wad on the chair by the door. It looked a lot like the pile of laundry on the floor, only smaller. He yawned and pried himself out of bed. Dull light behind the curtains drew him to the window where he peered out at the morning fog. The gray gloom seemed appropriate for the task he had for today: tell Sally the truth. Damn.

He shuffled into the bathroom on morning-stiff legs. After showering, he dressed and made his way to the kitchen, a place of despair if ever there was one. Where'd he leave that coffee pot? Scanning the room, he found it on the table next to an open cereal box and a wedge of dried-up toast. The pot was still half full with yesterday's coffee—or was it from the day before? He couldn't recall, shrugged. "How bad can it be?"

After lighting the stove with a stick match, he placed the pot on the burner then found a dirty coffee cup on the cluttered counter. The sink was full of unwashed dishes, and the floor needed mopping. Feeling hungry, he opened the refrigerator: two beers and half a pizza—with something brown growing on it. His appetite took a nosedive. He decided on breakfast in the cafeteria, closed the door, and headed outside to get the morning paper.

Paying little attention to the fog, he read the headlines. *Vietnam Tally Rises*. As much as he disliked bad news, he was glad the Vietnam War was someone else's problem.

The aroma of boiling coffee returned him to the kitchen. After tossing the newspaper on the table, he poured a cup and sampled the stale brew. It wasn't too bad. In fact, this bachelor's life suited him just fine, though sometimes, since he'd met Sally, he thought it might be nice to have her around—like that would ever happen. The way she cried for William, it didn't seem possible that she'd ever consider dating the doctor who didn't try to save him. How could he make her understand. He did what he had to do.

The doorbell rang.

It wasn't even 8:00. "Christ." He headed for the door. The doorbell rang again, this time with urgency, as if it would get him to the door any faster. "I'm coming."

He looked out the front window and shook his head in disbelief. Dr. Larson was standing on the porch, wearing a three-piece suit and a striped tie, looking too pressed and polished for this early in the morning. Eugene opened the door a crack. "What are you doing here?"

"We've got to talk." Larson pushed his way inside.

Eugene stepped back, more out of shock than congeniality. "Come right on in," he said sarcastically. "Want some coffee?"

"If it's fresh."

"Just made it." He led the way to the kitchen, grabbed the pot off the stove, and filled another dirty cup. "Hope it's hot enough." He handed it to his boss.

Larson sniffed the steam and frowned as if he detected a strange odor.

"Cheers," Eugene said, offering his cup in salutation. "Let's drink to our success."

Larson nodded and sipped from his cup. His face soured. "You call this crap coffee?" He looked around the kitchen. "And when are you going to clean up this place? You live like a pig."

"I work eighteen hours a day, for Christ's sake."

"That's no excuse."

Eugene wasn't in the mood for a lecture. "I don't have the luxury of a maid, not like you and your live-in surrogate."

"Leave Melanie out of this."

"It's always about Melanie." Eugene sat in a chair at the table. "The deal was room and board, John. Bedding her wasn't anywhere in the contract."

"She's more of a pain in my ass than anything." Larson took another swig of coffee, scowled, and set the cup on the cluttered counter. "How can you drink this shit?"

"I'm immune." He took a defiant gulp. "What do you want to talk about?"

"First thing this morning, I want you in the lab. Setup the IV's for the clone. I need three drips: a sedative, an antibiotic, and ten milliliters glucose. Meanwhile, I'll start on the blood work—"

"Now hold on one second, John. Give the kid a chance—"

"Clone," Larson interrupted. "He's a clone, not a kid."

Eugene ground his molars. Though his boss's attitude toward clones was firm, Eugene resolved himself to be equally adamant about Geoffrey's human status, but he wasn't in a mood to argue about it this morning. "Whatever you say, John. I still think Sally should nurse him."

"No."

"Why not?"

"It's too bonding...too personal. Why torture her with it?"

"She needs it. Geoffrey needs it."

The look on Larson's face remained blank and uncaring. "This isn't about what *they* need."

"You're making a big mistake, John." Eugene's coffee started tasting bitter.

"I want to get started on the tests right away." Leaning against the counter, Larson crossed his arms. "We need to prove the clones are the same persons as their donors."

"So what? You can't publish our findings. Colonel Harrison will have your hide."

Larson slumped. "Someday I will."

"Time is the true test of BZ-21. Don't rush it. Let the kids grow up."

"Clones," Larson spat.

"See how they mature."

"They'll be exactly the way they were, thanks to my restriction enzyme. I'm sure of it."

"So what's the rush? The tests can wait."

Larson spit in the sink. "If word of this leaks out, some high and mighty politician might put an end to our project."

"Quit." Eugene slammed down his coffee cup. "Nobody cares about bioengineering. Everyone with government contracts are building weapons and space hardware, while the rest of the world is busy watching astronauts walk on the moon and soldiers die in Vietnam. Give Sally and Geoffrey a week...that's all I ask."

"This is my project," Larson reminded Eugene.

"You're a true pioneer, John, but at what price, our compassion, our humanity?"

"There's always a price."

"All I see is suffering, human suffering, clone suffering...call it what you like." Eugene got up from the table, grabbed his coffee cup, and tossed it in the sink of dirty dishes. "And what's to become of the clones? Have you thought that far ahead?" He dumped the dregs of Larson's coffee. "What are you going to do with Morris? He's a killer. That's what he does."

"He's just what Colonel Harrison needs."

"And you're going to keep him locked up?"

"If we have to."

"And what about Tuliver's fortune, will you deny Geoffrey that, too?"

Larson looked at his watch as if waiting for a train. "That's not my problem." He moved toward the front door. "Besides, he's my clone. Anything William wanted doesn't matter anymore."

"Don't bet on it, John."

"I already have." He opened the door. "Just be at the lab in thirty minutes."

"I'll be in the cafeteria eating breakfast."

"Then make it fast."

Eugene stood in the doorway and watched his boss walk down the sidewalk that wound through a wooded courtyard toward the main building, his dark figure receding in the gloom.

"You stupid son of a bitch," Eugene muttered. It was the same old argument with the same old stalemate. *Clones aren't human. They don't need nurturing. They have no rights.*

He slammed the door. His stomach filled with foreboding. The first human clone was in for a rough time, and the project was on a collision course with disaster: for Geoffrey, the victim of Larson's medical tests, and Morris, the fetal time bomb.

But as long as Larson considered the clones inhuman, Eugene held no higher hopes for them than the condition of his kitchen.

Chapter Twenty-One

S ally heard her bedroom door open and footsteps approach her bedside.

"Are you hungry?" Dr. Marshall asked.

His voice hit her with a jolt of adrenaline. She squeezed her eyes shut, hoping she wouldn't hear it again. He'd lied to her and pumped her full of drugs. Now, with William gone, she felt trapped.

"Sally?"

Feign sleep.

"She was awake earlier," Chet said.

"Thanks for keeping an eye on her."

Footsteps. The door clicked shut. *Don't go, Chet. Don't leave me alone with this son of a bitch.*

"Sally, wake up. I need to tell you something."

She clenched her jaw. Hadn't he said enough last night?

He gently shook her shoulder. "Sally."

His persistence made her want to lash out at him with cat claws and rip out his eyes. "Leave me alone."

"Have some orange juice."

"Go away."

"Oatmeal and toast?"

"I hate you." She buried her face in her pillow.

"Hate me all you want. You still have to eat. Come on."

Turning her head, she opened her eyes slowly. Blinking, she scanned the room, her gaze landing on the bed stand and a breakfast tray. Food. She was starved. Then she saw Dr. Marshall in his white lab coat, noticed a forlorn look in his eyes. Was something wrong?

Geoffrey? She felt a chill. "Is Geoffrey all right?"

"He's doing fine."

"I want to see him."

"Eat something."

Sally pushed off her covers, kicked her legs over the edge of the bed, tried to get up but couldn't get past the pain in her stomach. "I want to see him," she rasped. "Right now."

Dr. Marshall put a firm hand on her knee. "No, Sally."

"He needs me."

"You're not going anywhere." He lifted her feet and swung her legs back onto the bed.

She kicked him, but the lingering ache of childbirth had left her too weak to do any real harm. "Damn you."

"Don't damn me, Sally. Damn William or damn Dr. Larson if you like, but not me. I told them to tell you the truth, but they wouldn't listen."

"About William...that he was going to die?"

Eugene raised his eyes to hers. "That...and Geoffrey."

"There's something wrong. I knew it."

"Not that."

"Why won't you let me see him?"

He swallowed, looked at her straight on. "I hate to tell you this, but he's not going home with you, Sally."

Her chest felt suddenly heavy. "Of course he is." She couldn't breathe. "He's my baby."

"I'm sorry, but he's not...not legally. He's the property of Blythe University."

"But I'm his mother."

"Listen, Sally. Carl drew up a contract between William and Dr. Larson. It gave William all rights to the clone, if he lived, but in small print, if he died, all rights were transferred to Blythe University. Your name wasn't mentioned anywhere."

She sat up, choking on shock. They'd never make it stick. "That baby is not a piece of real estate. I'll...I'll sue you. The whole world will know about your damn project."

"Come on, Sally, a human clone? No one will believe you."

"They'll investigate, cops, Congress..."

"We'll deny everything. Here, drink some orange juice."

He held out the glass to her.

She slapped it out of his hand, sending orange juice everywhere. "How could you let that happen?"

"William was only interested in himself." He swiped at juice spots on his lab coat. "Carl betrayed him. It's not my fault."

Of course it was his fault. "You could have warned me but you didn't. You're just as guilty."

"Don't be too quick to judge me, Sally." He reached inside his lab coat and pulled out *The Lost Diamonds*. "This is yours."

Her heart jumped when she saw William's book. She tried to grab it, but Dr. Marshall kept it just out of her reach.

"William cloned himself so he wouldn't lose his fortune."

Ridiculous. "He needed bone marrow—"

"It's all right here." He wagged the book. "William did it for his money. We told him he could have his life back, his fortune, everything. So he wrote this book so he could find it again...after he grows old enough to understand."

"That's not possible." Did he think she was stupid? "He can't come back. He's dead."

Dr. Marshall looked at the book in his hand. "No, he's very much alive."

"What?" Did they revive him after all? "Where is he?"

"There's something you have to know about his clone, Sally."

"William's all right?" It was too good to be true. Her heart raced. "Can I see him?"

"You already have." Dr. Marshall looked at her, nodding, a slight smile on his lips. "Geoffrey *is* William."

She almost laughed but felt a jolt as she remembered the clone's eyes, those staring, curious eyes. They'd looked like William's eyes, but they couldn't be—not really.

"We used a powerful enzyme to clone him. Geoffrey is *not* William's twin. He's William. He'll grow up with feelings of déjà vu, see shadows of a past life, experiences, and maybe even memories of places and people...us...you."

Even she knew that wasn't possible. "You're crazy."

Dr. Marshall handed her the book. "Maybe, but this book was his insurance. It won't do him any good though. The clone belongs to Dr. Larson like all the other lab rats around here."

"How can you say that? He's just a little baby."

"Believe me, Sally, he's not like any baby that's ever been born. That's why you can't take him home."

Clutching William's book to her chest, she felt the sting of betrayal, helplessness, and then a surge of anger. Who did these people think they were, stealing her baby? *It's not fair.* "You can't keep me from seeing him."

"That's not up to me."

"Try and stop me." She hit him with the book.

He yanked it away from her.

"It's my baby," she screamed and pounded on his chest with white-knuckled fists. She was a mother bear protecting her cub. "Give him back."

"Sally, stop it." He stood there, took the beating.

"It's my baby." She kept whaling on him. "Bastard."

He grabbed her wrists with iron-strong hands. "After all the work we put into this project, Larson's not going to let you walk out the door with his prize."

"Go to hell." She spit in his face.

He pushed her back down on the bed, wiped spittle from his chin with his white sleeve. "This isn't a maternity ward. It's a university. We're doing important research work here."

Lying on the bed, she covered her face with both hands, fought back tears with a wave of anger. "God damn Dr. Larson, damn your university, damn your work, and God damn Carl Savage for betraying us." She gritted her teeth, propped herself up on an elbow, and pointed at Dr. Marshall. "And most of all, God damn you for letting it happen."

"Come on, Sally—"

"You knew all along! You didn't care enough about me to stop it." She wanted to hit him, pound on him again, make him hurt like she was hurting. But she didn't have the strength to fight him, only words to throw out, hateful words meant to cut deep. "I thought I could trust you, Dr. Marshall. You're worse than the rest of them."

He rubbed his temple. "I've got a career here, Sally. This is my life. I did what I had to do."

"And I'll do what I have to do, even if it takes dragging you through every court in this country. And don't think I can't. William left me a lot of money. I'll spend every dime to get Geoffrey back."

"And I wouldn't blame you. But keep your voice down. Colonel Harrison won't be as understanding."

Cold fear shot through her. The military—what did they want with Geoffrey? How far would they go to shut her up? "They wouldn't...would they...k-kill me?"

"Don't put it past them, so be careful what you say." He handed her a breast pump. "Larson won't let you nurse Geoffrey. I want at least an ounce of colostrum in the bottle. Call me when you're done."

She stuck her chin up in defiance. "And if I refuse?"

"I'll send in the team to do it for you."

"You wouldn't."

Dr. Marshall tossed the book onto the bed next to her. "Don't try me." He left. The door slammed behind him.

She dropped the breast pump and clung to *The Lost Diamonds*. Tears flowed. William's wealth couldn't save him from his genetic defect, but could it have bought him a new life? It was hard to believe. *Geoffrey is William.* Was he really starting his life over? She hoped it was possible, more than anything, but how would she know for sure if she never saw him again?

"Oh, William. What have you done?"

Chapter Twenty-Two

After she used the breast pump, Sally examined the colostrum she'd collected in the bottle, nutrients and antibodies Geoffrey needed. It wasn't much, but it was the only thing she could do for him right now. Disheartened, she pressed the call button, paging Chet, and then arranged the bed sheets over her bare legs. She hoped he knew something about Geoffrey.

A moment later, Chet came in, quietly closed the door. His shoulders were slouched, his eyes downcast. "You finished?"

Showing him the bottle, she blurted out, "Have you seen Geoffrey?" But he said nothing, just looked at the floor. Keeping silent was highly unlike him. "He's not okay, is he?"

"I gotta get back to the lab."

"Chet...don't do this to me. Don't keep me in the dark like the rest of these bastards."

He shrugged. "I can't—"

"Please tell me what's going on."

Looking up, he sighed. "Don't worry." He approached the bed, took the bottle from her hand. "I gotta go." He headed toward the door.

She couldn't have been wrong about Chet. He was like a brother to her. He wasn't like Dr. Larson or Dr. Marshall. They must've made him keep quiet, threatened him or something. "Wait."

Slowly, he turned toward her. "Please, Sally, don't—"

"Help me, Chet. I must see him."

"He's fine, really."

Sitting forward, she challenged him. "Look me in the eyes and tell me that."

He shook his head. "I-I can't."

She knew it. Something was wrong. "What are they doing to him?"

"Believe me, Sally, you don't want to know."

"Damn it, Chet. This is killing me. He's my baby. Don't make me get out of this bed and pound it out of you."

He showed her a wan smile. "I believe you would."

"Then tell me."

"Sally..." He exhaled. "It's Dr. Larson and his damn medical tests. He doesn't care about Geoffrey. I can't bear to watch what he's doing to that baby."

A sudden welling of tears in Chet's eyes surprised her. She didn't know the ex-Marine had it in him, but it proved Geoffrey was in trouble. "They're hurting him. I knew it."

He rushed back to her bedside and took her hand. "I didn't know it would be like this. That poor kid: all those tubes and needles and wires stickin' him. Larson's taken blood samples and urine, and he even scraped tissue from the back of Geoffrey's throat. I didn't sign on to this project to watch Larson torture baby clones."

"Where is he?"

"In the lab."

She'd been there before, a cold and technical place, and the smell, sharp as formaldehyde. It was no place for a child. "We have to get him out of there."

Chet sat next to her on the bed, exhaled in despair. "There's nothing we can do."

"What? There's got to be something—"

"Are you listening? There's no way, Sally. Security has doubled since last night. I have to use a special passkey to get into the lab, and Colonel Harrison has posted around-the-clock guards. It's impossible to get Geoffrey out of there."

She refused to believe it. There had to be a way. "Help me get him out. Chet, please, think of something."

"Where ya gonna take him, Sally? The lab is only the first problem. There are guards in the building, patrolling the halls...and outside, the courtyard, the perimeter. It'll take an army to break him out of here."

"Call the cops."

"They're not gonna believe me. A human clone? I hardly believe it myself."

"Then sneak him out yourself."

"If I get caught, they'll kick me out of school."

"There are other schools, Chet."

"But those soldiers have guns."

"Since when have you been afraid of guns?"

He nodded, bit his upper lip, and thought a moment. The hurt in his eyes turned to anger. He slapped his knee and stood. "I'll see what I can do."

"Thank you, thank you, thank you." She reached up and squeezed his hand.

"Meantime, I have to get this bottle to Dr. Larson. I'll be back soon."

"Hurry."

He brushed his hand against her cheek. "I will."

His touch felt warm, sincere. She was right about him, after all. He wasn't like the others. She could trust him.

As Chet turned to leave, he stopped abruptly at the door.

"What is it?"

"I know I closed this door when I came in. Look."

The door was slightly ajar.

"Did you notice anyone open it?"

"We were talking." She hadn't paid any attention to the door. "I don't know."

Cautiously, he pulled on the handle, opening the door.

Sally's heart almost stopped when she saw Dr. Marshall in the hall. He was in mid turnaround, as if he were walking away and changed his mind. Had he overheard their conversation?

"Dr. Marshall," Chet said. "Are you coming in?"

She held her breath.

"Ah, Chet. There you are. Do you have the bottle?"

"Yes, of course." He handed it to the doctor. "I was just leaving for the lab."

"I'll walk with you." Dr. Marshall examined the bottle's contents. "Nice work, Sally," he said through the open door then looked at Chet. "Let's go."

As the door closed, she exhaled. Damn! Could he have heard what they were talking about? She should have been more careful. Dr. Marshall could ruin everything. Geoffrey was in trouble, and Chet was his only hope.

Chapter Twenty-Three

Their footsteps echoed down tiled corridors as Dr. Marshall and Chet Brady walked toward the lab. Chet wasn't convinced that his boss hadn't overheard his conversation with Sally, and he expected a confrontation that was slow in coming. The silence made his stomach jittery. He feared being taken off the Tuliver project or suspended from Blythe all together. But Dr. Marshall remained mute.

They turned left down a hallway, passed the entrance to the library, and pushed through a set of double doors that thudded back and forth on their hinges. At the top of the stairs, Eugene broke the silence. "Do you have your pass key?"

"Sure do."

They walked up another set of stairs to the main lobby.

"Don't lose it. Anybody can use it to get into the lab."

That was obvious. Why had Eugene said it? "I'll be careful."

He followed Eugene across the main lobby and into the cafeteria where Chet spotted the tall red candy machine and its giant glass sphere filled with a million colorful balls. Not one to pass up the sweets, he said, "Want a jawbreaker, Doc?"

"No thanks."

Chet rushed to the machine and dropped a penny into the chrome slot. Twisting the knob, it clicked until a jawbreaker clanked down a chute and landed in his hand. "Yellow," he announced, popping it into his mouth. The hard candy flooded his mouth with lemon flavor.

Leaving the cafeteria, they walked down another bright

hallway while Chet bit the jawbreaker into pieces and chewed it. He followed Eugene around the corner to a hall that led to the lab.

"Halt!" A guard's voice echoed like thunder down the corridor.

Chet stopped, swallowed the candy. He hadn't seen this guard before. Dressed in camouflage fatigues, the man's muscles bulged under tight shirtsleeves. He wore a Colt .45 on his belt, the security strap unsnapped.

Dr. Marshall kept walking toward him.

"I said halt, mister," the guard shouted. "That means now."

"I'm unarmed," Eugene snapped back. "You're not going to shoot me."

"I will if I have to." The guard's hand hovered over the butt of his weapon.

Heart pounding, Chet quick-stepped up to Eugene, grabbed his arm, yanked him to a stop. "A confrontation would be highly unwise."

"He's a wimp."

"But he's a *big* wimp."

The sergeant blocked the doorway with his body. "Orders are orders. I check everybody that comes through here."

"They teach you to guard babies in boot camp?"

Chet felt needle pricks in the back of his neck. *Not a smart thing to say, Doc.*

The guard's cheeks reddened. "I didn't ask for this assignment. I'd rather be in Nam, pumping lead into Charlie. Instead, I pulled this duty, and I'm pissed off as it is, so don't push your luck."

"We work here," Eugene said. "I've got the baby's bottle, so let us through."

"Not until you show me some IDs."

Chet pulled his student card from his pocket. "He's just doing his job, Doc."

"That doesn't give him the right to order us around."

"Get used to it," the guard said. "We're gonna be stationed here for a long time."

"Let's give him what he wants." Chet hoped to defuse the situation.

Eugene scowled, put his ID card with Chet's, and handed them to the guard. "You don't have to play tough guy with us. We're not impressed."

The guard checked the IDs against a list on his clipboard. "You're cleared. Don't forget to sign in."

"Sign in, sign out," Eugene spat. "What are we, prisoners?"

"Something like that." The guard let them pass.

Walking to the lab, Chet hurried his pace to keep up with Eugene. "Why did you have to give him a hard time?"

"I wanted him to remember us."

"He could have shot us."

"But he didn't, and the next time he sees you, he'll know you belong here, if you know what I mean."

No, Chet didn't. At the lab door, he used his passkey on the lock and wondered what Eugene was up to. He'd been acting strangely since they left Sally's room. Had he heard them talking? Why hadn't he said anything?

Inside the dimly lit lab, the sharp smell of formaldehyde lingered in the air. A light over the counter reflected off a man's white lab coat. It was Dr. Larson hunched over a microscope, his eyes pressed to the double lenses.

"Get a load of this," Larson said, not looking up.

Eugene handed Chet the bottle. "Add some formula to this."

"Won't that be too hard on a newborn's stomach?"

"This is no ordinary newborn," Eugene reminded him.

"Right." As a prerequisite for the Tuliver project, Chet had taken a class on mothering, not very macho, but necessary. His big hands were more suited to work grenades and machine guns than bottles and diapers. However, having the routine down pat, he retrieved a baby bottle from the drawer as Eugene approached Larson at the counter.

"What have you found, John?"

"Look." Larson rolled his chair out of the way.

Bending to the microscope, Eugene recognized red blood cells. "So?"

"They're the clone's, crossed and matched Tuliver's exactly."

"That doesn't surprise me."

"But this will." Larson picked up a scroll of paper, unrolled it on the counter. It looked like a lie detector test printout with three traces. "Check this radio-spectrograph of the clone's cells. It measures the length of the chromosomes and compares them to cells of the same age. The shorter the chromosomes, the older the cell. The top trace is Sally's, the middle one is the clone's, and the bottom is Tuliver's."

Eugene looked up. "Geoffrey's matches Sally's?"

"The clone's cells are the same age as hers."

"My God...how did that happen?"

Baby bottle in hand, Chet squinted. "Geoffrey's thirty?"

"That's right," Larson said. "Using the nuclear transplant procedure, BZ-21 duplicated Sally's age from her egg."

"Of course," Eugene said. "Her egg cell mass was greater than his nuclear mass. The enzyme duplicated her mitochondrial DNA."

Larson peeled the latex gloves from his hands. "Starting the clone's genetic clock at thirty years. He'll feel like a sixty-year-old man when he's only thirty. And there's something else. When the clone is thirty, its sixty-year-old bone marrow cells will short-circuit again, start dividing and mutating like before."

Eugene winced. "Leukemia."

"The same thing that killed William."

"Thirty years, that's all he's got?"

"Give or take a couple."

Chet didn't like the sound of that. He got a can of formula from the cabinet shelf. "Is there anything we can do about it?"

"We can't turn back his genetic clock," Eugene said with a look of dismay. "If only there was a way to locate the genes that trigger tumors and splice them out beforehand."

Larson pulled the slide from the microscope and dipped it in an alcohol dish. "Someday we'll be able to map the human genome and cure this kind of cancer with gene splicing therapy."

"But will it come in time to save Geoffrey?" Chet grabbed a can opener from a drawer and popped a hole in the formula can.

"We still have the growth spurt problem to resolve," Eugene reminded them. "We got lucky this time, but it might happen next time, or maybe the tenth time. It's a crap-shoot either way."

Chet wondered why the doctors were willing to risk the life of a surrogate mother. He remembered what the calf had done to the cow. Good thing that didn't happen to Geoffrey. He poured the formula in the bottle, added Sally's colostrum, and shook it.

Larson turned off the microscope lights. "Right now, I'm more concerned about BZ-21's presence in the clone's body, what effect it will have on its overall growth rate and health."

"The enzyme must be diluted to infinity by now." Eugene leaned on the counter.

"I'm going to take some tissue samples tomorrow: liver, pancreas, spleen. Exploratory surgery. See if I can find any trace evidence of BZ-21."

"Surgery? Christ, John, give the kid a break."

Larson glared at him "It's a clone. Not a kid."

Chet felt a chill. "Not a kid?"

"You heard me," Larson barked.

"So what if he's thirty years old? He's just a baby. You can't start cutting him up." Chet gulped, his argument thwarted by Larson's icy stare. Truth was, Geoffrey was *not* a normal baby. He *was* different. And they had made him that way.

Eugene patted Chet's shoulder. "He's probably hungry by now. Let's go."

"Lock him up good when you're done." Larson flicked off the countertop lights and left through the double doors.

Chet watched him go, despising the doctor's cold, scientific approach to Geoffrey. Sally was right. They had to get him out of here before Larson ended up killing the kid that wasn't a kid.

"Forget about him," Eugene said.

"He makes me so mad I could just..." Chet jammed a nipple on the bottle and followed Eugene across the lab to a chamber in the far corner. It looked like a walk-in freezer with walls thick as a bank vault. At the window, Chet looked in, saw Geoffrey lying on his back in a crib made of glass with round holes in the sides. From the ceiling, a mass of wires dangled down to him, their terminals taped to various places on his diaper-clad body. He looked like a marionette lying there, peacefully awaiting his next performance.

Eugene unlocked the heavy door, and Chet followed him inside. At the infant's glass bedside, Eugene smiled down at him. Chet could see why. Though Geoffrey looked helpless, he seemed at peace. His little lips moved in a sucking motion as his bony chest rose and fell with gentle breaths. The unmistakable smell of a newborn baby hung in the air.

Without removing his gaze from the child, "The bottle," Eugene said, hand extended.

Chet gave it to him and watched as Eugene stroked the nipple across Geoffrey's tiny lips.

"Here you go, little one," Eugene cooed. "Would you like some of this?"

Chet was surprised at Eugene's gentle crib-side manner.

Suddenly, with startling force, Geoffrey sucked the nipple into his mouth.

Eugene's eyebrows arched. "His suckling instinct is very strong." The bottle surged in his fingers with each gulp. "I wonder if he knows he's done this before."

"You think?"

Eugene smiled. "Maybe."

Chet could tell the doctor had a soft spot for the little guy. "I think he likes you."

Suddenly, Geoffrey spit out the nipple. His eyes flew open and stared at Eugene, a piercing stare that made Chet's heartbeat skip.

But Eugene didn't move. He didn't blink, as if he didn't want to risk severing his connection with the clone.

Chet's temples pounded as Geoffrey studied the men leaning over him. His brown eyes rolled in a circle, darting to Chet's face, then to Eugene's, and back again. Chet smiled at Geoffrey but refrained from making baby noises. Eugene had the market on that.

"Hi there, little guy. How yah doin'?"

Geoffrey responded with a baby noise of his own, sounded like "da da", and then he sucked the bottle nipple back into his mouth. Now content with his companions, he made short order of the formula. His eyes slowly closed.

Eugene set the empty bottle on the counter. "I heard you and Sally talking," he whispered. "About Geoffrey."

Chet's heart banged against his ribs. Dr. Marshall knew they wanted to get Geoffrey out. Chet had to say something fast. "She's worried about him...and me too."

Nodding, Eugene dabbed a tissue around Geoffrey's mouth. "I'm not going to stop you."

Chet took a quick breath. "What?"

"Help her get him out of here. Tonight. After Larson's done with his surgery tomorrow, this baby won't be fit to travel."

Chet blinked, wondered if he'd heard the doctor correctly. He looked into his eyes, saw tenderness and a welling of tears. Chet had never seen him like this before. But he understood why. Geoffrey had worked his way into the doctor's heart, too. He'd become personally involved, a bad thing for the doctor—but a good thing for the patient. "All right." Chet followed Eugene out of the chamber. "But how am I going to pull this off?"

Taking a pencil from his pocket, Eugene placed it in the doorjamb and gently closed the thick chamber door. The pencil cracked but kept the latch from locking.

"What about the guard?" Chet asked. "How are we supposed to get around him without him sounding the alarm?"

Eugene removed a vial from the medication safe and found a

hypodermic needle in a drawer. "Put him to sleep with this. He won't expect you to stick him. You're on the list, remember?"

"Y-yeah, right," Chet replied, his throat tightening. Now he understood Eugene's previous antics with the guard.

"Get Sally and Geoffrey to Chicago, and while you're there..." He pulled a folded paper from his pocket. "Take this birth certificate to the Cook County courthouse." He tucked it into Chet's lab coat pocket.

This would be a risky mission, Chet knew, like many of those he'd been on with Special Forces in Vietnam. And like back then, he'd be pitted against an enemy that would kill him to stop him, but in this case, the bad guys weren't the VC; they were American soldiers with one directive: contain the first human clone at all costs. It was easy to understand why Eugene wanted *him* to rescue Geoffrey and Sally, but why would he sabotage his own project? Chet locked eyes with Eugene. "Why are you doing this?"

"I'm not doing anything. You are. This child deserves a normal life, don't you think?"

"Sure, but—"

"I can't risk my career to help him, if that's what you mean."

"But I should risk my education here?"

Eugene shook his head. "I'll cover for you. Just get them out before it's too late."

Chapter Twenty-Four

The setting sun's glow painted the horizon bright yellow. Through a dusty attic window in the spire atop Blythe University, Chet scanned the courtyard and stone-hedged perimeter below. On the dirt road paralleling the wall, Colonel Harrison's patrol jeep rumbled by, floodlights illuminating the dust that swirled in its wake. He counted three soldiers, two riding up front and a third manning a 50-caliber machine gun mounted on the roll bar. The sight reminded him of the MPs who'd patrolled the perimeter around Phan Rang Base, Vietnam. Like them, these soldiers were well trained and not to be taken lightly.

As the jeep disappeared around a corner, he saw a squad of foot soldiers marching down the sidewalk that wound its way through the wooded courtyard. He counted twenty men with M-16s slung on their shoulders. Geoffrey Scott Michaels, the first human clone, was well guarded.

In the fading light, he noticed a creek flowing through the field beyond the courtyard and into a tunnel that burrowed under the perimeter wall. On the other side, the creek emptied into an irrigation canal that cut across a meadow and under an array of towering power lines to a stand of trees and a highway bridge in the distance.

As twilight distorted the landscape into indistinguishable shapes, Chet turned his attention to the university grounds. A twelve-foot-tall iron gate marked the only way in and out of Blythe. Several armed guards paced back and forth. A Blackhawk helicopter sat idly by. In the parking lot, his tan '65 Volvo station wagon glistened under the lights. His plan was risky: smuggle Sally and Geoffrey out in the back seat of his car. They'd be in Chicago before anyone realized they were missing. He just had to get past those guards.

The sky over Cedar Lake slowly turned black.

***

In the lonely confines of her room, Sally pushed her dinner tray aside. The potatoes were untouched, and a chicken leg lay on the plate, half-eaten. With Geoffrey on her mind, she was feeling guilty. She knew she was to blame for all this, just as much as William, Carl Savage, or Dr. Marshall. She brushed back a fallen lock of hair and wondered how she could have loved William with such blind devotion. Her own selfishness, wanting a baby, had gotten her into this mess. She thought she could never forgive herself if Geoffrey had to pay the price for her self-gratification.

The door creaked open. Chet stalked in.

Her pulse quickened. "What's going on?"

He glanced up and down the darkened hall before closing the door. "Let's go."

Go? She'd never seen that look in his eyes, serious, focused, and scary. And instead of wearing his lab coat and slacks, he wore a black jacket, blue jeans, and brown hiking boots. "Where are we going?"

He pulled her off the bed to her feet. "Get dressed."

Her fingertips felt numb. "We're getting out of here?"

"It's all arranged." Chet tossed her a pair of blue jeans from the dresser drawer.

"But how?"

"You let me worry about that."

Fear stabbed her chest. She slipped out of her hospital gown and into the jeans. After pulling an old *Beatles* sweatshirt over her head, she grabbed her tennis shoes from under the bed and hastily laced them. Her body ached, but she refused to give in to the pain. She threw on a black parka and slung her purse over her shoulder. Scanning the room, her mind started racing. Was she forgetting something?

"Come on."

Just as Chet was about to lead her down the hallway, she remembered. "Wait." She ran to the nightstand and grabbed *The Lost Diamonds*. After stowing it in her purse, she ran back to Chet waiting in the hall. "I'm ready." She wondered what she was getting into. Her tennis shoes squeaked on the tile floor, but they'd made the first landing of the stairwell undetected.

Chet stopped abruptly. "Take this." He handed her a silver passkey. "It'll get you into the lab. In the far corner, you'll find Geoffrey in a sterile chamber. Just pull on the door handle. It'll open."

"What are *you* going to do?"

"The hard part." He took a syringe from his pocket. A clear liquid quivered in the cylinder. "I'm going to knock out the guard with this."

"Really?"

"Just leave it to me." He cupped the hypo in his hand and hid the plunger up his sleeve. "I'll do all the talking. When I stick him, you run for the lab. Got that?"

Though apprehension flooded her brain, she nodded and wondered about Chet as they climbed the remaining steps. He sure was brave. At the top, her stomach cramped with a surge of worry. How brave was she?

Following Chet through the lobby, she thought about the happy times at Blythe University. She'd made a lot of friends here, but some of them had suddenly turned into enemies. The place seemed so different to her now, hostile and unfriendly, and she wondered why she hadn't noticed this before. It must have been because of William. Everything seemed so much better when he was around.

Chet stopped in the hallway on the other side of the cafeteria. "The guard is just around this corner." He brushed her hair back with his fingers. "Just relax." His touch was soothing, his voice calm. "And smile."

She clutched the key in her hand and forced a smile. "This okay?" Her knees trembled. After one last deep breath, she followed him around the corner.

"Halt."

The biggest man she'd ever seen blocked their way. She grabbed Chet's arm and wondered how he was going to pull this off. The corridor seemed to close in around her. Chet walked on as though he were unconcerned. She took a quick breath and brightened her nervous smile.

"Evening, sergeant," Chet said as if they were at a cocktail party.

The guard nodded then looked at Sally. "Who is she?"

"The baby's mother. She wants to see him."

"You know I can't allow that."

Sally clasped her hands under her chin. "Just for a minute."

The big man's voice softened. "Lady, if it were up to me—"

Chet lunged at him with the needle, but as if by instinct, the guard blocked Chet's arm, knocking loose the syringe. It slid down the hallway and clinked against a baseboard. With a crack, Chet caught a left hook on the side of his head. He hit the floor like a rag doll.

"You dumb shit," the guard roared as he bent over and lifted Chet's flaccid body with powerful hands. "I'll kill you for that."

Sally's chest tightened. Remembering Chet's instructions, she fought panic and waited for an opportunity to run. As the guard slugged Chet again, she slipped around behind him and ran through the double doors. A sign with an arrow pointing left read: *BIO LAB*. The passkey was in her fingers. Her heart was in her throat.

***

A burst of speckled light exploded in Chet's brain. He didn't remember hitting the floor. An instant later he was being lifted like a child's doll. Panic raced through his mind.

The second blow didn't hurt as bad. Adrenaline had already

numbed his sense of pain. The flight or fight instinct took over. He grabbed the sergeant's shirt collars with both hands and ducked his head between his arms. The big man could only punch him in the ribs.

Chet dropped to the floor, pulling the guard down with him. He tried to throw him over his head, but he was too heavy, and Chet ended up underneath the guard.

"You're gonna die, fucker."

Gasping, Chet tried to push the heavy man off. He tried to roll. He tried to buck. He couldn't breathe. Ceiling lights began to spin. Chet struggled harder, but it was no use; he couldn't break free. So this was how he was going to die. What would become of Sally and Geoffrey? He saw his wife standing at his grave during the funeral. Tears flowed from her eyes. She didn't look good in black.

That thought drove him into a frenzy, kicking and punching, but the guard was unmovable.

"Think you're a tough guy, huh?" The guard pressed his beefy forearm down on Chet's throat, blocking the flow of air. Locked nose-to-nose with his killer, Chet began blinking in and out of consciousness. He smelled onions.

The guard suddenly stiffened. His eyes crossed and rolled up in their sockets. A groan came from his throat. He went limp.

"What the hell?" Chet wriggled out from under the unconscious guard and gulped air. A motion down the hall caught his attention. Someone in a white lab coat had just dashed around the corner. He thought it looked like Dr. Marshall.

Struggling to his feet, Chet looked down at the guard. He was lying on his stomach, an empty hypodermic needle protruding from the back of his neck.

Chet swallowed. "You gotta be shittin' me."

Chapter Twenty-Five

Sally made it to the dimly lit lab, found the sterile chamber, and pulled on the door. It opened with a squeal. She rushed inside, saw Geoffrey and had to fight back tears. "Oh my God." He looked helpless tethered to tubes and wires that Dr. Larson had rigged for his medical experiments. Blinking away a tear, she ran her fingers through Geoffrey's fine hair. He was sleeping, his tiny hands curled into fists, his toes twitching. "What have they done to you?"

She set her purse on a counter cluttered with medical supplies and equipment and tugged on the tubes and wires hanging from the ceiling. They were securely fastened. With no idea what they were for, she feared removing them from Geoffrey's little body might harm him. Not knowing what to do, she cupped her hand over her mouth. "Oh dear." But she had to do something—and quickly.

With trembling fingers, she peeled off the tape that held a wire to his chest. It came away freely. Relieved, she removed two more wires in the same manner. "All right." She breathed a sigh of—

A beeping alarm rang out. She flinched and looked toward the counter where a heart monitor displayed a flashing red light. "Oh dear." Someone was bound to hear all the racket. The machines were probably monitored from a central control room somewhere. Dr. Marshall and Dr. Larson could already be sprinting toward the lab to investigate. And the soldiers. Clenching her jaw, she knew time was running out.

She grabbed a calming breath and quickly plucked the remaining wires from Geoffrey's tiny body. It amazed her that he was still sleeping through all the noise—not to mention all the pulling and prodding. She wondered if Larson had drugged him the same way Dr. Marshall had drugged her. The bastard.

Pushing the tangle of wires aside, she turned her attention to the tubes. There were three of them. One went up a tiny nostril. She assumed it was oxygen, pulled out the tube and tossed it aside. The next tube was attached to his chest with a suction cup. As she started peeling it off, his skin began to stretch up with it, like taffy. She hesitated, fearing she'd hurt him. But the wailing alarm spurred her to yank it off quickly. Still, he didn't stir. She turned to the last tube. It was an IV, the needle piercing a vein on the inside of his thigh and taped in place. She began to sweat. This was going to be the hard one. Looking around, she spotted the medical supplies on the counter. She grabbed a wad of cotton and a strip of tape.

First she peeled off the tape that secured the needle to Geoffrey's thigh. Blood pounded in her neck. The beeping alarm was driving her crazy, making it hard to concentrate. She readied the cotton wad in one hand, and with the other, she pulled out the needle. A line of blood jetted from the open wound.

He jerked.

"I'm sorry, Geoffrey." As she applied the cotton, he started wailing and kicking, making it difficult for her to keep thumb pressure on the wound. She thought her heart was going to explode. "It's all right," she whispered. "It's all right." She taped the cotton to his thigh, and gathered him into her arms.

"Hush little baby, don't you cry."

His sobbing subsided quickly as she rocked him. He seemed happy to be held, just like William. She wrapped him in a blanket, grabbed her purse from the counter, and ran out of the lab. Now for the hard part. She made her way down the hall toward the door where the guard had been stationed. She expected to see Chet lying dead on the floor and an army awaiting her appearance. Cautiously, she opened the door a crack. She saw Chet standing over the guard, shaking his head. The side of his face was swollen, but he'd obviously won the fight. Relieved, she pushed through the door.

"You okay?"

Speechless, Chet pointed down the hall, wide eyed as if he'd seen a ghost.

"What is it?"

He shook his head. "Ah...never mind. We gotta get out of here."

As he led the way down the hall toward the cafeteria, she heard heavy footsteps tromping down a nearby stairwell. Three soldiers burst through the doors, guns drawn. The alarm must have alerted them. They looked mad as hell.

"Stop."

Sally clutched Geoffrey to her chest and ran as fast as she could, her purse swinging violently on its strap. Her insides ached, but she kept running. The soldier's footfalls, thumping on the floor behind her, were getting closer and closer.

"Leave us alone," she shouted.

"Give it up, lady."

She hoped they wouldn't shoot her.

Running through the cafeteria, she saw Chet stop at the jawbreaker machine.

"What are you doing?"

"Keep going." He shoved the machine over. It hit the floor, and the glass sphere shattered with a bang. A million jawbreakers rattled across the tile floor and into the path of the oncoming soldiers. They slipped on the rolling candies and tumbled to the floor, groaning.

Seconds later, Chet caught up with her. "This way." He pushed open the main lobby doors.

Running as fast as she could, she followed him across the parking lot to a Volvo station wagon. Geoffrey started crying again. Gasping air, Sally patted his back, trying to comfort him. "It's all right...mommy's here."

Chet keyed the door lock. "Hurry."

She jumped into the back seat.

"Get down."

Sprawling on the seat, she rubbed Geoffrey's back, trying to quiet him. Chet threw a blanket over her, the door closed, and a second later Chet got in behind the wheel. The engine cranked and started. Feeling like an ostrich with her head in the sand, she held her breath. *Go, Chet, go.*

"Hang on."

Tires squealing, he peeled out of the parking lot just as sirens pierced the night. The alarms had gone off, alerting all the soldiers. Rocking violently on the seat, Sally felt like an escaped convict running from the hounds.

Fishtailing, the car sped up.

She sat up and peered over the seatback. "Where are we going?"

"Stay down."

Ahead, she saw the main gate aglow with floodlights. Armed soldiers blocked the gate, their rifles pointed at the approaching Volvo. "What are we going to do?"

"Hang on!" Chet hit the brakes and spun the Volvo around. Acrid tire smoke filled the car. Sally looked out the back window, saw a patrol jeep tear out after them, the machine gun muzzle on the roll cage flashing white fire. She ducked down on the seat as the back window shattered and bullets ripped into the car. Shards of glass shot through the air like shrapnel.

"They're going to kill us."

"Not if I can help it." Chet cranked the wheel. The Volvo careened off the road, bounced through a ditch, and sped across the wooded courtyard. The jeep's bright headlights were right behind them, and from every direction, muzzle flashes lit up the night. "Foot patrol." Chet yanked the steering wheel, just missing a tree.

Bullets pummeled the fenders and doors, shattered windows, and tore into the car's interior. Volvos were supposed to be the safest cars ever built, but surely they weren't meant to hold up under this kind of punishment. As the deadly rounds popped and clanked around her, Sally shielded Geoffrey with her body. Terror punched her in the chest. She had to fight for each breath. Geoffrey bawled. Gunfire banged. Engines roared. "Chet," she yelled over the mayhem.

"We're not giving up."

The Volvo skidded to a stop. Behind them, the jeep's brakes squealed and the machine gun went silent. The headlights were blinding. "Get out of the car," an angry voice demanded.

Sally's temples throbbed. "I thought we weren't giving up."

"We're not." Chet shoved the shifter into reverse and threw his elbow over the seatback. "Watch this." He popped the clutch and floored the accelerator. Sally held on to Geoffrey and braced herself. The Volvo slammed into the jeep with a bang. Headlights burst on impact, cloaking them in darkness.

A soldier moaned.

Geoffrey shrieked.

A bullet shattered the windshield.

Clutching her terrified infant, Sally smelled the pungent mist of antifreeze hissing from the jeep's radiator. Maybe now they had a chance to get away.

Chet ground the transmission into first gear, careened the Volvo around a tree, and headed out across an open field. Behind them, rifle reports cracked through the night. Chet wrestled the steering wheel back and forth as the Volvo bounced along.

"I hope you know where we're going." Sally hugged Geoffrey and wondered if she was rescuing him or getting him killed.

Zing! A bullet ricocheted off the roof. *Clack! Clack! Clack!* Vegetation slapped the underside of the car. *Boom!* A rear tire blew out.

The Volvo swerved and skidded into a creek. The engine roared. Tires spun. But the car didn't move.

Geoffrey wailed at the top of his lungs.

"Damn it." Chet slammed his hands on the steering wheel and kicked open the door. "We're gonna have to hoof it from here." He pulled her out of the car.

Cold creek water flooded her shoes. And mud. Could it get any worse? The gunfire stopped, but she could hear loud voices approaching in the dark.

"This way, men."

"My purse. It's on the floor."

Chet ducked inside the car to get it.

"Where are we going?"

"There's a tunnel about a hundred feet downstream. It'll take us under the perimeter wall to an irrigation canal." He handed her the purse and, as she slung it over her shoulder, he pulled a tire iron from the spare tire compartment. "Stay close behind me and keep quiet."

Geoffrey stopped crying. Sally flinched. It was as if he understood they were in danger of being discovered. How could that be?

"First squad, follow me."

Chet said, "Let's go."

Holding Geoffrey close to her chest, she trudged through the creek, straining her eyes to keep Chet in sight. He was merely a black shadow in a gray landscape dimly lit by the distant lights of Blythe University.

"They went this way," a soldier shouted.

With Geoffrey in one arm and pushing bull rushes aside with the other, she followed Chet's sloshing footsteps. Something abrasive scraped her leg. The strap of her purse got caught on a branch. As she freed it with a firm tug, a bird fluttered from the tangle, scaring the shit out of her.

Plodding on, she thought about the time she and William had walked down to this creek, the day she learned she was pregnant. Never would she have believed that one day she'd be back here—running for her life.

"Lock and load."

The soldiers' angry voices, the cold water, the reality of what she and William had done, what a mess she'd made of her life. But there was no going back now. She had to save Geoffrey or die trying.

Slogging onward through the muck, she hoped her pounding heart wouldn't give away their position. It seemed like miles before they reached the concrete mouth of a tunnel, which looked like a dark hole into hell. However, at the far end of the tunnel she could see a faint dot of light. It wasn't much, but it was hope. Chet ran in ahead of her.

She stopped to catch a breath, heard the chirping of crickets and the croaking of frogs. And as if that wasn't bad enough, the stench of stagnant water, slime, and decay hit her like a club. "It's gross in there."

Chet stopped. "Come on."

"I'm going to be sick." She held her breath and tread into the abyss. Chet waited, took her hand and led the way. The farther they went the more the cold corrugated steel walls closed in on her. A chill caused her limbs to shiver. Mud, slime, and fungus under her shoes made each step treacherous. It wasn't long before she noticed their presence had silenced the resident creatures. She hoped she didn't step on one.

A flashlight beam cut through the darkness behind her and cast her shadow on the silt. "Halt!" *halt! halt!* echoed down the tunnel. "Or we'll shoot!" *shoot, shoot!*

Geoffrey started crying again.

"Leave us alone!" *alone! alone!* Sally thought her heart would burst.

A muzzle blast reverberated through the tunnel.

"Chet!" *Chet! Chet!*

"Come on." He pulled her along. "We're almost there."

Approaching the end of the tunnel, Sally noticed the light from a farmer's barnyard began to take on a strange pattern, like a tic-tac-toe game. Another rifle report banged, and sparks cascaded down the tunnel wall beside her. Geoffrey wailed.

Chet pulled her to a stop. "Shit!"

Sally saw it too. Her heart sank. They'd reached the end of the line. A grate of steel bars blocked the exit. "We're trapped."

Grabbing the bars, Chet shook the barrier. A rusty padlock on an old iron latch clanged in defiance. "It's locked."

Sally turned and looked down the tunnel. Approaching flashlight beams swept back and forth.

"Come out with your hands up!" *hands up! hands up!*

Defeat hit her like a low punch. They'd tried so hard to save Geoffrey from this horrible place. "It's over."

A bang, like metal striking metal, jerked her attention back to Chet. She saw him reaching through the bars and striking the old padlock with the tire iron. "It's not over till I say it's over." A couple more whacks and the lock broke loose with a sharp snap.

Sally felt dizzy with relief.

On rusted hinges, the grate squealed as Chet shoved it open.

"They're getting away!" *away! away!* The tunnel erupted in gunfire.

Bullets cracked and ricocheted past Sally's head. She saw a two-foot drop from the tunnel to the canal, and holding Geoffrey firmly, she jumped into knee-deep water with a splash. She almost lost her balance, stumbled forward but stayed on her feet.

Chet landed in the water right behind her, turned and swung the gate closed. Then he jammed the tire iron into the steel loops where the padlock had been and twisted them around until the latch was bent beyond use. "It'll take a torch to get that open." He tossed the tire iron into the bushes and brushed his hands together. "That'll hold 'em a while."

Geoffrey stopped crying.

"Let's go."

The tree-lined irrigation canal was harder to traverse than the creek. Sally's shoes kept sinking in the mud, and she was falling behind Chet. The smell of cattle manure tainted the air. She heard the wail of sirens in the distance.

They'd made it. Geoffrey was safe at last. He made little gurgling sounds from inside his swaddling.

Hurrying, she caught up to Chet, and as they splashed through the water together, her eyes sought his in the darkness. "Thanks."

"Don't thank me yet." His voice was cold as the water. "We've still got to make the highway and hitch a ride." He put a hand on her shoulder. "Then you can thank me."

Suddenly, the air-slapping sound of chopper blades hammered the night air.

Geoffrey stiffened in her arms and started crying again.

Chet whirled around. "I don't know where it's coming from."

Then an airborne searchlight turned night into day. Sally winced as the cone of light swept left to right. She saw her shadow angle right and then suddenly shift left as the chopper circled around them. Her knees buckled with fear.

Chet shouted, "Run."

The chopper's downdraft lashed at the tree limbs overhead like a hurricane wind. Sally ducked, and sheltering Geoffrey from the onslaught, broke into a clumsy run behind Chet. She sloshed drunken-like through the water and mud, every muscle aching. The blinding searchlight was locked on them, following their every move. There was no escape. Tears of despair clouded her vision.

Half staggering, half running, she followed Chet down the canal, which flowed into a small meadow. The next clump of trees, a mere silhouette on the landscape, was a hundred yards downstream, just past the power lines. The highway and freedom might as well have been a million miles away. It was no use. Sally lungs burned from exertion. She had to stop running, rest.

Chet pulled on her arm.

"It's too far," she shouted over the chopper's whine. "We'll never make it."

"Just keep going."

Pivoting around, the chopper swung in front of them, dropped down, and hovered over the canal, blocking their way with a wall of water kicked up by the powerful downdraft. Chet stopped, clutched Sally under his arm as they stood before the military menace. Whining turbine engines and slapping rotor blades inched closer.

The noise was deafening. The bright light was impossible to look at. Getting closer, the chopper teetered in the air as soldiers jumped off.

"They're coming," she cried and held Geoffrey as if it would be the last time.

Just then, Chet scrambled up the muddy bank. "Give me your hand." The chopper rose and hovered above them again, the searchlight beaming down, intense as the sun. Weeds and bushes thrashed all around her. Fighting the furious downdraft, she stretched out her arm and felt Chet's strong hand grab her wrist.

He pulled her up the bank and out of the canal. "We have to make it to those trees. They're not far."

They looked far, she thought, and took off running after Chet. The ground was uneven, dangerous to negotiate. She held Geoffrey tightly, tried not to jar him around too much. Vegetation slapped her jeans, threatened to trip her. She followed Chet, first to the left and then to the right, a zigzag course he must've learned in the Marines. The chopper followed them, changing direction with each turn they made. Shadows darted to and fro.

Suddenly, gunfire rattled the night. Geysers of dirt flew up next to her.

"They're going to kill us."

"Warning shots," Chet shouted. "Or they would've killed us by now."

She knew the pilot wasn't going to take his eyes off them for an instant. There was no eluding the chopper.

Ahead, she could see the clump of trees. Chet was right. They were so close. Again, rapid-fire burst down through the searchlight beam. Dirt spit up around her, closer this time.

Sally screamed.

Chet dodged right.

She stayed close behind him, cringing as bullets ripped up the ground beside her. Then muzzle bursts flashed from the canal. Foot soldiers started firing and running toward them. Bullets were flying everywhere. Fear tunneled her vision, but she could see the shadowy cluster of trees close ahead. They were going to make it. They had to.

The chopper pilot must've realized how close they were to the trees, how close they were to cover, because he pulled up and slewed around in front of them. Flying tail-high and backwards, the chopper blocked their escape with a hail of machine gun fire.

Chet suddenly dropped to the weeds.

"No." Sally fell on her knees at his side, cradling Geoffrey and fearing the worse "Are you shot?"

Chet reached up and pulled her to the ground. "Stay down."

Just then, the chopper backed into the power lines. Rotating blades struck high voltage wires. A sizzling display of sparks exploded like fireworks. Twisted blades snapped and turbine engines coughed as the chopper swayed in the electric web. A bright blue charge of electricity surged through the aircraft, eerily illuminating the interior and silhouetting the skeletal remains of the pilot and crew until the high-tension wires snapped. The chopper spun to the ground with a thunderous crash and burst into flames. A yellow and red fireball mushroomed high into the night sky.

Sally shielded Geoffrey with her body as debris rained down around them, hot and smoldering metal, mostly, and one body part she recognized, an arm bone with finger bones clenched in a fist.

Crackling, severed power lines whipped down from the towers to the ground, spewing jagged sparks that flashed and popped. The foot soldiers gave up their chase and stood like statues in the glow of the crash.

Chet scrambled to his feet and pulled Sally into a run, guiding her around the burning wreckage. She could feel the heat on her face and clutched Geoffrey to her chest protectively. Her tilting shadow stretched toward the highway where the headlights of passing vehicles looked like angels flying by in the night, angels that would deliver them from hell.

Chapter Twenty-Six

On northbound Highway 41, Hank worked the big steering wheel of his Kenworth with ease. A honky-tonk radio station played the kind of steel-guitar-twanging music that kept him awake on the long haul from Lafayette to Chicago. In the trailer behind him, a load of electric motors was destined for some refrigerator factory on the east side.

The freighter ahead of him, loaded down with cement sewer pipes, thundered along at ten miles over the speed limit. Hank kept up the pace. His Cummins diesel purred as eighteen wheels rumbled north toward Cedar Lake, two miles ahead, according to the sign he just passed. Spitting a slug of chewing tobacco into a spittoon on the doorpost, Hank smiled. *Ain't life grand?*

Suddenly, a flash of light caught his attention, off the highway to his left, then a ball of fire churned up and dissolved into the black sky, leaving behind a glow on the ground. His heart rate hit overdrive. "Holy tarnation, what was that?" He let off the throttle. The freighter up ahead pulled away as if nothing had happened. Was the driver blind?

Hank couldn't make out what was burning. As his rig decelerated, he had to downshift. Cars went around him, honked. Was he the only one who saw the fire?

He coasted across a bridge and pulled to the shoulder. The parking brake set with a shrill rush of air. Engine rattling, he sat there a moment and watched the fire burn as traffic whizzed by. Maybe it was an airplane crash, being out in the open as it were, or a gas line explosion. Maybe he should report it.

After flipping on the emergency flashers, he grabbed his CB mic. "Breaker, breaker. This is Hank the Tank at the Cedar Lake Bridge. Anybody got their ears on?"

"Muskogee Raider back at yah, Tank."

"What's your twenty there, partner? You seen a big fire?"

The CB radio crackled. "Two miles north of Cedar Lake haulin' hogs to St. John, Tank. Only fire I seen was in my Betty's big blues when I kissed her goodbye. That was two years ago. Over."

"Anybody else seen a big fire, come back?"

Silence.

"Do I got a state trooper out there?" Hank asked, knowing the CB's range was limited to three miles over uneven terrain.

Raider came back, "Don't ya wanna hear about my Betty?"

"Maybe later." It was a bad time of night to raise anyone. "Tank, over and out." He wiped perspiration from his brow. As long as he was stopped, he might as well take a break. He reached for his thermos and pulled out the cork. The aroma of coffee permeated his cab. After filling his mug, he took a quick sip, and jammed the thermos between his legs. "Ah." He slapped the cork back in place and reached for the radio volume knob as *Cathy's Clown* began to play.

"Here he ca-ha-ha-ha-ums," he sang along, "that's Cathy's Clown." Everly Brothers harmony filled the cab.

Bam, Bam, Bam.

Hank's heart had a blow out. He damn near spilt his coffee. "What the hell?" He turned down the radio. Someone was banging on his door.

"Help us." A woman's voice came from outside.

"Open up, please." It was a man's voice this time.

Bam! Bam! Bam.

Swallowing hard, Hank checked his rearviews. Nobody had pulled up behind him. Who the hell was out here in the middle of nowhere this time of night?

"Open up, mister. We need a ride."

Goddamned hippies. "Get the hell away from my rig." He set the coffee mug on the dash and shoved the shifter into gear. *Leave them freaks in the dust.* Then he heard a cry—a baby cry? "I don't believe this shit." He couldn't drive off and leave no baby out here. What the hell was going on? He put the transmission in neutral. "What in tarnation are you folks doin'?"

"Our car hit a power pole," the man's voice said. "Caught fire...over by the canal."

So that was it. Hank rubbed his cheek. Must've been a damn big car.

"We need a ride to Chicago."

"Please, mister," the woman's voice said. "Will you take us?"

The baby was wailing.

Sounded like a nice enough family, but he knew better than to drop his guard, not that he could think of any reason someone would want to hijack his load of electric motors. But just to be safe, he fetched the revolver from under his seat. "I'll unlock the door, but you be sure to climb up here real careful like, ya hear. Don't move too fast. I'm a jumpy old fart, I'm warnin' ya."

The woman said, "We don't want any trouble, sir."

No trouble? *They ain't seen trouble 'til they mess with Hank the Tank.* He kept the gun low, worked the electric door lock switch.

Click!

"Nice and easy now."

As the door opened, the dome light winked on. He was ready for anything. "Don't do nothin' stupid."

A mud-splotched man with muscular arms climbed into the cab, showing his palms. "We just need a ride, mister."

Hank's gun hand began to sweat. "What the hell happened to you?"

"It's a long story." The man reached down and helped a woman into the cab, redhead, splattered with mud. She coddled a whimpering baby wrapped in a dirty blanket.

"Thank you, sir," she said. "I'm so cold."

They were a sorry sight.

The man closed the door. The light went out, but the instrument lights illuminated the whites of their wide-open eyes.

"I think you all better sit real still for a minute." He showed them his gun. "We ain't goin' nowhere 'til you square with me. You runnin' from the law?"

The Cummins rattled as he waited for an answer. "Well?"

The swaddled baby murmured, an innocent kind of sound that struck Hank's heart really hard. He'd never had a baby in his truck before, hadn't even seen one since cousin Margaret dropped twins twenty years ago. Curiosity overcame caution. He clicked on the map light and twisted its flexible stem, shining the beam on the blanket.

"You want to see him?" the woman asked, shaking pretty bad as she uncovered the baby's face.

Hank peered at the child, cute little guy. "What's the tike's name?"

"Geoffrey," she said, shivering.

"Chicago?" the man put in. "Are you going that far?"

He regarded the grimy couple and their happy baby. Seemed harmless enough. "Sure." Hank put his pistol back under the seat and spat into his spittoon. "But you have to put up with my singin'." He released the brakes and wound up the Cummins. After lurching the big rig onto the highway, he turned up the radio.

"Here he ca-ah-ah-ah-ums, that's Cathy's Clown."

Chapter Twenty-Seven

The Pentagon

Colonel Harrison shouted into his telephone. "You idiots." His crack military team had failed to prevent the clone's escape, jeopardizing the Tuliver project's secrecy. He couldn't believe it. "How many casualties?"

"Three men and one aircraft, sir. Sally Mayfield stole the clone. She's responsible."

"The surrogate?" He wrote her name on a scratch pad. "Find her." After slamming down the receiver, he turned to a corporal at the front desk. "Get my staff car."

"Yes, sir."

Harrison folded the note, put it in his pocket, and slapped a khaki cap on his head. "And get the Learjet ready."

"Where to, Colonel?"

"Cedar Lake."

"Right away, sir."

Harrison pushed through the double doors of the com-center and rushed down a barren corridor toward his office. In less than twenty-four hours, Dr. Larson had managed to lose his clone. They had to get it back before the whole damn world found out.

In his office, he turned on the light and went directly to the chair behind his desk. Pulling open the bottom drawer, he grabbed a black leather holster and his Colt .45. As he ejected the clip, he noticed the picture of his son on the desktop. A sharp looking young man dressed in an Army uniform, Sergeant Daniel Harrison had served his country well, but he came back from Vietnam in a flag-draped coffin. He was only nineteen years old. There was no cloned soldier to take *his* place in the rice paddy. Harrison slammed the clip back into the Colt. If the damn politicians in Washington weren't running this war, his son might still be alive. He shoved the drawer shut and dialed the phone.

"Beth, did I wake you?"

"Billy and I are watching Saturday Night Live."

Leaning back in his chair, Harrison rubbed the side of his neck. Billy had taken his brother's death pretty hard. But at fifteen years old, he'd recover quickly. With school, football, and girls, his life would soon return to normal. But Harrison worried that the armchair generals in Washington might drag out the Vietnam War long enough to claim Billy's life, too. Unacceptable."Tell him I said hi."

Audience laughter came over the line. "Your father says hello, Billy."

"I'm trying to watch this."

"When will you be home?"

"I have to fly to Blythe tonight."

"But you just got back this morning."

"Complications. I'm sorry."

He heard Billy laughing with the TV audience. Beth released a restrained chuckle, too. "Be careful, dear. We miss you."

"Sleep tight." He hung up the phone and sank back into his chair. Someday, he swore, when he became a General, lowly Colonels were going to take care of *his* pet projects, but until then, he knew he was duty-bound to serve his higher-ups. With sadness and the highest respect, he saluted his dead son, pulled his fatigue jacket from the coat rack, and left for Andrews Air Force Base.

***

On the tarmac, Learjet engines whined to life. A white marker light on the tail blinked, and strobe lights pulsed on the wing tips. The staff car rolled to a stop, and Colonel Harrison swung the car door open.

"Have a nice flight, sir," the driver shouted over the noisy jet engines.

Harrison only nodded and marched to the steps leading up to the aircraft. A flight attendant waved him aboard. Dressed in her sharply pressed WAF uniform, her smile was as bright as the shiny silver bars on her collars. She saluted him at the door.

"Evening, lieutenant," Harrison said as he pulled off his hat, shoved it smartly under his left arm, and returned the salute. "Sorry to drag you out like this again."

"Glad to be of service, sir." Her smile didn't waver.

He ducked inside the cabin. The fragrance of perfume lingered lightly in the air.

The first officer pulled back the cockpit curtain. "We're ready when you are, sir."

Harrison settled into the plush velour of his favorite seat and cinched his seatbelt. "Then what are we waiting for?"

The lieutenant swung the door closed and secured the latch.

With a hiss, the cabin sealed. Engines revved and the jet began to roll. Harrison watched out the window as the aircraft gently rocked and thumped along the taxiway.

A few moments later, the line of blue taxiway lights swung away, and a row of green runway lights appeared. The jet stopped. He watched the lieutenant tug on her seat belt.

The engines wound up to a thunderous roar, and the aircraft accelerated down the runway, slowly at first, then faster and faster until he was pressed into the back of his seat. The nose pitched up, airfield lights dropped away, and landing gear banged into their compartments. The heavy inertia of takeoff quickly gave way to the floating sensation of flight.

Below, the lights of Washington D.C. glowed like a carpet of Christmas tree lights. He had mixed feelings about the most powerful city in the world. The politicians down there were ruining everything. They'd tainted the very core of what made this country great. George Washington and his band of revolutionaries had no idea that their military agenda would become a chaotic system so complicated that nobody had any real control over the battlefield. The President thought he had to restrain his military operations in Vietnam because he was worried that Russia would get involved. Didn't the whacko realize that Russian-built guns and rockets and surface-to-air missiles were killing Americans in Vietnam? Get in there and kick some ass, Harrison grumped, but no, the military couldn't do a damn thing about it. They were fighting a war with their hands tied behind their backs. No wonder Vietnam was raging out of control. And Daniel had paid the ultimate price for the President's incompetence. Harrison clenched his jaw.

The Learjet rolled left as it climbed into the night sky. Indiana was more than two hours away. He reached in his pocket and pulled out the note he'd scribbled. *Sally Mayfield.* He wondered who the hell this woman thought she was. And why did she agree to be the surrogate mother of the world's first human clone? Was she a patriot or a traitor? Certainly she must realize her precarious position. If she thought she'd be famous, she was wrong. She'd be dead first.

Chapter Twenty-Eight

East Chicago

Dawn. Sally climbed out of Hank's truck cab, felt the morning's icy air seep through her wet pants and shoes. Her breath vapors swirled around her head as Chet gave her a hand down to the pavement. The air-horn blasted a goodbye.

Geoffrey flinched under his blanket.

She waved as Hank and his load of electric motors rumbled off down the road. He'd made the long ride pleasant, sharing his coffee, telling jokes and talking about his thirty years in trucking. She'd only slept about an hour.

Chet ushered her towards a diner. "We'll need to take a cab the rest of the way," he said when they were seated at a booth in the back corner. The aroma of bacon and coffee filled the air. "Do you have any money?"

Cradling Geoffrey, she opened her purse and pulled out the now battered copy of *The Lost Diamonds*. Staring at it a moment, memories of William whirled through her mind: the Diamond Building, Paradise Park, the times they shared together under the mist of his magnificent fountain—all gone—

"Sally?"

"Huh?"

"Money?"

"Oh." She set the book on the table and resumed rummaging through her purse. The din of conversation and clinking silverware sounded alien. It had been more than a year since she'd seen anything outside of Blythe University.

"Money, let's see." She yanked out an address book crammed full of loose notes, coupons, and other papers she thought she'd need some day. "In here, somewhere." She found a stack of hundreds wrapped with rubber bands. "Here we go." She tossed it to Chet. "Should be enough for breakfast and a new car."

Chet's mouth fell open. "What?"

"Don't worry, there's a lot more where that came from. William left me a bundle."

Stuffing the money into his jacket, Chet said, "Thanks."

"No, Chet. Geoffrey and I thank you. You were brilliant and brave." She crammed her things back into her purse. "We wouldn't have made it without you."

"But it wasn't just me," Chet whispered. "I wasn't the only one helping save Geoffrey. I swear I saw Dr. Marshall—"

"Don't talk about him." A hot flash of anger stabbed her stomach. She didn't want to hear his name, hear anything about him. She leaned forward and spoke through clenched teeth. "I know what kind of bastard he is."

"But he's not—"

"He betrayed us, Chet. He lied to me. And he didn't warn William that Dr. Larson and Carl Savage were going to steal Geoffrey from me. Dr. Marshall could have prevented all this."

"There must've been good reason."

"He chose his precious career over loyalty to his patient. I'm sure he won't rest until Geoffrey is back at Blythe."

"I don't think so."

"Thanks to you, Geoffrey has a chance. So take the credit. You deserve it."

Chet ran a hand through his tousled hair. "I'm sure you're wrong about him. He—"

The waitress interrupted. "What can I get you?"

Sally looked up at her. Standing six feet, she wore a food-stained apron and chewed gum noisily, an order pad held open in her hand, pen ready. With red painted lips, she cracked a smile as she looked over her customers. "Golly, you two sleep under a truck?"

Just then, Geoffrey cooed under the blanket.

"Oh, my goodness. Looky here." She leaned over and pulled the blanket off the baby's face. "It's a newborn. What're you folks doin' out here with this little thing? Can't be mor'n a day old."

"Two," Sally said with a wan smile.

Chet cleared his throat. "Our car broke down about twenty miles out. A trucker brought us in this far."

"We're headed to my mom's," Sally added to the ruse. "I'd like two eggs over easy, toast, and coffee."

"The same," Chet said. "And we need a cab."

"Fix you kids right up." She cracked her gum as she walked off toward the kitchen.

Sally noticed how Geoffrey's eyes followed the waitress. "It's weird," she said, whispering. "He doesn't fuss much."

Chet nodded.

"He watches us. It's almost as if he knows what's going on. He's much too alert for a normal newborn. And those eyes, they're different. Focused. They seem older, wiser, like William's eyes. And I think he understands what we say."

"Could be." Chet played with his spoon. "Dr. Larson said Geoffrey is already thirty years old."

"Don't be ridiculous. Just look at him."

Chet rubbed his stubbly face. "He's not what he seems, Sally. And you know it. You've seen it in his eyes, the way he acts. And there's something else you should know."

The waitress set a hot cup of coffee in front of Chet. "Here you are. Food's a comin'."

"Thanks." He frowned as if annoyed with the interruption.

"And extra cream for the young mother," the waitress added, cracking her gum. "Don't hesitate to ask for more."

"I won't," Sally said even though she liked her coffee black. The waitress moved to the next table.

"Sally, there's something you need to know."

"What's that?"

"Dr. Marshall said—"

"I don't care what he said." She patted the back of Chet's hand. "Drink your coffee and shut up about him."

"But he thinks—"

"Stop it!"

Chet held his breath for a long moment then picked up his cup. "Have it your way."

Pulling the blanket over Geoffrey's face, Sally didn't care what Chet thought about Dr. Marshall or what he'd said. *Geoffrey's not normal. She's not his mother.* She already knew that from the moment she saw him. And she knew Geoffrey wasn't her son. He was a motherless child. A clone, not conceived in the natural way, but manufactured in a lab, primed with some concocted enzyme that made him a freak of nature. She didn't need to hear it all again.

Turning her attention to the steaming coffee cup in front of her, she took a slow sip and stared into the black brew, her faint reflection quivering back at her. Everything was going to be all right, she hoped. Or was it? Truth was, she feared nothing would be all right. From here on out, soldiers would be looking for her. Harrison, Larson, Marshall, they'd hunt her down like an escaped prisoner. They'd lost their precious *investment*, along with some other basic human traits like kindness, compassion, and honesty.

Looking down at the bundled child in her lap, the sleeping clone, the motherless child, she had no idea how she was going to protect him from the consequences of what those men had done.

Chapter Twenty-Nine

Blythe University, Dr. Larson's quarters

One month later, Melanie stood at the window and examined the swirling lines of frost that etched the glass. She tried to ignore her swollen abdomen that throbbed from a heavy load. Pregnancy had become a daily torment. The money seemed far too little for the burden she'd agreed to bear. Her legs and ankles, swollen like tree trunks, had become bone-white and streaked with varicose veins. Gone was her thin and attractive figure of which she was once so proud. A tear trickled down her cheek.

"What's the problem?" Dr. Larson asked, tying a plaid tie. His voice felt as cold as the frost on the windowpane, his once loving touch gone from her life. The loneliness had become unbearable.

"Something is wrong with the baby, John."

"You worry too much." He threw on a long gray coat.

She could smell his aftershave from across the room. "Why won't you listen to me?"

"Your next checkup is in two days. It'll all be over in a month."

She turned away from the icy window. "Look at me, John." She opened the front of her robe. "The Titanic wasn't this damn big. I need to see Dr. Marshall. Today. I can't take it anymore." Lumbering over to a chair at the kitchenette, she plopped herself down. "I want him to cut this baby out of me, a-sap."

Larson buttoned his coat, and as he pulled on a pair of black gloves, he stared down at her with uncaring eyes. "You got what you asked for. The university has paid you well, so stop your bitching."

Adrenaline hit her bloodstream, which caused the clone to kick and roll violently. She didn't know what was worse, the pain inside her abdomen or the ache in her heart. Both were torture. Before she could say anything else, the door slammed with a rush of cold wind. He was gone. "Damn it, John." What was wrong with that man?

She had to lay down. Shuffling like an old lady, she moved toward the bedroom; her bulging abdomen throbbed with each step. The clone was struggling as if he were caught in a trap, desperate to get free. Angry.

Clenching her jaw, she wondered how she could make it one more month. Her back hurt so badly she couldn't take another step. At the doorway to the bedroom, she stopped to rest, clung to the doorjamb, and gulped air. Her fingers hurt from the strain of holding herself up.

Only a few more steps to the bed. She could make it—one step at a time. *Come on, Melanie.* Dr. Larson was right—*stop your bitching. You got what you asked for.* Go to bed. Get some rest. Releasing her grip on the doorframe, she put one foot forward. Her stomach cramped so hard her knees buckled. She cried out and fell. A dizzying blackness overwhelmed her.

***

Sitting behind his desk, Dr. Marshall watched Larson set the coffee pot on the burner.

"Sally's been gone a month," Larson griped. "There's still no sign of her." He rubbed fog off the window and looked out across the campus. "Colonel Harrison couldn't find an apple on an ant hill."

Eugene leaned back. "I thought they had a lead."

"This?" Larson removed an envelope from his coat pocket, tossed it to Eugene.

It had been opened. He removed the paper from inside—a deposit slip. "For a rental?"

"But she didn't move in."

Making a mental note of the address, Eugene said, "They're

doing the best they can." But he hoped they'd never find her.

"Bullshit." Larson slopped his coffee. "Get the Chicago police involved. They'll find her."

"Real smart, John. I can see the headlines now. *Massive Manhunt for Woman and Clone.* How long will you spend in jail?"

"You're not going to start with that *unlawful confinement* or *violating her civil rights* crap are you?"

"This situation must be kept quiet." Eugene got out of his chair and walked toward his boss. "Besides, you've got another clone to worry about."

"1122B?"

"Morris Brennon's clone."

Larson huffed. "Melanie is worrying enough for both of us."

"How's that?"

Larson took a sip of coffee. "She does nothing but bitch lately, it's too heavy, it hurts too much, she's big as the Titanic. What did she think this was going to be, some kind of rowboat ride?"

"But Melanie is a strong woman, John. Strong body. Strong willed." Eugene knew enough to listen to his patients' concerns. "Are you sure she's just bitching?"

"Sounds like it to me. I don't know much about pregnant women, but if I were her, I'd be bitching too. She's getting pretty big." He made a round-belly motion with his hand. "Maybe you should have a look at her, make sure the clone's okay."

Eugene wasn't sure if that meant anything. Pregnant women get big, usually bigger than they expected. He stepped back to his desk and flipped through pages in his calendar. "I saw her three days ago." He remembered clearly. "She was fine." Then he recalled the cows, six out of twenty went from stable to critical in less than twenty-four hours. He felt the blood drain from his face.

"What is it?" Larson asked.

"I'm thinking about the calves."

"The growth spurts?"

"Thirty-three percent...all the surrogates died. Let's get her in here and have a look."

"I'll call her right now." Larson left the room in a hurry.

Eugene sat at his desk, wondering if Melanie was in trouble, or perhaps Dr. Larson was exaggerating. Definitely, Sally was in trouble, probably moving around the country, trying to stay out of sight. He was glad she hadn't been captured. Chet Brady had done a good job rescuing Geoffrey from the lab. Speaking of which, Eugene picked up a postcard from his desk, a picture of the Rocky Mountains towering above the town of Boulder, Colorado. Chet had transferred to the University of Colorado. Written on the back, he reported his wife had joined him there. They were living in a little ranch house in the foothills.

Wish you were here.

Eugene felt good about that. He'd done the right thing. Just as he set down the card, Larson stormed in.

"There's no answer. She couldn't possibly have gone out. Something's wrong."

Not good, Eugene thought. "Let's go."

A cold wind blew snowflakes through the air as Eugene followed Larson back to his quarters. He keyed the lock and pushed open the door. "Melanie."

They checked the kitchen, the bathroom, and then raced to the bedroom where they found Melanie sprawled on her back, her eyes wide open and a blue hue washing her cheeks. Eugene had never seen a woman's abdomen this big. It churned and bulged from within.

"She's distended." He knelt beside her and put his hand on her convulsing belly. The clone kicked it away. "John."

Larson was on the phone. "Get a gurney over here right away. And alert the team." He hung up. "Damn it. That clone better be okay."

Eugene palmed Melanie's eyelids closed, stood, and stepped back, horror engulfing him. The clone was trying to get out. "Look." Her abdomen was turning black and blue before his eyes. Stretched beyond limits, blood vessels broke, and blood blisters formed under her skin, the bruise growing like an ink spill on fine white paper. Eugene suppressed a wave of panic.

"He's picked his own birthday," Larson said.

"God help us."

The door burst open. A gurney rolled in. Three students helped Eugene lift Melanie to the pad.

"The team's on station," one assistant said as they rushed through the snowstorm toward the lab. The gurney wheels shuddered with speed along the icy sidewalk. "They're not prepared for this."

Eugene shook his head. "None of us are."

Inside the delivery room, Larson went upstairs to his position behind the observation window. Technicians and student assistants scurried about their duties.

"Pulse, 150," one announced. "Blood pressure, 60 over 40. We're losing her."

Melanie's abdomen boiled and bulged.

"The clone is ripping her insides apart," someone said.

It was happening—what Eugene feared the most. "Jesus."

A technician taped heart monitor leads into position. A faltering, ominous beep echoed through the room. A student slid an oxygen mask over Melanie's mouth and nose. It fogged lightly from her shallow breaths.

"She's not stable enough for anesthesia."

Eugene pulled on latex gloves. "Give her a local. I'm going in."

As a technician prepared the hypodermic, Eugene lifted Melanie's eyelid. Her pupil looked like a big black hole, the blue iris only a thin ring, unresponsive to light. "Fixed and dilated. Never mind the anesthetic." He selected a scalpel from the tray, swallowed. This procedure wasn't new to him. It was the seventh time.

Suddenly, the heart monitor sounded a steady, shrill tone. Eugene's stomach clutched. He was out of time.

"Defib," a technician announced, paddles in hand.

"Wait." Eugene knew an electric shock could kill the clone, but without it, Melanie wouldn't survive. No matter what he did, one of them was going to die—but which one? Sweat trickled down his forehead as he looked up to Dr. Larson standing in the window. "Who do I save?"

"The clone."

Eugene knew it. The goddamned clone was more important than the surrogate. Again. But he wasn't giving up on Melanie that fast. "Keep the paddles ready," he told the technician. "When the clone clears the table, hit her."

The defibrillator charged with a high-pitched whine.

Surgical steel glistened as Eugene made the first cut from hipbone to hipbone through Melanie's abdominal skin. His hand guided the scalpel carefully, precisely. Only a small trickle of blood appeared. He'd hoped for more.

Then he made the second cut, through the muscles of her abdominal wall. An unexpected gush of bloody fluid spilled out, flowed to the floor, and pooled in the gurney's shadow. The nauseating stink of bile and feces knifed through the air.

"My God," a student said, gagging.

"God had nothing to do with this." Eugene pushed aside a tangle of intestines. He'd never seen anything this bad before. Pressing on, he made the final cut into the torn and churning womb. It was completely drained of amniotic fluid. Two students held the incisions open so Eugene could reach in and extract the clone.

1122B fought him. Kicked him.

"Hold still, damn it."

He finally grabbed one slippery leg and then the other. Using both hands to get control of the writhing clone, he pulled it out of Melanie's womb, feet first. The sight of him sent bile up the back of Eugene's throat: bald headed, round cheeks and rolls of slimy wet and wrinkled red fat. Eighteen pounds—maybe twenty, with long fingernails, long toenails, and four front teeth. Eugene could hardly hold on to the squirming clone. He didn't have to slap its back or tickle its feet to coax life into it. Fluid and air rushed in and out of its lungs with a hissing sound.

A student ran from the room, puking. One of the assistants tied the umbilical cord and cut the clone free of Melanie.

Eugene stepped back. "Hit her."

"Clear."

The defibrillator discharged like a shotgun. Melanie's mangled body jerked. Her spine arched upward from the surge of voltage and instantly slammed back down to the gurney pad. But the heart monitor continued to report a steady alarm.

"Again." Eugene ordered. The clone writhed in his grasp, hissing and wailing, as the machine recharged. Eugene held his breath. A sick sense of loss crept into him. He didn't want to accept it. Melanie was badly damaged, more internal injuries than could ever be repaired.

"Clear."

The high voltage thumped her again but left her lying limp, blue, and lifeless.

The thin yellow line on the heart monitor screen didn't even flinch as the piercing alarm echoed through the room. She was dead. There was no bringing her back. "Turn it off."

The alarm quit; the clone's hissing was the only sound.

Eugene felt drained, his heart drowning in sorrow. He looked at the monster in his grasp, hissing and swinging its fists at everyone around. And just like Morris Brennon, it was a killer. His first victim lay motionless on the blood-soaked gurney. Eugene's sadness turned to guilt and then to anger.

Holding the clone up to the observation window, he shouted, "Look what you did, John. 1122B lives and Melanie dies. And for what, to prove your enzyme is better?"

Larson nodded. "A few lab rats have to die in the process."

"That's unacceptable." He dropped the demonic clone on the prep table and ripped off the bloody latex gloves.

"I quit."

Chapter Thirty

Somewhere in Chicago, ghosts and goblins skittered down a tree-lined sidewalk and fanned out across lawns toward eerily lit porches in the neighborhood.

"Trick or Treat."

To Sally, these inner city streets weren't any scarier tonight than any other night. After relocating twice, she'd ended up in this rundown redbrick slum, but only after a shady landlord agreed to take cash, renting it to her off the record, or so he'd promised. She felt safer this way, but just a little.

As she walked toward her house, she held Geoffrey tighter. He was wrapped in a dark blue blanket, the bundle in her arms looking more like a load of laundry than a swaddled child. And to compliment the ruse, she wore a long, heavy gray coat, sewn and patched, with frayed cuffs and collars. An old black knit scarf completed the ensemble and kept out the chilly night air.

An hour ago, she'd donned these old clothes, darkened her face with makeup, and sprayed silver highlighter on her hair. Even Dr. Marshall wouldn't recognize her in this getup, she'd thought as she put together the disguise. Confident she'd not be recognized, she'd ventured out to a convenience store several blocks away.

Though the night air nipped of winter, Geoffrey gurgled and cooed under his blanket. He liked to go for walks with her, just like William. In her pocket, she carried their rewards for braving the cold: a can of baby formula, a shiny new rattle, and a Snickers bar. After all, it was Halloween. In her purse, which she'd hung on her shoulder under her coat, she carried her most prized possession, *The*

Lost Diamonds. She took it with her wherever she went. William seemed closer to her that way.

Two little hobos ran past. She thought about Geoffrey's first Halloween adventure. Maybe she'd dress him up like a ghost, use a white sheet with eyeholes and a pillowcase for his candy. Or perhaps he could be a pirate with a black patch over one eye, a broad-striped jacket, and a hook for a hand to carry his bag of treats.

As the cold north wind blew leaves along the sidewalk, her imagination wandered to their first Christmas together. For sure, she'd take Geoffrey to have his picture taken with Santa. He'd probably fuss when she put him in the jolly man's lap. There was so much to look forward to, so much to do before Geoffrey grew up—to be William again, if she were to believe Dr. Marshall. On one hand, she wanted to believe him. She wanted William back. On the other, she couldn't imagine being his lover after raising him as a son. Her head hurt thinking about it.

A black cat ran in front of her. The bitter wind seemed suddenly colder. Blythe University was a long time ago, or so she tried to convince herself. Two months had gone by. Still, she was sure they hadn't stopped looking for her.

Reaching the weathered picket fence in front of her house, she stopped, her heart suddenly banging out of control at what she saw on her porch. Under the dim light fixture stood the silhouette of a man at her door. With her breath lodged in her lungs, she cowered behind the gate, eyeing the stranger whose back was to her as he knocked on her door. A long coat draped from his shoulders. He wore a hat, like Carl Savage. She stifled a scream. How did he find her?

She thought about running, but her sense of logic took over. It was Halloween. It couldn't be Carl Savage. The man standing at her door was too tall. He could be a boy in a costume. Sure. That was all, just some high school kid out looking for treats.

Emboldened, she took a breath of relief and pushed through the gate. "Young man, aren't you a little too old for trick or treating?"

The dark figure turned toward her. Fear twisted her stomach when the porch light revealed his face in the darkness.

Dr. Marshall.

She screamed, but it sounded normal for this Halloween night. No one would come running to her aid.

"Sally?" He took a step toward her. "It's all right."

His voice sent a chill down the back of her neck. She clutched Geoffrey in her arms and backed through the gate. "No." She turned and broke into a run.

"Sally, wait."

"Leave us alone."

"Wait."

She heard him bang through the gate behind her. Terror ripped through her like a hurled spear. Hot adrenaline spilled into her veins. She ran down the middle of the street, but he was right behind her, his footfalls heavy on the pavement, strong and fast. Stumbling, she swallowed the urge to scream and ran harder. Rounding a corner, she saw colored lights decorating the street up ahead. Strains of music and haunted-house noises filled the night: screaming victims, howling werewolves, and booing ghosts. A crowd of costumed partygoers jammed the sidewalks, their laughter and revelry rising as she neared. Salvation. A Halloween block party. Ducking low, she pushed her way into the buzzing throng, hoping to lose Dr. Marshall in the chaos.

Suddenly Dracula sprang out in front of her, his black cape spread wide, his white fangs gleaming in the streetlights. Sally looked behind her. He wasn't there. Through gaps between bodies, she got a glimpse of a marching band drumming along the street. But no Dr. Marshall. Where was he?

She turned around. A bony skeleton with a glowing skull took jerking steps toward her, arms outstretched. She spun the other way. An evil laugh cackled in her ear. Clutching Geoffrey, she turned again, saw a headless horseman holding a pumpkin in the crook of his left arm and grabbing for her with a white-gloved right hand. She clenched her teeth and pushed her way deeper into the crowd.

Across the street, revelers surrounded a grandstand decorated in pumpkins and witches made of papier-mâché. Dark-suited men sat in chairs neatly rowed behind a podium where a big man wearing a wizard's costume addressed the crowd.

"Ladies and gentlemen. Welcome to the ninth annual Chicago Ghost Stomp."

As another round of cheers rose, Sally scanned the masked faces behind her. She held Geoffrey close to her chest. The crowd pressed around. She couldn't see over them. Fear began to set in. Where was Dr. Marshall?

A policeman caught her eye. He stood on the other side of the street, just beyond the marching band that was followed by costumed drunkards dancing and twirling in the street as if it were a Mardi Gras party in New Orleans. They were loud and boisterous. Unruly. But she had to make it past them to the other side of the street. She had to get the policeman's help.

Filled with determination, she darted into the dancing horde. They reeked of alcohol and tobacco. They were laughing, cheering, yelling. Their revelry echoed all around her, adding to her sense of chaos and panic. They bumped her, pushed her, and detoured her from her goal. Feeling like a pinball in an arcade game, she gasped for air and fought her way through the crowd, cradling the blue bundle in both arms protectively. But the drunks swarmed her and blocked her way.

"Hey lady, want a drink?" A cowboy dressed in a brown leather vest, six-guns, and spurs shoved a Jack Daniels bottle in her face. The alcohol vapor stung her eyes. She pushed it away. The booze spilled all over her coat. Though she tried to brush it off, the spill spread and made her coat stink of liquor. Standing in the middle of the street, she searched the crowd for Dr. Marshall. Had he spotted her yet? Where was he?

A strong hand grabbed her arm from behind. Her heart lunged with fear. Instinctively, she tried to jerk away from his vise-like grasp. "No." When she turned, she saw a hairy-chested man dressed in a green caveman suit. His face was heavily bearded. Relief swept over her. It wasn't Dr. Marshall. Then she noticed an angry glare in the burly man's eyes. What had she done to make him mad? "Let go of me."

"Get the hell out of our party, ya old bag." He shoved her toward the curb.

She tripped and fell to her knees on the sidewalk, one hand on the ground, the other desperately clutching the bundle in her arms. Behind her, the sound of laughter. But Geoffrey remained silent, as though he knew his cries would give her away.

As she struggled to get up, a pair of shiny black shoes stepped into her field of vision. Oh no. Dr. Marshall. Slowly, she looked up. It was the policeman. She was safe.

He grabbed her coat collar and yanked her to her feet. "Now lady, you know the rules. No panhandling."

She looked into his cold eyes. "Officer—"

"And no vagrants allowed around this party. If it weren't for you people, I'd have the night off."

"You don't understand. I'm—"

"Whew." He grimaced, fanning the air in front of his face. "You stink of liquor, old woman. I should haul you in for drunk and disorderly."

"Me? What about those guys?" She indicated the unrulies.

"They bought tickets for this show." He turned her toward a dark alley and booted her in the rear. "Now git. Don't let me catch you around here again."

She turned to complain but spotted Dr. Marshall searching the crowd across the street. The dark alley was far better than dealing with him. Silently, she backed away and slipped into the shadows.

As she moved down the alley toward a cone of light by a dumpster, the party sounds faded away. Once under the light, she put her back against the dumpster and slid down to a crouch, out of sight from the street.

The alley's dankness seeped into her like a poisoned fog. Urine and vomit soured the air. Peering into the darkness beyond the small ring of light, her mother's memory came back. Suddenly, New Orleans seemed like only yesterday. She shivered, wondering how she'd ended up in a dark alley again.

At least they were safe from Dr. Marshall. She pulled back a flap of blanket covering Geoffrey's face. He was sleeping. At peace in his little world, he twitched his lips. His tongue, tiny and pink, moved in and out as if he were playing with it.

Sadly, she watched him, her heart aching. She missed William. Was it too much to hope Geoffrey was really William reborn? And even if that were true, they could never be together the way they were before the cancer. Life didn't repeat itself. Their life together was over. Now all she had to show for it was Geoffrey.

She touched the child's cheek, thinking how Colonel Harrison could find them, no matter where they went: New York City. Dallas, Texas. No-name-little-town, USA. If she ever had an address, a phone, registered a car, or took a job, they'd find her. If she tapped the trust fund William had left her, they'd find her. If they did, Geoffrey would end up back in the lab at Blythe University. Her eyes stung with tears as she realized that he would never be safe as long as he was with her.

A squeaky voice came from the shadows. "What a darling little child."

Sally's heart raced with fear. "What do you want?" She covered Geoffrey and tucked her knees up tight, pressing him against her chest. "Go away."

A shuffling noise came from the alley as a dark silhouette formed just beyond the light, slowly rising in front of her.

"Who are you?"

"Name's Mildred," the voice replied. "But for a closer peek at the child, you can call me Millie."

Hesitating to say *go away* again, Sally took a calming breath. Show no fear, she remembered. In this world of the alley people, fear was a sign of weakness. The strong dominated the weak, got the best sleeping places, and laid claim to the finest dumpsters. She'd learned that from her mother in the alleys of New Orleans. Besides, if Mildred had meant her harm, she wouldn't have announced her presence.

"Come into the light...where I can see you, Millie."

The dark form came toward her. A face appeared in the light not three feet away, an old woman's face with a bent nose and gray strands of hair protruding from cavernous nostrils. Black gaps separated yellow-stained teeth. "And what's your name, deary?" A thin-boned hand reached out to her.

"Sally." She expected the old woman to offer her a poisoned apple.

Millie's black eyes pinned the blue bundle. "And your child?"

"Geoffrey. His name is Geoffrey." She pulled back the blanket so Millie could see his face.

"Ah, a fine boy child." She touched his forehead with a bony finger. "What'r you two doin' in my alley, girly?"

Sally looked into the old woman's eyes, hoped to find compassion, but only saw scrutiny. "We're hiding."

"Say it's a lie." Her eyes flickered. "You can't hide in my alley."

"I didn't know." Some homeless people were very territorial.

Millie sniffed the air. "You smell of booze."

"Some cowboy—"

"Go back to *The Loop* where you belong."

"I didn't come from *The Loop*."

"You look like it. You smell like it. Must be it then."

Glancing down at her old gray coat, the black scarf, blue bundle, and smelling of Jack Daniels, Sally realized how easily she'd been mistaken for a homeless woman. How well she looked the part. Her disguise had worked better than she'd planned. "Millie. I can't go home."

"The child needs a home, deary."

"But he's not safe there."

"No?"

"A man was chasing us. A bad man. He wants to take Geoffrey away...to a bad place. I can't go back now."

Millie touched her chin. "Not go back?"

"Not ever."

"And where is the father?"

Sally bowed her head. "He's dead." It was the only answer that made any sense.

Scrunching up her nose, Millie said, "The child can't stay here."

"I'll move along, right away." She started to push herself up the side of the dumpster to stand, but Millie stopped her.

"The child's not safe here." She pointed down the alley in both directions. "Someone will snatch him, maybe while you sleep. Sell him off for a bottle of cheap wine."

"They wouldn't."

Millie nodded.

Things must've changed since the last time Sally lived on the streets, or perhaps she was too young to know about all the dangers. There had to be someplace where Geoffrey would be safe. "I don't know what to do."

The old lady looked over the sleeping child. "What to do?"

Sally caught a whiff of Millie's coat. It smelled just as putrid as the alley the old woman called home.

"Let me think." Millie crouched in front of her under the light. Hunched over and squatted, she shuffled sideways, opened her big brown coat. It bulged from bags sewn to the inside liner, bags stuffed with everything she owned. From one bag she pulled out a piece of old fried fish. At least that's what it smelled like.

"Want some?" She pushed it in Sally's direction.

It was slimy green. "You go ahead, Millie."

With a toothy grin, she replied, "Eating helps me think."

As Millie nibbled on the food in her hand, Sally eyed the

strange coat, not unlike her own. Bags could easily be sewn inside it. One couldn't live a simpler life.

"Mother Mary of the Saints," Millie blurted out in her squeaky voice. She chucked the last of her meal. "Yes. She can help you. I'm sure she will."

"Who? How? Put us up for the night...find a place we can hide?"

Millie turned her solemn eyes on Sally. "You've nowhere to hide, no home, no family. The child will die or be snatched away, or the bad man will come to take him. Mother Mary is what you should do, at the orphanage. You have no choice."

Sally sucked air. "Give him up for adoption?"

"Or lose him to death or worse. You chose." Millie thrust her face toward Sally. "Got any sweets?"

"Y-yes," Sally stammered, remembering the Snickers bar. She pulled it from her pocket. "Will this do?"

Millie snatched it from her hand. "My favorite."

As Millie wrestled with the wrapper, Sally looked down the dark alley. Dotted by lights from small windows, it looked like a world far removed from where she had come, a world where a person could be lost forever, if one chose. But it wasn't a world befitting a child. He'd have no bed to call his own. No toy box. And what about school, and friends to grow up with, and Senior Prom? Her head swirled with questions, but she feared Millie had the only answer. Adoption.

Feeling hopeless, she pulled Geoffrey closer. If he really was William, how could she give him away? She wondered if he'd remember her from his past life. More likely, he'd think of her as his mother, grow up and get married—She blinked away a tear—No, she'd rather not know where William's new life takes him, and he shouldn't know how his life began again, as if he'd believe it.

Cradling Geoffrey in her arms, she sobbed quietly and thought about the book in her purse. *The Lost Diamonds* was supposed to guide Geoffrey back to his past. But William's plan was a fantasy, the last hope of a dying man. The book could ruin Geoffrey's life, make him crazy finding out he was someone else. She didn't want that to happen to him.

However, adopted into a real family, Geoffrey could grow up normally. He'd have a future as long as he didn't know about William Tuliver, or Sally Mayfield for that matter. She had to let him go.

Then she'd have to live on the streets. If Harrison ever caught her, they'd make her tell them what she'd done with their clone. The government had ways of getting information out of people: truth serums, hypnosis, and torture. She wouldn't put anything past Larson and Harrison.

Living on the streets was the only way to insure that Geoffrey's secret was safe. She looked at Millie munching on the Snickers bar. "You're right. I don't have a choice."

"Follow me."

Chapter Thirty-One

After a long walk in the chilly night air, Millie and Sally came to the steps of an orphanage. A light burned in a window on the second floor of the gray stone building. Surrounded by a wrought iron fence with a squeaky gate, the place looked gloomy to Sally, loveless. And she was supposed to leave Geoffrey here?

She followed Millie up concrete steps to a heavy wooden door that groaned when they went in. Geoffrey didn't make a sound. After climbing a creaky stairway, they found themselves in a dimly lit hall. A door at the other end was ajar, and from it, a sliver of light angled across the floor. The sign read: *Administration.*

Mother Mary seemed delighted to see the old woman, as though they'd known each other for many years. They hugged briefly, Millie in her bulging coat, Mary in her black and white habit. "And who is this?" She lifted a corner of the blue blanket. Her face gleamed white like she'd never sinned.

"His name is Geoffrey."

"He's a little cutie. When was he born?"

"August 20th," Sally said as she followed Mary's gaze to the child's face.

Geoffrey's eyes opened, but they looked different, sad instead of curious. Sally wondered if he knew why she'd brought him here.

As Millie took Mary aside, Sally gazed into Geoffrey's eyes. He stared back at her blankly. A sadness she'd never known came over her. She wanted so badly for him to understand why she had to do this. "I hope you know, little one...I do love you more than anything." His eyes didn't move. "Whether you're William or Geoffrey doesn't matter. I love you both the same, and I want you to be safe, even if it means I must live without you. I don't want to...please understand... I'll miss you."

He reached for her face with his hand, touched her nose, and wiggled his little fingers. Her heart skipped as she realized he was waving goodbye.

Mary approached. "Millie told me everything, and I have just what the child needs. A young couple, the Jordans, just lost a child, stillborn, and she can't have another. Geoffrey will be like a gift from God."

Sally looked at Geoffrey. His gaze was on Mary now. Gently, she handed the blue bundle to the lady in black and white. "Take care of him." Sally's eyes welled with tears. If she was doing the right thing, then why did her aching heart tell her not to leave him here? How could she bring herself to say goodbye?

"He'll be fine," Mother Mary assured her.

Sally took the can of formula from her pocket. "He'll need this."

"Thank you."

Geoffrey murmured in Mary's arms.

"And Geoffrey thanks you," Mary added with a smile.

Putting a finger to her lips, Sally kissed it and touched it to his little mouth. "Goodbye, Geoffrey." She thought her heart would stop beating any second.

Millie tugged on Sally's coat sleeve. "Let's go."

Together, they walked out into the cold night, the wind swirling around them. "Now go find your own alley." Millie turned and disappeared into the shadows.

Shoving her hands into the warmth of her pockets, Sally suddenly felt lonely. As she started to walk away, her fingers touched the rattle she'd bought Geoffrey earlier. She took it out of the pocket, remembered the look on his face when he first saw it, and thought to rush back inside to give it to him. But when she turned and looked up at the orphanage, the light in the window went out. It was too late. How quickly things had changed. Now Geoffrey was gone, and she had only this rattle to remember him by. Clutching it to her chest, she vowed to keep it forever.

An hour passed as she walked the side streets and alleys, reminiscing over the events that had brought her to this place in her life: living on the streets of New Orleans, moving to the farm in Illinois, then meeting William Tuliver and working in the Diamond Building, going to Blythe University filled with hope, and now back on the streets. It seemed her life had gone full circle, and all for what?. A clone? Was that all? She'd wanted a baby. She'd gotten what she wanted. Geoffrey meant everything to her. That he was a clone didn't matter. He was a child that deserved a normal, happy life.

"Go to hell, Dr. Marshall," she muttered. "And take Larson with you." She felt a great deal of satisfaction in screwing them out of their *investment*.

Freezing, she came upon a group of homeless people in a dank alley all huddled around a barrel, a smoky fire burning inside. She squeezed her way between two indigents, avoiding their faces, not wanting to see them, and not wanting to care. And she didn't want anyone to care about her either.

From now on heartache would be her companion, loneliness her destiny, all for the love a clone. On the streets of Chicago, she'd disappear into the realm of human despair. Dr. Marshall would never find her. And without her, they'd never find out what she'd done with Geoffrey, a secret she'd carry to her grave.

After warming her hands over the dwindling fire, she reached into her coat and pulled out William's tattered book. *The Lost Diamonds* was the only way Geoffrey could ever find out that he was once William Tuliver. She thumbed the pages thinking how crazy William's fantasy had been. He was dead. He wasn't coming back. It was over.

At that, her eyes welled with tears. One ran down her cheek

and fell into the barrel, sizzling when it hit the glowing embers inside. A small flame hungrily licked the air. She looked at the book and back to the flame. It was the only way to set them free. "Goodbye, William."

She tossed *The Lost Diamonds* into the fire.

Instantly, the pages curled and burst into flames. With a whoosh and a flash of light, William Tuliver's link to his clone was severed forever. And like the smoke that swirled away on the wind, any hope she ever had for her future was gone, too. At least Geoffrey would never know what they had done.

A deep sadness swept over her, black and heavy like the night. Succumbing to the heart-wrenching sorrow of losing everyone she loved, she fell to her knees and cried.

PART TWO

The Lost Clone

Terry Wright

Chapter Thirty-Two

Thirty years later, Chicago

Athump in the dark awoke her with a start. Karen Carlyle cast a quick glance toward her husband sleeping beside her. She held her breath and listened, heard the nightstand clock ticking, the wind outside her window. But what had made the other sound: a door closing, a window opening, an intruder's shin bumping the coffee table—?

Thump!

It was louder this time—or perhaps closer. Heart pounding now, she felt a chill and hugged the blankets around her neck. Someone was in the house.

"Roger?" she whispered.

He snorted.

She elbowed him. "Wake up."

"What the—?"

"I heard something...downstairs."

"It's probably just the wind, dear." He turned his back to her, pulling covers with him. "Go back to sleep."

The wind? Of course. Jeeze. What an imagination she had—but for good reason. The nightmares. It was just last night she dreamed the same dream that had haunted her for the past thirty years—ever since she'd witnessed Morris Brennon's electrocution. She saw the electric chair smoking, Morris Brennon standing, a growl in his throat as he ripped wires from his burn-blistered arms. Prison guards fell to his lethal ax.

How did he get an ax?

"I'll get you for this, bitch," he roared and busted through the observation glass.

She stumbled backward, broke a heel, twisted her ankle, and tried to run. But the air thickened to mud.

Run!

She slogged in slow motion to the steel door, pushed and pushed and finally got past it, found herself in a room with a steel chair bolted to the floor, a table, a mirrored wall. Moving through the room, looking for a way out, she tripped over a body on the floor. Fred Flanagan—he was lying in a pool of blood, his throat splayed open.

Scream!

She looked up, saw Morris chained to the steel chair: writhing, thrashing, shouting: "I'll get you for this, bitch." The enraged killer broke the chains, rose to his feet like an awakening monster, muscles bulging.

No!

She started crawling, but he cornered her, grabbed her. His breath was foul as sewage, and the stench of his burned flesh made her stomach lurch.

"I'm glad you're going to the chair," she screamed. "I'm glad...I'm glad."

His hairy-knuckled hands ripped off her clothes. Clutching tatters, she stared into his face. "You're crazy."

Morris unbuckled his belt. "I'll know what came in your mail." He unzipped his zipper. "I'll know what you had for dinner." He dropped his pants. A throbbing erection moved toward her. "I'll know what your hubby said..." He climbed on top of her, his fat body heavy, his intrusion painful. "After he did you in the ass."

Thump!

Karen's heart jumped. It was just the wind, she convinced herself. Sometimes she could be such a big baby. Pushing the covers aside, she sat up on the bed. Lingering adrenaline heated her veins.

She arched her back and stretched her arms. The motion of her reflection in the mirror caught her eye. Aerobics and skiing had kept her shapely and fit. At 52, she believed an investigative reporter had to look good for the cameras—just in case she broke a big story and made the ten o'clock news. The younger women at the Chicago Tribune envied her, or so she had heard.

Wide-awake now, she sat in the shadow-streaked bedroom, stared into the mirror, and listened to sounds in the night. Roger's gentle breathing. The ticking clock. How was she going to get back to sleep? A glass of milk, she decided, stepped into her slippers and slinked to the bedroom door.

Thump!

She swallowed hard. It was just the wind, a loose board, a tree branch hitting the window downstairs. Determined to beat back her fear, she charged down to the kitchen. As she opened the refrigerator door, the interior light bathed her with relief. Big baby. Reaching for the milk carton, she noticed the Tupperware lid was off the bowl. Last night's dinner was uncovered, but none was taken. How strange? Roger must have come down for a snack but changed his mind. She replaced the lid, thinking he didn't need the extra calories anyway.

She put the milk carton on the table and reached for a glass in the cupboard. In the refrigerator light's glow, she caught a glimpse of yesterday's mail strewn all over the counter. Her heart clutched. She'd stacked it in a neat pile before she went to bed. How could that be?

Terror stabbed her chest. She felt suddenly isolated, cold and vulnerable. The reoccurring nightmare raced through her mind. Last night's dinner, yesterday's mail. She shivered. Morris Brennon's threats—her imagination raced through a nightmare turned real. No way.

Thump!

"Roger?" She spun around, fists clenched. Biting her lower lip, she scanned the kitchen shadows, looking for any hint of motion, any sound. She wasn't alone. Was it Morris Brennon or just his haunting memory? She wasn't sure, but whatever it was, she about pissed in her panties.

"Is anyone here?"

Silence.

"Christ." There was nothing in the kitchen but her wild imagination. She took a long breath. "Get over it, Karen." Roger must've looked through the mail when he came down for a snack. Sure, that was it, but her heart still banged as she rearranged the mail in a neat stack. Why didn't she feel any better?

Trembling, she poured a glass of milk, the ax murderer's memory playing havoc with her mind. He'd scared the hell out of her back then, during the interview, but she hadn't let him see her fear, refused to give him the satisfaction. She only wished the recorder was on when the killer started talking crazy, telling her he'd be back to get her. Nobody believed he'd told her that. They all accused her of making it up just to sensationalize her story, which had sold a lot of papers and made her a household name around Chicago.

She closed the milk carton, knowing her fears were irrational. Moving to the open refrigerator, she steeled herself to the facts. She was an investigative reporter. Her whole career was based on finding facts. And the facts in this case were clear: Morris Brennon was dead, executed by electrocution. The killer got what he deserved. His loony threats didn't matter. He was just talking crazy.

And she was just a big baby.

She swung the refrigerator door shut, plunging the kitchen into darkness. The facts. There was no boogieman going thump in the night. She took her glass of milk into the living room, sat in her favorite recliner, and tucked her knees under her nightgown. A streetlight beaming in through the window dimly lit the room and painted the shadows of swaying tree branches on the wall. Her heartbeat calmed. She took a sip of milk and relaxed, safe in her home, safe from the nightmares and the crazy—

Thump!

Every muscle in her body seized. That sound didn't come from outside.

From a dark corner came the rasp of heavy breathing, deep and airy.

That wasn't the wind.

"Roger...?" She couldn't breathe. "Is that you?"

"You're the best, baby."

Fear punched her in the stomach. Those were Roger's last words—tonight—before he rolled over. But it wasn't Roger's voice. It was the voice that haunted her dreams. Morris Brennon.

She tried to suck in a breath but it wouldn't come. *I'll know what your hubby said after he fucked you in the ass*—Oh, my God. It can't be—

Thump!

She slumped in the chair, wishing she could sink into the cushions and disappear. Hot adrenaline spilled into her bloodstream. Wide-eyed, she searched the shadows for the voice. It couldn't be Morris Brennon. He was executed thirty years ago. There had to be another explanation. She had to be hallucinating—or gone completely mad.

Thump!

A shadow streaked up the wall. She gasped, knowing it was nothing her imagination had conjured up, for the shadow was a long-handled ax, its wide blade smeared across the ceiling.

Her jaws locked. Terror rifled through her limbs, contracted her muscles in waves, and made her tremble uncontrollably, the cold milk spilling on her nightgown and shocking her out of paralysis. The instinct to survive hit her like a board.

Run.

She threw the glass and leaped from the chair just as the wind from the falling ax blade whooshed by her head. Sprinting toward the stairs, she screamed, a loud piercing scream, like no scream she'd ever screamed.

"Roger."

A lamp crashed to the floor behind her.

"Roger."

She scrambled up the stairs, stumbling on the hem of her nightgown, smelling urine. Heavy footsteps followed her, and ragged breathing.

The bedroom door was closed. She swore she'd left it open.

"Roger." Why wasn't he answering?

Clumsy with panic, she pulled and tugged and pushed and kicked at the door until it flew open. She ran in and leaped on the bed.

"Roger." She shook him. "Wake up." She shook him hard. But something was wrong. Roger wasn't responding. He felt wet and sticky, and the sheets were soaked with—she gagged. What was that awful smell?

The bedroom light flicked on. In the sudden brightness, she squinted but couldn't believe what she saw. Roger's face—it was caved in—his skull cracked wide open—red goo in his hair, blood and brain matter pooled on the sheets. She looked at her sticky hands. Blood red. "Oh God, no."

She spun toward the door, saw a huge man standing in the doorway, a finger on the light switch, a bloody ax in the other hand. It was him. Morris Brennon. Just as she remembered, bald and toothy, fat and ugly, and not a day older. He grinned that sickening grin, and he swung the ax like a pendulum above the floor.

She bared her teeth. "What have you done?"

"Go to hell, bitch." He raised the ax over his shoulder and lunged forward.

She screamed, rolled right, and fell off the bed. Morris landed on Roger's body and twisted around like a wild beast. His boots got tangled up in the bloody sheets. Cursing, he struggled to free himself.

Fighting nausea, she ran down the stairs, screaming, hoping the neighbors would hear and call the cops. She had to get out of the house. She had to make it to the front door.

Heavy footfalls barreled down the stairs behind her.

She didn't look back, just ran.

At the bottom of the stairs, the door only steps away, a heavy sharp blow drove her to the floor. Her chin hit hard. She couldn't inhale. Pain. Like nothing she'd ever felt before. Blood staining the carpet. Her back on fire. She knew what it was, but she couldn't believe it. Morris Brennon's ax. My God, he was killing her. How could this be happening? He was dead, damn it. Dead.

Fighting for breath, she pushed herself to her hands and knees and began to crawl and weep like a child. She was so close to the door, only inches, but it may as well have been a million miles.

Gasping like a fish out of water, she knew Morris Brennon was looming above her, his black eyes glaring, cold and indifferent. How could he be alive? She remembered the interview, what he'd done to those nurses—oh God, no, she didn't want to die like that.

Morris cackled. "I told you I'd be back."

She coughed up blood. The bastard was enjoying himself. Had he waited thirty years for this moment? How..?

Pain! Her limbs started jerking spastically. She fought for air. Her arms gave out, and she fell to her belly. Gritting her teeth and clawing at the carpet, she tried to drag herself to the door.

Morris reached down and ripped off her nightgown, tore it like tissue paper. The rape would begin. Death would be better.

Bastard!

Spitting blood, she wondered why he wasn't dead. Electrocuted. She was there. She watched him die. How did he get here?

Her right lung had collapsed, she was sure of it, the pressure paralyzing, the ax blade in her back grating against bone. *Roger, help me.* Oh God, he was gone. Morris Brennon had butchered him. And now it was her turn to die.

Crawl, damn it! Crawl!

She reached the door, clawed at it with her fingernails.

Morris circled above her like a vulture. She could smell his sweat and hear his raspy breathing. What was he waiting for?

Fighting for air, gurgling noises leaked from her throat. She choked on the blood, coughed. It would be so easy to give up now. God, she didn't want to die.

A cool breeze swept across her face. The door had miraculously opened. For the briefest moment, a wisp of hope rose inside her. Morris was letting her go. Had he changed his mind? Or was he playing with her—like a cat toys with a mouse before the kill.

She summoned up all her strength, and teeth clenched, she crawled out on the porch, leaving a smear of blood. With all her might, she tried to scream, but only a squeak came out. Crawling, she made it down the steps to the cool cement sidewalk. It felt like sandpaper against her bare breasts. The street. She had to make the street. Maybe someone would come by, someone would help her. Maybe—

Suddenly, Morris Brennon's heavy boot stomped on the small of her back. "Far enough, bitch."

She clawed at the concrete, tearing off fingernails, but couldn't move. Her strength drained. "Please...no," she moaned, blood bubbling from her mouth.

"I'm gonna do yah just like them nurses," Morris growled.

"How...how did you...get back?" She managed.

"You'll never know."

"W-why?"

"You made a bundle off my story...but you didn't tell it right. The truth wasn't good enough for you and your readers. Well, your readers are gonna love this." Morris yanked the ax out of her back.

Air rushed in like acid. She looked up—saw the ax coming down. Her scream was the last sound she heard.

***

Flashing emergency lights lit up the predawn darkness on Dover Street. On the lawn in front of a white stucco house in the middle of the block, Detective Spence Ritter lifted a bloodstained sheet from a corpse. The coppery smell of blood hit him. He saw the woman's head had been severed at the neck and tucked under her right arm, which was broken and bent in morbid angles. Rib bones protruded from her back. There was no doubt in his mind. She'd been hacked up with an ax, over and over, violently, a clue that the killer had let out all his rage on this woman. Her blood-soaked nightgown was bunched up around her waist. The killer had posed his victim, on her knees, ass up in the air, the anus torn open and bloody. Streaks of semen glistened down her inner thighs.

Ritter's stomach turned over. He'd seen a lot of this kind of thing during his ten-years with the Chicago PD, blood and gore and death, what one human being had done to another. It never ceased to appall him. He hadn't gotten used to it, and he was sure he never would. But he'd never seen anything as gruesome as this.

"The neighbors heard a scream and called 911," a policeman told him. "Got here in under ten minutes. This is the way we found her."

Ritter dropped the sheet and turned away from the killer's handiwork. "Who is she?"

"Karen Carlyle."

"The Tribune's investigative reporter?"

"The same."

"She must've really pissed somebody off this time."

"There's more." The policeman pointed to the house. "Roger Carlyle. He's dead too."

"Jesus," Ritter said. "And sexually assaulted?"

"Posed and sodomized, just like her."

"What kind of monster would do this?" Ritter knew the answer. This killer's MO reminded him of a homicide case his father had worked on forty years ago, the most prolific killer the Midwest had ever seen, Morris Brennon. It ended with his electrocution in 1969.

Was there a copycat on the loose?

Ritter feared the slaughter had begun again. "Call forensics in. Dust everything. It's going to be a long night."

Chapter Thirty-Three

The announcers voice echoed across the tennis court. "Love, thirty." Jeff Jordan shook his head and setup to serve again. This game was killing him. Tossing the ball up, he swung the racket high and slammed down on the ball as hard as he could. It popped off the strings with a thump, good power over the net, right into the service box.

But Rick Atkins was on it. A tough opponent, tall and lanky with a wedge-shaped nose and stringy blond hair, Jeff had beaten him before. This time he wasn't doing so well. The ball came back at him fast. He ran to it, got there late. A wild swing sent it over the net, but it hit the right sideline.

"Out," a line judge called.

"In," another insisted.

Jeff wiped sweat from his brow with a weathered Wilson band on his wrist. "Make up your mind," he mumbled.

Rick was playing tougher than usual, like he had to win. But Jeff wasn't making it easy for him, in spite of the fact that this wasn't one of his better days. His joints ached, especially his right hip. Arthritis? He felt sixty years old instead of thirty, sluggish and easily tired. The sun, the heat, and Rick were beating him up.

He took a deep breath, tried to relax. Oak and poplar leaves rustled in the breeze. Cicadas buzzed. His fingers tingled. He made a fist with his racket hand, flexed his fingers a few times in an attempt to restore circulation. It didn't help.

The normally quiet crowd in the stands began to mumble as if annoyed with the pause in play. The sideline judges were huddled in conversation, debating whether or not the ball was out or in.

Jeff really didn't care. He just wanted to get it over with. From where he stood on the court, he saw sunbeams gleaming off the roof of his black '59 Cadillac limo parked at the curb. He recalled the first time he saw the car—at the Cheap Heaps car lot, dirty and dented and badly in need of repair. The classy tailfins had attracted him the most. He couldn't resist buying the junker. It took him two years to restore it. He'd done all the work himself in the auto repair shop he owned.

Looking to the stands, he saw his parents waving at him. He held up his racket to them. Colorful umbrellas shaded their smiling faces. They were his biggest fans. Next to them sat his wife, Lois Jordan. She was eight years younger and the love of his life.

She threw him a kiss.

He pretended to catch it in mid air. Before the match, she'd playfully said she didn't care if he won or lost, she'd still love him either way. And she mentioned having a baby again. He told her he still wasn't ready to be a father. The shop kept him busy—too busy to start a family. Maybe someday.

Holding the racket in both hands, he glanced at the clock on the clubhouse tower. The match had started two and a half hours ago. The third set was the toughest yet, a seesaw battle of wits and power strokes. He'd won four games. But Rick had won five. The pressure was on. He ran a hand through his prematurely graying hair and wished the game was over.

The umpire said, "The call is *out*. Love, forty."

"Match point," the announcer said.

Jeff bounced the ball on the court, two, three times, stalling, trying to psych himself up again. His feet felt heavy as cement blocks. The racket weighed a ton. *One more time,* and with all his strength, he served the ball. Rick returned it with a cannonball forehand. Running up to the net, Jeff slammed the ball back to him. But Rick returned it with a blazing backhand. The ball sailed past Jeff like a missile.

The Duplication Factor

The crowd cheered. Rick raised his racket in victory.

Exhaling, Jeff was glad it was over. He didn't think he had the energy to swing that racket one more time. Tucking it under his arm, he met Rick at the net and shook his hand. "You worked hard for that. Congratulations."

Still smiling and waving to the crowd, Rick said, "What happened to you? It's like you just quit on me."

"I don't feel so good."

They walked together toward the sideline. Rick patted Jeff's shoulder. "Then let's get the hell out of this sun." He pointed to the clubhouse. "Cold beer?"

"Get your trophy and say goodbye to your fans. I'll meet you there."

Jeff handed his racket to the ball boy and watched Rick for a moment as he walked back and forth in the front of the stands, waving. Disappointment washed over Jeff. He really wanted to win this ladder match. The NTA title was at stake. But this preliminary match had taken its toll on him physically. He deserved to lose.

Throwing a towel over his shoulder, he turned toward the clubhouse, saw Lois standing by the gate, leaning on the chain-link fence. Five-foot-four with short red hair, her freckles were as red as her sleeveless blouse. The sun had given her white legs a little more color than usual. She wasn't the prettiest woman he'd ever seen, but she was the best. As he approached her, she put a pout on her lips. "Sorry."

He chuckled. "It's not that bad."

She threw her arms around his neck. "You did great."

His sweaty body responded to her touch with goose bumps. As he gazed into her hazel eyes, a ripple of anxiety ran through him, that same feeling, the one that had haunted him ever since he met her. He couldn't help thinking he'd looked into those eyes before, somewhere. But where? When? Every time he got that feeling, it left him empty, without an answer, without a cause.

He closed his eyes and kissed her. She kissed him back like she meant it.

"All right kids..." Dad's voice reached him from down the fence line. "Save it for later."

Lois stepped back, the diamond necklace she wore glinting in the sunshine. Diamonds fascinated Jeff, their symmetry, their clarity, their brilliance, and he'd given her lots of diamond jewelry, all that he could afford.

He turned toward his approaching parents, their faces beaming with pride. "We're not kids anymore."

"You weren't much of a kid when you were a kid," Mom said and kissed his cheek. "You grew up much too fast."

"Great match, son." Dad patted Jeff's shoulder. "Better luck next time."

"Rick outlasted me, that's all."

"How's the book coming along?"

"Don't get him started on that now," Mom said.

"He doesn't mind talking about it."

"As long as you don't mind listening." Jeff smiled. "It's nearly finished."

As they headed toward the clubhouse, Lois took Jeff's hand. "He's going to be a famous author someday. You'll see."

"He should be," Dad said, "for all the time he spends down at Paradise Park, typing on his laptop."

"I like it there, Dad. It inspires me...the oak trees, the fountain, and the Diamond Building. My characters know that place well, and it feels as though I've been there before too, you know, like in a past life...or something."

Mom gave him a nudge with her elbow. "Don't go on about that again."

Jeff shrugged off her negative attitude, just as he'd done so many times before. She was tired of hearing about his problem—his déjà vu. *"You're being overly sensitive,"* she'd tell him. But he disagreed. There was something special about his feelings for Paradise Park.

The Duplication Factor

Walking toward the clubhouse, he thought back to a time when he was a young boy riding his bicycle. Paradise Park and the fountain made him tremble every time he peddled past it. The place frightened him, as if a monster of some kind waited in the shadows of the giant oak trees. He didn't dare go in there.

Then one day, the fountain's roar seemed especially loud, carried to him on the breeze. Curiosity got the best of him. He swallowed his fear, dropped his bike on the grass, and though his heart raced and his head felt dizzy, he walked into the park, slowly, as if each step would be his last.

The oak trees rustled overhead like a choir of welcoming angels. Feeling soothed, he made his way toward the roaring fountain. He remembered the sound of children playing, their screeching and laughter nearby. People were everywhere, strolling the sidewalks, lounging on benches, and picnicking on the grass. They all became a blur as he moved among them like a ghost.

Heart pounding, he approached the massive fountain, stood at the wishing pool for a long time, taking in the whoosh of geysers and the sound of splashing water. Déjà vu. He was home, but he didn't know why. Slowly, he reached out his trembling hand, ever so carefully, palm up, and touched the diamond clear water falling from the sky. The feel of it, cold and clean, washed away his fears. The spray on his face made him feel alive. An eerie calm came over him. From then on, he couldn't stay away.

"Jeff?" Mom's voice brought him back to the present. "You all right?"

Looking at his mother walking beside him, he wished he could explain it to her. Many times he'd tried. But she refused to acknowledge his problems, his feelings. He couldn't find the words to make her understand. Putting his arm around her shoulder, he gave her a quick hug. "I'm okay, Mom."

"You scare me when you zone out like that."

"Sorry."

Dad pulled open the clubhouse door. "All aboard."

Jeff followed his mother inside. Air-conditioning made the heat of the tennis court seem far away. The aroma of buttered popcorn aroused his appetite. Tennis shoes squeaking on the hardwood floor, he walked past rows of photos hanging on the wall: tennis greats Jimmy Connors, Pete Sampras, Billie Jean King, and many others, all smiling with rackets in hand.

Leading the way to a table that overlooked the tennis courts, Jeff pulled out a chair for Lois and motioned his mother to a seat across from her. "Rick will be along as soon as he's finished showing off for the crowd." He threw his towel over the chair next to Lois and sat. "This place will be packed."

"I'm sorry you didn't win, dear."

Jeff sighed. "It's just a game, Mom." He signaled to Ralph the bartender. "Four drafts."

Ralph nodded and started lining up glasses at the tap. A television above the bar attracted Jeff's attention. Grim-faced, a news reporter stood in front of a white stucco house cordoned off with yellow police tape. He was speaking into a microphone.

"Turn that up, Ralph."

The bartender set a foaming beer aside and reached for the remote. "Damnedest thing. Karen Carlyle was killed right in her own front yard."

"I hadn't heard. She's the reporter, right?"

"It's been all over the news," Mom said. "Horrible."

The TV reporter pointed to an upstairs window. "Roger Carlyle's body was found up there. Police say it was as bloody a murder as they'd seen around here in forty years. Back to you, Susan."

The scene switched to an anchorwoman in the studio. Looking like a model, not a hair out of place, she sat behind a counter, her face sad. A picture of Karen Carlyle appeared in the upper right corner of the screen. Though her brown hair had light streaks of gray, her face glowed with perfect makeup, and deep brown eyes sparkled with a telltale beauty of days gone by.

"Karen Carlyle's career spanned thirty years for the Chicago Tribune," the anchorwoman said. "Early on, she gained prominence as an investigative reporter with her award-winning interview of the ax murderer, Morris Brennon."

Jeff's heart rate shot up. "Morris Brennon? What's she talking about?"

"It launched her career," the anchorwoman said.

"The same Morris Brennon?" Lois asked.

"No way. He's the ax murderer in my book. I-I made him up." Swallowing shock, Jeff couldn't believe his character had just come to life.

The anchorwoman continued, "Because an ax was used in the murder, investigators fear this is the work of a copycat killer. Karen Carlyle, dead at fifty-two. Chicago will miss her."

Jeff stared openmouthed at the TV, his hands clenched together on the table, squeezing. His hip throbbed. As Ralph delivered the beers, Mom put a gentle hand on Jeff's hands. "You must've heard about him and subconsciously used his name in your story."

Gritting his teeth, he felt sure that wasn't how it happened. He leaned back, took a swig of beer, and looked into his mother's eyes. "You have to understand, I don't know Morris Brennon. It's my main character, William Tuliver, who knows him. I tell you, I'm writing what comes to me when I'm in Paradise Park. I get these weird feelings...like I've been there before."

"Don't be ridiculous. It's just your imagination."

"The story comes from inside me, like deep inside. I don't know where, but it's more real to me than just my imagination."

Mom sipped her beer then smiled faintly. He thought she was only trying to reassure herself. After all, whenever his life wasn't making sense, whenever he confided in her, she always discounted him, waved him off, wouldn't listen. He often wondered if she had been keeping a secret from him, or protecting him from something. If so, it had been a lifelong project. He needed to make her understand. "I was a strange kid, Mom, you said so yourself."

"All kids are strange."

"Strange enough to remember being born?"

"There you go again—"

"Now, son," Dad put in. "Just drop it. You're upsetting your mother."

"But it's true." Jeff kept his voice low but insistent. "I can still feel the pressure, the pushing, the pain, the sudden relief and the chill. And I remember seeing a face, a woman's face, fuzzy like in a dream, but I can still remember how sad she looked. Then I didn't see her anymore."

Mom glanced at Dad. Her eyes welled with tears, but she said nothing.

"You've been out in the sun too long," Dad said.

Lois patted Jeff's arm. Her eyes told him she understood. She was the only one. It was no use with Mom and Dad.

Looking up at the television again, he saw a commercial for dish soap. Ralph had turned down the volume. But Jeff could still hear that name: *Morris Brennon! Morris Brennon! Morris—*

He swallowed hard. "One thing's for sure...if *my* Morris Brennon is alive, no one is safe."

"How do you know that?" Lois asked.

"William Tuliver told me."

Chapter Thirty-Four

Blythe Biotech, Cedar Lake, Indiana

D r. Larson flinched when General Harrison stormed into the office and slammed his morning paper on the desk. "The son of a bitch killed her."

"I was afraid that would happen," Larson said, still amazed at what had appeared on the news. It proved beyond a doubt that 1122B was just like Morris Brennon.

"I told you to be careful with him." The General leaned on the desk. "How did he get out?"

Resisting the urge to growl back, Larson remained cool, straightened his blue and white zigzag-pattern tie. "It's not my fault."

"He was confined to the compound." The General pointed to the paper. "This detective Ritter had better not come snooping around here, John. He could ruin everything."

Teeth bared, Larson leaned forward. "You've got your damn soldiers. In six months you'll have your motherless army. That was the deal. I'm sick of babysitting your clones."

"If it weren't for my clones, your research department would have been belly-up broke a long time ago. Are you sick of those big checks coming in from the Department of Defense?"

"The money's been good," Larson conceded and leaned back in his chair. "I only wish Dr. Marshall could be here to see all this."

"He turned chicken-shit and ran," Harrison spat as if the man's memory left a bad taste in his mouth. "I'll bet he had something to do with losing your first clone."

"Not a chance." Larson knew Dr. Marshall was no traitor. "He saved 1122B's life. Now you've got your natural born killers, General. The clone proved that last night." He indicated the newspaper. "So get off my ass."

Harrison grumped and turned his attention to a green file folder on the desk: *Feeding and Formulating.* It contained all the records for the experimental intravenous formulas they'd developed for the clones of Morris Brennon. Some were better than others, but they all had the necessary nutrients. His clones weren't starving.

Rubbing his chin, Larson thought about how much things had changed since Dr. Marshall walked out. Blythe University had lost its charter due to some inconsistencies in the Board of Trustees' handling of all that government money rolling in. They cooked the books and got caught with their hands in the cookie jar. Some got jail time. The university crumbled.

Then along came Colonel Harrison and Carl Savage. They bought the compound, incorporated Blythe Biotech, and funded the operation with Department of Defense contracts. Senator Bennett was a big help getting appropriations pushed through Congress. He'd stuck the requisition in with an urban renewal program for Cincinnati.

Larson didn't care how they did it, how they cheated and lied, who they bought or who they sold out. His career had been saved, and his cloning research continued without interruption. And the world knew nothing of what they were doing at Blythe Biotech.

Along the way, Harrison had received many promotions. He was now a three-star general. Rumor had it number four was coming soon. He was overheard saying that having a Senator in his back pocket was better than Santa Claus himself. But the years had been hard on the old soldier. His glasses were thicker and his jowls hung lower than when he was a Colonel, back when the first human clone slipped through their fingers.

Larson thought about Geoffrey Scott Michaels, the clone of William Tuliver. They'd failed to find him—or Sally Mayfield.

She'd disappeared without a trace, and Larson held little hope of them ever turning up again.

An assistant appeared at the door. "1122B is back."

"Where is he?"

"In the cafeteria...and he's hungry as hell."

Harrison dropped the file on the desk. "I'm going to kill the bastard."

Pulling himself out of his chair, Larson said, "No you won't. He's your main man, remember? You wouldn't have your soldier clones if it weren't for his DNA. Now think about it. You wouldn't want your natural born killers to know you'd murdered their big brother, would you?"

General Harrison pulled his revolver. "I'm not afraid of those bald headed bastards."

It was the same old battle, 1122B against General Harrison, with Larson in the middle, protecting the clone. But this time the born killer had gone too far.

Chapter Thirty-Five

Chicago

In the hallway at the police station on West 63rd Street, reporters from the Chicago Tribune clamored like an angry mob. "We want answers," a reporter called out. One of their own was dead. Karen Carlyle had been brutally murdered. Detective Ritter didn't have the answers. He locked his office door, pulled the blinds shut, and sat at his desk, hoping they'd tire soon and go away.

"Who did it?" a reporter shouted through the closed door.

Ritter sipped on a cup of coffee, one he'd poured for himself an hour ago, and he lit up a Winston just as he noticed one was already smoldering in the ashtray, its long gray ash drooping. Usually, he didn't smoke, but he'd been under a lot of stress lately. The Carlyle case was as *high profile* as they got. Even the mayor was on his ass about it.

"Where's the chief?" someone shouted. "We want to speak to the chief."

With cigarette smoke burning his eyes, he thumbed through pages of a file he'd ordered up from *records*. If the killer was a copycat, this was the guy he mirrored. Morris Brennon. The folder, dusty and water marked, held reports detailing a multiple murder unlike any case in history. It took dozens of boxes of file folders to store all the information on all the murders he'd committed. But this folder was about his first victims: the three nurses in Champaign.

Forty years ago, the murder spree began. It ended in the electric chair on September 5th 1969, one of the last executions in Illinois before the Supreme Court declared the death penalty unconstitutional. *Cruel and unusual punishment*, they had called it.

"Ritter. Come out and talk to us."

Those high and mighty judges should have done a tour with the homicide squad in Chicago or any other major city before they'd made that ruling. Only then would they have seen what "cruel and unusual" really meant, like what Morris Brennon had done to his victims. The Supreme Court Justices didn't know the *real* horrors of murder: the blood, the smell, the heartbreak. They were so far removed from the reality of killing that they actually thought those poor convicted murderers were being abused. They had rights, Constitutional rights. They were human beings, after all, not animals. Ritter thought maybe if those self-righteous judges had known Morris Brennon, if they'd met him up close and personal, maybe then they would have seen the death penalty in the proper perspective.

Turning a page, Ritter's neck hairs prickled as the killer's mug shot stared out at him. His black eyes were hollow and cold and empty like dried up wells, dark and despairing. Morris had the pale look of death on his face, bald head, scruffy fat cheeks, and choppy teeth.

"Do you have any suspects?"

Ritter snuffed out his cigarette and examined the fingerprints displayed in two rows under the mug shot. *Left Hand. Right Hand.* The double loop pattern on Morris's left index finger twisted right and then back in an unusual way, almost complete whorls. He hadn't seen a fingerprint like that before.

Looking again at the killer's face, Ritter tried to imagine how horrible death must have been for Morris Brennon's victims, how *cruel and unusual* it was to have been slaughtered with an ax, how *cruel and unusual* Karen Carlyle's murder was. Ritter blinked, wondering if there really was a copycat killer. Or was it just a coincidence? He shook his head. He didn't believe in coincidences. There was no such thing in a murder investigation.

"Give us what you've got, damn it." The ruckus in the hallway escalated. Another loud voice peaked the melee. "Who's in charge around here?"

Then two knocks rapped on his door. The code.

Ritter moved to the door and opened it a crack.

A young man wearing a white lab coat braced himself against the throng of reporters. "The natives are restless, Lieutenant."

Ritter let him in. Cameras flashed in the hallway.

"How's the investigation going, Ritter?" a reporter demanded. "Any clues?" another yelled.

"When we've got something, we'll call a press conference. You know the rules." Ritter slammed the door then turned his attention to the lab technician. His face was flushed as if he'd run all the way up from the fingerprint lab. "What do you have?"

He waved a manila envelope in his right hand. "The prints from Carlyle's place...they were everywhere, like the perp didn't care. Our computers came up with nothing. The FBI is checking now."

"Let's have a look." Ritter pulled the glossy black and white enlargements from the envelope, fanning out five pictures on his desk.

Refrigerator. Kitchen counter. Staircase wall. Staircase railing. Bedroom light switch.

The last picture grabbed his attention, a double loop pattern on the light switch. He couldn't believe his eyes. His temples pulsed from a sudden rush of blood. He'd just seen that pattern only moments ago. How was that possible—?

Photograph in hand, he shuffled through the old file he'd been studying. Maybe he was mistaken. He'd only glanced at the prints, but he prided himself in his eye for detail. The little things made the biggest differences.

And sure enough, there it was in black and white, just as he'd seen it: left index finger, double loop pattern. Heart thumping, he examined the lines carefully. It was an exact match. Morris

Brennon's fingerprints were all over Karen Carlyle's house. The killer had used his left index finger to turn on the bedroom light. Morris Brennon had to be the killer.

Ritter grimaced. But how could that be? Morris Brennon was dead, executed by electrocution thirty years ago.

Cruel and unusual punishment, remember?

Chapter Thirty-Six

Westside Medical Center

"*D*r. *Marshall, report to obstetrics. Dr. Marshall.*" Not a day went by that Eugene didn't hear that page over the intercom, as if some greater power knew whenever he was in the cafeteria, pouring his first cup of coffee, or sitting down with the morning paper. He'd just buttered a hot cinnamon roll.

"*Dr. Marshall...stat.*"

It had to be Mrs. Simmons again. He looked at his watch. This was the third time in two days she'd come running in with false labor pains. How many times would it take before she understood? She wasn't due for another month. *That's thirty days and thirty nights*, he had told her. Stomach cramps were not labor pains. If she'd lay off the pickles and ice cream she wouldn't have the stomach cramps.

Tossing a napkin over his cinnamon roll, Eugene pushed his chair away from the table, grabbed his cup of coffee, and rushed from the cafeteria, leaving behind the clatter of plates and silverware and the chatter of doctors and nurses who didn't know Mrs. Simmons existed.

In obstetrics, he stopped at the counter and talked with his head duty nurse, Miss Aggie Page, a pleasant woman of plump proportions, giddy and joyful of her job. Eugene always thought her life was like an ongoing beer commercial where everyone smiled all the time. "It's Mrs. Simmons again." Her smile never wavered.

"How am I going to convince her to stop this?" he asked, more out of frustration than expecting a helpful answer.

Nurse Aggie giggled. "She's in labor room 213. Suzie is with her. Have fun." She flitted her fingers at him and returned her attention to the appointment book.

Grabbing a breath, he headed for the labor room and the incomprehensible Mrs. Simmons.

"I just know it's time." She rubbed her swollen belly as she lay on the labor bed. "The contractions," she gasped, "are every three minutes now."

Suzie, a young assistant with fluffy blond hair and a concerned brow, handed Eugene a fresh pair of latex gloves. "You better have a look, doctor."

"Thanks." He pulled the gloves on with a snap then lifted Mrs. Simmons' hospital gown. Working her abdomen with both hands, he decided the fetus was lying on its back, cradled in the womb as if reclining in a hammock. Gently, he pressed down on the lowest curve of her abdomen with the palm of his hand, gauging the tautness of her muscles there and felt nothing unusual.

With the stethoscope, he listened to gasses gurgling in her intestinal tract, more pickles and ice cream.

Lifting her knees and spreading her feet apart, Eugene thought how he didn't want to do this examination. It wasn't necessary, but she would insist if he refused. She always insisted. Maybe she hoped he'd find something in there that her instincts told her didn't exist. Sitting on a stool, he looked at her, surprised to see she'd already shaved as if she were certain that today would be the day.

Inserting the vaginal speculum, he examined the shiny surface of her cervix, the puckered opening to the womb. It was covered with clear mucus. He saw no sign of dilation, no leakage, nothing to indicate that labor had begun.

After retracting the speculum, he looked at her for a moment, not at her vagina or her swollen breasts, but at her face as she peered at him over her bulging abdomen. Her eyes were full of hope. He could only guess how badly she wanted his report to be good news.

Her pregnancy would end today, he wished he could tell her. But that was not the case.

He sighed and stood. "Sorry, Mrs. Simmons. Your baby isn't ready yet." Pulling the gown over her, his heart sank when he saw tears welling in her eyes. "Where's Henry?"

She shook her head and looked toward the wall, tears now streaking her cheeks.

Eugene knew the answer: Patrick's Pub on Van Buren Street, down by the rail-yards, his usual haunt. Henry prided himself in pilfering the railroad men's paychecks with a toss of the dice. But too often, in the end, Henry was the loser. Eugene thought perhaps loneliness had driven Mrs. Simmons to this delusion that it was time for the child to come into her world. He patted her shoulder. "Get dressed. I'll call a cab for you."

Ushering Suzie out of the labor room ahead of him, he followed her and closed the door with a gentle click. He tried not to listen. He tried not to hear the cries of the lonely woman, Mrs. Simmons, but he couldn't shut them out no matter how hard he tried.

"Will she be all right?" Suzie asked him.

"In thirty days." He hurried to the reception counter where Nurse Aggie looked at him with concern. Her eyes searched his as if a replay of the events in labor room 213 could be seen reflecting back at her. He blinked. "Why the hell did I ever want to be an obstetrician?" he asked, though not really wanting to hear her opinion on the matter.

Nurse Aggie beamed her trademark smile. "Because you're good at it, Dr. Marshall. Look at the schedule you keep. Three deliveries yesterday." She pointed to a heavily scribbled page in her appointment book. "And two in hard labor this morning, not to mention one false alarm, of course." Meaning Mrs. Simmons. "And I bet your afternoon is jam-packed with patients at the clinic."

She was right. He'd probably see eight or nine expectant mothers in various stages of pregnancy before he saw the end of this day. Leaning on the counter, he scanned an array of baby pictures

Nurse Aggie had displayed and a clutter of stuffed animals she kept handy to give the newborns. "Call a cab for Mrs. Simmons." He glanced down the hall. "Is there any end to this?"

"Not in this world," Nurse Aggie handed him a clipboard. "215."

He recognized Mrs. Braggs' chart immediately. A duty nurse had written *ten centimeters* on the last line. He quickly referred to his watch. That was half an hour ago. "I better check on her."

"And another thing," Nurse Aggie said. "Miss Gustafson wants something stronger for the pain. I told her you'd be in to see her soon."

"I can't be everywhere at once." He started moving down the hall.

"Maybe you should clone yourself," she called after him.

Eugene staggered. Memories bombarded him. Thirty years ago he'd walked away from Dr. Larson and Blythe University. For months after that, he'd searched for Sally, sat watch over her rented house, hit all the cafés, motels, and boarding houses he could find, hoping beyond hope that one day he would locate her—and Geoffrey.

Dizziness engulfed him. He leaned against the wall, pinching the bridge of his nose, his mind in a whirl. If only he could have told her how sorry he was for the choices he'd made back then, his career over his duty to his patient, his loyalty to Dr. Larson over his responsibility to her, and all the lies by omission. He knew it would have been hard for her to forgive him, to believe that he truly loved her, or to take him into her confidence once more. But he really wanted her to try.

Back then he needed to tell her how he felt, but he couldn't find her. He'd looked everywhere. Eventually, he realized it was too late to make amends. Time passed, easing the pain, the longing, and the worry about what had become of her. But the guilt lingered like a fungus on his heart.

So he filled his days and years with the task of bringing babies into the world. Real babies. Not the clones of self-centered rich men or heinous killers, but babies with real mothers and fathers, with genes from both of them, the way nature or God had designed things to work.

"Are you all right, doctor?" Nurse Aggie had rushed to his side, set her hand on his shoulder. He felt suddenly small, unguarded and vulnerable in this curious position leaning against the wall. His head cleared almost as quickly as it had muddled. He pushed himself upright and smoothed the front of his smock. "I was just thinking...that's all."

She eyed him curiously. "You look a little pale."

"I'm all right." He showed her a phony confident smile.

She patted his shoulder as if she thought he needed comforting anyway, and then headed down the hall, her white shoes squeaking on the tile floor.

Shivering, he put the past out of his mind and hurried toward labor room 215, wondering how much time he had wasted during his relapse. It seemed like an hour. Mrs. Braggs had probably delivered her baby by now, and he was sure Miss Gustafson had died from her pain. A glance at his watch allayed his fears. Only a few minutes had passed.

Standing in the doorway to room 215, he thought Mrs. Braggs looked to be in rough shape, her flushed face contorted, her cheeks rounded and panting. Sweat glistened on her forehead. Her husband held her white-knuckled hand.

"Doctor," she moaned in a haunting voice of desperation.

From the next room, Miss Gustafson screamed in agony.

Eugene took a deep breath. The baby doctor's work was never done—not in this world anyway.

Chapter Thirty-Seven

Paradise Park

A breeze rustled the oak trees, a mere whisper compared to the roaring fountain and its relentless splashing. Wearing his favorite Dockers, a white T-shirt, and tennis shoes, Jeff sat on a shaded bench in front of the pool. His laptop sat next to him, but he felt no urgency to begin writing.

He took in the scent of freshly mowed grass. How he loved it here, in the park at the foot of the towering Diamond Building. Sunshine glistened off its windows like a beacon, guiding him, stretching the limits of his mind, pulling thoughts from his head that had no logical reason for being there.

In the grass around him, pigeons strutted and cooed and pecked at the ground. He moved his foot. They leaped, batted air, and darted toward the buildings across the park. After admiring their grace and ease of motion, he looked up to the fountain's pinnacles, which gave off a fine mist to the breeze. Paradise Park Fountain was a breathtaking work of fluid art. He was proud of it, as if it were something he had created. However, he thought its name was boring and meaningless. If it were his fountain, he'd have given it a different name. So when he wrote about it in his book, he gave it a name that meant something special to his main character, William Tuliver.

Jeff thought about his reason for doing that. Something troubled him. Deep inside, he felt someone there, a presence he could not explain, a mother he remembered as if in a dream, or perhaps another life, if that were possible. She was an unhappy mother, distraught over the death of her son at Pearl Harbor. He could feel the weight of her anguish, the misery she carried with her everywhere. Her sorrow crept inside his heart and lingered like a disease, sometimes depressing him so badly he'd have to force himself to think of something else. So while writing his novel, he gave that same sorrow to William Tuliver's mother, whose younger son had been killed at Pearl Harbor. Her sorrow motivated William to build the fountain, and in his book, Jeff named it *Mothers' Tears*.

And in his story, William Tuliver was rich beyond belief. He had an affinity for diamonds and named his company *Diamond Auto Parts*. Jeff had used that brand of replacement parts in his auto repair shop, so it worked perfectly into his story. The Diamond building in Paradise Park was also the perfect setting for William's headquarters. Whenever Jeff gazed up the face of that magnificent building, he felt the same sense of pride that the fountain gave him. Atop the Diamond building, William enjoyed a lavish office. He was a successful businessman. Unfortunately, the Japanese wanted to take over William's company, but he wasn't about to sell it to the country that had killed his brother.

Also, William was an advocate of the workingman and an admirer of the spaceman. He believed in the American judicial system. *Slow but sure*, he had always said. William stood for everything that Jeff thought was important in life. Tingling with pride, he felt like a master of clay, molding an American patriot who lived the American dream.

But a story was nothing without conflict, so Jeff gave William an adversary, ruthless and cunning and greedy. Carl Savage wanted all of William's American Dream. But William wasn't about to give it up without a fight, or so he'd thought until he became sick with cancer. In a desperate attempt to finance a cure, he scarified his principles and sold his company to the Japanese for a fortune in diamonds.

When William's health deteriorated, he walked with the aid of a diamond-studded black walnut cane. Jeff figured that if his character was going to walk with a limp, he was going to walk with a limp in style.

And then there was William's best friend and chauffeur, a lanky tennis player like Rick Atkins. Jeff named him Andrew Cobb and gave him a '59 Cadillac limo to drive, just like the one Jeff had restored and drove every day. Andrew was like a brother to William, not just an employee. To Andrew, William would divulge his deepest and darkest secrets.

Jeff thought his characters were so real that he couldn't help but wonder who he was writing about, William Tuliver or Jeff Jordan. Sometimes, like now, he felt as though both of them were the same person. Between his feelings and the déjà vu that plagued him, he felt trapped within his story, writing the book as though he were on the inside looking out. He had to force himself to believe it was just a novel.

That had become more difficult, when unbelievably, Morris Brennon had turned out to be a real person, the news report of the ax murderer coming to mind. Even now Jeff struggled with how that could have happened. Maybe Mom was right. He must have heard that name before. There couldn't be any other explanation. In the story, Morris Brennon had murdered more than a hundred people, William's parents among them. At the trial, Morris's first victims, three nurses, got all the attention. William's old and feeble parents weren't even mentioned. But none of this was real, he assured himself. It was just a story.

He liked the characters he'd developed, Sally Mayfield being his favorite. If ever there was a love affair between a writer and his heroine, this was the hottest one of all. As Jeff wrote about Sally, he used Lois as her model. The way she looked, the way she talked, her strengths and her fears all came out on the pages. Especially the part about her wanting a baby. Lois became the mold for Sally.

He blinked; confusion now clouded his thinking. Or was it the other way around? Was he in love with Lois because she was so much like Sally? His heart beat faster. Which was the mold and which was the clay?

Looking at the laptop, he decided to get busy. He had some serious writing to do. A literary agent, Stan Thompson in New York City, had expressed an interest in representing his work. Hopefully, Stan would sell *The Lost Diamonds* to a publisher.

Sitting comfortably in his favorite place, Jeff planned to finish his book. In the final chapter, William would succumb to his disease and leave his fortune in diamonds entombed beneath his precious fountain, *Mothers' Tears*. The spoils of his own Japanese invasion would be buried forever in William's favorite place.

The words began spilling from his mind even as he removed the laptop from its case.

Chapter Thirty-Eight

Blythe Biotech

A door slammed, the sound echoing down the hallway just outside the cafeteria. Morris Brennon tore off another mouthful of fried chicken breast. Bones and bird debris lay around the table where he ate, alone as usual. Everybody around here was scared to death of him.

They damned well should be.

Footsteps came next. His jailer was coming, probably to give him a bunch of crap about Karen Carlyle. The bitch really thought she saw Morris Brennon. Funny part was—she did. What a rush. Killing her gave him the hardest boner he could remember.

Belching, he eyed the pile of chicken parts next to a carton of milk and a big piece of apple pie on his tray. The intruder had better not spoil his appetite. Chewing chicken, he thought how he especially liked the breasts, the legs being his second favorite. But most of all, he liked thinking about the dead chicken and how he was eating its flesh. He only wished he could have been there to kill it, to chop off its head with an ax and watch its neck squirt blood. Like last night. *C&K all the way.* Last night he had a blast. Morris Brennon knew what he liked.

The cafeteria's double doors banged open. Morris kept eating, didn't lift his gaze to see who had entered. He already knew and didn't give a damn.

Sitting in the shadow of his jailer now, he could smell General Harrison's cologne. Dr. Larson was standing next to him, his arms folded across his chest. They had a lot of nerve acting like saints, keeping him here, a caged animal, some kind of exotic pet. But they weren't saints; they were worse than anyone, what they did, what they were doing now, to his brothers, the clones. He couldn't remember how many times he'd told Dr. Larson how he felt about that...and how much he hated the General, the master jailer with his high-and-mighty henchmen, the soldiers with all the guns.

Dr. Larson had tried to help him understand, but he'd failed. So they'd made a deal. Dr. Larson had promised him a free night out in exchange for his tolerance of the big shot General. A night away from this rat hole was a good thing. The General was another matter all together. At that, Morris spit out a chicken bone and glanced up. "What are you lookin' at?"

"Why did you kill her?" General Harrison barked.

Chomping on another piece of chicken, Morris ignored the question. He wasn't scared of the General. The asshole had no control over him, not like he had over his soldier clones.

"Speak up, mister."

"The bitch got what she deserved, so get out of my face." He guzzled some milk, spilling it down his chin and onto the front of his blood-spattered T-shirt. "Them other two just got in my way. A little sideline fun was all."

"What other two?" Dr. Larson asked, his face turning white.

"Don't matter none."

"Like hell," General Harrison shouted. "Just because Dr. Larson told you all about Morris Brennon, it doesn't mean you can go around acting like him."

"Who's acting?" Morris tossed another leg bone aside, stripped clean of the dead chicken. He smacked greasy lips and reached for another breast on the tray.

The General grabbed him by the wrist. "You son of a bitch."

Morris flexed his thick biceps, shot out of his chair, and went nose-to-nose with the General. "At least a son of a bitch is somebody's son. I'm nobody's son. I'm a duplicate, an exact copy of a killer, thanks to the doc and his goddamned enzyme crap. So don't put no shit on me. It's hereditary. You got what you asked for." He pushed the General away.

Harrison didn't look so tough all of a sudden with his eyes wide and his mouth hanging open. He stepped back from the table and scowled. "I'll...I'll lock you in isolation for that, mister."

Stiffening, Morris felt a sudden chill. Not isolation, anything but that. He'd never forgotten being locked up down there, caged like a wild dog, fed through a slit in the door, eating among his feces and the rats. And the basement was always so damn cold, the smell inescapable, like syrup. "I'd rather die," he said to the master jailer.

"That can be arranged."

Dr. Larson tugged on the General's arm. "Forget it." He indicated the door. "I'll talk to him."

"He's impossible." Harrison grumped and stalked away.

Larson sat in a chair across the table and stared at Morris.

Looking down at his food tray, he realized he'd lost his appetite for the dead chicken and even for that big piece of apple pie. "Shit." He sat, still not looking at Larson. All he wanted to do right now was kill the General, chop him open with an ax and rip out his heart.

"You've really pissed him off this time," Larson said.

"He's shit," Morris spat. "If it weren't for you, I'd have killed that bastard a long time ago."

"It's been hard, I know."

"You don't know nothin'."

"I've been like a father to you," Larson said softly.

Morris glared at him. Sure, Dr. Larson *had* been like a father, and a teacher, and a coach. From the teacher he'd learned reading, writing, and arithmetic, a little biology and science. From the coach he'd learned about sports, competition, and the ethics of fair play, a total waste of time. From the father he'd learned other things like keeping his room clean, brushing his teeth, doing his laundry. "You were a lousy father."

"I did my best to help you grow up normal."

"I'm stuck in this stinking shit hole surrounded by soldier boys and guns. How could anything be normal?"

"We gave you free run of the grounds."

"Big deal." Morris picked up a chicken leg, stared at it a moment as his mind went back to the tunnel, his favorite place on the grounds of Blythe Biotech. That was his secret place, a place to do secret things, to play the secret game, C&K. Catch them and Kill them.

C&K all the way, he would say.

Dr. Larson hadn't taught him the game. Nobody had. Somehow he just knew the rules, what few there were. *Rule number one*: be very quiet. *Rule number two*: strike without warning. *Rule number three*: enjoy. What a turn on.

In the tunnel, there were only frogs and snakes to C&K. A poker stick through the head was sufficient to win, but after a while, he got bored. It wasn't until after he'd snatched a butcher knife from the cafeteria kitchen that the real fun began. C&K got B&B. Bloodier and Better.

As Larson sat staring at him, Morris recalled the time when a stray cat had wandered into his tunnel. *C&K all the way*. He caught the damn thing and cut off its legs with the butcher knife. Wriggling helplessly in the mud, it meowed its fool head off. He watched it bleed to death, his pants bulging with excitement. And that wasn't the best part.

"What are you thinking about?" Larson asked.

"When I was fifteen...remember Sergeant Miller?"

"I try not to. That was horrible what you did to him."

"He deserved what he got." *Miller the Pillar* his buddies had called him. *Miller the Pile* was more like it. Recalling the bastard, Morris curled his upper lip. "Every time I walked through the courtyard, that pile of shit sergeant always made fun of me, called me a fatso and said I was ugly as the butt of a dog."

"What did I tell you about sticks and stones? You should've

ignored him."

"How could I? He kept saying shit like, *'Look at the big fatso,'* to his soldier pals. They'd laugh. And he'd go, *'Bet you'd have to tie a pork chop around his neck to get a dog to play with him.'* They'd all laugh some more. And, *'The fatso has to sneak up on the toilet to take a shit.'* Well they ain't laughing now."

"You didn't have to kill him."

Grinning, Morris remembered how perfectly he'd played the game that night, how he stalked *Miller the Pile* through the darkness. *C&K all the way.* Be very quiet: rule number one. He'd caught him coming out of the port-a-john, both hands busy with his zipper and buckle. Rule number two: strike without warning. He'd killed the bastard with the butcher knife right between the eyes. *Now who's laughin'?* Rule number three. *Ha, ha, ha!* He looked at Dr. Larson. "It was funny."

"The General wasn't amused." Larson frowned. "He locked you in isolation for that stunt."

"Everything changed after that."

"How?"

"I remember I was crouched behind the locked door and overheard the General telling you that the killer clone was out of control."

Leaning forward, Larson clasped his hands on the tabletop. "You weren't supposed to hear that."

"'What's a killer clone?' I must've asked you a hundred times."

"I know. Every time I came to take blood samples and made you piss in a cup."

"Like I said, you were a lousy father."

"I needed those things."

"And I needed to know why."

"I was afraid to tell you."

Morris tossed the chicken leg on the plate. "Was the truth so bad?"

"You took it pretty hard."

"How'd you like to find out you were some freak of nature, a duplicate of some fricken ax murderer who'd been electrocuted? Talk about a tough load to haul."

"That's why I didn't want you to know."

"Cloning, what a stupid thing to do."

"It's important research."

"For you maybe. What's in it for me?"

"You proved that Morris *wasn't* responsible for what he'd done. Killing was in his genes, preprogrammed since conception. The guy never had a chance for a normal life."

"You don't need to convince me of that. Look at the mess you made outta my life."

"But you got used to it."

Morris grinned. "You think?"

"Did I miss something?"

"When you told me about Karen Carlyle, brought that tape and all the articles she'd written about Morris Brennon, I finally understood. I knew who I was, why I was here, and what I was going to do. The bitch had to die. I promised her."

Larson shook his head. "You said there were two others. Did they deserve to die?"

"Does it matter?"

"What makes you think you're so important that you can get away with murder?"

Morris slammed his fist on the table. It wasn't that hard to understand. "I'm the first human clone, damn it. Morris Brennon, a celebrity, a fat cat on easy street."

Larson leaned back in his chair. "You're wrong."

Morris grimaced. *How could I be wrong?* "What are you talking about?"

"There was another clone...Geoffrey Scott Michaels...one that came before you, one I never told you about."

"Like hell. Where're you keeping him?"

"He got away."

"From this shit hole? How?"

Larson's eyes narrowed. "I thought I could change you, help you grow up to be a good person, a doctor perhaps, or a teacher. I had great hopes for you, but no matter what, you're still a killer...just like Morris."

Glaring at Larson, Morris growled, "When are you going to get it? I *am* Morris Brennon."

Larson sat upright. "And you killed Karen Carlyle to prove it."

"At least now she won't be tellin' no more lies." Sensing his appetite return, Morris took delight in his recollection of last night's events. He'd played the game perfectly. *C&K all the way.* But now he feared the master jailer would make good on his threat to lock him in isolation. That would be unacceptable. He'd rather be dead. Picking up a chicken leg and pointing it at Larson, Morris said flatly, "I can't stand being locked up, you know that."

"It's a possibility," Larson replied and stood.

"You better tell the General to back off."

"Harrison doesn't listen to me any more than you ever did." Larson headed for the door.

"What about another night out, huh?"

"You're not going anywhere, 1122B."

"My name is Morris Brennon, damn it."

"You still have to pay the consequences for killing Karen Carlyle." Larson stormed out.

Morris threw the chicken leg at the closing door. He'd better not be locked up in that shit hole again, especially after last night. Freedom felt good. He'd thought about not coming back. He wanted to keep going, to get as far away from Blythe as possible, but when he thought about it really hard, he figured this was the only home he'd ever known. This was where he felt safe. The outside world scared the hell out of him.

Besides, he couldn't leave his brothers behind. He knew they were feeling the same as him; after all, they had his genes too. Surely they despised the master jailer for confining them down there in that cold basement room.

Grabbing another piece of chicken, Morris growled and thought about the General.

C&K all the way.

Chapter Thirty-Nine

New York City

Raindrops spattered on the plate-glass windows of Stan Thompson's 27th floor office as he sat at his desk. His rain-slicked overcoat and dripping umbrella hung on a rack by the door, the one he'd just slammed shut on his way in. The foul weather matched his mood. He leaned back in his overstuffed chair and scowled at the piles of manuscripts surrounding him, *the slush pile* they called it in his business. There seemed to be no end to the relentless flow of paper—and rain.

Thunder boomed.

He turned in his chair and looked out the rain-streaked window. Madison Square Park sopped below him. Wind thrashed the trees, and pedestrians scurried along, ducking under umbrellas and coat sleeves. Stan gritted his teeth as he returned his attention to the problem at hand: Jeff Jordan. Who did he think he was trying to fool? It was obvious he wanted to get away with a copyright infringement.

Just then, the door swung open. His secretary strode in, her hairdo wilted by rain, her drab beige pantsuit and blouse looking just as dreary as the day outside. A pen teetered behind her right ear, and a dainty pair of reading glasses balanced low on the bridge of her nose. Her eyes pierced him with a disapproving glare, probably because of his inappropriate entrance, which was entirely unlike him.

"Here's the last of it." She held out a stack of paper and didn't smile. "It's the same all the way through. Jeff Jordan did a good job of copying the story, the chapters and scenes, they're all the same. The text is different...but still pretty close."

He pointed to an unoccupied corner of his desktop.

She set down the papers and glared at him.

"Thank you...and...well..." He showed her a puppy dog face. "I'm sorry about my temper tantrum. This whole thing is just so bizarre."

Her eyes softened. "So what if this one got away? There's another to be found somewhere in these piles." She wagged a finger around the cluttered room, a slight smile on her face. "You never know what talent, what stroke of genius lies hidden in this garbage heap."

Slush pile. Stan thought to correct her but chose not to ruin her first smile of the day. She was right about one thing. Most of it *was* garbage. Maybe one out of a thousand deserved consideration for publishing, like Jeff Jordan's manuscript, *The Lost Diamonds*, the one he'd pilfered from some poor dead author.

Thunder boomed again.

"Take a letter," he told his secretary. "Dear Mr. Jordan."

Grabbing the pen from her ear, she sat in a chair opposite his desk and crossed her legs, legal pad ready. "Give him hell, sir."

Standing, he crossed his arms and stood with his feet spread. "I thought I had seen all the scams before, but this one is the most flagrant of all. You didn't even try to cover up your hoax, to hide it in some way, like changing the title."

He looked at the ream of paper setting on the corner of his desk: The Library of Congress, Copyright Certificate for *The Lost Diamonds* by William Tuliver, July 1970.

"But we have foiled your little scam." He paused in front of the stormy window. "New paragraph...In the normal course of investigating a manuscript for representation, we stumbled upon the facts. *The Lost Diamonds* already has a registered copyright.

"Of course, it's not unusual to find like titles, but we wanted to be sure the stories were different and investigated further. We requisitioned copies of the certificate and manuscript from the United States Copyright Office." He picked up the stack of paper and thumbed the pages. "Funny thing. The book is almost an exact match to your manuscript. Of course, you already knew that."

He gave his secretary a sly glance, squinting one eye, but she was busy writing and didn't see him gloating. "New paragraph...And you also know the author's name...William Tuliver, your main character. Before his death, he transferred the copyright to a Mr. Geoffrey Scott Michaels, whomever that is, but I'm sure you knew that too."

Feeling as though he had solved the world's greatest mystery, Stan took a breath. "New paragraph...In light of the fore-stated findings, this agency has decided not to represent you."

Thunder cracked again.

Chapter Forty

The Clone Room

In the darkest part of Blythe Biotech, down in Basement Level Two, at the far end of a hallway, Dr. Larson stepped off the elevator. He heard the familiar sound of bubbling water, a soothing sound that could lull a man to sleep, but he knew that was just an illusion, a mask on the face of danger.

Shivering from the chilly air, he flipped up the collar of his lab coat as he approached two heavily armed soldiers standing guard in front of a steel door. Breath vapors wisped from their lips.

"Evening, Dr. Larson," one guard said.

Larson nodded. "Let's get this over with."

The guards stepped aside.

Standing at the door, Larson looked over the thick steel panels, painted black, and the huge chrome rivets that held them in place. It was the last obstacle between the clones and Blythe Biotech's complete annihilation. He straightened the lapels of his lab coat and turned to a control panel with a flashing green LED.

"Everything is quiet in there, sir," a guard said.

Keycard in hand, Larson took a calming breath and inserted the card into the slot. A solenoid clicked. An electric motor whined. Mechanisms engaged and levers moved. The door slid open with a grating sound.

He stood at the opening to a short hallway crisscrossed by dozens of red laser beams. Beyond them, another steel door remained closed.

On a keypad to his right, he punched in his user code. Resonators clunked. The red lasers went out, and bright ceiling lights flickered on revealing black walls dotted with diamond-cut laser ports. The air felt much colder in here, the burbling louder. He could hear the hum of distant water pumps. Stepping forward, the door slid closed behind him. The locks clicked. His neck hairs prickled. No man's land. He looked up at the cyanide gas jets, Blythe's last line of defense should the clones escape their vats. Quickly, he moved forward to the next door and its keypad terminal.

A green LED glowed. He knew that meant the computer sensors and circuits monitoring the room beyond the door were intact and functioning properly. However, because the clones could think and reason to possibly circumvent the security system, there was also a video monitor he could check.

Flicking the switch that turned it on, he carefully worked the panel-mounted joystick, panning the camera across the room he was about to enter. Green LEDs twinkled throughout the dimly lit span and reflected off rows of glass cylinders lining the walls and huge glass vats set on the main floor. The clones were sleeping, exactly what he'd expected this time of night, but something he never took for granted. If one clone got out, they could all get out. If they all got out, it would result in mass murder on a Biblical scale.

Satisfied everything was safe, he slipped his keycard into the slot. With a click, the door slid open. He stepped out of the passageway and onto a platform overlooking the clone room. Behind him, the ceiling lights flickered out, and the red lasers blinked on with a buzzing sound. The door slid closed and locked. General Harrison had said he'd never lose another clone. This heightened security proved that the General meant what he'd said.

Larson stood on the platform overlooking the vats and inhaled. The smell wasn't entirely unpleasant, but sweet—like maple syrup, so thick that he could taste it in the cold moist air. Some days the sweet smell made his stomach sick, days when the clones were especially active in their vats, stirring up the fluid more than usual.

But keeping the room temperature a chilly thirty-three degrees made the smell more tolerable.

By the dim light, he could see the mist spilling from the vats and swirling down to the floor where it drifted knee-deep like an autumn fog. The phenomenon was due to the warm fluid in the vats, which the computers regulated at a constant 98.6 degrees, reacting with the room's cold air.

During the day, things were much different in the clone room. Because the ceiling lamps were on, the mist would refract light into colorful rainbows—clonebows, they were called. And the place was noisy, filled with activity. Teachers attended the clones. Video monitors presented their studies. Reading, writing, and arithmetic classes were followed by intensive military training videos. The clones learned all the intricacies of M-16 assault rifles, laser guided rocket launchers, tank warfare and even hand-to-hand combat, the most effective use of the bayonet, the quickest way to kill a man. Everything from battlefield strategy to digging latrines was covered, over and over, day in and day out.

No one taught the clones anything about religion, philosophy, history, or family values. Weapon systems didn't need to know that shit, General Harrison had said.

Larson checked the environmental scanner—*NORMAL*—then made his way down a steel staircase to the fog-swept floor. Above him, scaffolds and catwalks hung from the ceiling on cables and traversed over the vats. Conduits ran the length and width of the ceiling, two hundred feet in either direction, carrying wires and tubes from the LSC, the Life Support Computer, to the eight-foot-tall glass vats and the smaller cylinders lining the walls.

Pumps hummed. Liquid gurgled.

On his left, a black electrical transformer sat darkly behind a wire-mesh barrier. Thick black cables fanned out from the transformer, sending power to various components in the clone room. A large sign warned: *KEEP AWAY - HIGH VOLTAGE.* The eye sockets of a skull and crossbones symbol stared at him as if daring him to come too close.

A few steps forward, he came to the LSC's main control panel, which gleamed hospital white, stretched twenty-five feet long and stood waist high. Its monitors, lights, and gauges glowed and pulsed with a mesmerizing rhythm. Twenty-four hours a day, seven days a week, this electronic sentry stood watch over the nation's newest weapon system.

Larson took a moment to quickly scan the instruments monitoring the clones' vital signs: things like heartbeat, temperature, blood pressure, and breathing rate. Each clone had a number similar to the one he'd given 1122B. Arranged in twenty-one vertical rows, twenty-five numbers deep on the console, each number had two LEDs next to it, one red and one green. Row after row, the LEDs glowed green. A glowing red LED meant a clone was in trouble, possibly life threatening. It had happened before. Things didn't always work right. Pumps failed, heaters shorted out, filters clogged.

Drowning clones were not a pretty sight. They'd thrash around in the honey-colored fluid, straining against the shackles that held their feet to the bottom of the vat. It happened to 1334A. Its red LED had suddenly started flashing. As technicians tried to assess the problem, the clone fought for its life. Larson swore he could hear it screaming, a fluid-choked guttural kind of scream. Its eyes were wide with terror, its teeth bared in anguish. Technicians worked frantically, trying to unclog an air pump screen. 1334A was turning blue. A bolt broke. Threads stripped. The clone clawed at the glass wall of the cylinder, fingers bleeding, until finally it went limp and bobbed on its shackles. An acceptable loss.

Shaking off the memory, Larson scanned a row of meters on another panel. They told him the temperature and acidity levels of the fluid in the vats. This was no ordinary fluid. The Oxygenated Fluorocarbon Emulsion Fluid, or OXYFEM, gave off the sweet odor that permeated the air. Clones breathed the fluid in and out of their lungs, taking in the oxygen and releasing carbon dioxide. Laced with the latest version of his enzyme, BZ-47, fluorocarbons in the

OXYFEM passed the clones' waste products into a filtering system. Cleaned of feces, urine, CO_2 and even excess salt, the OXYFEM was then re-oxygenated by fresh air from the pumps, like water in a fish aquarium.

Looking at a pressure gauge, he confirmed the correct flow of air from the pumps to the OXYFEM. The needle vibrated in the green band. Rising and popping air bubbles filled the room with the burbling sound.

Larson leaned against the console and looked over the misty vats. Back when this all began, Colonel Harrison had told him to get rid of the surrogates. He found the technology for that harder to come by than perfecting the duplication factor itself. But the Pentagon pumped in money, and with the help of scientists from Cal Tech, they'd successfully engineered the first mechanical womb. Surrogates were no longer needed. And the clones could be kept in these vats until it was time for their emergence, when they were matured and trained.

But even with that accomplishment, mass-producing clones had more hurdles to clear. The duplication factor could not crunch time enough to meet the Pentagon's eight-year criteria. It wasn't until he'd reformulated his enzyme that things began to progress. Fed massive quantities of anabolic steroids and the growth hormone Thyroxin, the clones grew faster. In spite of the risks of irritable and aggressive behavior, liver problems, jaundice, and heart palpitations, he had filled the clone room vats with 524 duplicates of 1122B, aka Morris Brennon.

Never mind the long-term effects, General Harrison had said. Liver failure, cancerous tumors, and enlarged hearts some twenty years from now were of no concern to him. Twenty years was a respectable service life for a weapon system. Larson didn't have a problem with that. The clones weren't real people anyway. They didn't have to live a long time.

He turned to the suction gauge on the main bank of filters. The needle quivered in the *safe* zone. The LSC had everything under control. He checked the digital clock. *Emergence* was scheduled for December 31, 1999 at 11:59 PM. The hours and minutes counted down a second at a time, the numbers glowing blue on the console, only five months before the start of a new millennium, the twenty-first century, and a new era for the military. That's what General Harrison had told him. An army of killer clones would be under his command.

Something bigger than big was about to begin.

Chapter Forty-One

Washington DC

A black Lincoln Continental idled at the curb in front of the Pentagon. Twin American flags, clipped to masts on the front fenders, swayed lazily in the breeze. General Harrison returned a salute from the driver who held open the back door. After ducking inside, Harrison nodded to his youngest son, the only son he had left...after Vietnam. Colonel Billy Harrison sat with his arm propped on the seat divider and a satchel on his lap. "How's it going, Pops?"

Billy always called him Pops instead of Dad or Father.

"I'll let you know after we're done with the President." The door closed. General Harrison worked a switch on the panel. A motor hummed, raising a glass partition that sealed them off from the driver.

"I don't think he'll bend on this," Billy said coolly.

Harrison didn't reply. He focused his eyes on the road ahead as the car pulled away from the curb and joined the flow of traffic. His mind was 560 miles away, on Blythe Biotech and his clones. If the President vetoed the Bennett Bill, Harrison would be forced to use them.

"He won't give up his power as Commander in Chief," Billy said. "I wouldn't if I were him."

Harrison looked at his son. The silver eagles on Billy's collars seemed to clash with his boyish face. He looked much younger than forty-five. Colorful ribbons adorned the left breast of his jacket, and his shoes were spit-polished black. In that uniform, he looked as sharp as Daniel Harrison had looked—back then—before a Viet Cong sniper's bullet killed him.

"Your brother and 58,000 soldiers died because four Presidents," he held up four fingers, "failed in their responsibilities as Commander in Chief. They succumbed to Congressional pressures, special interests, the news media, and campus unrest. Their *popular vote* was more important to them than the soldiers that wallowed in those stinking rice paddies. They couldn't make up their minds, escalate, deescalate, attack and retreat, jab and cover, pussyfooting around until we lost the damn war. They don't deserve the power to decide the course of battle."

"But the—"

"The Bennett Bill will combine our armed forces into one fighting unit and establish a new rank and order of leadership. The President will be out of the loop. He should never have been there in the first place."

"A flaw in the Constitution, perhaps?"

"If professional military men had control of the Vietnam War instead of those ass-kissing politicians, Daniel wouldn't be dead."

"That's been eating at you for a long time, Pops."

"And now it's time to do something about it. When I take over, we'll fix this screwed up system once and for all. By the time you take my place, the hard part will be over. Have you got everyone lined up?"

"All except Admiral Griggs. He said *no* again."

Harrison shrugged. "Then he goes on the hit list."

"The clones had better be able to pull this off," Billy said with taut eyebrows.

"Of course they will. They don't have any of that *Mom and apple pie* Americanism. They'd just as soon kill the Admiral as a cockroach."

"And the President?" Billy asked. "Kill him too?"

"If he's stupid enough to veto this bill."

The car hummed down the highway. Turning his eyes to the satchel in his lap, Billy fingered the strap. "What do you suppose Mom would have said about all this?"

Harrison bit his lower lip. "I sometimes think, that if she were still alive, I wouldn't have bothered trying to fix any of this. I would have had better things to do...with Beth...and you wouldn't have had to listen to me complain about losing her *and* your brother."

"Well, *I'm* still with you, Pops."

Harrison nodded but said nothing, not wanting to get all mushy about it.

Turning to the window, Billy sniffled. "There was a time when I wondered if you even noticed me. I mean...well...it seemed as though Daniel and Mom got all your attention."

"I didn't—"

"You thought about them all the time, Pops. Still do, I know."

"But—"

"I felt like I had to compete with them for your affection. First Daniel, and then Mom, they each took a big piece of you with them." He turned and faced his father. "Well...in case you didn't know, I miss them too, Pops. But unlike you, I stopped grieving a long time ago. I went on with my life."

"I didn't realize..." Harrison rubbed his cheek. For the last thirty years, his grief over Daniel's loss had consumed him. The mourning process never ended, which kept Daniel alive in his heart. But ten years ago, when Beth died of cancer, he was overwhelmed with grief for both of them. His only release from the sorrow was the retribution he planned against the system. Things were going to change, but in the process, he'd failed the only son he had left. "It's been tough for both of us, son."

Billy smiled. "Everything is all right now, Pops. Since the project at Blythe, I've put it all behind me. If what we're doing is right or wrong, I don't care. We're together now. I'm with you on this because I love you."

"I know." Harrison braced himself as the car made a hard left turn. The White House was just up ahead. 1600 Pennsylvania Avenue, their future address.

At the gate to the White House driveway, Secret Service agents, dressed in dark suits, their coats unbuttoned, approached the car. General Harrison lowered the partition. After examining IDs and confirming their appointment to see the President, the agents waved the car through the gate. Tires screeched as the car stopped at the entrance.

"Here goes nothing." Billy pulled himself out of the car. Harrison followed his son into the White House. After a short wait, the President's aide led them into the Oval Office.

"Morning, gentlemen," the President said in a Southerly lilt. "Make yourselves comfortable." He motioned to plush chairs in front of his formidable desk. Behind him, crossed flags, one with the Presidential seal and the other, Old Glory, hung in limp silence. Missing was the entourage that usually attends a bill signing: no Senator Bennett, no legislators, no table with a dozen pens laid out, and no press photographers and reporters. This lack of formality stabbed Harrison's chest, sharp as any blade.

The President seemed relaxed, sitting with his hands clasped on the desktop, a formal document spread out in front of him, complete with the presidential seal. He'd combed his graying hair straight back. Thin-framed reading glasses sat low on the bridge of his nose. A slight smile accentuated his clean-shaven face. His eyes shifted back and forth between his guests.

Being in this office was nothing new to General Harrison. Many times he had sat in this chair, and in front of different Presidents. His position at the Pentagon had a lot to do with his access to the Oval Office.

The Chief of Staff entered through a side door. He carried with him a file folder. "Let's get on with it, shall we?" He set the folder in front of the President.

Billy handed his father a similar file, which he had pulled from his satchel. General Harrison didn't open it. He set it on his lap. "I want you to know, Mr. President, a lot of time and effort has gone into drafting the Bennett Bill."

"I see," the President replied. "But you fellas missed the mark, don't you think?" His Southern drawl was tainted with a hint of sarcasm.

"On the contrary." Harrison grumped. "The numbers show a significant reduction in operating expenses with a combined military structure. And the simplified chain of command will boost battlefield efficiency to a level we've only dreamed of."

The Chief of Staff, standing next to the President, huffed. "It also gives the military too much power, with no checks and balances. That's not what our forefathers had in mind when they founded this country."

"They made a mistake," Billy said bluntly.

The President leaned back in his chair, eyeing the Colonel. "Interesting concept...but I'm curious about one thing. How did you boys get enough support to push this bill through Congress?" He shifted his glare to the General.

Harrison cleared his throat. "Do you remember the boys who went to Vietnam, the protesters who flocked to the capitol, the students who burned their draft cards, and the silent majority? Where do you think they are today, Mr. President?" Harrison leaned forward. "I'll tell you where they are. They're sitting in the Senate and the House of Representatives. And all the way down through the political scheme of things, some became governors and others are mayors of large cities and small towns. Still others are state legislators and county administrators. None of them have forgotten the fiasco of Vietnam. Today, they are calling on the Presidency to account for those mistakes."

"The Vietnam War was a difficult conflict," the President said, pulling his glasses from his face. "But take a look at the Gulf War. The system worked there, and we won that war, quite decisively I might add."

Billy shook his head. "I'm sorry, Mr. President. You're

mistaken. We went in and kicked some ass, sure. But when the political agenda was met, namely the liberation of Kuwait, the military was put back on a leash. We should have been allowed to go all the way into Baghdad and take out Saddam Hussein. But the Commander-in-Chief back then buckled under the pressure of the politically correct and left the bastard in power. The Gulf War is just another example of politicians shackling the military. It's going to take another war before the military can accomplish what they wanted to do from the git-go."

"Face it, Mr. President," Harrison said. "For all the right reasons, the American people don't want you to have the power of Commander-in-Chief anymore. Too many good soldiers get killed. So it has to end right here, today."

The President pinched the bridge of his nose and set his glasses back on. "You're right, gentlemen. Mistakes were made in the past, but that doesn't mean the system is at fault, only those charged with running it properly. Your bill is going into the garbage...where it belongs." With a stroke of his pen, he signed the veto document in front of him.

The Bennett Bill was dead.

General Harrison stood, hot blood coursing through his veins. He thought of his clones and what they would have to do to rectify the mistake. "A decision you'll certainly regret, Mr. President."

Chapter Forty-Two

Chicago

Ⓘn his auto repair shop, Jeff stepped back from under the hood of a Ford Taurus. He eyed a fuel pressure gauge attached to the fuel rail. "Give her a try, Lou."

The engine cranked with a moaning sound that told Jeff she was in bad shape. She didn't wheeze or puff. She didn't even try to fire. Jeff always used the word *she* or *her* whenever he referred to an automobile. Those mechanical marvels possessed wondrous form, like women, and they were just as complicated in design, with an uncanny mastery of power and motion. But on the other hand, like this little three-liter job, a car could be stubborn, even vengeful in her refusal to cooperate. Last night, this one had left her owner walking.

"That's enough, Lou."

The starter went silent. An air wrench rattled from under a pickup truck at the other end of the shop. Lingering hydrocarbon from the tune-up bay tainted the air. The phone rang.

Jeff shook his head. "The fuel pressure's okay. Do a compression test." He dashed for the phone, spent a few minutes talking with a customer about the clutch they were putting in his pickup. Halfway through that conversation the other line rang, which he put on hold, and a parts driver brought in a steering gearbox for the Chevy on lift number two.

"That's right," Jeff said into the phone. "Six hundred bucks." He inspected the gearbox and signed the parts driver's invoice. "Is four o'clock tomorrow all right?"

"I'll pick it up then." He hung up.

After that, Jeff answered the call holding on line two. It was a telemarketer. "Have I got a deal for you."

"No thanks." Jeff hung up and headed back to the Taurus where Lou was unscrewing a compression gauge from cylinder number four. "Looks like she's jumped time."

Jeff gave the car a quick inspection. Her radiator seams were infested with corrosion. The windshield was cracked, the left fender dented, and the original paint color was hard to determine. The seats were stained and ripped, and the carpet, what he could see of it through the trash, probably hadn't seen a vacuum for the last fifty thousand miles. He shook his head. *Junk.* "I'll write an estimate."

"Jeff," a mechanic called out from bay number three where a dented Toyota's charging system had failed. Jim was trying to fix it.

"What's the problem?"

"Are you sure this is the right regulator for this piece of shit?"

Jeff hurried toward the Toyota, his hip protesting with a needlelike jab of pain. The aspirin he'd taken earlier was wearing off. Examining the new regulator, he could clearly see that it didn't look like the original part. "What part number is it?"

"VR338 it says here." Jim handed him a bright orange box with a blue stripe down the middle. It had a silver diamond logo with *Diamond Auto Parts* printed across it in gold.

Every time he saw that logo, every time he held a box from Diamond Auto Parts, he got that same feeling, like whenever he looked into Lois's hazel eyes, or when he sat on the bench in front of the fountain in Paradise Park. The feeling made his stomach turn over. He took in a slow breath to quell a sudden sense of misplacement. He imagined himself standing in the corporate office atop the Diamond building, taking in the view of the city and holding a woman in his arms, her hazel eyes welling with tears, her red hair shining, just like he'd written in his book.

"Is it going to work or not?" Jim asked.

Jeff started. He wondered if Jim had seen him slip into his little trip that left him dizzy and short of breath. If so, he must've thought his boss was loony. Jeff's personal problems were something he'd always kept from his employees. He matched the pin configuration of the new Diamond Auto Parts regulator with those in the wiring harness. They matched. "Give it a try."

The phone rang again. "Damn." He ran back to his office.

After talking to a lady about a noise she thought she'd heard in her engine last week, he started typing up an estimate to repair the Ford Taurus when the mailman walked in wearing his neatly pressed uniform with black stripes running down the leg seams. R*acing stripes*, he called them.

"Howdy." The mailman set a handful of mail on the counter, and as he did every day, he picked through the bowl of candies, and then left as quickly as he came. Must have been the racing stripes.

He looked over the completed estimate for the Ford and thought about calling the customer but decided to look through the mail on the counter first. Mixed in with the usual bills and the fabulous credit card offers, he spotted a letter from Stan Thompson, a discovery that took precedence over everything. Heart racing, Jeff peeled open the envelope.

As he read the words Stan Thompson had written, he thought the air in the room had suddenly vaporized into some kind of poisonous gas that left him gasping. "*Seen all the scams before...cover up your hoax...The Lost Diamonds, copyright...William Tuliver...Geoffrey Scott Michaels...this agency has decided not to represent you, not to represent you, not to represent you.*"

Jeff's knees wobbled. What the hell was this all about? He read the letter again, still unable to grasp its meaning. *Hoax? What Hoax?* He leaned against the counter, shaking, wondering how William Tuliver could have been the author. William Tuliver was the main character in his book. Stan Thompson must have made a mistake. Surely he was confused. The main character couldn't be the author. Besides, William Tuliver wasn't even a real person.

Then Jeff remembered the news broadcast in the clubhouse. Morris Brennon turned out to be a real person. There was no doubt about that. And what if William Tuliver was just as real as Morris Brennon? Did that mean Sally Mayfield was real, too? And what about Andrew Cobb and *Mothers' Tears*? What if they all were real? What if *The Lost Diamonds* wasn't fiction? That could mean only one thing. Jeff Jordan wasn't real. Jeff Jordan was the hoax. Jeff Jordan was the freak, the freak, the freak...

His knees buckled. Everything went black.

The next thing he knew, a bright light shined above him. An antiseptic smell irritated his nose, or perhaps it was the tubes coming out of his nostrils. Panic raced through his muddled mind. Where was he? What happened? He tried to claw at the tubes, but his hands wouldn't move. They were tied down. He squinted against the blinding light, and writhing, he felt someone grab his arms, a cold and clammy grip. As he fought to free himself, he heard a voice.

"Son?"

It was a familiar voice. *Dad?* "Dad!"

"He's coming out of it," a woman's voice said.

"Mom?" Jeff struggled harder.

"Now, son, take it easy," Dad said.

The straps hurt his wrists. He bared his teeth and flailed his head back and forth. "What are you doing? Let me go. Let me go, damn it." He kicked but got no response from his legs. They were tied down, too.

"Jeff," a woman's voice said. "It's okay."

"Lois?"

"I'm right here, Jeff. Try to relax."

He felt his heart banging in his chest and thought it would explode. His head ached. In the bright light, a faint silhouette appeared above him, hazy, featureless.

"Where am I?"

Something cold landed on his forehead, a wet towel perhaps, or ice cubes in a plastic bag. It felt good. He wanted more, some on his face and on his neck and chest. He was on fire. The bright light was burning him. He squeezed his eyes shut, hoping it would go away.

"Stay with us, son," Mom said. "Stay awake."

Mom the disbeliever. "What happened?"

"You've had a nasty fall. A concussion maybe. Open your eyes, son."

Jeff trudged through the muck in his mind. A nasty fall? Did he trip over an air hose? Did he fall off a cliff? How did he have a nasty fall? Where had he been? What had he been doing?

Slowly, a foggy recollection of his office came to mind. In the blur of his thoughts, he saw a letter.

His eyes blew open. "The letter. Where's the letter?"

"I have it," Dad said. "Must've given you a horrible fright, the nerve of this guy Stan Thompson. Who the hell does he think he is anyway?"

Things started coming back, slowly at first, and then in a whirl. Stan Thompson had discovered something wrong with Jeff Jordan. And somehow, William Tuliver had everything to do with it. Jeff closed his eyes again, blotting out the bright light and leaving him with questions that battered his brain. Who was William Tuliver? Where was he? Did *The Lost Diamonds* hold the clues to finding him?

"Open your eyes, son," Dad said in a voice that sounded hollow and distant.

"Stay awake," Mom pleaded.

As if every bridge he'd ever crossed had just collapsed behind him and every road he'd ever traveled came to a dead end, he now felt trapped somewhere between Jeff Jordan and William Tuliver. He mentally retraced his steps, wondering if he had missed a crucial turn or some critical signpost that could have led him in a different direction. Or was the letter from Stan Thompson exactly that: a new direction to go, a new road to travel? Where would it take him in the end?

"Open your eyes, son. Stay with us."

Chapter Forty-Three

Menard Correctional Center

Detective Spence Ritter had been driving for an hour and forty minutes. The rented car's seat felt like a concrete slab. His back ached, and the hum of the engine and whining tires made him groggy. Glancing at the empty thermos on the seat beside him, he wished he hadn't downed all his coffee on the flight from O'Hare to St. Louis. He hated long trips. But the Karen Carlyle case had taken a bizarre twist. After three days mulling over fingerprints and crime scene photos with the precinct brass, he decided to pay a visit to Menard Correctional Center. The evidence warranted retracing the last moments of Morris Brennon's life.

The way things looked, the killer had somehow ducked the electric chair. Ritter swallowed dryly. He had to find out how that could have happened. Did the wrong man end up in the chair that day? Maybe Morris Brennon switched cells and clothes with another prisoner who looked like him. Or perhaps his sentence was commuted to life, the record failing to show that, and he could have made parole then returned to his old ways. Ritter gripped the steering wheel tighter. And why did Morris kill Karen Carlyle?

The car rumbled over a bridge, crossed the fog-shrouded Mississippi River, and rolled into the quaint town of Chester, Illinois, home of Popeye the Sailor Man. Morning sunshine hadn't heated the autumn air enough to lift the haze that swirled through the streets. He turned left and sped toward the prison, a half-mile up river.

Moments later, in the prison parking lot, he stopped in front of a hundred-year-old redstone building. It stood like a dark monstrosity on the foggy bank of the Mississippi. A hot flush crept up his neck. Only the gruesome image of Karen Carlyle's hacked up body suppressed his urge to turn around and speed away. He shut off the engine and got out of the car.

Standing at the granite steps, he peered up at the black doors leading into the armpit of Illinois' correctional system. They'd called it Menard State Prison back when Morris Brennon was here. Its present title, Menard Correctional Center, did nothing to lift its dismal aura.

He looked up the four redbrick columns that reached to a third floor balcony. There, another four columns jutted up to a steeply gabled roof. Narrow barred windows stared down on him like the weeping eyes of an old man. In stony silence, Ritter rubbed gooseflesh on his arms. Morris Brennon's secret was hiding somewhere inside. He took a deep breath and started up the steps.

A guard met him at the door. His uniform, a brown shirt with matching tie and tan trousers, looked freshly pressed. A black nightstick hung from his thick belt, and a big ring of keys dangled there, too. He didn't smile.

"Detective Spence Ritter, Chicago PD." Ritter flipped his badge out for inspection.

"This way, detective."

After a quick pat down and metal-detection scan, he surrendered his Glock .40 and followed the stoic guard through several iron gates. There were no windows where the guard took him. Their footsteps echoed off block walls painted lime green. The whole place was dimly lit and smelled like dirty socks. When the last gate creaked shut, a sudden sense of loss swept over him. The thought of all the things that couldn't be done in here numbed his insides.

Turning down another corridor, he moved quickly past the cafeteria clamoring with noisy prisoners and smelling of greasy bacon, dish soap, and floor wax, enough to kill any man's appetite.

"Right in there, detective." The guard motioned him through a big steel door edged with rivets. It clanged closed behind him, the echo reverberating as if trapped forever within these prison walls.

But this hallway was much different from the others he had just traveled. The floor was tiled in alternating black and white squares, and the doors lining the corridor were trimmed in finely engraved cherry wood. Shifting his eyes around, he got a sense of time travel, of being suddenly in a different place, a brighter part of Menard Correctional Center, if that were possible.

A few yards down the hall, a short wimp of a man stepped from a doorway on the right. He wore a black vest over a white shirt with broad collars and stood with one hand buried in a pocket of his gray slacks, the other holding an unlit pipe to his lips. He had jet-black hair and piercing eyes that looked Ritter up and down as if sizing him up for a fight. "Detective Ritter, I presume."

"The one and only."

"Welcome to Menard CC. Hope you had a pleasant trip."

"I nearly fell asleep." Ritter shook the little man's hand and thought how he looked more like a bank teller than a jailer. His grip was firm, his nails well manicured, and his smile pleasant. "You must be Mr. Foster."

"You can call me Brent, assistant warden and water boy. Mr. Cowan is away at Stateville. Before he left, he filled me in on your concerns about Morris Brennon. Come in. Coffee?"

"If it's strong."

The office looked like an old-time parlor where men of wealth might have gathered to converse and smoke cigars. Antique walnut furniture with flower print upholstery flanked a massive hardwood desk. Tall brass floor lamps glowed softly. The air smelled of rich coffee. Brent poured a cup. Ritter was surprised at how quickly he felt at ease with the little man.

They sat together on a davenport in the middle of the room facing barred windows. Mr. Foster talked about Menard CC, going on and on about the history of the place, the crowded conditions, and the most common complaints of the inmates. "They call them inmates now, you know...instead of convicts."

Ritter took a sip of coffee, unimpressed.

Foster didn't light his pipe but held on to it as if it were a security blanket. Fifteen minutes flew by before Ritter got down to talking about Karen Carlyle's death and his discovery of Morris Brennon's fingerprints at the crime scene.

"There are two things that bother me." Ritter put his coffee cup on the table. "One, Morris Brennon was executed in 1969 and we have a perp with the same prints, a one in sixty four billion chance, or two, he wasn't executed and you guys let him out of prison."

"I assure you," Brent said with certainty, "he was executed. I've called on an eye witness who can set you straight on that." Clamping the idle pipe in his teeth, he handed Ritter a file folder. "I also had this brought up from archives, just for you. However, before you get yourself all dusty going through it, I'd like you to meet him."

"Is he a credible witness?"

"Impeccably." Foster raised his voice. "Fred, you can come in now."

An old man appeared in the doorway. He held a brown felt hat in both hands. His thinning gray hair was mussed. Dressed as though he'd been fishing, he wore tan pants and a green flannel shirt. A bushy gray mustache under his bulbous nose made his face look heavy. He cast a wary nod in the detective's direction. "That him?"

Foster turned to Ritter. "Fred Flanagan was Morris's cellblock guard back then. He's agreed to take time out from his busy retirement to meet with us today." He waved the old man in. "Please. Sit down, Fred. Tell Detective Ritter your story, just like you told me."

The old man shuffled in and plopped into a chair by the desk. Fog-filtered sunlight through the barred window illuminated his weathered face with an eerie glow.

Ritter said nothing as his interest in the old man spiked.

Settling back in the chair, Flanagan set his hat on his knee and fixed his eyes on the detective. "Well, it was September 5th as I recall, 1969. I remember the sun comin' up that day, big and bright on the horizon, like it hadn't a clue 'bout what was going to happen." Flanagan's eyes narrowed. "Ever seen a man fry?"

A tingle prickled the hairs on Ritter's neck. "No."

Fred smirked. "Well, I have. It was near on 6:45 in the morning. Warden Evans came into the room where 'bout twenty witnesses includin' myself, and a slug of reporters had gathered around. He said to us then, *'Gentlemen, there'll be no more smoking and you're to be as quiet as though you were in a church.'* I remember thinkin', *Just get on with it.* Morris Brennon's time had come. Ya see, I had promised the bastard I was gonna watch him burn in the chair."

From that Ritter understood the men hated each other.

"So me and the rest of them followed the warden out across the prison yard to Cellblock B. We went in and sat in three rows of chairs facing a glass wall. This room we was in was kinda dark, and I can still remember the smell of fresh paint. Yeah, we had to spruce the place up a bit. Hadn't been used in eight years before this party." The old man's eyebrows arched. "Morris Brennon was a special case, ya know."

Nodding, Ritter was well aware of Morris's notoriety.

Fred grabbed his hat and leaned forward. "It was 7:10 when the room on the other side of the glass wall flooded with light. Darn near blinded me 'til my eyes got used to it. Then I could see the big wooden chair, black as coal and lookin' like some kind of a God-awful throne. I heard gasping in the room around me but paid the wimps no mind. I was there for the show." He inspected the brim of his hat before he went on. "It wasn't but a minute later when Morris Brennon came into that room. The ceiling light was gleaming off his bald head. He was with a chaplain and four uniformed guards. They'd split his pant legs up to his knees and cut off the sleeves of his shirt. But they'd left the shackles on him, by golly. I'd warned them, don't take no chances with Morris Brennon.

"Well, without even hesitatin', Morris walks right up to that chair and pulls himself into it like he was gonna get a haircut. The guards strapped him down and offered him a black hood. He refused and turned a gnarly smile at us sitting there behind the glass wall. *See ya all later*, he said, whatever that meant. An asshole to the end, he was."

Ritter fidgeted in his chair, beginning to feel uneasy.

"It only took a minute to get him ready and read the warrant. Then they zapped him with twenty four hundred volts, a sight I'll never forget. He started shakin' some at first, then more and more 'til it got so bad he was thrashing against the straps. I started tremblin' at the look of him. Then his mouth flared open and his tongue stuck out like it got swelled up and turned to stone. My stomach cramped, but I couldn't take my eyes away. He was wailing somethin' awful. Toward the end, blood spewed from his mouth and nose, then his eyeballs popped out and hung by the nerve cords. His body jerked and stiffened and finally fell limp in the chair. Smoke was comin' out every opening.

"He was dead at 7:13. I was on the floor, pukin'."

Ritter hadn't noticed the silence in the room, nor realized how long it lasted. Foster patted sweat from his forehead. Fred just sat there, twitching his mustache. Ritter took in a sense of the old man, an eyewitness to be believed.

Foster got up from his seat. "Thank you, Fred. You can go now."

Rising from his chair, Fred cast a long glance at the detective. "He's dead, I tell ya."

Ritter swallowed, not having found words to express his thanks to the old man who was now shuffling out the door and setting the hat back on his head. It wasn't until Ritter turned his attention to the file in his lap that he realized he was trembling. But he still thought the death penalty, as barbarous as it was, was justified for Morris Brennon.

"Are you satisfied now?" Foster asked, looking blankly into the bowl of his pipe.

Ritter shook his head. "There's still the matter of the fingerprints. How did a dead man's fingerprints get all over Karen Carlyle's house?"

Foster looked up from his pipe. "You're sure about that?"

"Without a doubt." Ritter began thumbing through papers inside the file. He came across a list titled *VISITORS*. Karen Carlyle's name appeared there several times. "Nobody else came to see him?"

"No," Foster replied with a sigh. "Morris had no family, no friends. No one claimed the body. You'll find his ashes buried in grave number 59 at Stateville Cemetery on Canton Farm Road."

Ashes were of no use to Ritter, no fingerprints, no clues. He returned to his search of the file. The infirmary report caught his eye. *August 1, 1969.* "Why did Morris see the doctor on August first?" he asked Foster.

"Let's have a look." The little man went around behind the davenport, leaned over Ritter's shoulder, and flipped through the medical log. "Ah, here it is." He pointed to paragraph eight. *Tissue resection of right forearm.*

Ritter grimaced. "Why would they cut out a piece of his arm?"

"Maybe he had a cyst or something," Foster replied.

"But he'd be dead in a month." Ritter skimmed the pages and found three other entries where Morris Brennon had visited the infirmary. The same doctor had signed him in and out each time. "Who is this guy? Says here, *Dr. Larson, Blythe University, attending physician.* I thought you had your own doctors here."

"It's not unusual to have other physicians come in."

"But the same one every time seems odd, don't you think?"

Foster walked to the window, the pipe again clenched in his teeth. "Could be Dr. Larson had a special interest in Morris Brennon...or perhaps...it's just a coincidence."

Ritter frowned. There were no coincidences in a murder investigation.

Chapter Forty-Four

Chicago

An autumn breeze blew clattering leaves across the driveway as Jeff Jordan pulled into the garage and shut off the engine of his classic '59 Cadillac limo. Something about her elegant form gave him the same feeling he got from the fountain in Paradise Park. He caressed the bone-white steering wheel. For the first time in his life he began to think he might soon find the cause of his déjà vu. But first he had to find William Tuliver.

"Are you all right?" Lois asked, sitting next to him, her eyes teary.

He gave her a gentle nudge. "I don't think so."

She didn't say anything as they got out of the car.

Inside the house, Jeff tossed his car keys on the kitchen table. The place smelled like chicken soup. Lois had prepared dinner before she left to pick him up from the hospital. Two days ago, he had fainted and banged his head against the counter. As concussions went, this one could have been worse, the doctors had told him. His headache was gone, and if he never ate another cup of cherry Jell-O, it would be too soon.

Lois closed the door and pulled off her coat. "Stan Thompson made a mistake." She followed him across the kitchen.

Lifting the lid on the crock-pot, Jeff took in a big whiff of simmering broth. "He knows his business better than that." He set down the lid, turned to face his wife, and gently put his hands on her shoulders. "You read the letter. *The Lost Diamonds* has already been written."

"That's not possible, Jeff. Something is wrong."

"Something has always been wrong, but don't you see, I've been right all along. The déjà vu means something after all."

"So tell me, Jeff." She stared into his eyes. "Just what exactly *does* it mean *after all*?"

He dropped his gaze. "I'm not sure. I only know that it does."

"Does what, Jeffrey?"

His hip throbbed. She never called him Jeffrey. It sounded wrong coming from her. It sounded like the Jeffrey in Geoffrey Scott Michaels.

Lois glared at him. "Tell me what you think it means when you work your ass off writing a book that's already been written. Are you somehow mentally linked to this guy Tuliver? Are you possessed by his spirit or something?" She brushed his hands from her shoulders, turned her back on him, and wept.

"Lois, please. I don't know what it is. I don't even know who I am anymore. Nothing makes any sense. I feel numb. But whatever it means, I *will* find out." He put his arms around her waist. "Just hang in there with me."

"Jeff, I'm scared," she sobbed out, leaning her head back against his chest. "I don't want to lose you."

He held his wife tighter. "Lose me? How do you figure?"

"You don't know who you are. You've always had your doubts. Now I'm having mine. What if...when you find out... Well...what if I don't know who you are anymore? What will happen to us?"

Kissing the top of her head, he sighed. "Nothing is going to happen to us. I love you."

"How can you say that? You don't even know who you are."

Jeff thought his heart had plummeted down a well. Never before had she doubted his love. "Don't give up on me, Lois." He rocked her a little, wishing he had never written that damn book. "I'm sure, in the end, we'll find there's some logical explanation for all this."

"I'm not so sure," she said through tears and turned around in his embrace. "This thing you've had with the déjà vu, well...I've always dismissed it as a little quirk in your personality." Sniffling, she fidgeted with a button on his shirt. "But when I heard Morris Brennon's name on TV, I freaked. I knew then there was more to your problem than just some weird feelings." She searched his eyes. "It scares me to think what might happen when you find out your mother's been keeping a secret from you."

"What makes you say that?"

"I've seen the denial in her eyes. She never listens to you, Jeff. She doesn't want to hear what you're telling her."

"I know."

"Ever notice how she turns her eyes away whenever you talk about your feelings? Why is that?" She buried her face in his chest.

He stroked her hair. "I know Mom's been difficult at times, but she means well."

Lois looked up. "Does she?"

"Of course."

"She's keeping something from you, Jeff. Some big secret."

"That's nonsense," he lied, now remembering how he'd thought the same thing in the clubhouse that day of the tennis match. A reoccurring question gnawed at him then. Would a mother keep a secret to protect her son from the truth? How horrible could the truth be to make her do such a thing? Often he'd tried to think of what she might be hiding, but for now, he didn't want Lois to know he had the same concerns. After all, she was worried enough already. "Everything's going to be fine. You'll see."

Lois threw her arms around him, squeezed him as though she would never let him go. Her nose brushed his cheek. He turned his lips to hers, lifted her into his arms, and carried her up the stairs. Their lips never parted.

Chapter Forty-Five

Jeff closed the bedroom door quietly, leaving Lois to sleep a little longer. He wanted to linger there with her, but his mind wouldn't let him rest. He could still smell her perfume, taste her lips on his tongue. They'd made love as if it was their first time, or maybe as if it would be their last time.

Wearing only a pair of boxer shorts, he shuffled into the study, favoring his painful hip. Under the bright light of his desk lamp, he set his manuscript down in front of him. He felt a sense of mystery, the enigma of *The Lost Diamonds* making his hands tremble. It was the most bizarre thing he'd ever heard of, but somewhere within these pages were clues to William Tuliver and his connection to him. But which parts were real and which parts were fiction?

In the first chapter, William Tuliver owned Diamond Auto Parts, and his office sat atop the Diamond Building. Jeff thought that would be the logical place to start looking for him. Besides, Jeff always wanted to go inside that magnificent building, though he wondered if anyone would even recognize the name William Tuliver. He pulled a tablet from the drawer and made a note:

#1: William Tuliver, the Diamond Building

He had also written that Sally Mayfield was William's secretary and lover. If she were a real person, where could she be found? As he thought about her, he figured she wouldn't be someone's housewife with six kids. He thought she'd be alone, grieving over William's death. But where? He made a note of that also:

#2: Sally Mayfield

And then there was Andrew Cobb, William's loyal aide and best friend. Maybe he was living somewhere in the Chicago area, driving a cab or perhaps working as a chauffeur for some other wealthy baron. Worthy of noting, he jotted that down:

#3: Andrew Cobb, chauffeur

He turned a few pages—to the part about the Dragon Man. What had become of Carl Savage? He'd probably be a mob boss by now. There was one way to find out. Jeff put the fat man's name on the list:

#4: Carl Savage.

A few chapters later, Morris Brennon appeared in the book. There was no mystery about him. The ax murderer was executed nearly thirty years ago. Though Jeff wondered if William's parents were on Morris Brennon's list of victims, he decided not to put that question on his list. Something inside told him he didn't really want to know.

He closed the manuscript and placed the neatly folded letter from Stan Thompson beside it. Then Jeff thought of one more clue from the letter, William Tuliver's heir, Geoffrey Scott Michaels. Where could he be found?

#5: Geoffrey Scott Michaels

Jeff set down the pen. The end of his story came to mind. The way he'd written it, there were diamonds, the ones the Japanese paid William for his company. This quickened his heartbeat. If everything else was real, then somewhere under *Mothers' Tears*, in the massive pumping station, there was a fortune to be found. His mouth went dry when he realized his problem. He had written that William hid the diamonds down there but exactly where, he didn't say, he didn't know. Quickly, he jotted that down with the other clues.

#6: THE LOST DIAMONDS

Chapter Forty-Six

The drive to the Diamond Building took Jeff twenty minutes. Morning traffic problems aside, it went well but not nearly fast enough. He parked the Cadillac under the carport in the space marked *Executive One Only*. The black limo looked as if it belonged there. Walking toward the entrance, his hip felt stiff and sore.

After pushing his way through the revolving door, he stood inside a massive lobby. He'd never been in here before, but he'd imagined it this way: crystal chandeliers, plush carpet, and rich upholstery. It all looked familiar, even the face of the old man standing behind the reception counter.

"How can I help you?" the man asked.

Limping a little, Jeff walked up to him, stared into the old man's eyes, and felt a chill of recognition. That overwhelming feeling came over him again. Déjà vu. A name came to him. Impossible, but he couldn't help saying it. "Hello, Ron."

The old man's eyes widened. "Do I know you?" He paused for a moment, staring, and then he gasped. "Jesus H. Christ. You're the spittin' image of William Tuliver, by God. You must be his boy."

Jeff hadn't expected that reply. His spine tingled, and he felt lightheaded. William Tuliver *had* been here after all. Jeff stumbled for a response to the old man. "Am-am I his son?"

Ron stood statuesque, flushed, his palms flat on the counter as if glued in place. "I'll be damned. William and Sally lit out of here some thirty years ago...to have a baby I hear tell, at some special hospital—"

"Sally?"

"Huh?"

"Do you mean Sally Mayfield?"

"Who else? You're their son, right?"

Jeff started shaking. His hip stung. This seemed so impossible. Sally Mayfield his mother? William Tuliver his father? "I-I really don't know," he stumbled. "But that's why I've come here...to find William Tuliver." Jeff suddenly wondered if he really wanted to know any more. "I'm Jeff Jordan...I think." He offered Ron a handshake.

Ron, looking like he'd seen a ghost, accepted gingerly. "I better get someone down here to help you, Jeff Jordan." He picked up the phone and spoke without dialing. "There's a gentleman down here looking for William Tuliver."

For the next few minutes, which seemed like an hour, Jeff paced the lobby. He'd been here before. He could feel it in his bones. He loosened his tie and unbuttoned the collar of his white shirt, hoping to breathe a little easier. By now, he was oblivious to the pain in his hip. But as hard as he tried, he couldn't stop trembling.

The elevator dinged, and an Asian woman stepped out. She stood five feet tall, flashed dark eyes, and wore red lipstick. Her blue flower-print dress hung silkily down to the top of her white sandals. Long black hair flowed behind her as she approached. "Mr. Jordan?" She smiled.

Jeff nodded, nervous.

"Hello. I'm Toyoko Nakamura." She bowed deeply. "The CEO of Diamond Auto Parts."

Staggering, Jeff couldn't believe it. The Japanese owned William's company—just like in the book he wrote.

"I'd be pleased to help you. Come with me." She turned gracefully back toward the elevator. Jeff followed her, his head screaming *RUN*.

Upstairs, in the corporate office on the 66th floor, he approached the plate glass windows overlooking Chicago. Though

The Duplication Factor

he'd never been up here, he'd imagined the view—just this way.

Toyoko stood beside him. She held a thick photo album in her arms. "Maybe this will help you find what you are looking for, Mr. Jordan."

On a desk, she laid open the book. *Annual Reports, Diamond Auto Parts, 1940, 1950, 1960,* the cover read. Colored tabs separated the decades. Jeff sat in a chair Toyoko offered, and with heart hammering, he wished he hadn't come here but knew he had to press on.

He pulled on the first tab, immediately shaken by what he saw. A black and white photo of himself stared back at him. He was dressed in an old fashioned suit. The caption read, *The CEO of Diamond Auto Parts, William Tuliver.* He must have been thirty years old when this photo was taken. Jeff's breath hitched, but he forced himself to remain calm. "Hello, William Tuliver. Finally, we meet."

"Fine looking father," Toyoko said, looking over his shoulder. "Like son, I'd say,"

Jeff looked up at her. Could she be right about that? Could he be William Tuliver's son? He looked at the book again, his fingers trembling so badly he could hardly turn the pages. With each one, he felt his life turning upside down and spinning out of control. He sucked short breaths, imagined he was floating above himself, not really doing this thing, only seeing it happen to some other poor slob.

As he flipped through pages of reports and figures, he found many more pictures, all black and white, most of motley work crews, dressed in flannel shirts and blue jeans, holding various types of tools and posing in front of buildings under construction. One was labeled *Atlanta, Georgia, 1941,* another *Richmond, Virginia, 1943.* It was obvious William Tuliver's company was growing.

He pulled on the next tab, *1950.* There, with William Tuliver, stood a young man of lanky proportions, a narrow face, wedged nose, and stringy blond hair, the spitting image of Rick Atkins. *Andrew Cobb,* the caption read. Jeff swallowed dryly, half in shock, half bewildered. "Hello, Andrew."

There were more pictures of construction sites and a few photos of men and women dressed in their Sunday best, seated around a large conference table. *Stockholder's meeting, 1955,* the caption read. He could smell Toyoko's perfume as she watched him turning pages. There was no way she could know what this was doing to him.

The next tab, *1960,* brought up a picture of an older William Tuliver with thick gray hair and a robust smile. But that wasn't the thing that nearly stopped Jeff's heart. It was the car in the picture. William posed at the fender of a 1959 Cadillac limo, black and shining like new. Andrew Cobb sat in the driver's seat, smiling broadly. For all Jeff knew, it could be the same car he'd rescued from the Cheap Heaps car lot. He wondered if the serial numbers would match. Wouldn't that be something to write home to Mom about, he quipped, whoever Mom was.

The next few color pictures showed construction of the Diamond Building as its steel skeleton stretched skyward, from a hole in the ground to the finishing touches. A huge crane held the blue DIAMOND sign in place for workers to secure just above the top floor. William Tuliver stood off to the side with his legs spread, hands on his hips like the proudest man in the world. In the next picture, William struck the same pose, only this time in front of the fountain in Paradise Park. Jeff felt a jolt in his chest. *Mothers' Tears.*

The next turn of the page gave him Sally Mayfield. The resemblance to his wife, Lois, nearly knocked him out of his chair. A few misplaced freckles, a different curve of the ears but exactly the same face, the same hazel eyes and short red hair. His temples throbbed like mad.

"Hello, Sally," he said to the picture and smiled nervously. "Or should I call you Mom?"

Chapter Forty-Seven

Jeff Tuliver, as he now knew his name to be, worked the steering wheel through traffic, the '59 Cadillac humming down the highway toward the Cook County Courthouse. A picture of William Tuliver lay on the seat. Toyoko wouldn't let him take the original picture from the album, but she made him a photocopy. He thought he'd never forget the way she looked at him as they rode the elevator down to the lobby. Her eyes told him she knew that seeing that book had somehow changed him. "If you need anything else, please feel free to ask," she had said as he walked away from the Diamond Building.

Clue number one had been solved. He'd found William Tuliver, his father. But one question answered spawned more unanswered questions. Like, if he was the son of William Tuliver, then how did Geoffrey Scott Michaels become his heir like Stan Thompson implied in the letter? And how did Jeff Tuliver become Jeff Jordan? A lump formed in his throat. Could Lois have been right? Had Mom kept a horrible secret from him?

A horn blared, jerking Jeff's attention back to his driving. He swerved right and took the next off-ramp. A few minutes later, in the courthouse parking lot, he locked the car then hurried up the steps.

Courthouses always seemed so hollow, each footstep and word echoing on forever down cavernous halls. He found the door with "*CLERK*" painted on the glass and went inside. There, an equally hollow looking woman stood behind a counter with a long line of people in front of her. Her every move was in slow motion.

After taking a form from the counter, he filled in his request for a copy of Geoffrey Scott Michaels' birth certificate. No better place to start looking for him than from the beginning. He also filled out another request: William Tuliver's death certificate. He stood there waiting, standing behind an old woman who smelled of cheap soap.

When it was his turn, he handed the clerk his requests.

"Are you family?" she asked in a raspy voice.

"I think Geoffrey is my long-lost brother. I've been searching for several years now," he lied. "William was my dad." No lie.

"That'll be six dollars at the cashier's window over there." She pointed to a room across the hall. "Bring your receipt back and have a seat." She motioned to a bench along the wall, already crowded with people. "We'll call your name when it's ready."

After waiting in another line at the cashier's window, paying the county for its trouble, and enduring the throng of bodies on the bench, someone finally called his name.

Outside in the limo, Geoff peeled open one of the envelopes the woman had given him. He slowly extracted the paper from inside. It was a copy of William Tuliver's death certificate, which immediately caused his hands to tremble. The date hit him like a wrecking ball. *August 20, 1970.* His father had died on the same day Jeff was born. It must've been an emotionally trying day for his mother.

He set the death certificate on the seat and opened the other envelope. *Certificate of Live Birth*, it read across the top of the paper bordered with a lacy frame. *Geoffrey Scott Michaels.* And that was the end of the good things he read there.

Mother: Sally Mayfield. Father: Unknown.

Jeff couldn't catch a breath. Why didn't Sally know who the father was? Gripping the steering wheel, he tried to figure out what that meant. William Tuliver was his father, but who was his mother? Sally Mayfield was Geoffrey Scott Michaels's mother. The date: *August 20, 1970.* Jeff's chest tightened. They were both born on the same day. His mouth fell open, and he slumped in the seat. A passerby might have thought him dead, sitting there limp and pale.

Could Geoffrey and Jeff be the same person? After all, their first names were similar. Or were they twins? Maybe they were separated at birth somehow. But why did they have different last names?

Why? Why? Why? What the hell did it mean?

His hip throbbed. The photocopy on the seat beside him had convinced him of one thing; William Tuliver was his father, without a doubt. The birth certificate proved Sally Mayfield was Geoffrey Scott Michaels' mother. The way it all looked, Sally Mayfield gave birth to an illegitimate child and William Tuliver made him heir to his fortune. Why would he have done something like that, forsaken his own son? Or had he? Maybe Geoffrey was Jeff's long lost twin brother, the only heir left after that horrible day Jeff became misplaced. It had happened before: nurses confused mothers with babies and switched armbands; or deranged women stole newborns. Could that have happened to him? And where was Geoffrey Scott Michaels now? Did he know about Jeff Tuliver? Did he have the answers?

And again, the other heart-wrenching question gnawed at him. Who was Jeff Tuliver's mother? Ron said it was Sally. Had Mom been hiding his real mother from him all of his life? Or was she shielding him from another truth? Dad couldn't be his real father. Maybe she had a torrid affair with William Tuliver and hid that from her husband. Again, he wondered if Lois was right about Mom. Was she hiding a truth more horrible than she would dare reveal?

Exhausted from the strain on his mind, he rested his forehead on the steering wheel, the birth certificate now lying on top of the death certificate next to the photocopy of William Tuliver on the seat. Jeff Tuliver sighed. The only way to make any sense of this was to solve clue number two. He had to find Sally Mayfield.

But first he had to talk to Mom.

Chapter Forty-Eight

A t nine in the morning, Jeff Tuliver stood in front of his parent's house on Ash Street, the Cadillac limo gleaming behind him. He was wearing a fresh shop uniform, white shirt and navy blue slacks, thinking he'd show up for work sometime today. Holding the photocopy of his father, William Tuliver, he savored the memories of the place where he grew up. It was a simple corner house, sided with white aluminum panels and trimmed in pink. Lace curtains were drawn over the windows. A slab walkway, cracked with age, led up to the front porch. He pictured his red tricycle parked there, next to the milk box that, too, was long gone. A leafy elm tree still shaded the lawn. Dad always kept the grass perfectly manicured.

He thought there was nothing special about the way he grew up here. Like most boys, he went to school and to church and to Boy Scouts for a time. He loved frogs, hated girls, and was in a constant battle with the Honaker brothers, the neighborhood bullies. He could remember hooping basketballs in the driveway, slugging home runs in the ballpark across the street, and racing his ten-speed through traffic. In all these things, he seemed to be a normal growing boy, except for those feelings that haunted him every day. And he always felt as though he was much more focused, much more driven than the other kids his age. He got better grades in school and more trophies in sports. His friends called him *Ace*. The bullies called him *Brown-noser*.

Jeff walked up the sidewalk to the porch, his hip paining him some and his stomach churning. Mom and Dad didn't know he was coming here like this, with questions. But no matter what answers he came away with, he knew his parents deserved a great deal of credit for the love and care they'd given him all his life. He only hoped that the truths revealed today would not be as horrible as the ones he'd imagined yesterday.

Wearing a Chicago Bulls sweatshirt and green stretch pants, Mom answered the door. Her hair looked freshly brushed. "Jeff," she said cautiously. "What is it?" He caught her eyeing the picture in his hand.

"I've something to show you. May I come in?"

"Please."

Inside, a lingering aroma of bacon drifted in the air. "I see I'm late for breakfast."

"I'll make you some if you like." Mom ushered him through the living room.

"Not now, thanks." Jeff saw Dad, or whoever he was, standing in the doorway to the kitchen. He was dressed as if he had some work to do in the yard: old blue jeans spattered with different colors of paint and a blue short-sleeve shirt to match. He hadn't shaved. Mom stood next to him now, clutching his hand. The looks on their faces were a mix of surprise and fear.

"Shouldn't you be at the shop, son?" Dad asked.

"Jim and Lou can handle it." Jeff switched on the dining room light. "Shall we sit here...at the table?" He pulled on a chair. "Mom?"

They sat together in silence, the tension in the air brittle as old bones. Jeff Tuliver, standing between them, set the photocopy of his father on the table in front of them. They stared at it openmouthed.

Dad spoke first. "Nice picture, son. Where did you come up with the old suit?"

Mom said nothing. She only stared.

Jeff shook his head. "It's not me, but I want to know why I look exactly like this guy."

Mom said nothing.

Dad looked at the picture and again at Jeff. "If this isn't you, then who is it?"

"William Tuliver."

"Your main character?"

"He's my father."

Dad gasped. "Sweet Jesus."

Mom burst into tears, wailing in a way Jeff had never heard before. "Oh God, no. Don't let this happen." She clasped her hands in front of her chest.

Dad said nothing. He only stared at the photocopy of William Tuliver.

Jeff put a gentle hand on his mother's shoulder. He felt sad for her. This horrible secret she'd carried for so long now seemed destined to tear her apart, but he refused to feel responsible for that. What she had done was not his fault. And if she had kept this secret from her husband, she would now have to pay the price for doing so. "I need to know, Mom. Are you my mother?"

Tears streamed down her face. Her eyes were read and cheeks flushed. "Jeff, please," she cried. "Don't make me say the words. Go home to Lois. Go back to your shop. Go away from here and come again another day."

"Mom, I've got to know."

"No God, no. You don't have to know." She looked up at him this time, looked into his eyes as if searching for his soul. "Please, Jeff. You only think you need to know."

"I'm not leaving until you tell me the truth."

"And when you hear it, you'll be gone forever."

Jeff dropped to one knee at her side and put his hand on hers, clasped in her lap. "The truth cannot change the fact that you have been the only parents I've ever known. You'll always be Mom and Dad to me. I love you now. I'll love you then. But you must tell me. Are you my mother?"

"I've always been your mother."

"Did you give birth to me, Mom?"

"What do you want from me?"

"The truth."

"I'm...I'm sorry..." She shook her head violently. "No...I'm not sorry about this, Jeff, only sad for having kept it from you."

"What did you do, Mom?"

"Don't tell him," Dad said.

"Dad, please, let her speak."

Mom whimpered. "You won't understand."

"Mom?"

She sniffled. "You're adopted."

The word hit Jeff Tuliver like a sledgehammer. "Adopted?"

"We loved you from the moment we saw you and took you into our lives and hung onto you as if you were our own son."

A lump stuck in his throat. "Adopted?" Jeff said it again, still trying to grasp the meaning. He felt off balance, his mind dizzy. *Adopted* wasn't what he was expecting. He'd thought his mother would confess to having an affair with William Tuliver, but this new revelation caused him greater concern. Why had his father put him up for adoption and given Geoffrey everything? God, nothing made any sense.

With tears in his eyes, Dad looked at Mom. "You better tell him why."

She pulled her hands from Jeff's gentle grasp and clung to her husband's arm. "Please. Don't make me do this."

Dad clasped her hands. "He needs to understand, dear."

Mom again turned her eyes to Jeff, the son that wasn't her son. "Because...it was because I couldn't have any more children," she sobbed out. "Not after Randy died." She tore her eyes away from him and buried her face in her husband's arm. "Oh God, it was all my fault. I couldn't bring him into this world. I killed him. I killed him."

Holding his wife tightly, Dad looked at Jeff, his eyes overflowing now. "Randy died in childbirth, Jeff. Our grief was unbearable. We thought an adopted child would replace our dead son. You were that child, Jeff, a gift from God. But your mother's guilt never faded."

Jeff Tuliver's eyes stung with tears. He stood numbed by the sorrow he had unleashed upon his parents. Though he felt stripped of his past, abandoned by William Tuliver and lost from his mother, whoever she was, he could see that their loss was much greater. A dead son and the guilt his mother carried must have been a heavy burden for them both. As they hid from the truth, they also hid the truth from him.

"Why didn't you tell me this before?"

Mom looked up. "You are my son. I couldn't have it any other way. We loved you like you were our own."

"So we chose to live the lie," Dad said. "But it wasn't easy. The more you grew, the more we realized how different you were from us."

"You were a strange child," Mom said. "Almost eerie the way you caught on to things. We were afraid you'd figure it out on your own."

Dad handed Mom a tissue. "We had to be careful not to let anything slip."

"But we knew this was coming," Mom put in, sniffing.

"We couldn't sleep that night," Dad went on, "after we heard about Morris Brennon, as hard as it was to admit, we realized then that your déjà vu was real. Your book was going to haunt us. It was our punishment for not telling you what we'd done. And then this." He tapped the photocopy of William Tuliver on the table. "This is too weird. You're a dead ringer for this guy. How did you find him?"

"My book." Jeff shook his head. "My history is all there."

"How's it possible to write a book like that?"

"I don't know, but I'm going to find out."

Chapter Forty-Nine

In the weeks that followed the revelation at his parent's house, Jeff Tuliver struggled with a sense of his own identity. He searched the archives for Andrew Cobb and clue number three, hoping he would have information about Sally Mayfield. She had to be the mother of twins, one inheriting everything, the other lost somehow, abandoned and adopted. However, all attempts to locate her had ended in frustration. Jeff was sure Andrew could tell him who his mother was or what his relationship to Geoffrey Scott Michaels might have been.

After an exhausting search of the Illinois Cemetery Registry, Jeff was relieved to know Andrew Cobb had not passed away, at least not in Illinois. He decided to visit Toyoko again.

"What you ask of me is not right," she said as they stood together at the plate-glass window overlooking Chicago.

"You're the last hope I've got. Andrew is the key. He can help me."

She regarded him a moment, her beautiful Asian eyes searching his. "What is so important to you?"

"I've lost my family, my father, my mother. Certainly you understand the importance of family."

"Yes. Family. There is great honor there."

"Or disgrace," Jeff said sadly. "Please help me find out what happened to them. Andrew Cobb is the only link I have left."

"But the company records are confidential."

Jeff felt the air leak out of him. "Then I will fail."

Toyoko regarded him a moment then asked, "You will keep

this in your highest confidence?"

"I promise." He bowed slightly.

"Very well. This way."

Relief made him lightheaded. He rode with her in the elevator three floors down to the file room where rows of shelves held the archives of Diamond Auto Parts. At the front of the room, she stopped at a computer terminal and typed in a security code that appeared as Xs in the login window. A moment later, Andrew Cobb's employment data appeared on the screen. She selected *print* with the click of her mouse button. The printer buzzed and rolled out a sheet of paper, which Toyoko retrieved and handed to him. "I hope this will end your search and bring you peace."

Jeff examined the record. Dates of employment, salaries, insurance benefits, and lots of other information were listed first. Then addresses, PO boxes, and finally, the mailing address for Andrew's pension check. Jeff's heart rate went up a notch. *River Bluff Nursing Home. Rockford, Illinois.*

"Thanks." He kissed her cheek then dashed for the elevator.

"Good luck, my friend," she called out after him.

***

It took an hour and a half to drive to Rockford, the home of the Ice Hogs just west of Chicago. Lunch was being served when Jeff Tuliver arrived at River Bluff Nursing Home. The whole place smelled of ravioli and garlic bread.

A nurse met him at the reception counter. She was a solemn woman with sagging cheeks and thin gray hair. "Andrew is in the hospice center. Congenital heart disease, liver failure, and a touch of Parkinson's. Poor man drank himself into this place."

Jeff's stomach felt sick as he followed the nurse's heavy gait down the hallway. "How long has he been here?"

"Seven years. You're his first visitor."

"Do you know where he'd been before that?" Jeff asked as they walked together toward the hospice wing, the sterile-white halls echoing his words.

"He talked of chauffeuring for the Kennedy clan in New Hampshire for a spell, least 'til his drinking got to be a problem. Then he drove a cab in Chicago 'til his drinking got him in trouble. The poor man turned his insides to mush, but he never told anyone why he'd done it."

But Jeff thought he knew why. Andrew Cobb carried with him secrets he wished he weren't privy to. He probably knew that Geoffrey Scott Michaels was illegitimate and why William Tuliver put his son up for adoption. If he had it figured right, Andrew knew everything. He was William's best friend. And Jeff knew Andrew's life wouldn't have turned out like this if William Tuliver hadn't put pressure on him to keep silent about what he'd done to his family.

Standing at the door to room 32, the nurse stopped Jeff short of going in. "He's not a pretty sight."

Jeff went inside anyway.

The room shined brightly with flowered wallpaper and pictures of mountains and meadows. A vase of red and pink carnations adorned a table in the corner. In front of the window, a plush brown chair sat under a reading lamp. The air smelled faintly of urine. On a steel-framed bed, the skinny shell of Andrew Cobb lay covered to his waist with a blue blanket. His pallid skin was spotted with black welts and spider webbed with varicose veins. A tube ran out of his nose, and his cheeks were caved in. Wires from a faintly beeping heart monitor were taped to his bony ribcage. Andrew Cobb was not long for this world.

Standing at his bedside, Jeff saw the old man's eyes were closed. His mouth hung agape. He had no teeth. If it weren't for the shape of his nose, there would be no resemblance left of the man in the pictures. Watching him suck hollow breaths, Jeff felt pity for Andrew Cobb, for the way he'd lived and for the way he would die.

Jeff shuddered, a tear stinging his eye. He sensed he was about to endure another loss in his life, though he didn't understand why he felt that way. "Andrew," he said softly. "Andrew Cobb?"

Terry Wright

The old man's eyelids began to rise slowly. His vein-webbed eyeballs rolled down, revealing bright blue irises. They rotated toward Jeff and fixed on his face.

The heart machine began beeping loudly. Andrew gasped. His eyes shot open wide as if he'd seen a ghost. "William Tuliver," he said in a rasping voice.

"I look a lot like him," Jeff said, his heart beating as hard as that confounded machine.

Andrew frantically looked him up and down. "It can't be."

"I didn't mean to startle you."

"You said you'd be back."

"But I haven't been here before. My name is Jeff Tuliver."

"No." Andrew's eyes were filled with terror.

"I'm William Tuliver's son."

"No..."

"William's my dad."

"No...he's not."

"Of course he is—"

"William never had...*cough*...a son."

Jeff thought the old man was confused. "I know everything about him. Go ahead. Ask me something, anything."

Gulping, Andrew's Adam's apple bobbed. "Tell me then," he rasped. "What did William name his fountain?"

Too easy. "Paradise Park Fountain."

"You don't know shit." Andrew turned away. "Get out of my room. Can't a man die in peace?"

"No wait." Jeff had another thought. In *The Lost Diamonds*, he'd named the fountain... Why not? Everything else had turned out to be true. "It was *Mothers' Tears*."

Andrew's eyes got big again. The beeping machine got louder. "By God." He coughed. "I-I never thought I'd see the day. William Tuliver...you're back, you did it...you made it back."

Jeff put a hand on the old man's shoulder, thinking Andrew had flipped out. "No. No. I'm Jeff Tuliver, William's son."

~272~

Andrew shook his head. "I told you...William didn't have a son."

"Sure he did. I look just like him."

"Because you *are* William Tuliver."

"What?"

"It's true, William. You're William."

"What kind of drugs are you on? He died thirty years ago."

"I-I know." Andrew's voice cracked. "I buried you. That's the beauty of his plan...don't you see? You are William, cloned and reborn, I tell ya."

Jeff took a step back from the bed, aghast at the old man's words. The drugs must have been working overtime on that feeble brain of his. *Cloned?* "You're high, old man."

But Andrew's eyes were fixed and certain. "Try to remember," he said weakly. The heart machine was still beeping fiercely. "Cancer in your bones was killin' you, so you got yourself cloned and named your new self Geoffrey Scott Michaels."

Fighting panic, Jeff had everything he could do to keep from running to the door. "*I* am Geoffrey Scott Michaels?"

"I was there when you were born."

"So that means..." A barrage of names flashed through his mind. Jeff Jordan wasn't Jeff Jordan after all. He was Jeff Tuliver who was really Geoffrey Scott Michaels, whose mother was— "Oh my God. Sally Mayfield is my mother."

"I-I wouldn't call her that...if I were you," Andrew said hoarsely. "Don't think she'd approve." He coughed.

"But I'm her son."

Andrew trembled. "No you're not. You're William Tuliver, the man she loved more than was good for her."

"She gave birth to Geoffrey Scott Michaels. Me. I saw the birth certificate. That makes her my mother."

"You don't catch on too good, do ya? You're a clone...an exact duplicate. You *are* William Tuliver. You and that maggot lawyer Carl Savage made it all nice and legal. Didn't you figure that out from the book?"

"What book?"

"The one you wrote: *The Lost Diamonds*. It was supposed to show you the way back to your past life. Must've got ya this far."

Jeff fell into the chair by the window. His head throbbed. Andrew Cobb knew about a book William Tuliver wrote. The only way Jeff could have written the same book was if he'd already written it once before, when he was William Tuliver. That was the only way to explain it, the only way it made any sense. It all became perfectly clear. "You're right. I'm William Tuliver."

"And I've been keeping somethin' for you—" Andrew coughed. "In the closet over there. I was gonna have them bury it with me, just like you said."

"I said that?" William found it hard to believe they'd talked before. He pulled himself out of the chair, and on weak legs, moved to the closet and opened the door. Inside, he saw a diamond-studded black walnut cane hanging on the hook by its rhino horn handle. It looked like the same cane he'd written about in *The Lost Diamonds*—William Tuliver's cane. He began shaking.

"Go ahead," Andrew said. "It's yours. Take it." The heart machine hadn't let up its rapid report.

William lifted his cane from the hook, surprised at how heavy it felt. The walnut finish was polished smooth and the rhino-horn handle had been intricately carved with some kind of cryptic designs. It felt rough in the palm of his hand. The diamonds glistened magnificently. A black rubber cap padded the cane's tip. He set it to the floor and gave it a lean. It was perfect. Then he felt a sudden chill as he realized he was really back—back from the dead. The cane was the tie that binds. He thought his chest would burst.

But even as he accepted this revelation, he rejected it with his next thought. Looking down on the pale and panting Andrew Cobb tethered precariously to that beeping machine, he couldn't help bu think the old man was wrong about the cloning part.

"Human cloning isn't possible, Andrew, not now and certainly not thirty years ago."

"It was a secret project," Andrew replied in a sandpaper voice. "You're the first human clone."

First? Did that mean there were others? "Who cloned me, Andrew?"

"Ask S-Sally." He gasped for air. "She knows...everything."

"Where is she?"

The heart machine started beeping erratically. Andrew clutched his chest. William grabbed Andrew's shoulder and shook him. "Where is she?"

He shuddered, gasping. His terror-filled eyes were fixed on the ceiling, his bony fists clenched.

"Where is she, Andrew?" William shook him again. "Where is Sally?"

Andrew choked. "C-Chicago." He gasped. "Th...the..." he coughed, "loop." A gush of air huffed from his lungs.

The heart machine sounded a steady tone.

Chapter Fifty

A light rain ticked on William's bedroom window. Faint thunder rumbled in the distance. Standing naked at the blinds, he closed them and turned toward the bed where Lois lay. By the light of a single candle on the nightstand, he saw her eyes were shut. She was lying on her back, uncovered. Her red hair glowed crimson as flickering candlelight danced over her nude body. The peach fragrance of her perfume drifted in the air.

She must have sensed his stare. Smiling, she raised her arms, beckoned him to come to her. "Listen to the rain. Isn't it wonderful?"

William let himself down on the bed, slowly, until he lay next to her on his back, his hand resting on the curve of her hip. Her skin felt smooth and warm, and his body grew aware of the sensation.

"Do you have to go?" she asked.

"I need to find her."

"Please don't," she whispered. "I just can't bear the thought of you out there chasing some phantom woman."

"I've got to."

"Then take me with you."

"There's something we need to talk about."

"What?"

He turned to face her. In the candlelight, he watched her breasts rise and fall with the rhythm of her breathing. "I want us to have a child."

She stiffened. "You're kidding."

"No more birth control."

Glaring at him, she frowned. "I need to know why, Jeff. Why

now?"

"My name isn't Jeff. It's William Tuliver. Please. Call me William."

"Does that mean I'm not Lois Jordan anymore? Am I Lois Tuliver now?"

"Yes." He knew it was hard for her to accept. Hell, he had a hard enough time believing it himself.

She rolled on her side, facing him, and propped her cheek on her hand. "What if I don't want to be Lois Tuliver? What if I like Lois Jordan better?"

Her tone was playful, and William took that as a lack of seriousness. "Please try to understand."

Lois stared into his eyes. "You can't be serious."

"As a heart attack," William said softly.

"This is insane." She started to sit up.

William grabbed her arm. "It's the only explanation."

"I don't buy any of this cloning stuff. It's not possible."

"It's a stretch, I know, but please, lie down."

The tension drained from her arm. She lay back, her gaze on the ceiling. "I married Jeff Jordan because I loved Jeff Jordan. I don't love William Tuliver."

"But we're the same person."

Lois looked at him. "I'm not so sure. You've change already, Jeff."

"William."

"God, it's so weird."

"That's how I've felt all my life, until now. Andrew Cobb convinced me. I'm William Tuliver. The diamond-studded cane was the clincher."

"When you brought it home, I freaked. It's just like you described in your book. I can't fathom what that means."

"It's proof that someone out there knows how to clone humans. I'm not the only one."

"What's that got to do with us having a baby?"

William turned on his side, put his arm around her. Rain struck the window and roof with more force. Thunder rumbled closer. Now was the time to tell her. "Because I'm d-dying."

She gasped and tried to push him away, but he held her tightly. "Listen to me, Lois," he whispered in her ear. "*The Lost Diamonds* is a true story."

"No it's not."

"In the end, William Tuliver dies."

"You made it up."

"Did I make up Morris Brennon? No. Did I make up the cane? No. It's real. It's all real. I wrote the same book twice. When Andrew told me William Tuliver died of cancer, just like I wrote in my book, I knew that was real, too."

"But that's not going to happen to you."

"My hip has been getting worse."

"It's arthritis."

"It isn't, Lois. Don't you see? Back then my motive for cloning myself was to stay alive, somehow, anyhow. I didn't want to give up my fortune. And it didn't matter who I hurt in the process. I was so self-centered that I didn't even care how the clone might feel about it. What I did was wrong, horribly wrong."

She hugged him. "I can't believe you're dying. I won't—"

"I don't have much time."

"Then do something...see a doctor. Maybe they can cure you this time. Damn it. You can't just come into my life, let me love you, and then leave me alone like this. You have to try, for me, for our child. You hear me?" Tears spilled from her eyes.

William didn't like to see her upset, but he had to make her understand. "I've already seen a doctor."

"Without telling me?"

"I didn't want to alarm you."

"But I'm your wife. I have the right to be alarmed."

William realized he'd done the same thing to Sally, but pressed on. "The doctor sent me to a specialist. Long story short, without chemo treatment I have less than a year to live."

"Then get the treatment."

"I admit...my first thought was to save myself, just like before."

"There's nothing wrong with that." She sobbed.

"Don't you see? Treatment won't save me, only postpone the inevitable. If I take chemo and radiation therapy, I'm going to be sicker than a dog. I may never get the chance to find out who cloned me. I'm the healthiest I'm going to be...right now...I need to set things right. Back then, I should've taken my chances, had a child with Sally."

"You talk about her like she's an ex-wife."

"I shouldn't even be alive right now."

"But you're mine," she cried. "I don't want you to die."

"I understand, Lois. If I get back in time, I'll get the treatments, surgery, radiation, whatever they want to try."

"But by then it might be too late."

"It's already too late." He patted her bare smooth shoulder. "That's why having a child *now* is important."

"I can't imagine my life without you, Jeff—"

"William."

She clung to him tightly. "I'll miss you."

"That's the way it has to be."

"But I don't have to like it...William."

He kissed her lips, her cheeks, and the side of her neck. Her tears tasted salty. The smell of her skin filled his senses.

"I want you so bad," she said breathily.

Though he'd been with her a million times before, this time was different. His mind was free of the déjà vu. He couldn't remember a time when he thought so clearly.

As he touched her, moaning sounds came from her throat. Her chest heaved with airy breaths. In the flickering candlelight, her skin glowed. She put her arms around him. Her fingers stroked his back, sending tingles to his toes.

His lips found her mouth.

Their tongues met.

He moved to take her.

In that moment of penetration, she gasped.

Lightning flashed in the window and splashed across the bedroom walls. Thunder boomed. Rain pelted the roof with fury.

William tensed and shuddered in the final act of love.

Chapter Fifty-One

William Tuliver parked his Cadillac limo in front of the funeral home and stared out the rain-streaked windshield. The stone steps were void of mourners he'd expected to see huddled under umbrellas and filing in to pay their last respects to Andrew Cobb. Beyond the black wrought iron fencing that flanked the old building, an array of tombstones stood, some plain slabs, others elaborate markers topped with crosses and statues of angels. They were neatly rowed and slick with rain.

The nursing home staff had told him that Andrew was to be buried here, in a plot he had already purchased for himself. A simple service had been planned for one o'clock. William glanced at his watch. *12:30.*

He thought about the announcement he'd placed in the obituary section of the Chicago Tribune. *Memorial Service Set For Andrew Cobb*, it read. William hoped it would attract the attention of one person out there who might have cared enough about Andrew Cobb to attend his funeral, one special person: Sally Mayfield.

Pulling himself out of the limo, William opened an umbrella. The rain was coming down hard. His hip ached from the cold damp air. He retrieved the diamond-studded cane from the front seat and swung the door closed. Looking solemnly at this gloomy place of death, he limped toward the funeral parlor.

Organ music drifted in the air as he climbed the stairs to the big wooden doors deeply engraved with the scene of a haloed crucifix surrounded by angels floating on clouds. Lanterns glowed on pillars at each side of the doorway. The brass handle was wet and cold. He gave it a pull.

Inside, at the end of the aisle between the pews, sat a coffin on a bier. It had been crafted of the blackest, shiniest wood William had ever seen. The handles were made of gold, and a velvet pall was draped over it, flowing to the floor. The head cover was open, and from where he stood, it revealed only a white silk liner. Closing his umbrella, he thought that Andrew must have spent his life's savings on this casket.

A photograph of Andrew sat propped up on an easel behind the coffin. His broad smile overpowered his narrow face. Stringy blond hair fell over his forehead and blue eyes sparkled. Andrew wasn't much of a looker, and William thought that had a lot to do with why he'd never married and had a family.

William glanced around the parlor. Except for Andrew Cobb, he was alone. A wooden cross adorned the front of a candlelit pulpit, and he detected the fragrance of vanilla wax. After checking the knot on his tie, William made his way toward the coffin, the rubber tip of his diamond-studded cane thumping on the floor with each step.

As he neared, he saw a bouquet of red roses first, resting on Andrew's chest. He was dressed in a black suit coat with wide lapels, a pleated white shirt, and black bow tie. His thin gray hair was combed straight back, giving him the look of an old man facing a stiff wind. William shivered at the sight of him lying there, pale and still, his eyes shut forever.

"I'm sorry, Andrew...for everything...I wish you could hear me." William choked back a tear. "You were the best friend a man could ever have. You deserved more from life than what you got."

He touched the coffin, felt like falling to his knees and weeping like a child. "I don't expect you to forgive me, Andrew...or Sally either. I need to fix this mess I've made, but I don't know how." He blinked, fought to maintain his composure. "Rest in peace, my friend."

Stepping back from the coffin, he took a seat in the front pew and looked back to the doors, which were still closed. He stared at them, wishing they'd open, hoping they'd reveal Sally Mayfield. But for the next twenty minutes, the organ music played, and the doors remained closed.

A young man wearing blue and purple robes came in through a curtain behind the pulpit. The large gold cross hanging around his neck seemed heavy. He introduced himself as Reverend James. "Shall we start?" he asked, looking around the empty place.

"Please do," William replied. Andrew had died a lonely man.

After a short eulogy about the dead going to heaven and sitting at the right hand of God, Reverend James said, "In spite of this man's sole departure from this earth, we can take heart in the fact that he outlived all his friends. Amen."

Reverend James closed the head cover. Two diggers in hooded yellow raincoats and gray overalls rolled in a rubber-wheeled pallbearer. They lifted the coffin onto it, not showing anything but cold eyes and stiff lips from under their hoods.

William stood, approached the coffin once more, and asked the preacher, "Do you know why Andrew wished to be buried here?"

Nodding to the diggers, Reverend James clamped a Bible under his left arm and followed them out of the chapel. "No," he said finally. "Only that we've instructions to bury him in plot number 237B. He bought and paid for it thirty years ago."

"That's strange." William paused. "Does that mean there is a 237A?"

The Reverend glanced at him sharply as they moved into the rain soaked cemetery. "Funny you should ask." He ducked under William's open umbrella. "This particular plot has A, B, C, and D. They were all paid for in advance, including our finest executive caskets. But it's not a family plot. Last names are all different."

William wondered whom Andrew had chosen to spend eternity with. "Do you recall their last names?"

"Not right off. But we can check the registry later." He patted his bible. "When we're done here."

They walked together following the casket down the sidewalk

past rows of gravestones. Rain pitter-pattered on the umbrella, and William's heart felt as heavy as the gray clouds churning above.

The tiny procession turned down a muddy row. Ahead, under a canopy, William saw a pile of dirt next to a hole the diggers had made with a mud-spattered backhoe parked off to the side. Soggy canvas covered the marker of the grave next to the one dug for Andrew. Propped up in a wheelbarrow, a new tombstone shined with rain. *Here Lies Andrew Cobb*, it read. William leaned against his diamond-studded cane and shivered.

The diggers lowered Andrew into the hole.

Stepping from under the umbrella, Reverend James made a sign of the cross over the grave. "Ashes to ashes. Dust to dust. I commend you to the house of the Lord." He turned and walked away in the rain.

William stayed and watched the diggers shovel dirt into the grave, which made a thumping sound on the coffin, a sound that dug deep into the pit of William's stomach. Rain pelted the umbrella now, the wind rising, but William watched them finish. It was the least that he could do for Andrew.

After the tombstone was set in place, they pulled down the canopy and removed the canvas protecting the grave next to Andrew Cobb. With the wheelbarrow piled high, they trudged away.

As he turned to follow them, William thought about grave number 237A, wondered whose it was, Andrew's grandmother perhaps, or a sister, or maybe someone he loved long ago? Stepping up to the marker, he read the words engraved in white marble:

WILLIAM TULIVER.
Born
JANUARY 10, 1910
Died
AUGUST 20, 1970

William fell to his knees, clutching the diamond-studded cane as he read the inscription again. He felt smothered, couldn't breathe.

His former body lay beneath him. Ashes and dust. The revelation turned his stomach upside down.

He dropped the umbrella and cane in the mud and folded his hands together, his face turned up to the drizzling sky. "God, what have I done?" He felt empty and alone. Lost. Someone had cloned him. He'd cheated death, but only temporarily. The same cancer would kill him again. Death would not be denied. Ever.

A clap of thunder rolled in the distance. He became aware of creaking wheels, rattling metal, and the shuffling of boots on cement. Thinking the diggers were coming back, he looked left and right, but no one was there. He turned around, noticed a figure hunched over the handle of a shopping cart, pushing it down the cemetery sidewalk. The pusher wore a long gray coat, covered with plastic bags that dripped rain. A brown trash bag flapped from the person's head like a makeshift scarf. The shopping cart was piled high with bags of different colors. A broomstick jutted straight up from the cart like a flagpole. The load seemed too heavy a burden for the small frame behind it.

William looked down again at his headstone and back to the shopping cart wheeling toward him. Standing, he felt annoyed at the interruption. He wanted to be alone with his past self. Cold rain streamed down his face as he watched this strange spectacle approach close enough now to see an old lady pushing the cart. As it creaked to a stop in front of him, he could only stare at the odd sight.

The old lady stepped from behind the cart. Locks of red hair, streaked with gray, protruded from under the plastic-bag scarf and fluttered in the wind. Her hardened face, wrinkled and freckled, showed no smile. She looked at the fresh grave with weary hazel eyes. "This where they buried Andrew Cobb?"

"Yes," William said, amazed that she was here.

"I came as soon as I could." She walked to the front of her cart, never taking a hand off it. "Poor man."

William couldn't take his eyes off her. Déjà vu sliced through him like the blade of a knife. A rocket lifted off to the moon. The trees in Paradise Park swayed. A fountain roared. It was Sally Mayfield, the woman he'd loved in a past life. His knees began to tremble.

"Was it a nice service?" Sally looked up from the grave. Her eyes met his and froze. "Oh, my God...William."

"Hello, Sally?" he said softly, his heart pounding like mad.

She fell back against her shopping cart, clung to it as if it were the ledge of a tall building. Her eyes were wide, and rain flowed down her startled face.

He offered her his hand.

She turned her back on him.

"Sally, please. There's something I need to ask you."

"I have to go."

"Are you my mother?"

"No."

"Did you give birth to Geoffrey Scott Michaels?"

She turned around, sneered at him. "I was just your incubator, William, a warm place for your clone to grow. You don't have a mother. God knows you don't deserve one." Her words were cold as the rain.

He stared at her with tears in his eyes. This emotional roller coaster was killing him. First his parents weren't his parents, then his father wasn't his father, and now his mother isn't his mother—and he's a goddamned clone. His whole life was falling apart. "Who did this to us?"

She shoved the shopping cart around and leaned on the handle. "Leave me alone, ya hear?"

"Please, Sally. Wait. Help me."

"I helped you once before. Look what it got me."

He reached out and touched the sleeve of her coat. "I need to know how this happened."

She jerked her arm away. "Figure it out for yourself. You got this far." She pushed the cart into motion.

"No. Wait." William stepped in front of the shopping cart,

which violently banged into his leg.

She backed off and rammed him again. "Let me go," she shouted, her eyes narrow and hard.

"Please don't be like this, Sally."

She pulled the broom handle from her basket and gave him a whack. "Let me go, I tell ya." She hit him again.

William grabbed the stick. "Stop it, Sally. You've got to tell me who did this."

"I'm not telling you shit."

The streets had hardened Sally, made her tough and unyielding. "Look." He pointed to his grave. "What am I doing here, Sally? I'm supposed to be dead."

"To me, you are dead. Now you're a clone, a freak of nature."

"Does that mean I'm not a human being, a person with feelings, needs, and desires like anyone else?"

"Not as far as I'm concerned." She yanked on the stick.

He wouldn't let her have it. He'd been reduced to a desperate man, soaked with rain, defending himself against an old woman and her stick. "Please, Sally. Talk to me."

"You got what you asked for, William. Don't expect me to help you feel good about it now."

William released his grip on the stick. "Maybe we can help each other."

She held up the stick as if to strike him again. Then looking at him for a moment, her eyes softened. "You're still one hell of a good looking man, William." She cast her eyes down. "I'm old and worn out. I can't help you."

"Then who can?"

"It was Carl Savage. He betrayed us. Sold you out like a lab rat, left me without my baby. The whole fucking army was chasing me. He's the one you should be looking for."

"Where is he?"

"Working a porno ring out of Las Vegas, last I heard."

"I've got to find him."

Thunder clapped overhead.

"You do that. Now let an old lady pass."

Trees whipped back and forth in the storm's fury. William braced himself against the onslaught, the rain stinging his face. "If I step aside, will you tell me where can I find you again?"

"Don't bother looking for me, William. I like my simple life. But someday you'll find me right here." She pointed to the next gravesite, 237C. "Maybe there I'll find the peace Andrew Cobb has found today."

William stepped back from the shopping cart, shivering from the chill of the rain and guilt in his heart. He'd made a mess out of everyone's lives. The ones he loved most had suffered the most. And whatever life Jeff Jordan might have had was ruined along the way. And now Lois would end up alone, too. He looked at the last empty grave. "237D is for me, isn't it?"

"About time, don't you think?"

"I'm not ready yet."

She reached into her gray coat and pulled out an old plastic rattle with a red handle. "This is all I've had to remind me of you, when you were a baby. I bought it for you one Halloween night before I gave you up for adoption." She handed it to William. "You can have it now."

Trembling, he took the little rattle from her bony fingers. "My God. This was mine?" It felt like a giant piece of his past.

"Before I go," Sally said, "Tell me, how did you know about Andrew Cobb?"

"He was a character in a book I wrote."

"*The Lost Diamonds*?" she asked flatly.

"What happened to it?"

"I burned it...thirty years ago. Never thought you'd write it again."

"I wish I hadn't."

She leaned against the shopping cart and gave it a shove. "The truth can be an ugly thing."

"Please don't go."

"Goodbye, William."

Feeling like the loneliest person in the world, he watched Sally push the shopping cart down rain-slicked rows of tombstones and disappear into the mist. After the last image of her faded, he turned to grave 237D and placed the old rattle on it. This was where he belonged.

In his first life as William Tuliver, the people he'd loved and those who loved him gave meaning and purpose to his life. Someone had found a way to duplicate him, but they couldn't duplicate the things that gave true substance to his life, the love of a good woman and the loyalty of a good friend.

And he had failed them both.

Terry Wright

Chapter Fifty-Two

Las Vegas, Nevada

"Flight attendants, prepare for landing," the pilot said over the intercom. The 737 started a smooth descent to the desert floor. The city at night, as William saw from his window, looked like an oasis of colored lights surrounded by a vast span of darkness. He sat back in his seat, cinched his belt a little tighter, and awaited the touchdown.

It had been snowing in Chicago when he left. A Canadian cold front blew in over Lake Michigan, smothering the city in its wintry grip and making for a miserable Thanksgiving weekend. In Las Vegas, the temperature was a balmy 72 degrees.

In the seat next to William, a man locked his tray into the upright position. Instead of a stranger, William wished Lois were sitting next to him. They were cleaning up the kitchen after their Thanksgiving meal when she told him she didn't feel like going. Her morning sickness had been getting worse, and she had an appointment to see an obstetrician on Friday. He was supposed to be the best baby doctor in Chicago, and William believed only the best was good enough for Lois Tuliver.

Engine whine subsiding, the jet sank in the air. He remembered arriving home from the shop that night, as if it had happened yesterday. Lois lit candles all around the house. She'd set the dinner table with her finest china, and champagne bubbled in slender glasses. The look on her face beamed as bright as the full moon. "What's all this?" he remembered asking her. It was the best news he had ever heard. William Tuliver was going to be a father.

He was happy that she had something else to be concerned about now, instead of worrying about his hip all the time, his cancer, and the treatments he'd postponed. She could concentrate on the baby while he looked for the people responsible for cloning him. The problem with his hip was destined to run its own course, but he'd have to force the issue with Carl Savage: clue number four. If he were anything like his character in *The Lost Diamonds*, confronting him would not be found on anyone's list of fun things to do, but he had to face him to get the answers he needed.

The jet banked left. City lights sparkled below the wingtip. He patted his coat pocket where he'd stashed the letter from the Nevada Gaming Commission. It had arrived on Wednesday. With Toyoko's help, he was able to find Carl Savage. Turns out he owned The Red Lace Saloon on Las Vegas Boulevard, a strip joint with a rowdy reputation. If Sally was right about Carl, the place was probably a front for some sleazy porno operation.

The landing gear came down with a thump. A chime dinged through the cabin twice. William braced the diamond-studded cane between his knees and turned to look out the window. Below, city lights whizzed by, and a moment later, tires rumbled on the runway and reverse thrusters roared.

Inside the terminal, people milled about, some dragging luggage behind them, others grabbing handles on waiting slot machines. The sounds of clunking coins and ringing bells filled the air. William pressed his way to a bank of phones, coined a slot, and tapped in his phone number.

"Hello?" Lois answered.

"I made it. Is everything okay?"

"I miss you."

"I'll be back soon."

"Be careful." She hung up.

William clutched the receiver in his hand, not wanting to let go of his connection to Lois. *Be careful*, she'd said. A tingle skittered up his neck. He knew he might be walking into a dangerous situation. In *The Lost Diamonds*, he'd made Carl Savage a brutal man with no moral convictions. There was nothing he wouldn't do for a dollar. He'd even claimed that he'd sold his mother's soul to the devil. Carl was like the worm in an apple, destroying everything that was good around him for only one reason, to fatten himself up for a greater purpose. William had to be careful dealing with the Dragon Man.

At that, he set down the receiver and made his way through the noisy throng, then outside to a taxi stand where a porter hailed a cab.

"Where to, buddy?"

"Red Lace Saloon." William got in.

"Ah, a little sin for the flesh." The meter started running. "I know the place well, and I'll tell ya, buddy, they ain't got nothing like the Red Lace anywhere except Vegas, no sir, not even San Francisco, and I been there a lot, too."

"Don't take the scenic route. I'm in a hurry." William settled into the back seat and tried to ignore the distinct odor of sour beer and cheap perfume. The cab made popping and grinding noises as she rumbled along. He figured there must have been a million miles on her.

They cruised past the Luxor's pyramid of glass with its towering pylon and magnificent Egyptian sphinx statues. It stood in ancient contrast to the Excalibur Hotel with its Medieval Castle façade across the street. Up ahead, the Statue of Liberty stood poised like a proud beacon in front of New York, New York. On down The Strip, William took in the frontages of Caesar's Palace, the Mirage, Circus Circus, and other gaming establishments. Excess seemed to be the main commodity in this town, plenty of everything to entice tourists into parting with their money, a perfect place for Carl Savage.

The cab turned right and rattled into a car-choked parking lot fronting a two-story building. Flashing neon lights lit the entire façade, some forming a curvaceous dancing girl kicking a shapely leg high above ample breasts. An array of red lights made up the lacy teddy she wore. THE RED LACE SALOON sign pulsed to the beat of music booming from the club's entrance.

William pulled himself out of the cab. Holding the diamond-studded cane under his arm, he paid the cabbie and sent him on his way in a swirl of tire smoke and black exhaust. Standing at the front doors, the smell of cigar smoke rolled out of the club. He knew that Carl smoked cigars and probably welcomed those patrons who indulged likewise. Taking in what he believed to be his last breath of fresh air, William stepped inside.

The music was loud, the beat stimulating. He craned his neck, tried to get a peek into the room beyond the door, but a bouncer blocked his view. He was a brute of a man with no neck and hairy arms tattooed in skulls and dragons. "That'll be twenty bucks, mister." His words hissed through gaps of missing teeth.

William fumbled out a twenty. "I'm here to see your boss, not get a date."

"Only date you'll ever get is in your hand, cream puff, so move along."

The bullies of the world were all alike. William walked into Carl's nest of sin. Oddly, the place wasn't at all like he'd imagined. Instead of a dingy bar packed with sleazy patrons and ruddy whores, he saw satin covered tables and richly upholstered chairs arranged in clusters around the barroom, which was dimly lit in blues and reds and swept by white spotlight beams. Illuminated cigar smoke swirled in the air. Everything vibrated to the beat of the music. The place was full of whooping and hollering men, most casually dressed, perhaps upper class white-collar workers.

Leaning on his cane, he spotted the reason for all their frivolity. A curvaceous stripper was dancing around a chrome pole on center stage. She wore a stars-and-stripes thong and no top. Catlike eye makeup, sultry red lips, and rose-colored cheeks gave her an animalistic aura. Long black hair cascaded down to her hips, which undulated to the music. Glitter sparkled all over the naked parts of her body.

Terry Wright

With each step William took toward the tables, cane in hand, the closer he got to her, the more he was aware of his rising heartbeat. She wasn't only beautiful, but she was a professional showgirl, an expert at keeping the audience's attention. Her eyes met his, and for the briefest of moments, he caught himself holding his breath. Then she flashed him a smile, wrapped a shapely leg around the pole, and rode it to the floor.

William slid into a chair by the stage, looked around trying to get a feel for the joint. Burly bouncers stood around here and there. Skimpily clad waitresses moved about the room, trays balanced on upturned palms and hips swinging. He put the cane between his knees, glad that Lois was safe at home. Glancing at the stripper and feigning interest, his attention was mostly on his peripheral vision as he searched the crowd of faces for one that might be Carl Savage— the way he'd imagined him to look: short and fat and ugly.

As if on cue, a petite blond wearing a red lace teddy and white high heels approached him, smiling. "Care to buy a lonely girl a drink?"

"No thanks."

She leaned over, facing him, her cleavage displayed without shame. "Then a lap dance, perhaps?"

"I'll have a beer."

She twisted her fanny toward him, looked back over her shoulder and winked. "Is there anything else you would like?"

"Make it a Bud Light."

"My room is upstairs—"

"Just get me a beer," William growled. "And forget the come-ons."

"Well!" She huffed and stomped off.

Not giving her another thought, he went back to watching the woman on stage and wondering where Carl Savage was, when a bouncer came up behind him and yanked him out of the chair by his suit coat collar. He nearly dropped his cane. "Hey!"

"Okay, wise guy," the bouncer bellowed. "What's your

problem?"

The little blonde was standing next to him, arms crossed, tapping her foot. "Kick him to the curb, man."

"What'd I do?" William protested. "Offend the boss's daughter?"

Just then, one of the bouncer's buddies approached with a hairy-knuckled fist drawn back. William didn't take time to think about it, just swung his cane with the force he would have put to his tennis racket. The rhino-horn handle hit the side of the bruiser's head, dropping him to the floor like a wet towel.

A woman screamed.

The bouncer shoved William into a table. Beer bottles, ashtrays, and patrons went flying. The bouncer came at him again. Fighting panic, William rolled over and jabbed the cane into the bouncer's nose. Blood spurted out. The goon staggered backward, palmed his face, and hollered, giving William time to scramble to his feet. He swung the cane again, a backhand this time, right into the bouncer's groin. That put the big man on the floor, writhing in pain, clutching his crotch with one hand and his face with the other.

The music stopped.

William crouched, gave the crowd a nervous look over, his eyes shifting back and forth, the cane poised to strike anyone else who made a move on him. He thought they all could hear his heart pounding.

"Well, well, well," came a voice that chilled the air. "What have we got here, boys, some kind of tough guy?"

William looked around for the origin of the voice, a voice that filled his head with déjà vu. At the top of the stairs, a fat man appeared, stood spread legged, a black cigar smoldering between his teeth. Thick gray hair hung to his shoulders, and he wore a light brown suit, a bulging vest, and baggy pants sharply pressed. Carl Savage. William clenched his jaw.

The fat man lumbered down the stairs. A spotlight followed him to the floor of the club.

William felt sick with fear but held out his cane in front of him. "Call off your dogs, Carl."

Waddling up, the fat man seemed unconcerned about William's threatening stance. More spotlights swiveled and poured over them. Carl pulled the rank cigar from his teeth and gave his bleeding bouncer a swift kick. "Get your ass out of here." Then he pointed to the bruiser lying unconscious on the floor. "You're fired." Then turning to William, "And as for you, young man..." His eyes bored into William's face, which was well lit by the spotlights. "You're..." Carl glanced at the diamond-studded cane clenched in William's fists. Beads of sweat appeared on his fat forehead. His mustache twitched. "You're..?" His face contorted in bewilderment, and then his brows arched. "Very impressive." He laughed. "Let's have us a little chat, say upstairs...in my office."

William felt his blood turn cold. Seeing Carl, it was as if the villain in *The Lost Diamonds* had just leaped off the pages, frighteningly real. However, William refused to be intimidated. He tapped his cane on the floor. "I ordered a Bud Light. The service around here stinks." He quickly glanced at the stripper who was standing there half-naked, holding onto the stage pole and scowling at him as if perturbed at the interruption of her performance. "Sorry, Miss." William tipped an imaginary hat.

She smiled.

"Somebody get this man a beer," Carl barked. "We'll be upstairs."

The music began again.

William followed his nemesis up the stairs, caught a whiff of The Dragon Man's cheap cologne. They went into an office, a cozy place complete with a gas fireplace in the corner and a built-in bar against the far wall. The smell of cigar smoke permeated the room. William hooked his cane on the edge of a desk. The petite blonde brought his Bud Light and left with her nose in the air. He took a gulp of beer and set it down. "Bet you never thought you'd see the likes of me again."

Carl pinched the loose skin under his chin. "William Tuliver, you look great."

"I don't feel so good." He folded his arms across his chest and leaned against the desk, ignoring a stab of pain in his hip. The music seemed far away.

"I see you've still got your cane."

"My hip's been bothering me."

"Again?"

"Nice place you have here." William changed the subject.

"Couldn't have done it without you, William." Carl chuckled. "The Diamond deal made me enough dough to get in good with the Chicago syndicate boys. They have a way of making honey out of horseshit, if you know what I mean."

"The mob, huh? Drugs?"

"Don't touch the stuff. Porn, William. It's all the rage. Everybody has some of it hidden somewhere...in a drawer, a closet." He touched his mustache. "You have any idea how many pedophiles there are in this country?"

"I don't *want* to know, Carl."

"So what brings you here?"

"I'm looking for the bastards who cloned me."

Carl's eyebrows dipped. "What do you know about it?"

William examined his beer bottle. "I've been reading a lot lately...about Dolly the sheep and stem cell research for starters. Seems I'm way ahead of the times."

Carl waddled to his built-in bar. "How did you find out?"

"I left an ugly trail."

"What makes you think I know anything about it?"

"Sally told me."

"Sally? Of course." His eyes narrowed. "That bitch screwed up everything."

William checked an instant desire to smash the fat man with his cane for saying that. "How do you figure?"

"She stole you from the lab. Because of her, Colonel Harrison got in deep shit with the Pentagon, and I lost a bundle on consulting fees. No clone. No money." Carl snuffed out the rank stub of his cigar and pulled the top from a bottle of scotch. "Do you know you're the first human clone?"

"Why don't I feel honored?"

"Don't let it get you down, boy." Carl poured a splash of scotch into a glass. He swirled it around before he downed the whole thing. "The government's been dabbling in human cloning for three decades, thanks to you."

"I haven't heard anything about it."

"That's because Area 51 is the big deal, has been for a long time. Seems people are more interested in aliens than anything else the government might be hiding."

"So they're getting away with it."

"It was all your idea, William. You insisted the government have this cloning technology."

"Well I was wrong."

"What, no more high and almighty patriotism, William? What happened to your principles this time?"

"Things change."

"That's a fact." Carl snorted. "So what have you been up to with your new life? Married? Got any kids?"

William didn't answer. He knew Carl had a way of getting information. It was a lawyer thing, and he wouldn't divulge any information readily either. William decided to dabble in small talk and maybe Carl would loosen up enough to start talking about the cloners. "Married," he finally said after taking another swallow of beer. "We have a nice home in South Chicago. My wife is pregnant. Her name's Lois."

"Congratulations." Carl poured another shot of scotch, which he carried with him to his desk. "Sally must've been heartbroken. You ending up with Lois and all." He plopped into his chair.

"Sally doesn't know anything about me. She gave me up for adoption thirty years ago. I don't blame her for what she did. It was all my fault, anyway."

"That was one hell of a crazy idea you came up with, William." Carl eyed the scotch in his glass. "I found a lab, you pumped in the money. Biggest deal I ever made. Then the government stepped in. Does your wife know anything about this?"

"As much as I do, but she's having a harder time believing it."

"Can't say as I blame her." He sipped the scotch. "So you were adopted. How did your parents react when you told them you were a clone?"

William shook his head. "I didn't tell them anything. They've got enough problems."

The fat man scratched his crotch. "Well then, it appears to me that your wife is the only person who knows this secret of yours."

"So far."

Carl leaned forward in his chair. "She's in danger, you know."

A jolt of adrenaline set fires in William's bloodstream. "What are you talking about?"

"They've been looking for you and Sally for a long time. If your wife breathes any of this to the wrong people, they'll zero in on her."

"Who's been looking for me, Carl?"

"The cloners."

William bared his teeth. "Well, I'm looking for them, too, and you're going to tell me where they are."

"Now don't get all riled up and jump into something you got no clue about. You gotta be careful of General Harrison. Things have changed a lot in thirty years, but I think I can get you in, through a back door maybe. You can sneak up on them—"

"I want to bash in their front door, Carl."

"You'll get yourself killed."

"I died once. I'm getting good at it."

"Ever since you got away, General Harrison's locked the place down tight. You can't get in through the front door."

"There's got to be a way."

Carl rubbed the fat on his chin. "Let me put you up for the night. You'll be quite comfortable at my villa on Lake Mead. I'll do some checking around, see what them cloners are up to. We'll make a plan." Carl arched his eyebrows. "You can't go in without a plan."

William downed the last of his beer. Something in his guts warned him: *Don't listen to Carl Savage. Don't trust him.* But he was right about needing a plan. Without one, the search for the cloners could end up a suicide mission. Carl Savage was a necessary evil. William had to trust him. "Okay."

Carl pulled himself out of his chair, a fat smile on his face. "Go downstairs and make yourself at home. Have another beer. It's on the house. Enjoy the show. I'll call my chauffeur." He picked up the phone. "You can leave whenever you're ready. And if you like, I'll fix you up with Cindy Star, the dancer you were ogling down there. She's my top draw."

"I'll pass." William picked up his diamond-studded cane and limped to the door. As he grabbed the doorknob, he turned to face Carl. "You better not be jerking me around."

"Hey, you're in good hands, my man. Now get down there and have some fun. I'll be along in a minute."

***

Holding the phone, Carl watched William walk out of the office and close the door. When the footsteps faded, he dialed. As the phone rang, he tossed back the last of his scotch. He'd been waiting for this day for thirty years. Payday.

The circuit clicked. "Blythe Biotech, Dr. Larson speaking."

"It's me, Carl Savage."

"What do you want, Carl?"

"I found your lost clone."

Chapter Fifty-Three

S craping like mad, the wipers on Detective Ritter's squad car barely kept pace with the snow building up on his windshield. He was warm enough though, wearing his Chicago Bears parka and black gloves. The heater whined fiercely, and the tires crunched through gravel and salt scattered by a plow hurling snow down Indiana Highway 41. Since noon, the Thanksgiving Day Blizzard had brought traffic to a crawl across the southern tip of Lake Michigan, but in spite of the weather, he had to make this trip. Captain Lou Billings, the Indiana State Police Commander, had called an hour ago with horrifying news. Karen Carlyle and her husband weren't the only ones hacked up with an ax in these parts.

Ritter accelerated around the snowplow. The squad car fishtailed through deep snow rutted with windblown tire tracks. Hunkering over the steering wheel, his heartbeat did double-time as he fought to maintain control. Billings had told him a forensic team was processing the crime scene just outside St. John. A work crew breaking ice on an irrigation canal had stumbled on the remains of two teenagers missing since late August, around the same time the Carlyles were murdered. A coincidence, Ritter thought? No way.

Approaching St. John, he spotted an Indiana State trooper's car idling at the city limits sign, his flashing overheads barely penetrating the snowstorm. It was Ritter's escort. He flashed his headlights. The patrol car spun onto the highway in front of him, picked up speed, and churned snow in its wake.

Three miles out of town, they made a left on Highway 231. The road, freshly plowed, took them east and then to a turnoff that skirted a heavily wooded canal. Rounding a bend, he saw a snowplow parked off to the side, and beyond it, flashing red and blue lights of a dozen or more police cars, and a step van marked: *CORONER*. Officers were huddled together like penguins.

Ritter braked behind his escort and climbed out of the squad car, bracing himself against the winter chill now biting his earlobes. A big black man, broad around the belly and wearing a long black coat, took a step back from the group of officers and batted his gloved hands together as if trying to ward off the cold. "Detective Ritter," he shouted. "Glad you could join our little party."

Ritter trudged through snow toward the officer, his face clearly visible now, a broad nose, high cheekbones, and thick eyelashes that busily blinked away snowflakes. A white scar sliced across his right cheek, an everyday reminder of a thug's bullet. Another half inch and Billings would have been dead. *Lucky Lou* everyone had called him after that.

"What have you got?" Ritter asked, keeping things official.

"Rita Jensen and Billy Don." Billings offered a gloved handshake.

"Positive IDs already?"

"The killer left their belongings, a purse, wallet, their money, but there's not much left of the kids."

"Badly decomposed?"

"Not to mention the scavengers." Billings pointed. "They're down there."

"Let's have a look." Kicking snow, Ritter followed Billings along a footpath that led toward the wooded canal. Entering a crime scene always gave Ritter the willies. It was sacred ground.

"You hear how they died?" Billings asked him.

"An ax, I was told."

"Right up your alley, I'd say."

Ritter didn't reply, wondering if he was suddenly an expert in the field of ax murders. He listened to the wind, the crunching of snow under his boots as he negotiated the slippery path down an embankment that sloped into a stand of trees and bushes. Beyond the thicket, the canal lay frozen. He thought it was an odd place for an ax murderer to strike, out here in the middle of nowhere. "Do you have the murder weapon?"

"We're still sweeping the area." Billings turned around

abruptly and grabbed Ritter's arm. "There's something else." He took in a slow breath. "Both kids were decapitated."

"Like Karen Carlyle...and Roger."

"Worse. The killer duct taped their heads together, lips to lips."

"He took the time to...what...leave us a message?"

"The way I read it, he's one sick bastard."

Ritter thought of Morris Brennon and shivered.

As they came upon an area swarming with investigators dressed in snow-dusted coats, Ritter got a sudden sense of the crime scene. *POLICE LINE – DO NOT CROSS* warned the yellow-taped barrier that cordoned off an area on his right. The ground had already been swept clean of snow, revealing a collapsed tent and what looked to be the remnants of a campfire. Bones and tattered clothing littered the scene.

On the left, an investigator squatted before two skulls propped up on a tree stump. He was flicking away snow with a small brush, being extra careful with the weathered and brittle duct tape that bound the skulls together in their eternal kiss.

Ritter stepped forward, dumbstruck at the sight.

Glancing up, the investigator said, "Talk about a camping trip gone bad."

A camera flashed.

Billings said, "No place is safe for our kids these days."

"Why were they camping down here?"

"The Rocky Mountains are too far away."

Scanning the area, Ritter tried to imagine how things must have looked to these kids back then. The trees would have been turning colors, the grasses long and green, and the canal water gurgling through this shaded campsite. It was a place of peace and beauty, a place that had turned to horror and death. *Cruel and unusual punishment* came to Ritter's mind.

He looked down the ice-choked canal that flowed south. Blinking, he wondered what had brought the killer and these two kids together at this particular spot. Was it coincidence that the killer had driven down the road, stopped here to take a leak, and stumbled onto them? Ritter shook his head. There were no coincidences. He knew the canal had to be the key. The ax murderer must have already been down here, possibly hiding out after killing Karen Carlyle, or maybe he'd used the canal for cover rather than travel the roads in plain view. If so, where was he headed—to another murder yet undiscovered, or was he going back to the place from which he came?

Ritter turned to the Captain who'd jammed his hands deep into his coat pockets. "This canal...where does it go?"

Stiff-armed, the big man angled his body upstream and then downstream. "Comes out of Lake Michigan, through Gary about ninety miles north, and branches out into the farmland around here."

"But where does it go?"

"As I recall..." Billings squinted. "This tributary runs under the old university and drains into Cedar Lake."

"What old university?"

"It's off limits nowadays. Government stuff—"

"What university?" Ritter pressed.

"I don't recall. That was some time back."

The investigator with the little brush looked up from his skull-cleaning chore. "My father went there. It was called Blythe University."

That name hit Ritter like a boxing glove. A doctor from Blythe University, Dr. Larson, had visited Morris Brennon at Menard State Prison on several occasions. Following up on that lead, and much to his dismay, he'd found no such place existed. It never occurred to him he should have been looking for a defunct university. Did Dr. Larson have a special interest in the condemned killer, and what kind of interest could it have been? Maybe it had something to do with whatever it was that they did at the university. He shielded his face from a sudden blast of wind driven snow. "What did they do at Blythe University?"

The investigator shrugged. "They were into genetic

engineering, hybrid stuff mostly, cattle and corn. Government's got control of it now, some kind of research center: Blythe Biotech."

"It's off limits," Billings reiterated.

Ritter inhaled cold air. "Biotech...like...cloning?"

"You watch too many late-night movies."

"But the government might...they could have..."

Billings shook his head. "Even *they* can't play God."

"But it all makes perfect sense..." Ritter couldn't control the sudden tremble coming from inside his chest. Thoughts of Dolly the sheep, cloned from a single cell, came to mind. And he remembered the medical report at Menard CC: *Tissue resection of right forearm.* For what other reason would a genetics doctor need tissue samples from a condemned man? Why else would he have gone to see Morris Brennon? Hell. A condemned murderer would be the perfect subject for an experiment in human cloning. No one had to know. No one would be around to point any fingers, to lay any claims to the clone, or draw attention to what they were doing at Blythe University. It all fit: the victim, Karen Carlyle, the vendetta carried out by the clone of the donor, everything but the fingerprints. Even identical twins didn't have the same fingerprints—unless they'd found a way to duplicate everything—including a killer—

Billings gave Ritter a shake. "You look like you're going to faint."

"I-I got a bad feeling about this," Ritter said, his voice cracking from the horror of his thoughts. As if the idea of human cloning wasn't bad enough, or the choice of donor unspeakably irresponsible, knowing the government had control of Blythe Biotech made Ritter's temples throb. He saw no limits to the terror racing through his mind. "We gotta get in there."

"You can't be serious."

"It's the best lead I've got."

"But it's heavily guarded."

Ritter patted the Glock under his coat. "There's got to be a way."

Chapter Fifty-Four

Westside Medical Center

Lois paced the waiting room floor in the obstetrics department. She stopped in front of the nurses' station, looked over the pictures of newborn babies and the assortment of stuffed animals on the counter. The duty nurse looked up from her appointment log and smiled. "He won't be much longer. Relax. Sit down."

Seating herself on the couch, she thumbed absentmindedly through a maternity magazine. She'd become accustomed to the antiseptic smell, the chatter of pregnant women, and the ringing phone that never let up. But her friend had told her this was the best doctor in Chicago. He was worth the wait to see and worth the inconvenience of taking a bus across town in a blizzard.

The reality of having a baby hadn't taken hold of her yet. Bouts of morning sickness seemed her only means to measure this stage of pregnancy. Whenever she tried to imagine her abdomen bulging out in front of her, or her breasts swollen and heavy with milk, a quiver of disbelief rippled through her body. But carrying Jeff's—or—William's child was the single most important thing in her life right now, an adventure she anticipated with pride.

"You may go in now," the nurse said.

Lois stood, put a hand on her belly even though it showed no hint of her condition, gave it a pat and said, "Here goes nothin', kid."

A young lady, maybe eighteen years old and wearing a pink lab coat, escorted her through the door. "Right in here." She directed

Lois to a narrow padded table covered with a sheet of white paper then handed her a skimpy white smock with only one tie to close the opening in back. "Put this on."

The revealing garment sent a chill down Lois's spine, but she knew she couldn't let her modesty come into this. No matter how nervous she felt about showing herself to this doctor, she resigned to be strong. When the young lady left the room, Lois laid the smock on the table, grabbed the hem of her sweater, and pulled it over her head.

Static electricity crackled in her hair as she inspected the sterile-white room. The counter, the cabinets, the floor, all looked sparkling clean. She undid her blouse buttons and examined a poster showing cross-sections of a pregnant woman's womb in various stages of development. It all looked so complicated.

Blouse and bra discarded, she donned the little smock and tied the string. A framed poem hanging on the wall caught her attention. It was titled *God's Garden*.

The world is a garden of dirt and sod,
the earth giving foods and waters.
A woman is a garden of love and God,
the womb giving sons and daughters.

Feeling a tingle inside, she pulled off her shoes, dropped her skirt and panties, and sat on the crisp paper-covered examination table. Her feet dangled over the edge.

Waiting was the hard part.

As she rubbed goose bumps from her arms, she thought about Jeff, or William as he preferred to be called now, in Las Vegas, wondering if he had spent a restful night at Carl Savage's mansion on Lake Mead. William had called before he went to sleep. He said Carl wasn't as bad as he first thought, and he told her how Carl had offered to help him find the cloners. The whole thing sounded so unreal. She hoped he'd come to his senses and get treatment for the cancer—before too long.

The young assistant came in again. She wrapped a blood pressure cuff around Lois's arm, took her pulse and temperature, and wrote a few things down. They talked about the snowstorm a little, how difficult the roads were, and how wrong the weather forecasters were most the time. Then she finally said her name was Suzie. Lois enjoyed her cheery demeanor and began to relax.

Squeezing the bulb of the blood pressure cuff pump, "I'm in my second year at the University of Illinois," she said, studying the gauge with the pulsing needle. "I've always wanted to be a nurse."

"I work for Azar's Computerware," Lois offered, her arm throbbing with pressure. "We distribute to all fifty states."

"Sounds boring." Suzie twisted a little valve on the gauge, which let out a hiss of air. Velcro made a ripping sound as she unwrapped the deflated cuff. "Dr. Marshall will be right in."

Suzie left her alone in the room. Lois flexed her arm a couple of times, thought of how little she knew about Dr. Marshall, only what her friend had told her. A lot of the things her friend told her didn't matter, like how distinguished he looked and that his smile was to die for. The parts about Purdue, his long-standing relationship with Westside Medical Center, and his bedside manner were most important. And he always took the time to get to know his patients.

The doorknob clicked. She turned, saw the doctor come in. As expected, he wore a long white smock, and a stethoscope dangled around his neck. His hair was touched with gray, and she thought the wrinkles on his clean-shaven face gave him an air of distinction. His brown eyes gleamed at her over a pair of reading glasses. "Mrs. Jordan, how are you today?" His smile seemed warm and sincere.

"I'm pregnant, Dr. Marshall."

"My friends call me Eugene." He shook her hand.

"I like that, Dr. Eugene."

"Just Eugene."

"I'm a little nervous."

"Well, don't be. I don't bite." The doctor inspected the file. He appeared to be skimming over notes Suzie had written earlier.

"Everything looks tip-top here." He put the file on the counter and looked her up and down. "You seem healthy enough for motherhood."

"It's my first one."

"The first is the most fun."

He stood in front of her, his hand on the side of her throat, probing a little, probably checking for things she didn't have. "My tonsils were taken out when I was six."

"Let's see." Eugene smiled. "Open."

She showed him a gaping mouth and stuck out her tongue.

"Very good, Mrs. Jordan."

Oh dear, Jordan—she'd forgotten—her last name was Tuliver now. "I'm sorry," she said. "I made a mistake...on your questionnaire. My name. I wrote Lois Jordan, but it's changed."

He looked into her ear with a chrome thing. "That doesn't sound like a mistake."

"It's my husband's idea."

Eugene looked in her other ear. "So where is he today? I thought he might have come with you."

"He wanted to, but something came up. He's in Las Vegas, looking for some guy named Carl Savage."

Doctor Marshall stiffened. "Carl Savage?"

He sounded shocked.

She turned to face him, surprised to see his wide eyes staring at her in alarm. "You know him?"

"You're sure about the name?"

"As sure as I'm not Mrs. Jordan anymore."

The doctor put a firm hand on her arm. "Tell me about that."

"You won't believe it."

"Try me."

She looked into his eyes. He seemed sincerely interested. Maybe she'd feel better if she confided in him. Besides, her friend said he could be trusted with anything. "My husband doesn't believe he's Jeff Jordan anymore. And if *he's* not Jeff Jordan, then *I'm* not

Mrs. Jordan."

"Who does he think he is?"

"Some guy he wrote about in his book."

"What book?"

Her stomach felt jittery. "Jeff had been working on a story about a rich man and his diamonds, something that was in his head, driving him crazy. He really is a good writer and finished the book in less than a year. But when he tried to get it published, he found out it was already written."

Eugene leaned on the counter, a bewildered expression on his face. He didn't look as if he believed any of it.

Hell, she hardly believed it herself, so why should he? "Never mind." She felt foolish for having brought it up. "You've got more important things to worry about."

"T-this book, Mrs. Jordan...was it called *The Lost Diamonds?*"

A poisonous silence choked the air. Heart pounding, she swallowed hard, unable to pull her gaze from Dr. Marshall's eyes. "How do you know about Jeff's book?"

White as a ghost, he managed, "Is h-he William Tuliver?"

Lois's blood pressure must've doubled. The doctor was scaring the hell out of her. "You know him?"

"Knew him..." Eugene's stare went blank, distant. "It was a long time ago...in a genetics lab at Blythe University."

Lois's chest tightened. "What are you talking about?"

He grabbed her shoulders and looked her straight in the eye. "Does William know where he came from?"

"He's just going through a tough time—"

He shook her. "Does he know, Mrs. Tuliver?"

"You're hurting me."

Eugene released her shoulders and stepped back. "I'm sorry. It's just that I was there when he was born. He was an experiment in human duplication, not a twin clone, mind you, an exact duplicate of William Tuliver."

"You mean...it's true?" Her heart banged against her ribcage.

"He *is* a clone?"

"His surrogate mother, Sally, she had an emotional investment in him. I helped her rescue him from the lab. They escaped. Gone without a trace...for thirty years."

Lois still didn't want to believe it.

Eugene wiped his brow. "We were messing with things that should have been left alone. The government got in on it. I quit."

She now realized that Jeff's problems were not brought on by anything that he had done. None of this was his fault. Jeff Jordan was a very special person. "Oh dear, what he must be going through," she whispered.

Eugene's eyes narrowed. "Has he found Carl Savage yet?"

"Yes."

A look of panic flashed in Eugene's eyes. "William's in big trouble."

Lois put a hand over her heart. What had he gotten himself into? "He told me Carl was going to help him find the cloners."

"It's a lie." Dr. Marshall tore off his stethoscope and threw it on the counter. "Carl Savage betrayed William once. He'll do it again."

"But why?"

"The Department of Defense offered him a reward for returning the clone, a million dollars."

"What are we going to do?"

"*We* aren't going to do anything, but I am." He started taking off his smock, paused a moment, and regarded her closely. "You look a lot like Sally, you know."

"So I've been told." It was hard to believe that Jeff had a past life with another woman. She meant William. She wanted to scream.

"No wonder he picked you for his wife. Probably didn't even realize it. Has he found her yet?"

"He said he talked to her."

Eugene's brows jumped. "Where is she?"

"I don't know. She showed up at Andrew Cobb's funeral

pushing a shopping cart."

"She's homeless?"

"A bag lady."

Eugene clenched a fist. "No wonder I couldn't find her. She gave up everything, the trust fund, the good life, all because she loved William Tuliver."

"My William Tuliver?"

Eugene blinked. "He probably had no memory of his first life, but he had a feel for it, like déjà vu, mostly because of that enzyme we used when we cloned him."

"It made a mess of his life, drove him crazy. Writing the book helped him deal with it."

"William wrote *The Lost Diamonds* as a guide for him to find his way back to his past life and his money."

"Jeff wrote the book, too."

"Something must have happened to the original one."

"Sally said she burned it."

"So William wrote it again. He's back...all right, the same person. Oh Christ." Eugene staggered backward. "1122B. Morris Brennon's clone. He must be back, too."

Lois felt a sting charge up the back of her neck. "You cloned a murderer?"

"Dr. Larson did. I was just the delivery boy."

"Do you think the clone murdered Karen Carlyle?"

"I'm sure of it." He wadded up the smock and tossed it on the counter.

"We've got to go to the police."

Eugene shook his head. "I have a better idea. Get dressed. I'll take you home first."

Chapter Fifty-Five

Lake Mead

William awoke to the sound of rap music and revelry outside his window. He threw on a pair of boxer shorts, and with the help of his diamond-studded cane, limped to the balcony outside the guest room of Carl Savage's mansion. Squinting against the bright desert sun, he leaned on the white marble parapet and took in the view of the grounds stretched out below. Green lawns, flower gardens, and palm trees edging the perimeter were in stark contrast to the red and rocky landscape that surrounded the estate. A mix of sage and cacti dotted the hills toward the horizon, cut by a roller-coaster dirt road. He thought that if it weren't for Hoover Dam and Lake Mead, man would have no reason to visit this area, much less live here.

Voices rose on a light breeze, giggling women and men's laughter. To his left, a crowd had gathered around the swimming pool. They wore brightly colored Speedos and bikinis, and their bronzed bodies glistened with tanning oil. Someone tapped a beer keg. It spit foam and incited more laughter. William glanced at his watch. *11:10*. A little early for a party.

In the driveway below, rows of parked cars basked in the sun: four Mercedes, three red Porches, a BMW, and several Cadillacs. An older Corvette had been parked next to a Gold Wing motorcycle. Sunshine glinted off keys someone had left in the ignition. But nowhere could he see the limo he'd arrived in last night, and he wondered if Carl Savage had left early to check on the cloners.

A bass horn blared from a 30-foot blue and white Bayliner moored at the dock. The boat pitched as a woman dove off the side. She was naked. Three men holding beer cans cheered. William took in a big breath of desert air, smelled the sage and thought Hugh Hefner might appear at any minute.

"Señor Tuliver, there you are."

Startled, he whirled around, saw a short Mexican woman standing in the balcony doorway, her long black hair flowing over ample proportions. Embarrassment heated his cheeks as he stood there in his boxer shorts, gripping his cane.

"E-excuse me," he managed to say. "I wasn't expecting anyone."

"Hurry," she said. "You put on nice clothes I laid out for you and go to party. I need to clean the room."

"But—"

"Go ahead." She motioned him back inside.

He spent the rest of the day in blue swimming trunks, a white Las Vegas T-shirt, leather sandals, and greasy sun block. He ate barbecued chicken hot off the grill, potato salad, and way too many chocolate chip cookies. Two young ladies kept him company while he enjoyed a couple of Bud Lights and watched the macho men playing water polo and trying to drown each other. As the day withered to dusk, the music got louder and his patience with Carl Savage dwindled. What was taking him so long?

After sundown, a cool evening breeze gave him goose bumps. He went inside and changed back into his traveling suit, but left the tie loose around his neck.

Back in the kitchen, he picked up the phone and dialed Lois. The music outside was so loud he could hardly hear the phone ringing, but there was no answer. How strange?. Could she have been delayed getting back from the doctor's office? After all, Chicago was in the midst of a blizzard. Or perhaps she and her friend decided to get together and swap baby stories over dinner. He hoped she was all right and hung up the receiver, thinking he'd try her again later.

Suddenly the music stopped. A deathly quiet hung over the backyard. No laughter. No conversation. William rushed to the kitchen door and looked out. Flood lamps now lit the grounds. Swarms of bugs spiraled in bright cones of light.

"You heard me," boomed a gruff and angry voice.

William's chest tightened. Why was Carl Savage yelling at everyone?

"Clear out of here, you faggots and whores. Party's over."

Partygoers started running every-which-way like a spooked herd of gazelles. A woman let out a sharp cry.

Standing at the back door, William looked around the yard, past the pool to the dock from which the Bayliner had roared away earlier. He couldn't see Carl anywhere.

"Move it," Carl shouted. William sensed urgency in Carl's voice and wondered why he was in such a hurry to get everyone out.

Car engines revved and tires squealed. William thought he should flee with the rest of them. Hip burning, he clutched his cane and sprinted to a window overlooking the driveway. The cars were gone, their taillights filtering through kicked-up dust on the desert road. Only the Gold Wing remained, its keys still dangling from the ignition switch.

Suddenly, the house went dark. Someone had cut the power. What was Carl doing? Heart drumming, William wondered why the yard lights were still on. He decided to find out. Fighting panic, he burst out the back door, his hip on fire, his stomach a knot of dread. He made it down the steps to the pool's edge and turned around looking in every direction for Carl. The grounds were deserted.

"Carl."

Silence.

"Where the hell are you?"

Then he heard a droning sound, faint at first, but getting louder, aircraft engines and the buzz of propellers out over the lake. He pivoted on his diamond-studded cane, his eyes searching the dark eastern sky. Blinking green and red lights appeared and dropped down toward the ink-black water.

The hairs on the back of his neck prickled.

Bright lights beamed on, landing lights, from a plane with twin engines and pontoons. A sea plane. The yard lights had served as a homing beacon for the pilot. If the plane was loaded with latecomers to the party, they'd certainly be disappointed. Or perhaps Carl Savage had invited them here for a different reason. Maybe they were the cloners. Was this Carl's way of helping? William stiffened, threw back his shoulders. "Bring 'em on, Carl."

Gritting his teeth, he watched the plane touch down. Within moments, the yard lights fully illuminated the aircraft as it approached the dock where the Bayliner had been moored. Cabin lights glowed and silhouettes moved about inside. The floats, nearly as long as the airplane, cut through the water like sleek canoes, and the propellers stripped water from the lake, swirling mist into the air. As it neared, its engines cut off, propellers jerked to a stop, and the aircraft glided up to the dock.

William leaned on his cane and watched, his temples throbbing. He feared Carl Savage had betrayed him and brought the cloners to reclaim their property. Clenching his jaw, William awaited the confrontation with a mix of fear and contempt.

A door under the left wing swung open. Two soldiers in combat fatigues and black boots jumped out. They manned ropes and secured the aircraft to the dock. Seeing M-16s strapped across their backs, William felt an instinctive urge to run, but he held his ground, until the next man emerged. He wore a baggy gray sweatshirt and blue jeans. The sight of this baldheaded man sent an icy chill down William's spine. Déjà vu hit him like a runaway truck. Morris Brennon. He looked as if he'd stepped out of the pages of *The Lost Diamonds*. Even from twenty yards away, William could see the killer's black eyes. The mass murderer was alive again. A clone. How could the cloners have been so stupid? The news broadcast of Karen Carlyle's murder came back, and he realized he would be

Morris's next victim. Hot adrenaline spilled into his veins. He gripped the cane midway and lit out for the dark mansion's back door.

"Hey," someone yelled. "That's him."

William made it through the door, slammed it shut, clicked the lock, and pressed his back against the kitchen wall. Temples pounding, he went to work on his breathing, trying to calm down. Peering out the back window, he saw Morris Brennon approach, his heavy footfalls climbing the steps toward the door. William darted a glance to the boat dock. Four soldiers stood guard at the plane. The killer had been sent in to do their dirty work. William had to find a place to hide.

Swallowing panic, he groped through the darkness, using his cane like a blind man. He moved from the kitchen, through the dining room, and stumbled into a pitch-black hallway. Feeling invisible, he turned around to assess the conditions behind him. The dining room was a dull shade of gray due to the outside light bleeding in. He could barely make out the black forms of the table and chair backs. There was enough backlight to silhouette Morris the same way, but not enough light for him to see into the dark hallway. William decided to make his last stand right here.

Gripping his cane like a tennis racket, he remembered the motorcycle in the driveway, the keys in the ignition. His plan was forming as the sound of shattering glass and splintering wood erupted from the kitchen. A surprise attack on Morris, knock him out cold with the cane, then commandeer the motorcycle and make a clean getaway across the desert. The soldiers on the dock couldn't stop him. They were too far away, and it was too dark for them to snipe him with their rifles. It was a makeshift plan at best, but good as any—

Heavy footsteps tromped across hardwood floors, getting nearer and louder.

William gulped, gripped the cane with both hands and set it on his shoulder. He positioned himself in the center of the hall and tested the clearance for a swing. Hitting the wall or the ceiling would mean certain death. All he needed was one good whack to put the killer down. The rhino-horn handle was heavy enough. It hadn't failed him at the Red Lace Saloon. It wouldn't fail him now.

Slowly, Morris Brennon's burly silhouette took shape in the gray dining room and moved toward the hall, growing like an ink spill.

William held his breath. His heart pounded. He readied the cane as if for a tennis serve, a forehand smash: ace, point, match. Biding his time to make his fateful swing, he went over his plan one last time: the ambush, the motorcycle, and the escape. But something was wrong. He had overlooked one important detail. Morris Brennon was approaching the dark hallway. The soldiers were standing guard on the dock. But where was Carl Savage?

The floor creaked behind him. A sudden flash of light sliced through his brain. Then nothing.

Chapter Fifty-Six

Aloud buzzing sound filled William's head, which ached with every beat of his heart. He felt sick. A stinging sensation hurt his face. The buzzing got louder. He became more aware of things around him. Again, he felt a sting on his cheek, but this time he realized someone had slapped him. He pried open his eyes. Carl's blurry features appeared before him.

"There, ya see? I didn't hurt him too bad."

William shook fog from his head. The buzzing sound—airplane engines, and he saw the interior of an aircraft, small and dimly lit, with plush seats, some facing each other— soldiers with guns, and Carl—leaning over him, grinning. William tried to rub his eyes, but his hands wouldn't move. His wrists had been bound with rope and tied to his belt. Panic raced through him like wildfire. He rolled his eyes back up to Carl. "You lousy bastard. I trusted you."

"Your mistake." He tapped William's head with the diamond-studded cane and laughed. "You should've known better by now."

The plane hit a bump of air. William fought an urge to vomit. His eyes searched the faces staring at him. No one seemed the least bit sympathetic to his situation.

Back in his seat, Carl folded his arms on top of his fat belly. He wore a white shirt and a loose black tie, looking comfortable, as if he were on a pleasure flight to Florida.

William blinked. "Where are you taking me?"

"We'll be landing on Lake Michigan, off Pelican Point. General Harrison is waiting for us with a helicopter. He's sure gonna be glad to see your ass." Carl cackled.

A general? The military was involved in human cloning. What had they been doing the past thirty years? They were going to take him somewhere in a helicopter. The pentagon? The White House? A firing squad? "Where am I going?"

"Home, William." Carl grinned like the Cheshire cat.

"You can't be serious."

"Home sweet home," came a gruff voice from behind him.

William twisted in his seat, looked back, saw the killer he'd written about in *The Lost Diamonds*, in the flesh, up close. He was every bit as ugly as he'd imagined. And frightening. "Morris Brennon."

"Welcome back," he said with a growl in his throat. "They used to call me 1122B. I was the second human clone. You were the first brat, ya know."

William stiffened. Being first born hadn't afforded him any special status with the cloners, especially after knowing they'd sent a killer to bring him back. "I thought you were going to kill me."

Morris laughed. "They don't want you dead. They want you home where you belong."

Mulling that over, William faced forward and wondered where he *did* belong. It had been his problem all his life, always trying to fit in, feeling like someone he wasn't, and now ending up being someone he didn't want to be.

Leaning forward, Morris spoke between the seatbacks. "We could've had a great time you and me, growing up together, being clone pals. We belong together."

"I belong with my wife."

Morris snickered. "All in good time, William."

Fear hit him like a lightning bolt. The unanswered phone call. Where was she? Wishing his hands were free to strangle the bastard, he turned back to Morris again. "What have you done?"

"She's in good hands," Morris said with a toothy grin.

William sank in his seat. A new terror overwhelmed him. *Not Lois...please...not Lois.*

Chapter Fifty-Seven

Detective Ritter sat at a desk in the State Police command center, Gary, Indiana. A ticking heater grate chipped away at his nerves. The floor shined, and the smell of fresh wax lingered in the air. In front of him, set out neatly like brochures at a convention, were copies of his reports detailing the events and facts that led him to believe a clone had committed the recent ax murders. Now it was up to Captain Billings to convince a judge to issue a search warrant for Blythe Biotech.

He glanced at his watch. 10:30, Saturday morning. The Thanksgiving Blizzard had finally released its grip on the Midwest and was now taking aim at New England. Ninety miles south of here, the killer was probably eating a leisurely breakfast unaware of his impending capture.

Though Captain Billings had initially balked at the contention that a clone had done the killing, Detective Ritter had challenged the seasoned policeman to come up with a better theory on the fingerprints they'd found at the crime scene. Somehow the government had duplicated Morris Brennon. It wasn't Ritter's job to explain how they could have done it, only that they might have done it. On that point alone, Billings agreed to a joint task force of Illinois and Indiana authorities to go in on the bust. *You can have the collar*, Ritter had told Captain Billings. *I just want to be there to take down the clone.*

Ritter's chief had already amassed a squad of officers, not only from Chicago PD, but from SWAT, as well. A division of Illinois State Police stood ready to roll, too. They would join up with their

Indiana counterparts as soon as the warrant made its way into Captain Billings' hand. The FBI would then supply backup agents for the operation. They planned to go in this afternoon.

The door burst open. Ritter spun in his chair. Captain Billings came in like the wind. "Our tactical team has just reported in. This is going to be a tough bust." His black face shined with sweat. "Blythe Biotech is heavily guarded. Armed soldiers. Jeep patrols at ten-minute intervals. Whatever those boys are up to in there, they don't want anybody to know about it."

Ritter nodded. "Or they don't want anything getting out."

"Like more clones?" Billings rushed into his office. "By God, I hope not."

Chapter Fifty-Eight

Bullied from the chopper, William stumbled, felt cold winter air against his face, a shocking change from Nevada's weather. In the mounting light of dawn, he saw a gray stone building, its spire reaching into the icy sky. Skeletal trees cast long shadows across the ground. Everywhere he looked, soldiers were huddled together: some among the trees, and others along the stone wall perimeter, their breath vapors swirling in the air. So this was home sweet home?

Everything had gone down just as Carl had said it would. A chopper was waiting for them at Pelican Bay, and they hastily switched aircraft and flew to this place they called Blythe Biotech. Now, Morris and a big soldier dragged him across a snowplowed parking lot. The others followed: armed soldiers, the pilots, and Carl Savage with William's diamond-studded cane propped on his shoulder like a rifle. The backstabbing bastard.

At the top of the steps leading to the front doors of the old building, a man wearing military fatigues and a green beret awaited them. Standing with his hands behind his back and his feet spread, he didn't smile. Three stars gleamed on his collars. A younger man in pressed dress blues stood next to him, displaying the same posture. Eagles adorned his collars and cap. They both looked important. It wasn't until William had been thrust in front of them that he noticed both their nametags read *Harrison*.

The older man looked him up and down like a side of beef on a hook. "So this is the twerp that got away." He shook a finger at William. "You know how much trouble you caused me, boy?"

William felt the weight of the man's eyes. An overwhelming aura of power radiated from his weathered face. Carl had said to be careful of the General. William began to believe the sleaze ball. "I'm not your boy," he said with as much contempt as he could muster.

"I'm his boy," the Colonel said blankly.

William glared at him. "Where's my wife?"

Colonel boy shrugged. "I don't know what you're talking about.

"Untie me."

Harrison cleared his throat. "I know we're off to a bad start, but things will look much better once we get in out of the cold. Shall we?" He motioned to the door with a gloved hand.

As the soldiers pushed William up the steps to the entrance of Blythe Biotech, he turned to Carl. "Right through the front doors after all, just like I said."

Carl grumbled back, "Big fucking deal. What are you going to do about it?"

William didn't have the foggiest idea.

Chapter Fifty-Nine

Turning off Highway 41, Dr. Marshall's red and gold Jeep Grand Cherokee sliced through the snow with ease. He worked the steering wheel with both hands, the 4x4 light glowing on the panel. The unplowed gravel road skirted an irrigation canal and wound its way through a winter wonderland left in the wake of the Thanksgiving Day blizzard. Hazy sunlight blinked at him through snow-laden tree branches lining the canal. Icy arctic air glittered like scattered stardust. Power lines sagged. The heater hummed in perfect tune with the engine.

Yesterday, after seeing Lois Tuliver home and canceling all his appointments, he'd tried to call Dr. Larson. *Information* had told him there was no listing for Blythe University in Cedar Lake, Indiana. An old phone number he'd found now belonged to a spinster in Kentland. Though her only phone call this month ended up being a wrong number, she'd rattled on about her grandson and the miserable time she was having with her roses. Eugene explained that he couldn't visit with her any longer and hung up.

Throttling around a downed tree, he thought about Sally Mayfield. Lois had told him that William saw her at Andrew's funeral, how they'd talked for the first time in thirty years. He envied William for that and hoped to talk to him about her soon.

As he muscled his Cherokee through the snow, Eugene also thought about why he hadn't married in all these years. After his failure with Sally, he went home to Vermont, but soon felt the need to return to Chicago, to find her, to tell her he was sorry. When he failed at that too, he buried himself in his work, always hoping that he and Sally would someday cross paths: maybe at the theater, maybe in a grocery store, maybe at the clinic. When that didn't happen, he figured she'd left town, started a new life somewhere far away. How ironic. She'd been there all along, living on the streets. She'd paid a steep price for the things he had done—and for the things he didn't do. His heart panged with guilt. He needed to find her, and after all this time, he hoped she would forgive him.

Up ahead, the turnoff to Blythe University came into view. He let his thoughts of Sally fade and squinted at a sign.

BLYTHE BIOTECH, INC.
U.S. GOVERNMENT PROPERTY
NO ADMITTANCE WITHOUT SECURITY CLEARANCE

Eugene braked and stared at the sign. What the hell happened? The university was gone? The government owned the place now? No wonder he couldn't find a phone number. And where was Dr. Larson?

Beyond the warning sign, a little ways down the snow-packed road, the rustic stone building and its gothic spire jutted up from a snowy landscape. The icy flat of Cedar Lake sparkled in the background. Eugene shivered. Was Dr. Larson still here, still making clones? It was just the kind of thing he was good at. The government may have kept him on their payroll. Besides, he and Harrison were attached at the wallets. Eugene was willing to bet Dr. Larson was still here, all right. If not, there was no way to get inside and find out what 1122B had been up to for the past thirty years.

At the main gate, a burly MP put down a snow shovel and snatched up an M-16 leaning against the guard shack. He held it with both hands, the barrel pointed upward, his eyes glaring out from under a frosted helmet. Clumps of ice clung to his mustache. "What's your business here?" he barked, his breath a mist in the freezing air.

Eugene motored down the window, spotted another gun-toting guard emerge from the shack, turtling his neck against the cold. A tone sounded from a speaker, much like the chime of a clock striking three. With that, Eugene saw a line of helmets pop up along the stone wall perimeter. Rifles clicked rounds into chambers.

Roaring, a jeep careened around the corner of the compound, flinging snow. A soldier wrestled with a machine gun mounted on the roll bar. Eugene felt a sting in his bloodstream. His reception committee didn't look very friendly.

"I'm Dr. Eugene Marshall," he said to the MP, now shivering at his window. "I need to see Dr. Larson."

The jeep slid to a stop in front of the Cherokee. Soldiers glared at him. Wisps of vapor snorted from their nostrils. The machine gun was pointed at him.

Inspecting the Cherokee's interior, the MP appeared to be checking for hidden passengers or packages in plain brown wrappers. "No visitors allowed," he growled. "Be on your way."

"I've driven a long way to see him."

"So you'll have a long drive back. Be off with you."

"You don't understand—"

The MP cocked his weapon. "Don't argue with me."

"I used to work with Dr. Larson...thirty years ago."

"I don't give a shit if you were married to him. Get out of here."

Eugene stared into the MP's hard eyes. He looked weary from the cold and short on patience. There was only one way to make him understand the urgency of this visit. "I know about the clones."

The MP stiffened as if knifed in the back. He stepped away from the window, his eyes wide with surprise. "I'll call my commander."

"Don't take too long." Eugene closed the window, turned the heater up a notch, and watched the MP talk on the phone. A lot of things went through his mind as he glanced at the soldiers along the wall. They looked like kids. He pictured them writing their moms and girlfriends and counting the days until their tours end. They didn't look like seasoned combat troops from Desert Storm. He wondered how well they would fare in a fight.

A gloved knuckle rapped the window, pulling Eugene from his thoughts. "Park it over there." The guard pointed to the side of the road. "We'll take you in the jeep."

Moments later, Eugene was seated in the passenger seat of a drafty jeep. A helmeted corporal, lanky and pimple-faced, drove. Behind them, some fat kid clung to the machine gun. They couldn't have picked a colder contraption to ride in. "You got a heater in this thing?"

The skinny soldier grumped. "You only gotta ride in this thing for a minute. We gotta do it all day, so don't be belly-aching about it."

Tall iron gates swung open, and the jeep lurched into Blythe Biotech's compound. The place didn't look much different than it did thirty years ago, back when his position here was more important than his patients. That had been a hard lesson. It had taken him a lifetime to amend those mistakes, dedicating his life to prenatal care for the sake of mothers and babies alike. Losing Melanie on the delivery table was never far from his mind. Though it had all started here, he didn't feel proud of this homecoming.

As the Jeep rattled toward the main doors of Blythe Biotech, he scanned the cars in the parking lot, noticed most of them were still buried in snow. In the corner, a big green helicopter with four rotors and a fat belly sat motionless. Void of snow and with exhaust vapors still curling from engine nozzles, he figured the chopper had recently landed. Dr. Larson had visitors.

Eugene's heartbeat jumped. This should be one hell of a reunion.

Chapter Sixty

Blythe Biotech

A million footsteps echoed off the walls as if an army were marching down the corridor. William had trouble walking without his cane, limped and staggered, but kept going. The general walked on his right; Morris Brennon had hold of his left arm. And like a shadow, Colonel Harrison followed his father. They stopped at an elevator. The door chimed and slid open.

"Where're we going?" William asked the General.

"To meet your maker."

"Is he a man, or is he a god?"

"What difference does it make?"

The ropes burned William's wrists. He was about to meet the cloners. They'd given him a preprogrammed identity. Jeff Jordan never had a chance to develop his own personality or excel in life on his own merits. He was already William Tuliver. Human cloning was wrong, but would they listen? Did they even care?

Leaving the elevator, the hallway they entered was freezing cold and smelled sweet as maple syrup. He thought of breakfast. He hadn't eaten.

Two soldiers guarding a door at the end of the hall snapped to attention. One said, "You all can't go in there at once."

"Open it up," the General ordered.

"The security system, sir?"

"Turn everything off. My clones aren't going anywhere. Make it fast."

Nervously, the soldier punched some numbers on a keypad. The door opened with a whine, revealing a black hallway and another door that slid open at the other end.

The General gave William a nudge. "After you."

He hesitated, his heart beating wildly. "What's in there?"

"You'll be quite safe, I assure you."

Kneecaps trembling, William stepped into the black corridor where he saw crystals on the walls and nozzles on the ceiling. It looked like a gas chamber, a freezing cold gas chamber. He emerged onto a platform that overlooked a dimly lit room. It was freezing in here, too. The sound of bubbling water filled the air. There was just enough light to see an array of huge glass vats filled with honey-colored liquid. An eerie mist covered the floor. It was spooky. He saw similar dark cylinders lining the walls, and a maze of scaffolds and wiring that hung from the ceiling. It was like a scene from a science fiction movie.

His hip ached.

By the stairs that led down to the main floor, he saw a transformer setting behind a black wire-mesh barrier. It hummed with high voltage. Thick, black power cables fanned out across the wall to conduits running above the vats. Rising from the misty floor, a long white console of monitors, gauges, and pulsing lights made him think of a supercomputer. Technicians wearing white lab coats tended to the equipment like ever-vigilant mothers caring for their young.

The General put an age-spotted hand on William's shoulder. "Come meet them."

"Who?"

"My clones."

William gulped. He was right. There were more than two clones. He followed the General down the stairs. Another man approached, six feet tall and lanky with a timeworn face. His black hair was splashed with silver. He wore a smartly pressed suit and a blinding orange and red tie. His eyes were fixed on William, in amazement it seemed.

"Here he is, Dr. Larson." The General stepped aside.

William thought the doctor looked important. He seemed to command respect, even from the General. And he seemed oblivious to the cold.

"Geoffrey Scott Michaels," Larson said with a smile. "Finally, I've got you back."

"My name is William Tuliver."

The doctor's eyebrows arched. "You don't say."

"I know what you did, you and your enzyme."

"Okay, William." Larson stared at him as if he could see all the way through to his soul. "Have it your way."

"Where's my wife?"

"She's fine."

"Why did you have to drag her into this?"

"Because she knows too much."

"You better not have bent a hair on her head."

"We were extra gentle." Larson pointed at the ropes binding William's wrists. "Must we, General? He's not going anywhere. Not this time."

The General motioned to Morris Brennon.

As Morris untied the rope, William quickly glanced around the clone room, examined the bubbling vats and the mist flowing down and covering the floor. He thought about making a run for it, but there were too many soldiers. And it was freezing cold outside. Besides, he wasn't going anywhere as long as Lois was here. Dr. Larson must have known that.

Standing before his creator, William wondered how many men could say they'd done that. He felt awe in Larson's presence, as a man would feel in front of his god. It didn't seem possible that one man could possess that much knowledge, to know how to create life at will, regardless of whether it was right or wrong. Did he deserve that kind of power? William rubbed his freed wrists. "Do you have any idea what you've done to me?"

"I gave you your life back, William, just as you wanted."

"But you shouldn't have."

"You should be thanking me. Not judging me."

William looked down at the mist swirling around his feet. It felt creepy. "What we did was wrong. Most people think human cloning is immoral, unethical and dangerous: the church, the government, even the United Nations has a declaration against human cloning as a cure for infertility. They'd have a fit if they saw what you did to me...to Morris. It's wrong."

Larson raised his chin. "They once said the same thing about Galileo when he searched the heavens with his telescope and saw that the earth was not the center of the universe. He went against the ethics of his time, challenged popular belief, and paid dearly for doing so. They cut off his head, but it didn't make him wrong."

"Galileo wasn't playing God."

"He was denouncing God, or the common conception of God at the time...and the relationship between heaven and earth. It took technology to prove the ethics of the time were wrong. Cloning is no different. It goes against the established thinking of our society now, sure, but in a hundred years, history will show where the ethics were wrong, again.

"By then, stem cell cloning will cure spinal cord injuries, make new hearts, new livers, new bone marrow for transplanting. You of all people can appreciate the value of that. The benefits to the human condition will be limitless. We'll be able to clone stronger men, sexier women, smarter scholars, and more talented artists. God should be happy that we improved his original design."

By now, William's right hip was throbbing. "The genetic reengineering of the human race? Are you serious? God would never approve of that."

Larson grumbled. "God has nothing to do with any of this. It's strictly biochemistry. You're a wonder of science, my boy. A goddamn miracle."

"You let the genie out of the bottle, Dr. Larson."

He leaned forward. "You haven't seen anything yet."

"What?"

"Let me show you something." Larson led him, limping, toward the console of gauges and flashing lights.

William held back, not because he wasn't interested in Larson's toys, but because walking was difficult without his cane.

"How bad is it?" Larson asked.

"What?"

"The hip."

"Bad enough."

"I was afraid of that," Larson said. "Carl, give him back his cane, for Christ's sake."

"I'm keepin' it," Carl spat.

"And you steal candy from babies? It's not a request."

"Give it back," Harrison growled or you're going for a swim." He cocked his head toward one of the vats.

Wide-eyed, Carl gave up the cane without further argument.

"Thanks," William muttered and leaned on it, wondering what it was about the vats that frightened Carl into submission.

"Now as I was saying..." Larson moved to the console with William right behind him. "This is the LSC, the Life Support Computer. From this station we control and monitor the environment in the vats." They walked down the length of the console together. "Here we have the medical stuff, heartbeats and temperatures, and over here we have the liquid filtration controls and over there," he pointed, "the air pump controls and monitors."

William thought it looked complicated. "What's it for?"

Larson made a motion to the center of the clone room. "Over here." They walked through the mist on the floor toward a bubbling vat. "Lights," Larson ordered.

The room brightened. Lights blinked on around the vats. William couldn't believe what he saw. In the honey-colored liquid stood a duplicate of Morris Brennon, baldheaded and fat faced, with thick hairless arms, a broad chest, and the legs of a weightlifter. He was naked, no bellybutton, and his little penis bobbed limply in the current. His skin looked dishwater wrinkled and transparent enough to see the blue veins and red arteries clearly. Shackles held the clone's feet to the bottom of the vat, and tubes and wires came out of his armpits. The clone looked pitiful in his liquid prison. Helpless. His big wide eyes, magnified fourfold by the fluid and glass, stared back at him, its mouth gaping like a fish, inhaling liquid and exhaling as if it were air.

Beyond the first clone, deeper into the vat, William saw a forest of identical clones, shackled in the same way, swaying in the current like seaweed, their wide eyes staring at him blankly.

"Oh God," William whispered. "What have you done?"

Larson put his hands on his hips. "This is your army of cloned soldiers, William, just as you wished."

"I did?"

"No more mother's sons going off to war. Your money got the ball rolling. Couldn't have done it without you, William."

He remembered his mother in *The Lost Diamonds*, how she'd suffered when her son was killed at Pearl Harbor. It was easy to believe that he wanted to spare other mothers that misery. But not this way. "I had no idea it would come to this."

"Careful what you wish for." Larson pointed to the first clone William had seen. "I'd like you to meet 1224A. Go ahead. Say hello."

"H-hello," William said and forced a smile.

1224A did not smile back.

Stepping up, General Harrison put a microphone to his lips.

"Watch this," Larson whispered.

"Company, ten-hut." The General's voice boomed over loudspeakers.

1224A and the rest of them went rigid in the vats. William scanned the cylinders along the walls, each housing a single clone, some of whom had not obeyed the General's command.

"Those are the problem cases," Larson said. "Watch how the

General handles insubordination."

Pointing what looked like a TV remote at the cylinder marked 1472C, the General pushed a red button. The clone thrashed about wildly in the fluid, its face contorted in pain.

"Electric shock," Larson explained.

Within a moment, 1472C also stood rigid in his cylinder, hands pressed flat against his thighs, his chin up and fat face forward. There were no other holdouts in the clone room.

Harrison blew into the microphone, getting everyone's attention. "Gentlemen," he said to his naked clones. "I want you to meet the first of your kind. He calls himself William Tuliver, but his case number is 1010C. He came from cell lot 100, the tenth fusion experiment in the third petri dish."

William whispered to Larson. "They understand all this?"

"Certainly. We taught them everything with videotapes. They read and write in English, excel in mathematics, and know all there is about everything military. 1224A..." He pointed to the rigid clone in front. "He's the squad leader."

"As you were, men," Harrison ordered.

The clones relaxed. Their arms floated freely.

"1010C will be coming around to meet you. Be nice and don't bug him with a bunch of personal questions. Tonight's movie is The Battle of Midway Island. I'm sure you'll enjoy it."

"They can talk?" William asked Larson.

"See the white slates tethered to the rigging. They write on them with grease pens just like scuba divers working a shipwreck. You'll see it's quite efficient as you make your rounds."

"Don't be mistaken," General Harrison put in. "These clones are genetically disposed to killing. They enjoy it. They lust for it. They're the perfect weapon system, tough, reliable, and replaceable."

William winced. "Replaceable?"

"They're not real people," Larson said coolly.

"Not real?" William grimaced. "Am I not real either?"

Larson shook his head. "Sorry."

William limped up to 1224A, the not-a-real-person thing banging around in his brain. The clone reached for his slate and began to write something. As William leaned on his cane and watched him, he thought about the pitiful life these clones had been forced to live, constantly at the mercy of General Harrison and his electric whip. William's existence had been a cakewalk compared to what these guys had been through. He reflected on how Sally Mayfield had rescued him from here, sparing him a life as Morris Brennon's clone pal. Sally was the real hero in all of this.

The clone's big eyes looked up from the slate and darted back and forth as if checking to see if anyone else was watching him. Larson and Harrison were standing at the LSC. Carl Savage and Morris Brennon had gone upstairs. The clone flipped the slate over for William to read.

"KILL US!"

William gasped, stepped back. "What?"

The clone rubbed the slate clean and pointed to the LSC. He had the look of a beggar on the street corner, pleading for help. Was their imprisoned life so miserable they'd rather be dead? Did the clone think he could only entrust another clone with his death wish? Shaking his head in confusion, William moved down the row of vats.

It didn't take him long to figure it out. At each of the vats, he saw the same despair on the faces of all the clones inside. He was standing in the midst of misery. None of the clones showed him a smile. They all had that same beggar's look, but there was something else in their eyes. Anger, and maybe even hate. William understood from the look of them how easily a life without freedom could foster feelings like that. These clones had been denied everything, even their own personalities. From conception to adulthood, they were trapped in Morris Brennon's genes. No wonder they'd rather be dead.

Suddenly, a woman's scream echoed through the clone room. The clones flinched in alarm.

"She tried to escape," a soldier shouted.

William spun around. Morris Brennon had hold of Lois from behind, a hairless arm locked across her throat as he wrestled her down the stairs. She wore a long white gown William had never seen before. Her nipples were clearly visible through the thin material.

"Get your filthy hands off me." She screamed.

William's chest tightened. "Let her go." He ran toward her, his hip on fire, his cane useless. "Lois."

The General grabbed William's arm. "Hold it right there."

He yanked free, spun around, but suddenly he was thrown to the floor face down in the mist with two soldiers on top of him. "Lois."

They wrenched his arms behind him, snapped on handcuffs, and pulled him to his feet. His diamond-studded cane disappeared under the mist. "Let her go."

Lois kicked Morris in the shin.

The General stepped up to her. "I warned you."

She spit on him.

He turned to William, pointed at him. "Let this be a lesson to you. Try to escape and you'll get the same thing."

"Leave her alone." William charged the General like an enraged bull, but before he made contact, a soldier decked him. He hit the floor, right on his bad hip. He tried to get up but caught a combat boot in the ribs. Air gushed from his lungs. Gasping in pain, and with the handcuffs cutting into his wrists, he managed to get up on his knees. "She doesn't have anything to do with this."

Harrison barked, "It's your fault, William. You told her you were a clone." He nodded to his men as if giving them a secret order.

Morris pushed Lois to the floor. She screamed. The mist scattered in a circle around her. A ceiling crane rumbled overhead, and a hook came down on a cable. Several soldiers clipped a leather strap to the hook and then buckled it around Lois's chest. She fought them and cursed them. They backed away. A motor whined. The cable lifted Lois into the air, kicking and screaming. "William."

Kneeling on the floor and fighting for air, he looked up, his heart pounding in his throat. "Lois."

"William." she cried out. "Help me."

The crane swung her across the room and stopped above an unoccupied cylinder full of honey-colored liquid. The motor whined again, lowering her feet to the cylinder rim. A soldier grabbed her right ankle and snapped on a shackle. It was attached to a chain that sloped down to the bottom of the cylinder. The crane motor whined again, dropping her into the liquid.

She screamed as she went down, kicking her free leg. The clip released the strap from the hook, and the crane swung away. A winch motor hummed on, tightening the chain to her ankle, pulling her down. She clung to the rim with both hands. "William."

The clones started thrashing in their vats like wild animals, stirring up the fluid until the cold air in the clone room became sickeningly sweet.

"Help me."

Gagging, William tried to stand, fell. His hip couldn't take the strain, and he couldn't use his handcuffed hands to help him get up. "Lois. Hold on."

The taut chain quivered as it pulled her down. Her knuckles turned white. Fluid lapped at her neck and then at her chin. She spit and coughed and choked. Finally drained of strength, her fingers let loose. She went under.

William couldn't believe his eyes. The cloners were drowning his wife. In spite of the fact that his hands were cuffed behind him and the fire in his hip, he managed to get to his feet. "General, please don't do this to her. I'll do whatever you want."

The old soldier's eyes showed him no sympathy.

"You're going to kill her." Rocked with a fear he'd never known, he looked around at the others, the soldiers and technicians. "Somebody stop him."

No one responded.

"You're all crazy."

A soldier knocked him to the floor. "Shut up."

"Damn you." His hip was killing him, and the handcuffs were digging in. Through tears, he looked up at the cylinder, hoping beyond hope that someone would get her out of there before it was too late. But no one did anything to help her.

She thrashed around in the liquid, her cheeks puffed out, and her magnified eyes were wide with terror. The chain had already pulled her foot to the bottom. She clawed at the glass. Bubbles trickled from her mouth, slowly at first, then suddenly gushed out of her. Kicking and jerking, she grabbed her throat, her mouth gaping, the fluid spilling into her lungs. She went into spasms, stiffening, convulsing, and choking. Somewhere between panic and chaos, she went limp, her eyes crossed and dazed. Like a jellyfish, the white gown she wore swirled around her and swayed in the current with the same rhythm as her hair. Her body floated perfectly still, her arms out in front of her.

"Lois." William thought his heart would burst. "You sons of bitches killed her."

The clones seethed in their vats, all flailing their arms and twisting about like demons trying to break their bonds with hell. Their brows were furrowed, their teeth bared, their fists clenched and muscles bulging.

Harrison shouted into the microphone. "Settle down, men." He pointed the remote control at the vats and worked the red button as if it were a trigger, firing it randomly at the raging clones. Harrison Jr. had a device just like it. They disappeared down the rows of vats, wreaking havoc. "Settle down, I order you." His voice boomed over the speakers.

The syrupy smell in the air thickened to nauseating proportions. William's stomach churned as he knelt in the mist on the floor, watching his wife floating lifeless in the cylinder. His chest convulsed with heart-wrenching sobs. She was gone. And so was his child and his only hope of setting everything right. Despair bulled him over. A dark cloud of sorrow sucked the air out of him. Never in his life had he felt so hopeless—so guilty. He could not have imagined this happening in his worst nightmares. "Lois," he cried. "Please forgive me."

Turning away, he couldn't bear the sight of her limp limbs and blank stare any longer. He looked at the pitiful clones shackled in the same way, the hate in their eyes as General Harrison and his bully son moved between the vats, administering their punitive shock therapy. Then he saw the sorrow-filled face of 1224A, who was penning the slate again. He showed William what he had written.

"KILL US ALL!"

Chapter Sixty-One

The column of patrol cars and step vans stretched a mile behind Detective Ritter. He rode shotgun in the command car. Captain Billings drove, the scar on his face clearly visible. His cheeks were taut, and his narrow eyes squinted against the snow-covered landscape. "We better be right about this." He glanced at his rearview mirror. "If there's no clone, we're gonna be in deep shit."

"We've been in deep shit before," Ritter replied, feeling confident. "I'll stake my career on this call."

"How can a clone have the same fingerprints as its donor? Hell, twins are clones of each other, and they don't have the same fingerprints."

"I wondered about that," Ritter said. "When I realized I was on the trail of a clone, I started reading everything I could find on the subject: the controversies, the laws, the procedures scientists used. An intriguing fact surfaced. Back in the late '60s, microbiologists discovered some kind of restriction enzyme that made cloning possible. A couple years later it was refined. Maybe by now, the government might have developed a better enzyme, one capable of exact duplication."

"Science fiction," Billings grumped.

"That's the scary part. Maybe it's not...anymore." The search warrant vibrated on the seat next to a yellow bullhorn. Ritter glanced back at his modern-day posse swirling snow in the air as they sped toward Blythe Biotech. They had enough firepower to win a war.

The radio squawked. "Tack Two, check in." The Feds, the US

Marshals, and the FBI couldn't keep quiet, always barking back and forth to each other as if they were more important than anyone else. But the Indiana State Police had the call on this one. This was their jurisdiction, their ball game. And Captain Billings was the coach. He'd given Detective Ritter the honor of serving the warrant, as a professional courtesy. After all, it was his murder investigation. The Feds were in on this only because Blythe Biotech was government property. If the administrators refused to cooperate with the warrant, the Feds would be on hand to step in. The task force had the bust covered, no matter how it went down.

Ritter settled back into his seat and folded his arms across his chest. A lump under his jacket pressed hard against his ribs. It was his Glock .40 with thirteen rounds in the clip. He hoped they'd all be there when this was over.

Chapter Sixty-Two

William Tuliver wept on the mist-covered floor. The bastards had killed his wife.

A hand touched his shoulder. He looked up, saw Larson standing above him, his eyes fixed on Lois floating lifeless in the cylinder. A hot jolt of rage surged through William. He shrugged off the hand. "Look what you've done."

"She'll come around in a moment."

Come around? "What?"

"She passed out. It's a perfectly normal reaction. Then her subconscience took over, reverting to a time when she was an infant in the womb. She's actually breathing the liquid. The OXYFEM will bring her around, you'll see. But rest assured, she won't be trying to escape again." Larson paused. "And neither will you."

William trembled as he looked into the eyes of the man he had momentarily thought of as a god. He saw no compassion, not even a glint of human kindness. William balled his fists still handcuffed behind him and sank back to the floor. Andrew Cobb was right when he said William Tuliver had made a deal with the devil. He'd made a deal with Dr. Larson.

A commotion came from the clone room entrance, soldiers storming in, and voices. "What have we here, John?" a man called down from the platform.

Larson's gaze shot to the top of the stairs. "Oh shit."

William looked up to see a tall and striking man with graying hair and a long brown coat standing with a soldier at each elbow. Carl Savage was with him.

"Dr. Marshall," Larson said. "Your timing is impeccably bad. You really shouldn't have come."

"John..." The doctor frowned, his hooded eyes darting about, casing the place as if he couldn't quite take it all in. "Have you been playing mad scientist again?"

"Now Eugene, don't be too hasty. This is my finest work."

"And I should have known your favorite maggot would be here." Dr. Marshall shoved Carl aside and made his way down the steps to the mist-covered floor. Harrison and his son reappeared, either having finished their morbid torture of the clones or distracted by the new arrival. Larson hurried to the bottom of the steps where Eugene stopped. "I see your taste in ties hasn't changed."

"I know what this must look like to you..."

"My, my, my." Eugene scanned the black power transformer, the LSC, the scaffolding above the vats, and finally his gaze rested on William, still kneeling in the mist with his hands cuffed behind him. "What did he do?"

"I didn't do anything," William said in his own defense.

Larson nodded to the General. "Get him up."

Harrison and his son pulled William to his feet. Another soldier stepped up and keyed the handcuffs.

Searching the mist, William couldn't see his cane anywhere.

Eugene stood in front of him now, looking him up and down. "Do I know you?"

William shrugged.

"It's been a long time," Larson put in. "Geoffrey Scott Michaels you may remember. He calls himself William Tuliver now."

"So I've heard," Eugene said, bobbing his head. "I delivered you, William. Helped you and Sally escape, too."

"What?" Larson barked.

"That's right, John. I set up the whole thing."

"Why?"

Shoving his hands into his coat pockets, Eugene panned the

room. "Because I didn't want him to be a part of this. And when 1122B was born, I realized I didn't want anything to do with the duplication factor either. Makes a man lose sight of who he is, where his responsibilities lie, what's right and what's wrong. But I can see you haven't learned anything. Look around you, John. Don't you see the misery here?" He pointed to the naked clones shackled in their vats. "Look at the sorry state to which you've reduced the human species."

"They're clones," Larson spat.

General Harrison, who'd kept quiet until now, must have sensed the need to defend his clones. "My men are not *a sorry state*, Dr. Smartass. They're soldiers, about to emerge and take their rightful place under my command."

Eugene huffed. "I can't see any good coming of that."

William shifted his eyes between the men and their conversation. There seemed to be no end to the finger pointing and insinuations. Frustrated, he looked at Lois and couldn't believe his eyes. She was moving, plying the glass with the palms of her hands and jerking her wide-open eyes back and forth, up and down, terrified and unsure of what had happened to her. His spirits shot up. "She's alive." A spark of hope ignited inside him. Had his unborn child survived the ordeal, too? "Lois." He sprinted to the cylinder.

She mouthed to him, "Help me, William. Help me."

He turned to the General. "Get her out of there."

A cackle came from his throat, like a hyena in the night. "I like her just fine where she is."

Eugene stepped in. "She's pregnant, for Christ's sake."

Harrison balled a fist. "Stay out of this, you traitor."

"General," a soldier's voice boomed from the platform above. "We've got problems outside."

Harrison groaned. "Now what?"

"There must be a hundred police cars. Some detective named Ritter has a search warrant. Looks like he brought some heavy firepower to serve it."

"Ritter, huh." The General snarled at Dr. Larson. "I warned you about him."

Larson shook his head, his brows furrowed in disbelief. "How did he find us?"

Harrison pointed at Morris Brennon. "Goddamnit. You brought this trouble here. It's isolation for you, mister."

The clone bared his teeth. "Over my dead body." He darted up the stairs and out the open security doors.

"Shall we stop him, sir," the soldier shouted.

"I'll deal with him later. We've got bigger problems—"

"What about Lois?" William pleaded.

"She's not going anywhere. Besides, I've got cops to deal with. Search warrant, my ass."

The General stomped up the stairs, his son right behind him. Dr. Larson and Dr. Marshall went up next with the fat lawyer, Carl Savage, falling in behind as they exited the clone room.

William turned to Lois floating in the cylinder. She looked like a doll in a water globe, so beautiful, yet so terrified. Pounding on the glass, she mouthed, "Help me, William. Help me."

"I'll get you out," he said, trembling. "Somehow."

Chapter Sixty-Three

Detective Ritter stood in front of the gate to Blythe Biotech, its black iron bars towering twelve feet above him. Cold air numbed his cheeks and turned his breath to mist. He held the search warrant in his left hand, the Glock in his right. On his left, two soldiers stood by the doorway to the guard shack, their rifles held at the ready. On his right, Captain Billings, wearing his long black coat, clutched a 12-gauge shotgun, his feet planted like Wyatt Earp at the OK Corral. Along the stone wall on either side of the gate, helmeted soldiers leveled M-16s on them. They looked like snot-nosed boys.

Covering Ritter, officers crouched behind their squad cars, pistols drawn. SWAT teams had taken strategic positions, kneeling among the trees and squatting in the snow-piled gullies, their assault weapons trained on the troops. Ritter shivered. It looked like all hell was about to break loose.

Beyond the gate, a jeep sped toward him. As it neared, he could make out a General wearing a green beret, riding in the passenger seat and a flashy colonel in dress blues, sitting behind him. Ritter clenched his jaw. If they played their cards right, nobody would get hurt.

The jeep slid to a stop at the gate. Military men piled out and stood there a moment as if sizing up the situation. The General stepped forward. "What is it we can do for you boys this afternoon?"

Ritter approached the gate, snow crunching under his boots, and held up the warrant. "We have reasonable cause to believe there's a killer in there. We want to have a look around."

The General held out his arms, palms up. "We're all killers here, detective. Isn't that right, men?"

His troops remained silent, their breath wisping from boyish lips.

"I take that as non-cooperative, General."

"Take it anyway you like." Smooth and practiced, the General drew his Colt.

Spotting the gun, Ritter's defenses kicked in. His instincts and training propelled him into the snow, diving first, and then tumbling. Gunshots cracked and rolled away like thunder. He saw Captain Billings fall. The place erupted in gunfire and screams.

Crawling through snow, Ritter made the stone wall where rifle reports banged above his head, hurt his ears. Ducking low, he scooted along the wall to a gully, slid down an embankment, and crawled toward the patrol cars barricading the road. He was shivering by the time he got there. From his position, crouched behind the taillight of a Ford, he saw the jeep speed away from the scene, back toward the building. Billings lay in a heap by the gate, motionless. Two soldiers were sprawled out in front of the shack, their blood turning the snow red.

"Hold your fire," Ritter yelled.

But no one could hear him. The gun battle blazed on.

***

The jeep sped toward the front doors of Blythe Biotech. Its windshield was shattered and the canvas top pulverized with bullet holes. The Corporal at the wheel panted hysterically. "What did you do that for?"

General Harrison didn't answer. He held his son in his arms, pressing the flat of his hand over a wound that gushed blood from Billy's chest. His dress blue uniform and multicolored ribbons were stained red. Billy stared at him with wide eyes, his mouth open, air gurgling in his throat.

"Hang in there, son."

"It's so cold...Pops."

"Jesus. I told you to keep low."

Billy gagged. "Sorry."

The General rocked his boy. "Oh God, don't take my only son."

"Am I going...to see Mom now...and Daniel?"

"Hush that kind of talk. You'll make it through this." Though he said the words, he didn't believe there was any way his son would survive this chest wound. Must have been a SWAT officer that placed that bullet so precisely. It was a heart shot. Left ventricle probably. He could tell by the way the blood pulsed from the wound.

The jeep careened to a stop in front of the steps. "I'll get some help," the Corporal shouted, bailed out, and bounded up the stairs.

"I smell cookies...Pops. Chocolate Chip...my favorite." Billy coughed. A spray of blood misted the air. "Do you hear music?"

Removing his bloodied hand from the hole in Billy's chest, Harrison clutched his son, buried his face in his neck. "I'm so sorry, son."

Billy's body quivered. "I'm not cold anymore...Dad."

Harrison flinched. He couldn't remember the last time Billy had called him Dad. "What happened to Pops?"

"I just figured it out," Billy said, gasping. "Pops died a long time ago...with Daniel...and Mom."

"What?"

Billy stiffened and groaned. His last breath wheezed past blue lips.

"No," the General wailed. But no one heard his cry. He sat alone in the freezing jeep, steam rising around him from his son's pooled blood. Gunfire cracked in the distance. He held his limp son in his arms. Billy's head flopped back. His mouth and eyes remained wide open. The General seethed with anger, his insides screaming for revenge. He wondered if this was his fault, after all he'd fired the first shot. It was meant for Detective Ritter who'd come knocking on the door, looking for trouble. This was all Ritter's fault.

Harrison released his dead son, peeled off his fur-lined general's coat, and covered him with it. All his plans had just died with Billy. The shortcomings of the government, the chaotic rank and file of the military, and even the President's undeserved position as Commander in Chief were no longer of any importance. Billy's killers were outside those gates. Revenge now took priority over everything. The General growled, a new mission in mind for his clones. Detective Ritter would pay with his life for bringing that search warrant here today.

Chapter Sixty-Four

From a shadowy corner of the lobby, Morris spotted Larson, Dr. Marshall, and Carl Savage watching the confrontation at the main gate through the front windows. Fools. He slipped past them and out to the tool shed where he'd stashed his ax, a beautiful, long-handled job. After putting a new edge on the blade, he gave it a few full-sweep practice swings into the bench. Wood splintered with a crack like breaking bones. Blood pulsed in his loins.

Quickly, he made his way back to the clone room entrance. The security doors had been left open when the General lit out with the rest of them. They must've been in a hurry to confront the cops outside. With one swing of his ax, he destroyed the keypads. Now the doors would stay open for the games to begin.

C&K all the way!

It was General Harrison's turn to play. The bastard had threatened to put him in that shit hole isolation for the last time. But William Tuliver would be the first to die, a little practice before the big game. He shouldn't have come waltzing in here thinking he was some kind of special turd in this toilet.

Morris worked his way down the stairs to the clone room floor. He held the ax in both hands. His heart pumped wildly. The clone 1010C, William Tuliver, stood by the cylinder where Lois pawed at the glass. Rule number one: be very quiet. He took another careful step down and crouched in the mist. All clear.

Shuffling across the misty floor, he carefully skirted the black power transformer with its ominous warning sign, *KEEP AWAY -*

HIGH VOLTAGE, and its electrical cables that fanned out across the wall. He slinked past the LSC control panel with its blinking green lights, paused, glanced left and right, then slipped between the first two rows of vats. He could feel the eyes of his clone brothers watching him. Rule number one was going very well. He was sure William was unaware of his presence.

C&K all the way!

Before he made it to the other side of the clone room where William stood, the sound of heavy boots came banging down the stairs. Curious about the ruckus, he backtracked and spotted the General, working controls on the LSC console. His uniform was stained with blood. Morris frowned, wondering what the idiot was up to now.

Chimes echoed through the clone room, a sound Morris hadn't heard before.

"What are you doing?" a voice boomed from the platform.

Morris looked up, saw Dr. Larson standing there, his hands clamped on the railing, his eyes fierce. "No, don't." he shouted and ran down the stairs. "You can't."

"I already did," Harrison proclaimed.

"Are you out of your mind? God, look at you. You're a mess."

"The cops killed my boy."

"Christ." Larson shuddered.

Holding the ax close to his chest, Morris worked his way back to the front row of vats, careful to stay out of sight. He chuckled at the news of Billy boy's death, the little brownnosing prick.

Harrison typed on the LSC keypad. "That son of a bitch Ritter and his gang of lawmen are going to kick the shit out of my men out there. They need help."

The warning chime stopped.

"You can't use the clones," Larson shouted. "We're not ready to contain them."

A buzzer sounded, pulsing an alarm.

"They'll kill everybody."

The Duplication Factor

The General went eye-to-eye with Larson. "That's the whole idea. The showers are ready. The uniform room is set up. The armory has plenty of guns and ammunition. We're going out there to kick some ass." He spun around. "Where are the damn techs?"

"They took off after you put Lois in the cylinder. They don't want anything to do with you anymore."

"The chicken-shit bastards. I'll do it myself."

"No."

"This is not an executive decision," the General sneered. "It's a military call."

"But it's not in everyone's best interest. This isn't Vietnam, General."

"That's right. This time it's my war." He grabbed Larson by his lab coat lapels, reared back, and punched him in the face. Larson dropped like a sack of beans.

Morris grimaced. The bastard General had gone too far. Dr. Larson may have been a shit father, but he was the only father Morris ever knew. Seeing him sprawled on the floor sent sharp spikes of rage through Morris's body. Just as he was about to pounce on the General, he saw William Tuliver rush to Larson's side, kneel and look up, his face wrenched with concern. The General had already moved behind the console, again working the controls.

The pulsing buzzer stopped abruptly. A female computer voice came over the loudspeakers. "*Warning. Emergence in ten minutes.*"

William shook Dr. Larson. There was no response.

Flexing his biceps, Morris puffed out his chest and bared his teeth. The General would pay for this outrage. Rule number two: strike without warning.

With a growl from deep in his chest, he leaped from his hiding place and charged the General, the ax cocked high. Time stopped. Maybe it was because Morris was so pissed off that tunnel vision had set in, or maybe there was something to the saying *blind rage*. Whatever it was, he didn't react fast enough to the General's quick draw. The muzzle blast was the first sign that Morris had made a major mistake. He should have moved in closer, or maybe waited for a better opportunity. Burning pain in his right shoulder gave him the second clue to his blunder. He dove to the floor, rolled, and slammed headlong into the LSC with a bang.

Another shot echoed through the room, then the click of clip ejection.

Enraged, Morris jumped up, spotted the General crouched behind the console, reloading his gun. Morris swung the ax, slammed it into the General's right wrist. The hand went one way, the gun the other.

Harrison let out a scream that sent the clones writhing in their vats. He backed up against the wall, clutching the spurting stub of his arm.

Morris cocked the ax and swung at the General's head.

He ducked and ran for the steps leading to the scaffolding above the vats.

Shouldering the ax, Morris went after him, taking care not to slip in the trail of blood the General left behind.

"Warning. Emergence in nine minutes."

Grinning, Morris thought this was too good to be true. The thrill of C&K made him oblivious to his own wound leaking blood down his arm. The ax handle became sticky. His adrenaline was pumping. He was on a high like no drug on earth. The endorphins of murder sent him into a trance. He only focused on the General, now clunking along the scaffold in front of him. Sayings like *the time of his life* and *the best party of all* rolled through his mind. *C&K all the way!* Rule number three: enjoy.

***

Kneeling at Dr. Larson's side, William shivered from the cold of the clone room and the terror of what he was witnessing.

The General stumbled along a scaffold above the vats. "Get away from me, you murdering bastard."

William scanned the mist around him. Somewhere under this

ungodly fog lay the General's right hand, a loaded gun, and the diamond-studded cane. But the only thing he wanted right now was Morris Brennon's ax. With it, he could smash the glass cylinder imprisoning Lois, but trying to get the ax could easily cost him his life.

"*Warning. Emergence in eight minutes.*"

On the floor, Dr. Larson moaned. "W-what was that? What did she say?"

"Something about emergence."

"God no."

"What does it mean?"

"Help me up."

Pulling Larson to his feet, William noticed the doctor's eyes were wobbling in their sockets. A commotion in the vats drew his attention. The clones were thrashing around in the fluid, their heads bent back, their angry eyes following the movements of the two combatants clanking along the scaffold above them.

"T-the LSC," Larson said hoarsely. "Help me get over there."

Now William missed his cane. With the doctor's weight leaning on him heavily, his hip throbbed more than ever. But, staggering together, they made it to the console.

Larson looked over the settings. "Christ. He's gone and done it now. The emergence clock has been set forward."

"I don't understand." William leaned on the console.

"The clones' shackles are going to unlock. They'll be free to rise up and emerge from the vats." Larson worked the keypad. "Damn. Harrison has set the LSC to release them all at once. It'll be mass murder." He turned dials and flipped switches. The monitor flashed red. *Changes Locked Out.* "I can't turn it off without shutting down the LSC. If I do, they'll all die."

The General screamed from somewhere above the vats.

William looked up to the scaffolding. The clone's ax had found the General's collarbone, which snapped with a sharp crack. He went down on one knee, his left hand on the rail, the bloody stub of his right arm cradled in his lap.

Morris cocked his ax again. He swung. The General's left hand flew off.

Harrison screamed in agony.

Horrorstruck, William watched the spray of blood and the tumbling hand fall.

"*Warning. Emergence in seven minutes.*"

The clone threw down his ax and lifted the General by his collar. "You wanted these cloned soldiers." Morris's gruff voice echoed through the clone room. "But you didn't treat 'em right. They're human beings, just like me, just like William."

The General spit. "You're all freaks."

"You expect them to serve you with that kind of attitude?"

"They'll follow my orders to the death."

"You think?" Morris bent the General over the rail.

"No, don't."

He gave Harrison a shove and down he went, a back flip into the honey-colored liquid.

William knew the General couldn't drown, not really.

Thrashing about, Harrison could barely swim with handless arms and a shattered collarbone. "Help me." he ordered his clones. He hacked and coughed.

The clones reached up for him, but instead of guiding him to the safety of the rim, they started pulling his legs down.

"No." With the crook of his arm, the General clung to the looms of wires and tubes, barely able to keep his head above the liquid. More hands took hold of him from below.

"*Warning. Emergence in six minutes.*"

"Stop. That's an order. At ease, men." The General went under. Now the only sound was the bubbling fluid and humming air pumps.

He thrashed about, kicking at the clones in the red-clouded liquid. But the clones didn't let him go. They handed him off, from one group to the next, working him toward the front of the vat and into the waiting arms of 1224A, their squad leader. He clamped the

General's head in the thick V of his right arm.

The General's face was wrenched in terror.

With a quick jerk, neck bones cracked. 1224A released the General. He floated to the surface, his head lolling at a right angle to his back.

"*Warning. Emergence in five minutes.*"

Again, 1224A showed William the slate. This time it read: *DO IT NOW!*

William turned to Larson. "It's the only way. Shut down the LSC."

"No." Morris's voice roared behind them.

William whirled around in time to see Morris rushing at him with the ax cocked high over his shoulder.

"You're not killing my brothers."

William ducked. The swinging blade just missed his ear. "Look at them," he shouted, moving backward and hoping to talk some sense into the crazed killer. "They want to die. They're miserable."

"*Warning. Emergence in four minutes.*"

"They don't know any better. I'll show them the thrill of the catch and the ecstasy of the kill. Together, we'll terrorize the planet. C&K all the way."

"I can't let you do that," Larson shouted and jumped on the clone's back.

Morris tossed him off like a bothersome child.

Larson's head hit the LSC with a nasty thud, and he slumped to the floor.

"Come on." The clone snarled at William. "Your turn to play the game."

The ax came around, this time slicing by his stomach as he jumped back barely in time. Panic raged through his mind like a Lake Michigan gale. Fight or flight. Kill or be killed. He was trapped, face to face with Morris Brennon's black eyes and toothy grin. For a moment, William could see his parents cowering from that face, pleading for their lives. Their last minutes on earth must have been as horrifying as this.

Drool ran out the corner of the clone's mouth. The ax came down again.

William bobbed and stepped back, but contacted the wall. He had no more room to maneuver. Fighting nausea, he noticed blood flowing from Morris's shoulder wound. It had to be working against his swing, his accuracy, and his power. It was the only reason William was still alive. But time was running out. The clones would soon be let loose. He had to get around the killer to help Dr. Larson, still lying on the misty floor, groaning. No one else knew how to shut down the LSC.

"Warning. Emergence in three minutes."

William bolted left, but the clone blocked his escape with a swing of his ax. Shuffling right, William's feet suddenly came out from under him. Something had tripped him. He landed on his right hip. Pain rifled up his spine.

The ax came down again.

He rolled right. The blade spit sparks as it hit the concrete floor and scattered the mist. In that brief moment, William saw the glitter of diamonds.

Rolling left, he grabbed his diamond-studded cane, swung up at Morris, and struck the side of his head with the rhino-horned handle.

The killer staggered but didn't fall. He held his ax and shook his head, giving William time to get to his feet, but his back was against the wall again. No escape. Power cables from the black transformer dug into his shoulder blades. Morris stood tall in front of him, the ax held high.

"C&K all the way!" He swung.

William ducked.

With a clank, the blade sliced through a power cable. It fell to the floor like a snake, wriggling, hissing, and spitting blue sparks.

"Warning. Emergence in two minutes."

William shuffled right as if he were on the tennis court, his eyes glued to his opponent who came at him again. Raising the cane in front of him with both hands, he deflected the ax blow. The blade hit the black barrier of the power transformer and got hung up in the wire mesh.

Morris let out a growl and tugged on the handle. The ax held fast.

Dropping to the floor, William scrambled between the killer's legs and got behind him. Morris's left hand grasped the wire mesh. His right hand yanked on the stuck blade. He grumbled and cursed.

William saw the cut cable spitting sparks, the clone struggling with the ax blade and the wire mesh. Up until now, this had been a battle for survival of the fittest, the meanest, or the strongest. Now it became a battle of wits, brain over brawn. William had to act fast. He grabbed the sparking power cable and jammed the hot end into the wire mesh.

A brilliant flash blinded him. Then the clone room lights went out as the cable sent high voltage surging through Morris Brennon's body. Crackling sparks popped and hissed from his fingers as he clung to the metal mesh with both hands and flailed about as if he were being flogged.

He screamed. His clothes caught fire.

In an instant, the smell of burning flesh overpowered the clone room's sweet-smelling air.

William scrambled to his feet and covered his nose with the palm of his hand, his stomach knotting from the stench.

A circuit breaker blew, cutting voltage to the cable. The room lights came back on.

Limp and smoldering, Morris's body dropped to the floor with a thump. His eyes had popped out of their sockets, and blood trickled from his mouth and ears. William turned his head away realizing Morris Brennon had just been electrocuted for the second time.

"*Warning. Emergence in one minute.*"

William ran to Dr. Larson and shook him. "Shut it down, now."

"What hit me?"

"There's no time."

Groggy, Larson got to his feet and staggered to the console. First, he worked the controls for the valves that shut off the air pumps. The bubbling sounds went silent.

"Hurry."

He turned knobs labeled, *FILTERING*. Water pumps stopped humming. The emergence clock quit ticking. He stepped back. "They're all going to drown."

William spun around, his eyes going to Lois still shackled in the cylinder. She would drown too. "We've got to get her out of there."

Turning to the crane and winch controls, Larson engaged the levers.

Nothing happened.

"Damn." He checked the meters. "Circuits down. It's the cable Morris cut."

"Shit." William tossed his cane on the console and staggered to the ax still hanging from the scorched transformer barrier. The handle was still hot, but bearable. With considerable effort, he pried the blade loose, and ignoring the pain in his hip, hop-skipped to the cylinder where Lois was imprisoned. He set his feet firmly apart, put the ax on his right shoulder, and waved her back with his left hand.

Lois, wide-eyed, pushed herself away from the glass.

He swung the ax with all his strength. The charred blade struck the glass squarely. The cylinder walls exploded. Honey-colored liquid spilled out, bringing Lois with it in a flood. William dropped the ax and caught her in his arms.

Larson ran up and unlocked the shackle on her leg.

She coughed and gagged. Liquid gushed from her lungs. Gasping air, she hacked, expelling more fluid. She clung to William's arm. Her fingernails dug into his skin.

But he didn't care. He just held her.

Chapter Sixty-Five

Outside, Detective Ritter shouted, "Hold your fire, men." A barrage of firearm reports replied. The SWAT team, laying down heavy saturation fire, seemed oblivious to anything but their private little war. And the soldiers, the snot-nosed kids, returned fire with just as much ferocity. Pistols discharged smoke and fire all down the line of patrol cars barricading the main gate. Just as Ritter had feared, all hell had broken loose.

He held the Glock with both hands, the muzzle pointed up, level with his right ear. The gun felt heavy, all thirteen rounds still in the clip, for now anyway. Kneeling, he peered around the Ford's taillight. A bullet pinged off the bumper, sending him back behind the fender. Gun smoke in the air stung his eyes. But in that brief instant when he looked around the car, he saw the doors of the command car, which Captain Billings had parked in front of the posse, still open. The car was ten feet from the closest cover, an Illinois cruiser parked two cars down the line. Ritter swallowed hard. The bullhorn should still be on the seat. He had to get it.

A quick tuck and roll got him to the next patrol car where an Indiana State trooper crouched behind the back tire, reloading. Ritter wondered if the cop was shivering from the icy air—or fear. A bullet zinged off the roof. It had to be fear.

He duck-walked to the rear bumper, took a breath, then tucked and rolled. A bullet zipped into the snow, spraying icy powder in his face, but he made it to the next car where two troopers were firing over the hood. The windshield shattered. They ducked behind the fender again. Clouds of vapor swirled from their mouths and mingled with the gun smoke.

"Cover me." Ritter motioned to the command car with a wave of his Glock. He scooted to the rear fender. "Ready?"

The officers nodded.

"Now."

They popped up and began squeezing off rounds, one after another, laying down a barrage of lead designed only to make the soldiers keep their heads down, if only for just a moment. Ritter spun, rounded the fender, and made a break for the command car, bullets pelting the snow at his feet. The cover fire wasn't working. A bullet zinged past his ear. Ritter turtled his neck. He was halfway there. A round ripped through the left sleeve of his jacket. He felt heat but no pain. In the next two strides, he began thinking how wrong he'd been about those snot-nosed kids. The General was right. They were killers.

Ritter dove into the command car's front seat. Windshield glass exploded, and shards rained down on him. He fumbled for the bullhorn, found the volume knob and cranked it to high. Sprawled low on the seat, he held the mike to his lips and stuck the bullhorn out the shattered passenger door window. "Cease fire, officers. Stand down." Gunshots dwindled, slowly at first. The soldiers too, eased up on their firing. "Everybody. Hold your fire."

Then it became quiet, an eerie silence that sent shivers up his spine. He had heard this stillness called the ghost of the battlefield, an empty space between the living and the dead where souls were relinquished for the best or worst of intentions. A wounded man's moan broke the haunting spell.

Ritter propped his elbow up on the glass-strewn seat and peered warily through the shattered windshield. Gun smoke hung heavy in the cold air, and steam rose from the cooling bodies of dead soldiers and policemen alike.

A sudden movement in the snow by the main gate caught his attention. Captain Billings sat up. He opened his big black coat and groped his bulletproof vest as if finding the slug was somehow important to him. Ritter couldn't help but smile. Lucky Lou had survived again.

On the other side of the gate, a striking man in a long brown coat approached. He waved a white flag, which looked to be made from a broom handle with a white towel. The soldiers turned their attention toward the strange sight, too.

"It's over," the man shouted. "Don't shoot. There's been enough killing today."

Ritter holstered his Glock, the one with all thirteen rounds still in the clip.

Chapter Sixty-Six

Lying on the mist-covered floor, William huddled over Lois as she gasped for air, her chest heaving.

Larson moved to put his hand on her forehead.

"Don't touch her," William shouted and bent his shoulder over her, shielding her from the man who played God.

Lois coughed. "William, I can't breathe." She hacked again, fluid dribbling from her mouth. "My baby." Her eyes were ringed in white. "Is my baby all right?"

"Your baby is fine," Larson said. "It was never deprived of oxygen." He took her wrist to check her pulse.

She yanked free of his grasp. "Stay away from me." She spit. "Get me out of here, William."

"Can you walk?"

Her hazel eyes locked on his. "I can run if I have to."

William glared at Larson. "We're leaving." He looked over the roomful of vats, whishing he could take the clones with him, give them a chance to live a rewarding life, instead of one filled with misery and oppression.

Waiting for death, the clones stood like statues. Guilt welled up inside him. It was his fault. His vision of a motherless army had merit in principle alone, but in reality, it was brutal and inhumane.

"I don't expect you'll ever forgive me," Larson said.

"It's going to be hard enough to forgive myself."

Larson smiled faintly. "Get out of here. Enjoy what's left of your second life, William Tuliver."

He pulled Lois to her feet.

The Duplication Factor

A soldier brought her a blanket, draped it over her shoulders.

"I'll show you to her clothes," Larson said.

As they walked past the first vat, 1224A held up his slate.

"THANK YOU."

William stopped and gave the clone a solemn nod. He wondered if he were given the same choice, would he have chosen death over the life of these clones? The answer was simple. Death. Morris preferred death to life in prison. He preferred death to isolation. His clones had made the same decision. After all, life was more than eating and breathing and going to the toilet. It was a mix of learning and loving, giving and taking, and establishing relationships that gave meaning to life. He had also come to realize that death was just a part of living, and that life was supposed to get better with the coming of each new generation. Snapping to attention, he gave 1224A a sharp salute, a salute to a soldier who had fought the toughest battle of all: cruelty and abuse.

For the first time, 1224A smiled.

Wishing there could have been another way to end the clones' misery, he grabbed his cane from the console. "I think I'm going to be sick."

"Come on," Lois said. They headed for the stairs.

Suddenly, the fat frame of Carl Savage appeared on the platform. William's heart jumped when he saw him draw a long-barreled gun out from under his vest. "You're not going anywhere, ya freak. Not 'til I get my money."

"What money?" William moved in front of Lois protectively. He waved her and Larson to go back down the stairs.

"The reward from the Department of Defense. A million bucks for finding their lost clone." Carl glanced to the vat where the General's body floated. "Looks like I'm gonna need you for leverage."

William moved up the stairs with slow, carefully placed steps. He glanced back once, down to the misty floor where Lois hugged the blanket, her eyes wide with fear. They'd come this far together.

He'd be damned if Carl would win in the end. William held up his hand. "Don't do anything stupid, Carl."

"Shut up."

"Leave my wife and baby out of this."

"You're in no position to barter with me."

"I'll do whatever you say."

Carl grinned. "Then you can start by giving me that damn cane."

"But I need it to walk."

Frowning, "I'm not going to let you beat the shit out of me with it like you did my boys in Vegas."

"You have my word...I won't—"

"Hand it over or I'll shoot you in the other hip."

"All right. All right. Don't get trigger-happy. You can have it." Gripping the rubber-tipped end, William lifted the rhino-horn handle up toward Carl, keeping it just out of his reach. As William had hoped, Carl fell for the temptation to lean forward on the balls of his feet. He grabbed the cane. William gave it a quick pull. The fat man fell headfirst and let out a yelp.

Lois screamed.

William hugged the wall as Carl tumbled past him, thumping down the stairs. He landed on his back with a huff, scattering the mist. The gun clanked down the steps after him and clattered on the floor. William scrambled after it.

Carl tripped him.

Grappling for the gun, William got to it first, spun around and pointed the barrel at Carl's fat forehead. "You back-stabbing son of a bitch." William cocked the hammer. "I've had enough of you."

"Drop it," a voice ordered from the platform above. The clicking of cocking firearms filled the clone room. William looked up. Several uniformed police officers stood behind a man dressed in a dark suit. They all had their guns trained on William.

"Detective Ritter, Chicago PD. Drop your gun."

"He deserves to die," William shouted. "Right here on the floor like the pig that he is."

"He's not worth it," Larson said.

"William, don't," Lois pleaded. "You'll go to jail."

The gun wavered in William's hand, but the hate poured out of him like a burst dam. His finger tightened on the trigger. He was going to do it, by God, he was going to do it.

"Don't make us shoot you," Ritter said evenly.

"William, please," Lois cried.

Carl's bug eyes were like a crazy man's. "Shoot me, you freak. You ain't got the guts."

"I'll send you to hell where you belong."

"Go for it."

"William, no."

"He betrayed me," William shouted. "Twice."

"It doesn't matter anymore," Lois said.

William blinked. She was right. Killing Carl Savage wouldn't be worth going to jail over. He looked at Lois, nodded, and dropped the gun.

"I knew you couldn't do it," Carl said. "You freak."

Officers bounded down the stairs. Detective Ritter picked up the gun, cleared the chamber, and stuck it under his belt.

"He tried to kill us," Lois said, clutching the blanket and shivering.

"Arrest him," Ritter told his men.

"On what charge," Carl growled.

"Assault with a deadly weapon, for starters. We'll pile on more charges after that."

"You ain't got nothin' on me."

The officers cuffed him.

William brushed his hands together. "Take a look into his Vegas operation, detective, the Red Lace Saloon. I hear he has mob connections in Chicago. And he's into child pornography. You'll find enough manure to bury the maggot."

"Damn you, Tuliver."

The officers hauled Carl Savage away.

As the hoggish lawyer disappeared though the door, a sudden commotion drew William's attention to the vats. The clones started thrashing about and grabbing at their throats, their magnified eyes round with terror. Some clones were clawing at the glass. Others were already floating limp on their shackles. 1224A's chest heaved. The big veins on his bald head swelled, and his white skin began to turn blue. He had the look of a man on the gallows, the noose tightening around his neck. His eyes darted back and forth, and his nostrils flared.

William couldn't watch. He tilted his head down, but he could still hear the honey-colored liquid splashing and surging in the clones' throes of death, those in the vats and those in the cylinders along the wall. A minute later, everything fell silent in the clone room.

Ritter's face turned white. "Who's responsible for this?" he demanded, his angry eyes on Dr. Larson.

"Not me," Larson said.

"Who's in charge?"

"I am, but—"

"Arrest him."

Several officers grabbed Larson's arms.

"For what?"

"Murder." Ritter pointed to the lifeless vats. "Mass murder."

Larson shook his head. "If a rat died in this lab, would you arrest me for murder?"

"What's that got to do with this?"

"Clones are no different. They have no more legal status than any other lab animal. No family. No birth certificates, no death certificates, and no next-of-kin. They're not real people, just an experiment. And they weren't murdered. They simply died because of an equipment failure."

The detective worked his jaw as if chewing on Dr. Larson's words, testing them in his head. "I'm looking for Morris Brennon."

William glanced at the singed body sprawled on the floor by the power transformer. "He killed my parents," he said to Ritter. "That's him, over there." He pointed to the dead clone, gathered Lois in the crook of his arm, and took her up the stairs, leaving the cops to sort out the whole affair.

*** ~

Ritter grimaced as he moved through the mist to the body on the floor. The burned clone's stench lingered thickly in the air. Morris Brennon's ugly face was still recognizable, even without eyeballs. His hands were charred black, the fingers burned clear down to bone. Ritter shook his head. If this was the killer who murdered Karen and Roger Carlyle, Rita Jensen, and Billy Don, he had no way to prove it. The fingerprints were gone.

And because he couldn't prove his theory that a clone had committed the murders, he would have to accept the fact that the Carlyle case would officially go down as unsolved. That thought didn't settle well in the pit of his stomach. The press would hound him forever. But standing there looking down at the dead clone, he found some satisfaction. The killing would stop. After all, that's what his job was all about.

He turned to the doctor, still in the officers' grasp. Larson was to blame for all this, but he was right about the clones. There was no legal precedent for their existence. Larson had done nothing wrong in Indiana. Though California had banned human cloning as a means to initiate a pregnancy, the United States had no such laws prohibiting the manipulation of human DNA. In Britain, France, Germany, and Australia, human cloning had been outlawed altogether, but not here in the land of the free and the home of the brave. Dr. Larson and scientists like him were free to manipulate genes in any way they wanted without fear of reprisal. *Designer babies* engineered to become super smart or super strong, blond or brunette, white or black, could be produced in labs of the future. Human cloning could infringe on our individuality, our freedom of choice to be who we wanted to be. He shuddered. What kind of future would that be for the human race?

Scanning the vats of corpses and the remains of Morris Brennon, his heart felt heavy. He asked himself if *Liberty and Justice for all* applied to human clones. Not wanting to be the one to make that call, he turned to his officers and gave the order. "Book him. Murder One."

"You can't do this to me," Larson shouted.

Ritter knew otherwise. "Let the courts figure it out. In the meantime, we've got one hell of a mess to clean up."

Chapter Sixty-Seven

The Diamond Building

Following Toyoko, William hobbled along on his diamond-studded cane as she led him through the executive offices. His hip was killing him, but clue number six was on his mind, *The Lost Diamonds*. He had explained to the chief executive of Diamond Auto Parts, that he wished to inspect the pumping station below Paradise Park fountain. He'd left something down there thirty years ago. She knew just the man who could help him.

They entered an elegant office adorned with mahogany furnishing and green and white curtains. Incense scented the air. The maintenance superintendent bowed. "Jeff Tuliver?"

William thought it best not to tell them his real name or confuse anyone with wild tales of human clones and how he'd come back from the dead. "Thank you for the private tour. I'm ready when you are."

"Very well, then," the super said, dangling a ring of keys from his fingers. He grabbed his coat off the back of his chair.

On the elevator ride down to the main lobby, William hung the cane over his left forearm. He could only hope this excursion would jar déjà vu in his mind and give him a clue as to where he'd hidden the diamonds—two hundred thirty seven million dollars worth.

Outside, a cold wind cut through Paradise Park. Skeletal trees clacked overhead, and the fountain splashed with a relentless rhythm. As he shuffled down the marble steps, he thought about how he loved this place and how much he was going to miss it.

The sidewalk to the pool wound its way between ridges of shoveled snow. In mid January, winter held Chicago in its icy grip. Because the park had been a focal point of Chicago's millennium celebrations, William thought it best to conduct this search after the festivities were concluded. The diamonds would still be there, he was sure. Besides, he and Lois had been busy fixing up the baby's room and visiting Dr. Marshall regularly. The auto shop he'd left in Jim and Lou's capable hands. Broken cars were the least of his problems these days, considering the cancer treatments he had to endure. Still the prognosis was bleak.

The super keyed the lock on a steel door to the pumping station. It opened with a creak. Inside the small atrium, he flipped light switches before proceeding noisily down a metal staircase. Gray concrete walls slanted into the depths and a musty odor lingered in the air. Humming electric motors and whining water pumps made the handrail vibrate.

"First level pumping station," the super explained.

In this room, directly under the pool, four huge stainless steel pumps sat on a concrete floor secured with bolts as big around as William's arm. Leaning on his cane, he scanned smooth concrete walls, looking for any seams that might indicate a hidden compartment, but nothing looked like a hiding place.

The second level housed the backup systems for the fountain and looked much like the first level. He saw nowhere to hide diamonds. William knew he wouldn't have put them anywhere that required shutting down the fountain to get to them, and he wouldn't have hidden them where normal maintenance operations could uncover them.

"See all you like?" the super asked.

William nodded, and they proceeded down to the third level. The air felt much colder. A waning light bulb flickered over huge stainless steel drums of deicing solution that kept the fountain operational all winter. William wouldn't have put the diamonds in there, either. Too great a chance of them getting sucked into the pumps.

The fourth level housed electrical stuff: the power transformers, switching stations, and even a new computer terminal had been added. Smooth concrete walls and floors looked just like the other levels.

Back on the third level, William examined the piping, followed each branch, tapping on them with his cane, testing to see if one might be a fake or lead to a dead end. But nothing seemed out of order.

The super hugged himself against the cold. "You've seen it all. Can we go?"

"Sure." William limped back up the stairs and out into the chill of Paradise Park. He thanked the super and said goodbye. Under the oak tree, the bench where he'd sat and written *The Lost Diamonds* was now covered with snow and ice. He knocked off the ice with his diamond-studded cane and swept snow away with the flat of his hand.

Sitting there, his eyes traced the fountain jets as they stabbed the frigid sky. He shook his head and wondered how he could have been mistaken about the diamonds. William Tuliver loved his fountain. He named it *Mothers' Tears*, in honor of his mother's sorrow. He romanced Sally Mayfield here. It had been his most important possession. The diamonds had to be down there, somewhere.

He tapped the cane on the frozen ground. The intricate carvings on the rhino-horned handle caught his eye. They looked like some kind of hieroglyphics, something foreign and old, but beautiful. He blinked. The cane was very important to William, too. It was special. After all, he'd entrusted it to Andrew Cobb, to hold for him until he returned, as a clone. It had to be as important as the fountain.

William examined the cane closer, the diamond studs and the rich black walnut. He tested its weight with both hands, remembering how he always thought it was heavy, he assumed because it was solid wood. But was it? Popping off the black rubber cap, he expected to see wood grain. What he saw was a tubular opening, and an inch inside it he saw finely grooved threads—and a silver plug—with a screwdriver slot.

He gasped.

Chapter Sixty-Eight

Chicago

There were times in Eugene's life that he thought he would never forget. As he slipped into his long brown coat and set a brown hat on his head, he recalled one of his favorites, the memory of that baby clone lying in the glass crib, sucking on a bottle Eugene held for him. That moment affected him, softened his heart, changed his attitude toward his work at Blythe University, and made him feel small. Geoffrey Scott Michaels, the miracle that he was, the first human clone, had again set Eugene's life in a different direction. William had talked to Sally. He said she was living on the streets of Chicago, homeless. Somehow, Eugene had to find her.

He pulled on a pair of black driving gloves and checked the pockets for his keys. Maybe he would find her today.

In the Cherokee, on the ride back from Blythe Biotech that Thanksgiving weekend, Eugene was convinced that Geoffrey Scott Michaels was in fact William Tuliver. It wasn't just the diamond-studded cane or the book, *The Lost Diamonds*, he'd written as a guide to find his past. It was the way Lois snuggled up to him in the back seat, and the look in her eyes, the same way Sally looked at William back then. The duplication factor had given William another life. He'd found another love, a spitting image of his last love. Unfortunately, they were both made to suffer for his wants.

He parked the Cherokee on Michigan Avenue, locked the doors, and took to the sidewalk. With his hands thrust deep in his pockets, he ducked against the wind that knifed through his coat and coaxed litter along the gutters. A train clattered on rails overhead. Gray clouds hung low and heavy with rain.

This was Sally Mayfield's world of brick walls, blacktopped alleys, and dumpsters. William had told him she was a bag lady. She could be found somewhere in the streets and alleys of downtown Chicago, wearing a long gray coat and pushing a shopping cart piled high with bags. He'd also warned him about her broomstick, the thing she used to defend her property from the snatching hands of beggars and bums. His stomach sickened from the thought of her living that way. She deserved so much more: a home in the suburbs, an SUV, the finest theater and dining Chicago had to offer. He had to rescue her from this life of poverty and misery.

And there was no reason for her to live like that anymore. General Harrison was dead, and Dr. Larson was awaiting trial. Geoffrey Scott Michaels had returned as William Tuliver. The circle was complete. Sally Mayfield was free, at last.

Eugene came to an alley where homeless people gathered around a big steel barrel belching smoke. Some were warming themselves. Others passed a brown-bagged bottle around, each taking a swig while the next looked on with anticipation. Huddling together, their tattered clothing fluttered in the wind. But nowhere did he see that shopping cart full of bags or the woman in the long gray coat.

Most of that afternoon went the same way, just as it had on many other trips he'd taken to this sad place. Each hopeful alley he explored left him disappointed. The fact that it was spring now, gave him little comfort. Searching wasn't any easier than it had been during the weeks of winter.

At day's end, a drizzling rain set upon the city and his earlier optimism dwindled. With a heavy heart he began to slosh his way back to the Cherokee, rain tapping on his hat brim.

Soon he'd be back to the warmth and comfort of his home. And tomorrow he would be at the clinic. There were mothers to care for and babies to birth. And he would take care of these responsibilities until the next time he could get away and renew his search, again as optimistic as he was this morning.

In all the times he had been down here, he had seen many faces of the homeless, the sick, and the forgotten. Whether it was alcohol or drugs, mental illness, or just dumb luck that had put them there, Eugene thought of them as a society onto themselves. They had their own territories, cliques, and rules of engagement. And he witnessed very little violence among those he encountered along the way: once a scuffle over a discarded cigarette butt and another time, a yelling match between two drunks. Sally must have adapted well. Thirty years was a long time to have survived like this.

He stood at the curb as a taxi splashed by. A heavy mist swirled in its wake. Gray dusk had coaxed the streetlights on, the rain now slicing through hazy, cone-shaped beams. The traffic light glowed red. A horn honked. The little green walking man lit up on the pole. Eugene looked left and stepped off the curb into a puddle.

It wasn't the cold water rushing over the top of his shoe and soaking his sock that sent a chill through him. It was a shopping cart piled high with bags that had rattled out of the fog. A broomstick jutted up from the basket like the mast of a ship on a stormy night, its captain concealed from view. Eugene's heartbeat jumped as he stood in the gutter, both feet sopping in the puddle.

The contraption rattled and squeaked nearer and nearer, to only a few feet away. Now he could see a woman pushing it, an old woman, judging from the way she was hunched over the handle, too old to be the woman he was looking for. Though she wore a clear plastic bag over a long gray coat and a brown garbage bag for a scarf, he thought she could be any old woman on these mean streets. He waited for her to pass, holding his breath as if he would drown in this storm. When he saw her face in the streetlight, weathered and slicked with rain, his heartbeat staggered. It was—it was Sally Mayfield.

Eugene jumped to the curb. "Miss."

The woman didn't look at him, just pushed on with her load.

"Please," he said shuffling at her side. "Sally Mayfield?"

The shopping cart squeaked to a stop, and the woman looked at him blankly. Suddenly, her eyes exploded with fear. "No." She broke into a run, the shopping cart wheels screaming with speed.

"Sally, wait." He lit out after her, but she darted into a foggy alley. He couldn't believe how fast she was getting away. The only thing he could reach her with now was his voice. He shouted the words without thinking. "I love you."

Sally stopped the hurtling cart, turned around slowly, the rain dripping from her garbage bag scarf. Her nose wrinkled. "What?"

Eugene took careful steps toward her, afraid he'd frighten her off like a stray cat. His eyes locked on her glare. "I love you, Sally Mayfield."

"You've got to be joking." She'd said it with a growl in her throat.

"I've always loved you, but I couldn't tell you because of my job at the university. You were my patient. Besides, I could see how much you loved William Tuliver. I was jealous."

As she stared at him with bewildered eyes, he recalled how plain she looked back then. Now, as he saw past the wrinkles that hard years had given her, he recognized the same face.

Sally lowered her eyes as if she were suddenly embarrassed to be seen. "That was a long time ago."

"Yes...but now there is a future for you, Sally."

She shook her head. "They might find me."

"It's over. Harrison is dead and Dr. Larson is out of the cloning business. They're not looking for you anymore. William Tuliver came back and ended what he'd started. You're free."

She scowled at him. "I've always been free, Dr. Marshall."

"I mean free to go home, to change your life."

"What would you have me change?" Sally glared. "What makes you think I want to change anything?"

The rain seemed suddenly colder and coming down harder. Or was it the chill in her heart that he felt, the icy tone of her voice?

"Come with me, Sally," he said softly, rain dripping from his hat brim. "We could do well together, you and I."

Sally leveled her eyes on him. "Just who do you think you are coming back into my life and telling me this crap?"

"I'm serious." Eugene's optimism was set aback by her harsh words, but he deserved to hear them.

"There's something you don't get about me." She stepped toward him. "I'm not your savior, and you're not mine. You had your chance. You could have told me the truth. You could have saved us from all this. But you didn't. So now you're left with the guilt. You may have let that consume your life, but don't ask me to help you feel better about it now."

"I made a mistake, a bad call. And when I came to realize the consequences, I helped Chet rescue you and Geoffrey from Blythe University. I tried to tell you how sorry I was that Halloween night, how I felt about you, but you ran away from me, just like you ran away from me now. I wanted to make everything right back then, for us and for Geoffrey, but you wouldn't let me."

Sally moved back to her shopping cart, stooped and worn. "There's no making up for what happened thirty years ago, Dr. Marshall. Not then. Not now. You lied to me. I lost my child. My distain for you will never get better. It'll never go away."

"Won't you even try?"

"I gave up trying. Maybe you should, too."

"But you can't possibly be happy like this."

Sally's brows lifted. "Happiness comes from accepting things the way they are. My mother taught me that when I was a little girl on the streets of New Orleans. I'm a survivor. I'm happy enough."

Eugene stepped back. "You're telling me you like this life?"

"I said *happy*, doctor. I didn't say I liked any of it."

"Then why not come with me? You can be *happy enough* without wallowing in all this poverty."

Sally shook her head. "I could never love you, Dr. Marshall." Her eyes narrowed. "In fact, I can only hate you. And my hate for you has been so much a part of me that I wouldn't know how to act if I let it go. So you see, we could never be together, *you and I.*"

Eugene stiffened, the rain now freezing him to the bone. He thought his soul had been ripped out of his chest and tossed into the gutter. Tears stung his eyes. Sally was right. There was no way to start again. Too much pain and sorrow cluttered the way. He saw the damage his decisions had done to Sally, what she had become because of what he had done.

And she was right about him. He always thought finding her would somehow help him deal with the guilt. Now he knew how wrong he was about that. The guilt was his alone to bear. But she'd given him a little hope when she'd told him that happiness came from accepting things the way they were. He didn't have to like it, but he could still find happiness in the life he was left with. She *was* his savior, and she didn't even know it.

He tipped his hat. "Goodbye, Sally."

She hunched over the handle. "Goodbye, Dr. Marshall. Try to enjoy the rest of your life." With that, she leaned on her shopping cart and disappeared into the fog and rain.

Chapter Sixty-Nine

Westside Medical Center

Summer sunshine flooded the room. A light breeze swayed lacy curtains, and the air coming in from outside smelled like freshly mowed grass. Pictures of flowers and meadows hung on pastel walls that glowed warmly. William thought it was mid June, the weeks having gone by in a blur since the doctors increased his pain medication. Cancer had taken claim to his body, zapped his strength a little at a time, and slowly whittled away at what was left of him.

"Are you hangin' in there okay, sport?" It was Nurse Aggie's voice, happy as usual. She would probably be giddy on judgment day.

"I'm thirsty," he said weakly.

"Here." She put a straw to his lips, and he drank some ice water. Seemed he couldn't get enough. Over the last few months, Nurse Aggie had been good about visiting him, bringing homemade cookies and banana bread. And some nights, when Lois went home to rest, Nurse Aggie would sit with him, read a story, or just tell him about things that mattered to her. He especially liked to hear about the women who'd delivered that day, the babies that went home, and which stuffed toy they took with them. But lately, he hadn't been up to listening. Because of the drugs, he slept most of the time. But today he was free of the medication, and though every bone in his body ached, he was glad to be alert for the upcoming occasion.

Nurse Aggie lifted the sheet and checked his catheter. He'd lost control of his functions, an embarrassing state that he found difficult to accept. But Dr. Marshall had told him how Sally accepted the way things were in her life. She was *happy enough*. Little by little, William took that advice and found solace in knowing that it came from Sally. He began to accept the fact that Lois would have to raise their child on her own, that he wasn't going to be there for them. Though he didn't like a bit of it, he was *happy enough*.

Nurse Aggie patted his shoulder. "It won't be long now."

He tugged on his bed sheet with bony fingers. Skinny and weak, every breath was torture. "How's she doing?"

"Just fine." Nurse Aggie showed him that trademark smile. "She's been in labor eight hours now. Should pop any time." The bed motor whined, lifting him to a sitting position. She gave his pillow a couple of slaps. "How's that?"

He winked and wondered how much longer he'd have to wait. Lois had assured him she'd be okay. And Dr. Marshall had promised to take good care of her. She'd said there was nothing William could do for her now. *Just rest and be ready to meet your son.* Ultrasound technology had given away that wonderful secret of the womb.

A tear stung his eye. Somewhere in this big medical place, Lois was giving birth. William thought about Adam and Eve in the garden, the forbidden fruit, and the punishments God put upon everyone for their sins; the pain of childbirth being one all women must bear. He never liked that story. Lois wasn't enduring the pain of labor because of some punishment dished out eons ago. It was a natural thing that all species must suffer through to ensure their survival. The duplication factor was nowhere in the scheme of things.

A horn honked from somewhere outside his window. William started, and then wondered how things were going at the shop. His employees bought the company from him, for a dollar. And his '59 Cadillac limo was safe, now on display in the main lobby of the Diamond Building, an historical tribute to William Tuliver. The serial numbers matched. It was the same car. On the day of the dedication, Toyoko had leaned over his wheelchair and kissed his cheek.

The Japanese were wonderful people.

"Get you anything else?" Nurse Aggie asked, ticking a fingernail on the IV drip tube.

William shifted his gaze to the diamond-studded cane hanging from the bed rail. He pointed to it with a shaky finger.

She slid it closer to him, where he could get hold of it. "Don't go anywhere," she said, smiled, and left the room.

William lifted the cane. It was much lighter now. He laid it on his lap, the diamond studs sparkling.

Of all the things he'd written about in *The Lost Diamonds*, this was the only thing he'd gotten wrong. But William Tuliver must have planned it that way, must have known his clone would figure it out for himself. William would never have risked someone stumbling upon his fortune. He would have wanted his diamonds close to him. And giving the cane to Andrew Cobb insured that he would get it back, or if he failed to find himself in his new life, the diamonds would be buried forever with his best friend, safe for eternity.

He caressed the rhino-horn handle. The memory of those diamonds spilling out on the table staggered his heartbeat. Inside the cane, William had hidden the finest cut diamonds on earth. There were hundreds of large pieces and thousands of jewelry grade stones. It took more than a month to sort them, get the appraisals, and make the exchanges. Trust funds had to be set up, and many donations were made. The most important thing was that his wife and son would not want for anything.

As for all the other things that his son had to learn in his lifetime, William would let him figure them out on his own. There'd be no book—no *Lost Diamonds*—to lean on. He would have to grow up like everyone else, learn how to love and be loved, and build relationships that will give meaning and purpose to his life.

William stroked the cane's smooth black walnut finish and held back tears. He knew Lois would pass the cane on to his son. The doctors had said there was a one-in-four chance that he may need it—that someday this genetic cancer might strike him down, too. Tears welled in William's eyes.

Footsteps came from down the hall. Gurney wheels squeaked and voices said, *"He's so cute"* and *"I can't wait for William to see him."* He dabbed tears from his eyes with the bed sheet and tried to steady his trembling hands. But it was no use. He hung the cane on the bedrail and swallowed dryly as he fixed his eyes on the hallway just outside his door.

The gurney came into view, Dr. Marshall walking alongside it, and Lois sitting upright. Red hair spilled over her shoulders. She held a baby wrapped in a white blanket. He couldn't see the child's face, only the top of his head. An orderly pushed the gurney through the doorway and into the room.

"William," she sang. "I have brought him for you to see." The gurney squeaked to a stop at his bedside. Lois's hazel eyes glistened with joy. "Look. He has your ears."

"They're b-beautiful ears," he said, his weak voice cracking. He had little power left in his lungs to speak. "May I hold him?" He leaned forward, and with his arms quivering from pain, reached for the child. Dr. Marshall helped situate the baby in his frail arms. Lois pulled back the corner of the blanket from the baby's face.

The room went silent. For several minutes, William stared at the child, contemplating the miracle that Lois had brought him. A son. Restraining tears of joy, his pain seemed numb, like it wasn't real anymore. Only the child filled his senses now, puffy cheeks, a wisp of thin hair lying over his forehead. His little fingers were curled into tight fists.

"What will you name him?" Dr. Marshall asked.

William didn't look away from the child's face. "Jeffrey Andrew Tuliver."

"Our son," Lois said softly.

A tear trickled down William's cheek. Jeffrey fidgeted. His

little eyelids opened, just a slit, and closed again. William didn't even see the color of his eyes, but it was in that brief moment that he realized a part of him was living in his son, and he would continue to live on in his grandchildren and their children and on and on until the end of the world—as life was meant to be.

A wonderful sense of calm came over him. His breathing slowed and his pain melted away. The child's face blurred.

William laid his head back on the pillow and looked at Lois. "I love you."

The smile she gave him warmed his heart.

His eyes rolled back, he gasped, and as he held his son in his arms, William Tuliver finally died.

About the Author

There's nothing mundane in the writing world of **Terry Wright**. Tension, conflict and suspense propel his readers through the pages as if they were on fire. Traditionally published in Science Fiction, Supernatural, and Horror, his mastery of the action thriller has also won him International acclaim as an accomplished screenplay writer. A longtime member of the Rocky Mountain Fiction Writers, he coordinated their annual Colorado Gold Writing Contest for six years, received their highest award for service, The Jasmine Award, and was nominated for the Writer of the Year in 2014.

Terry is a Vietnam Veteran (USAF – Red Horse - SAC), a certified pilot of single engine light aircraft, and an avid Harley Davidson enthusiast. After 36 years in business, he sold his auto repair shop and started publishing authors from around the world through his publishing companies, TWB Press and Amore Moon Publishing. When he's not writing and editing, he enjoys cross-country motorcycling. He lives in Centennial, Colorado, with his wife, Bobette, and their Yorkie, Taz.

Dear Reader,

Thank you for reading "The Duplication Factor." I wrote this book between 1998 and 2002. A literary agent loved it, and though he tried to sell it to New York publishers, he had no luck interesting them in a new author from Colorado. After eight years of disappointment, in 2011 I released the novel in e-book format, and in 2019 I released it in paperback. If you enjoyed the read, please post a review on Amazon. http://www.amazon.com/dp/B0055CP0IA

I invite you to visit the following links for my other works where you'll find more information, video trailers, and links to purchase. And while you're there, explore other TWB Press and Amore Moon Publishing e-books and novels. You're also welcome to visit my author website at www.terrywrightbooks.com where you'll find additional information about my award-winning screenplays.

— Terry Wright

The 13th Power Quest, Book 1
The search for the secret of the universe
Science Fiction novel, technology, action, adventure
www.twbpress.com/the13thpowerquest

The 13th Power Journey, Book 2
Mankind's first journey across the galaxy
www.twbpress.com/the13thpowerjourney

The 13th Power War, Book 3
And then came man, and war, and death
www.twbpress.com/the13thpowerwar

The Grief Syndrome
A futuristic Sci-Fi thriller, action, adventure
www.twbpress.com/thegriefsyndrome

Black Jack
A Denver detective searches for his wife's killer
Crime drama novel, thriller, action, mystery
www.twbpress.com/blackjack

The Pearl of Death
Novel based on the true story of the world's largest pearl
www.twbpress.com/thepearlofdeath

Undead in Paris (a screenplay)
Vampire wars: the old ways vs the new ways
www.twbpress.com/undeadinparis

Z-motors - The Job from Hell
Zombie short story, thriller, satire
www.twbpress.com/zmotors

Street Beat
A woman reporter matches wits with a serial killer
Crime drama short story, action-thriller, romance
www.twbpress.com/streetbeat

Return Me to Mistwillow
A dusty ghost town gets a visitor from the past
Ghost short story, Colorado history, action, thriller
www.twbpress.com/returnmetomistwillow

Wilderness Rampage
Action adventure short story, bad guys and a bear
www.twbpress.com/wildernessrampage

Find more authors and more titles at

www.twbpress.com